OXFORD WORLD'S CLASSICS

SELECTED STORIES

KATHERINE MANSFIELD was born in Wellington, New Zealand, in 1888. She was educated partly in London, and left New Zealand for Britain in 1908 with a journal full of maxims from Oscar Wilde. She acted on many of them, such as 'The only way to get rid of a temptation is to yield to it', with disastrous consequences for her health. She became a regular contributor to the *New Age*, and then to *Rhythm* which was edited by John Middleton Murry, whom she eventually married. Her first book, mainly of satirical stories, *In a German Pension*, was published in 1911.

Her life changed radically during the First World War: her only brother was killed in France and she contracted tuberculosis. At the same time she established close but volatile friendships with D. H. Lawrence and Virginia Woolf, and her story 'Prelude' became the second publication of the Woolfs' Hogarth Press. She had to winter in a warm climate on a small income; separation from Murry and from her family in New Zealand produced some of her most savage depictions of the fissured self, such as the damaged and dangerous narrator of '*Je ne parle pas français*', which appeared in *Bliss and Other Stories* (1920). One more volume of stories was published during her lifetime, *The Garden Party and Other Stories* (1922); too ill to travel, in many of these stories Mansfield recreated her childhood world, with a mordant insight into social relationships as well as an awareness of the transient glint of colour in a garden.

She moved constantly in search of health, and died in Gurdjieff's Institute for the Harmonious Development of Man at Fontainebleau in 1923. *The Dove's Nest and Other Stories* and *Something Childish and Other Stories* were published after her death; Murry also produced editions of her poems, letters, and notebooks. When she heard of Mansfield's death, Virginia Woolf felt that the only public that she valued was gone: 'When I began to write, it seemed to me there was no point in writing. Katherine wont read it.'

ANGELA SMITH is Professor of English Studies and Director of the Centre of Commonwealth Studies at the University of Stirling in Scotland. She has taught at universities in California, Wales, and Malawi. Her books include *East African Writing in English* (Macmillan, 1989), *Katherine Mansfield and Virginia Woolf: A Public of Two* (Clarendon Press, 1999), and *Katherine Mansfield: A Literary Life* (Palgrave, 2000). She has edited, with a critical introduction and notes, Jean Rhys's *Wide Sargasso Sea* for Penguin (1997).

OXFORD WORLD'S CLASSICS

*For over 100 years Oxford World's Classics have brought
readers closer to the world's great literature. Now with over 700
titles—from the 4,000-year-old myths of Mesopotamia to the
twentieth century's greatest novels—the series makes available
lesser-known as well as celebrated writing.*

*The pocket-sized hardbacks of the early years contained
introductions by Virginia Woolf, T. S. Eliot, Graham Greene,
and other literary figures which enriched the experience of reading.
Today the series is recognized for its fine scholarship and
reliability in texts that span world literature, drama and poetry,
religion, philosophy and politics. Each edition includes perceptive
commentary and essential background information to meet the
changing needs of readers.*

OXFORD WORLD'S CLASSICS

━━

KATHERINE MANSFIELD

Selected Stories

━━

Edited with an Introduction and Notes by
ANGELA SMITH

OXFORD
UNIVERSITY PRESS

OXFORD
UNIVERSITY PRESS

Great Clarendon Street, Oxford OX2 6DP

Oxford University Press is a department of the University of Oxford.
It furthers the University's objective of excellence in research, scholarship,
and education by publishing worldwide in

Oxford New York

Auckland Bangkok Buenos Aires Cape Town Chennai
Dar es Salaam Delhi Hong Kong Istanbul Karachi Kolkata
Kuala Lumpur Madrid Melbourne Mexico City Mumbai Nairobi
São Paulo Shanghai Taipei Tokyo Toronto

Oxford is a registered trade mark of Oxford University Press
in the UK and in certain other countries

Editorial matter © Angela Smith 2002

The moral rights of the author have been asserted

Database right Oxford University Press (maker)

First published as an Oxford World's Classics paperback 2002
Reissued 2008

British Library Cataloguing in Publication Data

Data available

Library of Congress Cataloging in Publication Data

Data available

ISBN 978-0-19-953735-8

9

Typeset in Ehrhardt
by RefineCatch Limited, Bungay, Suffolk
Printed in Great Britain by
Clays Ltd, St Ives plc

Contents

CONTENTS

ACKNOWLEDGEMENTS

I should like gratefully to acknowledge the help of colleagues, family, and friends in compiling the notes: Professor Vincent O'Sullivan, Dr Michelle Keown, Paul Keown, Professor Ken Arvidson, Peter Meech, Professor Grahame Smith, Dan Smith. I have also valued the advice and guidance of the editor of Oxford World's Classics, Judith Luna.

INTRODUCTION

'I am always conscious of this secret disruption in me.'[1]

Katherine Mansfield's vigorous and witty letters are full of questions. A week before her death they become more urgent: 'the question is always: *Who am I? . . . Is there a Me?*'[2] She was a restless traveller between continents and within Europe, and in her inner life there is always a sense of imminent danger but also of discovery, of being in-between. Her stories catch the fear and excitement of being between states, from the child Kezia leaving the safe house to explore the unknown garden in 'Prelude', or the small Fenella leaving her father and taking a ferry in the dark in 'The Voyage', to the middle-aged daughters of the late colonel who glimpse with dread and ecstasy what release from the tyrannical patriarch might offer. It is the nervous edge to the stories, their power to intrigue and disturb, that explains why they have never gone out of print since they were first published.

Colonial Life

Mansfield was born and brought up in colonial Wellington, in New Zealand, at the end of the nineteenth century. It was as far, geographically, as it could possibly be from London, the metropolitan centre of empire, and yet its inhabitants called it 'the empire city' and prided themselves on its bourgeois respectability, modelled on British life. When Vincent O'Sullivan says that Mansfield 'was born into a family, and a country, constantly checking themselves in a mirror'[3] he draws attention to the anomaly that the white New Zealanders who were Mansfield's contemporaries talked of Britain as 'home' even if they had never been there, and were preoccupied with mimicking a way of life that had evolved in a different hemisphere. The impression of living in-between, with home being neither here

---

[1] John Middleton Murry (ed.), *The Letters of Katherine Mansfield* (London: Constable, 1928), ii. 260. See n. 13 to clarify which edition of the letters is being used.

[2] Ibid. 266.

[3] Vincent O'Sullivan (ed.), *Katherine Mansfield: New Zealand Stories* (Auckland: Oxford University Press, 1997), 1.

nor there, is strong in Mansfield's early personal writing. It was her childhood experience of living in a society where one way of life was imposed on another, and did not quite fit, that enabled her to focus in her stories on what Virginia Woolf calls 'moments of being'. Many of her stories pivot on a fleeting disruption, when an established way of life is jolted by something other, strange and disturbing.

Mansfield herself had plenty of experience of these moments in the disjunction between Maori and pakeha[4] life in New Zealand, and again when she moved from colonial Wellington to the bohemian artistic life of London and Paris early in the twentieth century. The significance of disruption for her is suggested by a dream she had in 1920, when she had been away from New Zealand for twelve years. It straddles Paris and Wellington, heightening the impression of trying to inhabit two incompatible places. She dreams that she is in a café when Oscar Wilde (long dead by then) comes into it:

Oscar Wilde was very shabby. He wore a green overcoat. He kept tossing & tossing back his long greasy hair with the whitest hand. When he met me he said 'Oh <u>Katherine</u>!'—very affected. But I did find him a fascinating talker. So much so I asked him to come to my home. He said would 12:30 tonight do? When I arrived home it seemed madness to have asked him. Father & Mother were in bed. What if Father came down & found that chap Wilde in one of the chintz armchairs? Too late now. I waited by the door.[5]

The detail of the smart and shiny chintz invaded by the greasy but articulate Wilde suggests the complexity of trying to bridge the two worlds; Father was a bank manager and would not have welcomed any guest after midnight, let alone a decadent writer who might stain his domestic décor. His probable attitude is caught in the phrase 'that chap Wilde'. The pressure of being in-between and attempting to mediate oppresses Mansfield, who waits by the door to welcome the alien guest but also perhaps to make a quick getaway.

---

[4] As it is used by all ethnic groups in New Zealand, I use the Maori term 'pakeha' for white New Zealanders.

[5] Margaret Scott (ed.), *The Katherine Mansfield Notebooks* (NZ: Lincoln University Press and Daphne Brasell Associates, 1997), ii. 243. All subsequent quotations from the notebooks are taken from this edition (hereafter *KM Notebooks*). Inaccuracies in spelling and punctuation sometimes occur in the letters and notebooks and are reproduced as they appear.

One of the ways in which Mansfield was alerted to disruptive experiences was through her awareness of the position of the Maori in her society. Like most indigenous peoples in British colonies, the Maori in New Zealand had been dispossessed of their land and were expected by the British incomers to disappear as part of the process of cultural Darwinism; as early as 1838 a commentator wrote of New Zealand that 'the wiser course would be, to let the native race gradually retire before the settlers, and ultimately become extinct'.[6] The expectation was that the dominant settler culture would cause the supposedly 'inferior' race to die out without the necessity of active genocide. Of course European diseases did devastate the indigenous populations of new colonies; in Canada, Australia, and New Zealand large numbers of indigenous people died of such diseases as measles, smallpox, and tuberculosis after contact with the colonists, but there were more deliberate causes for disease and death. Mansfield's early writing shows her awareness of a repressed history of brutality and duplicity; Maori chiefs were deceived into making treaties with the invaders, whereas settler accounts of what happened represented the encounter as the triumph of white civilization over primitivism. As a young woman of 19 Mansfield writes that the New Zealand bush, outside the cities, 'is all so gigantic and tragic—and even in the bright sunlight it is so passionately secret'.[7] She sees the bush as haunted by a Maori history that is unrecorded and repressed by pakeha New Zealand, but sometimes that secret story erupts into the present. She writes about it obliquely, even in her diaries, but it is consistently there. When she does include Maoris in the stories she usually avoids racial categorization and invites the reader to perceive them first as part of the narrative, and then to realize that they are Maori. In 'How Pearl Button Was Kidnapped', the narrative perspective is mostly that of the small child, who notices the feather mats round the shoulders of her companions, and the green ornament round a woman's neck, but does not label these things as alien to her sense of her own ethnic identity, though the reader probably recognizes the green ornament as a tiki, a greenstone amulet, and infers that the 'two dark women' are Maori. The word 'kidnapped'

[6] Quoted in Robert Young, *Colonial Desire: Hybridity in Theory, Culture and Race* (London: Routledge, 1995), 9.

[7] Ian Gordon (ed.), *Katherine Mansfield: The Urewera Notebook* (Oxford: Oxford University Press, 1978), 55.

suggests a pakeha interpretation of the events in the story, but it is at odds with the reader's experience of what happens, since the child, the seeing eye in the story, perceives the dark women as her liberators.

Part of the tension implicit in Mansfield's dream of Oscar Wilde visiting her parents' home in Wellington arises from Wilde's sexual orientation; the empire city clearly expected its citizens to be heterosexual. Mansfield's transgressive impetus combined crossing racial boundaries with challenging sexual limits; in a series of frenetic entries in her notebooks when she was about 19, in Wellington, she expresses her erotic desire for Maata Mahupuku, a Maori she had known at school in both Wellington and London. She wonders whether there is a norm against which she can measure herself: 'Do other people of my own age feel as I do I wonder so absolutely powerful licentious, so almost physically ill . . . I want Maata. I want her as I have had her—terribly.'[8] At the same time she is sexually involved with male lovers, driven by what she sees as conflicting instincts. While Wilde, one of the dominant influences in her late adolescence, advocates resisting everything but temptation, bourgeois Wellington's social imperatives insist on repression and self-control. Her notebooks indicate that the impossibility of reconciling two such contrary ideologies is frightening, as Mansfield lectures herself on her own behaviour: 'As it is, with a rapidity unimaginable, you are going to the Devil. PULL UP NOW YOURSELF.'[9] The grammatical awkwardness is a measure of the intractability of the emotional disruption the writer experiences.

Incompatible paradigms, one way of being that will not fit another, are explored in Mansfield's earliest writing, in stories that she did not attempt to publish though they have now appeared because her notebooks have been published in full. 'Summer Idylle. 1906', a vignette about two girls in a beach house, written when she was 18, is full of inversions; the girl who is 'wrapped in the darkness of her hair' has a European name, Marina, and yet her colouring suggests that she is Maori: 'A faint thin colour like the petal of a dull rose leaf shone in the dusk of her skin.'[10] Her pakeha companion has a Maori name, Hinemoa. The story expresses the sexual magnetism Marina exercises over Hinemoa, 'a curious feeling of pleasure, intermingled

---

[8] *KM Notebooks*, i. 103–4.   [9] *KM Notebooks*, i. 111.   [10] *KM Notebooks*, i. 75.

with a sensation which she did not analyse'.[11] A Maori girl or woman as both an object of desire and a double, an aspect of the self, appears in 'Kezia and Tui', and sections of an unfinished novel that was to have been called *Maata* show Mansfield using her friend's Maori name for a narrative with a strongly autobiographical element. In her mature fiction, these externalized accounts of two ways of life being contrasted become internalized, the 'other' becoming part of the self as it does in Linda in 'At the Bay' or the unnamed woman in 'Psychology'. Mansfield wrote to her friend Koteliansky three months before her death of her own experience of incompatible ways of being: 'I am always conscious of this secret disruption in me.'[12]

Mansfield's awareness of disruption within herself and New Zealand society prepared her for the major artistic changes that were taking place in Europe at the beginning of the twentieth century. In her earliest diary entries she is preoccupied with what she calls 'the secret self we all have',[13] which is often at odds with the public persona. She was ready for the fissures and fragments of T. S. Eliot's 'The Love Song of J. Alfred Prufrock', and for Marlow's partial recognition of his repressed self when he is attracted to Kurtz in *Heart of Darkness*, because she lived in a society that denied part of itself, that repressed awareness of its own otherness. Maori culture was and is a powerful presence in New Zealand, evident then and now. For the empire city to deny it, together with the painful history of Maori and pakeha interaction, was to attempt partial amnesia, a willed forgetting or a denial of guilt. The claim that pakeha are civilized, and Maoris primitive, is undermined by a clear-sighted look at colonial history, in which pakeha cheated and brutalized Maoris; the pakeha are barbaric, untrustworthy, and greedy and so the stranger is not alien, definable as Maori, but part of the pakeha self. What is repressed is the knowledge that creating the empire city and mirroring the imperial centre in the colony, of necessity involves rapacity, greed, and duplicity.

[11] Ibid.

[12] *The Letters of Katherine Mansfield*, ii. 260.

[13] Vincent O'Sullivan and Margaret Scott (eds.), *The Collected Letters of Katherine Mansfield* (Oxford: Clarendon Press, 1984–96), iv. 278. All subsequent quotations from the letters are taken from this edition (hereafter *CL*), except for those from January 1922 until Mansfield's death in 1923, which will appear in the fifth volume when it is published. Punctuation, and occasionally spelling, are erratic in the letters and journals; I quote them as they appear in the text.

Mansfield had what she describes significantly as 'the *taint* of the pioneer in my blood'[14] (my italics). Her father, Harold Beauchamp, was born in the Australian goldfields, the son of an unsuccessful speculator, but worked his way resolutely up the social ladder in New Zealand to, eventually, a knighthood, becoming a director of companies like one of the members of Marlow's audience for his tale in *Heart of Darkness*. Mansfield and her three sisters and one brother were part of a lively household, encouraged to be interested in painting and music, and to read and discuss their ideas. In some respects the empire city was more progressive than the metropolitan centre; the franchise was extended to women in New Zealand in 1893, which would not happen in Britain for another twenty-five years. Though she did not actively support the suffragettes when she was in London, Mansfield's early notebooks show an interest in the issue that was to develop into incisive interrogations of patriarchy in such stories as 'Mr Reginald Peacock's Day' and 'The Little Governess'. As early as 1908 she writes: 'I do now realise, dimly, what women in the future will be capable of achieving . . . Talk of our enlightened days and our emancipated country—pure nonsense. We are firmly held in the self fashioned chains of slavery.'[15] In 1903 Mansfield was sent to London to complete her education at Queen's College, Harley Street, a school for girls which encouraged intellectual development rather than gendered accomplishments. She published stories in school magazines in Wellington and London, began a novel called 'Juliet', took cello lessons, and read Wilde and the French Symbolists with enthusiasm. By the time she returned to New Zealand in 1906 she was in love with London: 'London—it is Life.'[16] She curses her family with adolescent gusto for their provinciality: 'Damn my family—O Heavens, what bores they are. I detest them all heartily.'[17] Her antipathy to both New Zealand and her family was so determined that her father allowed her to return to Britain in 1908. When she could no longer visit her homeland, because she had contracted tuberculosis and was too frail to undertake the long sea voyage, she yearned to do so and memories of childhood became an impetus for

[14] Vincent O'Sullivan (ed.), *Poems of Katherine Mansfield* (Oxford: Oxford University Press, 1988), 'To Stanislaw Wyspianski', 30.
[15] *KM Notebooks*, i. 110.
[16] Ibid. i. 108.
[17] Ibid.

her writing, but the feeling was always ambivalent and disruptive. Her dreams provide a wry insight into her feelings: on 19 March 1914, she writes, 'Dreamed about N.Z. Very delightful', but on the following day the entry reads, 'Dreamed about N.Z. again—one of the painful dreams when Im there & hazy about my return ticket.'[18]

Literary Life in London

Mansfield's experience of colonial life prepared her for the disrupted forms and fractured expression of the writers and artists who became known as Modernists; she was already familiar with the concept of a multiple and fissured self, rather than the unified and organic sense of self proposed by some high Victorian fiction, such as George Eliot's *Middlemarch*. Her question '*Who am I?*',[19] asked only days before her death, is the unresolved problem that haunts Prufrock in T. S. Eliot's 'The Love Song of J. Alfred Prufrock', D. H. Lawrence's Birkin in *Women in Love*, and James Joyce's Stephen in *A Portrait of the Artist as a Young Man*. When she first returned to London in 1908, her search for an identity sometimes seemed to her contemporaries to result in a series of disguises; she changed her physical appearance so much that she was unrecognizable. Her first husband, George Bowden, said that the second time he met her she was dressed 'more or less Maori fashion' and 'looked like Oscar Wilde'.[20] John Middleton Murry, who became her second husband, thought her boyishly charming when he first met her. Other accounts of her describe her as wearing a kimono and using white make-up to give the effect of a Japanese mask, or appearing bizarrely in a funereal black suit and shiny black hat for her first wedding. As she experimented with projecting disparate images of herself, so she used different pseudonyms as a writer: the author of her stories in little magazines appeared as Julian Mark, Lili Heron, Boris Petrovsky, Elizabeth Stanley, or Matilda Berry. The familiar 'Katherine Mansfield' is itself a pseudonym as she was born Kathleen Mansfield Beauchamp, Mansfield being the maiden name of her beloved grandmother. Her first marriage, although she left her husband immediately after the wedding, added the option of

---

[18] Ibid. i. 280.

[19] *The Letters of Katherine Mansfield*, ii. 266.

[20] Antony Alpers, *The Life of Katherine Mansfield* (New York: Viking, 1980), 87.

'Bowden' to her range of possible names. Her lifelong friend and companion Ida Baker, whom she first met at Queen's College, described her as 'a born actress and mimic'.[21] Perhaps 'bred' is a more accurate description than 'born', in the light of colonial New Zealand's anxiety to mimic Britain. Several of Mansfield's early New Zealand stories, such as 'The Wind Blows' and 'Prelude', play on the link between clothes and an attempt to project an image which is undermined by weather or the intimacy of a small settler society.

Between 1910 and 1912 Mansfield had a series of encounters with writers and painters that radically changed her literary aesthetic. The first was with A. R. Orage, who was the editor of the first socialist weekly in London, the *New Age*, or, as Orage ruefully called it, the *No Wage*. He accepted for publication in the magazine her Bavarian sketches, which appeared together in book form as *In a German Pension* in 1911; Mansfield commented much later that Orage had taught her how to write and to think. The *New Age* was remarkable in its avant-garde editorial policy; it reproduced work by Picasso, and included translations of the fiction of Chekhov and Dostoevsky. Its essayists included Ezra Pound, and Edwin Muir, and it introduced to its public major new thinkers, such as Sigmund Freud and Friedrich Nietzsche, through translation and critical essays. Mansfield's lifelong fascination with Chekhov began when she wrote for the *New Age*. She recognized in him a writer who, like herself, was interested in posing questions rather than, like the Edwardian realists such as Bennett and Galsworthy, in providing answers. She wrote to Virginia Woolf in 1919: 'what the writer does is not so much to *solve* the question but to *put* the question. There must be the question put. That seems to me a very nice dividing line between the true & the false writer.'[22]

Mansfield's earliest letters and notebooks show her interest in the visual arts, which was sustained by her interaction with the *New Age* group; her Japanese image arose out of a visit to an exhibition of Japanese shrines, gardens, cultural ceremonies, martial arts, and artefacts, held in the summer of 1910 in Shepherd's Bush. Later in 1910 another exhibition in London caused an uproar; Virginia Woolf claimed, with characteristic ironic exaggeration, that it changed

---

[21] [Ida Baker], *Katherine Mansfield, the Memories of L.M.* (London: Michael Joseph, 1971), 233.

[22] *CL* ii. 320.

human character. In November Roger Fry brought to London the work of painters such as Cézanne, Van Gogh, and Gauguin, which had long been familiar in Paris, in the exhibition 'Manet and the Post-Impressionists' at the Grafton Gallery. Years later Mansfield wrote a letter about the impact on her of the exhibition, saying that Van Gogh's paintings in particular 'taught me something about writing, which was queer—a kind of freedom—or rather, a shaking free'.[23] This was a radical disruption of a positive kind for her; what was being displaced was the norm of realism. In his introduction to the catalogue for the exhibition, Desmond MacCarthy explained that Impressionism was so preoccupied with catching, for instance, a particular tree in a particular light that the 'tree-ness' of the tree escaped the painter: that the essence of the tree could better be conveyed through a pared-down reduction of the tree to its outline, such as might be offered by Matisse rather than Monet. Similarly a Cubist portrait, for instance by Picasso, offers a multidimensional approach to the subject, suggesting the varied simultaneous ways of looking and of being that also came to be encoded in T. S. Eliot's poetry and in Woolf's and Mansfield's fiction.

Murry and Rhythm

Mansfield's relationship with the *New Age* group was stormy, although she retained her admiration for Orage, so in 1911, in search of a new outlet for her work, she sent John Middleton Murry, the editor of a new little magazine called *Rhythm*, some kind of fairy tale, possibly resembling the story 'In Summer' included in the *Notebooks* (i. 174–6) but never otherwise published. It tells how Phyllis, a shepherdess, encounters the Yellow Dwarf, the child of gorse and broom, who enables her to meet Corydon, a musician wearing a garland of roses and little else. Murry rejected it. She then considered more carefully the editorial aspirations of the magazine, expressed in its first issue: 'it is neo-barbarians, men and women who to the timid and unimaginative seem merely perverse and atavistic, that must familiarize us with our outcast selves'.[24] The idea of the outcast and exile as part of the self was familiar to her from her life in New Zealand, and she sent Murry 'The Woman at the Store', a story set

---

[23] *CL* iv. 333.   [24] *Rhythm*, vol. I, no. 1 (Summer 1911), 3.

in the backblocks (the sparsely inhabited inland country) of New Zealand. He accepted it enthusiastically; they met and became lovers, and he introduced her to a group of expatriate writers and painters who lived in Paris. Their excitement about their cultural environment is expressed by the art editor of *Rhythm*, the Scottish painter J. D. Fergusson:

It was in these pre-war days that Middleton Murry and Michael Sadler came over and asked me to be the art editor of *Rhythm*. Peploe contributed to it. Later Murry came with Katherine Mansfield. We were all very excited with the Russian Ballet when it came to Paris. Bakst was a *Sociétaire* of the Salon d'Automne and used all the ideas of modern painting for his *décor*. Diaghilev made a triumph, surely even greater than he had hoped for. No wonder S. J. [Peploe] said these were some of the greatest nights of his life. They were the greatest nights in anyone's life— *Sheherazade*, *Petruchka*, *Sacre du Printemps*, Nijinski, Karsavina, Fokine. But we didn't spend all our evenings at the Russian ballet; there was the Cirque Médrano, the Concert-Mayol and the Gaité-Montparnasse.[25]

Diaghilev's Ballets Russes, fusing avant-garde music by Stravinsky or Debussy with Nijinsky's or Fokine's radical choreography and Bakst's Post-Impressionist costumes and sets, broke nineteenth-century moulds and academic traditions. The *Rhythm* group felt liberated to cross borders, both artistic and social. Pound's Modernist battle-cry was 'Make it new!' The *Rhythm* group's particular impetus for making it new was Fauvism, an inflection of Post-Impressionism initiated by Van Gogh and Gauguin and developed by Matisse. Its attempt to simplify and pare down line in sculpture and painting, to reveal deep structures rather than surface detail, resonated with Mansfield's own search for a new form for the short story. 'Fauve' means 'wild beast'; Murry and Mansfield, by 1912 the assistant editor of *Rhythm*, became known as 'The Two Tigers'. Mansfield's Fauvist passion for a sharp line never left her; she writes to Murry: 'Im a powerful stickler for form . . . I hate the sort of licence that English people give themselves—to spread over and flop and roll about. I feel as fastidious as though I wrote with acid.'[26]

Through the *Rhythm* group, Mansfield became part of an artistic milieu that both intrigued and exasperated her, as Murry himself

[25] Margaret Morris, *The Art of J. D. Fergusson: A Biased Biography* (Glasgow and London: Blackie, 1974), 47.
[26] *CL* i. 124.

did. They met Rupert Brooke and developed an intimate friendship with Frieda and D. H. Lawrence; by 1915 they had met the literary hostess Lady Ottoline Morrell and some of the Bloomsbury Group. Mansfield's letters to Morrell are often effusive and affected, giving the impression that she is looking in the mirror and trying unsuccessfully to mimic the natives of the imperial centre, though at the same time in letters to Murry she complains of the insiders' snobbery. The Lawrences and Mansfield and Murry were always short of money and moved from one rented house or flat to another; they were socially suspect and had to contend with family hostility because both women were married to other men at the beginning of their relationships. Though their marital situation did not perturb Morrell, her houseparties at Garsington made Mansfield feel an outsider, with no home, no children and deteriorating health. Mansfield's stories, unlike Woolf's novels, are characterized by a restless movement that is suggested by such titles as 'An Indiscreet Journey' or 'The Voyage'; even 'Prelude', a 'debt of love'[27] she paid to her childhood, begins with a family moving house.

The First World War and Illness

The First World War, which at first is barely reflected in Mansfield's personal writing, affected her increasingly directly; in 1915 her only brother was killed in France. A strange poem that she wrote about a dream soon after his death shows her trying to re-enter the familiar childhood world: 'We were at home again beside the stream.' However, the familiar has become unfamiliar as her brother invites her into a sacramental ceremony with him which will kill her, when he offers her poisonous berries:

> By the remembered stream my brother stands
> Waiting for me with berries in his hands . . .
> 'These are my body. Sister, take and eat.'[28]

This final sinister line, suggesting that the well-loved sibling relationship is drawing her into death, gives the reader an experience that recurs in Mansfield's fiction as the familiar is made strange. Kezia, in 'Prelude', stands as she has often done at an upstairs

---

[27] *KM Notebooks*, ii. 32.
[28] O'Sullivan (ed.), *Poems of Katherine Mansfield*, 'To L. H. B. (1894–1915)', 54.

window but 'As she stood there, the day flickered out and dark came. With the dark crept the wind snuffling and howling' (p. 82). Her terror is comparable with the moment in 'At the Bay' when the children, playing in the washhouse, suddenly and mistakenly sense that they have been abandoned by their parents. The familiar is transformed: 'It was true, it was real. Pressed against the window was a pale face, black eyes, a black beard' (p. 306). What seems to them an ogre or a vampire is Jonathan, a father who has come to collect his children, but their instinct is not entirely wrong, as the reader knows that Jonathan would like to abandon his family, but cannot summon up the energy to do so. Hints of the darkness shadowing a sunny day at the seaside occur throughout the story, most obviously when Kezia gets a terrified glimpse of her beloved grandmother's mortality.

During the war, Mansfield became intensely aware of her own mortality, and of the dark side to her physical pleasures: in February 1918 she bounded into bed, coughed, and began to spit blood. Diagnosed as suffering from tuberculosis, probably caused by gonococcal infection, she considered entering a sanatorium but decided against it because it would interfere with her writing, though from 1919 she had to spend the winter months in the Mediterranean or Switzerland as her health could not withstand a British winter. In a letter that contains a brilliant analysis of her own fiction she explains to Murry how she responds to post-war writing:

I cant imagine how after the war these men can pick up the old threads as tho' it had never been. Speaking to *you* Id say we have died and live again. How can that be the same life? It doesn't mean that Life is the less precious of [*sic*] that the 'common things of light and day' are gone. They are not gone, they are intensified, they are illumined. Now we know ourselves for what we are. In a way its a tragic knowledge. Its as though, even while we live again we face death. But *through Life*: thats the point. We see death in life as we see death in a flower that is fresh unfolded.[29]

She uses the shorthand of the literary language she and Murry shared when she says that her consciousness of death is of 'deserts of vast eternity', taken from Andrew Marvell's poem 'To His Coy Mistress' and referring to the long inactivity of the grave. Then she compares her own method with Murry's very explicit fiction:

[29] *CL* iii. 97.

But the difference between you and me is (perhaps Im wrong) I couldn't tell anybody *bang out* about those deserts. They are my secret. I might write about a boy eating strawberries or a woman combing her hair on a windy morning & that is the only way I can ever mention them. But they *must* be there. Nothing less will do.[30]

Mansfield's creative energy from 1918 until her death from tuberculosis in January 1923, at the age of 34, focused on finding a form for her fiction that would 'speak to the secret self we all have—to acknowledge that',[31] never explicitly. Characteristically this involves a moment of disruption, when the world as a character believes it to be is disturbed by a darker vision, as it is when Kezia confronts the possibility that her grandmother will die or when Miss Brill's sense of living as being part of a theatrical company is jarred by a young girl's perception of her. There is never any intervention or commentary by the narrator of the stories, no telling *bang out*, and the moment passes, but its significance for the consciousness that experiences it is not in doubt.

Writing the Secret Self

The secret self is not, of course, only concerned with disappointment or death. One aspect of Mansfield's mature fiction that becomes increasingly subtle is her control of comedy. Her early stories are overtly satirical; as she wrote to Murry: 'Ive two "kick offs" in the writing game. *One* is joy—real joy . . . The other "kick off" is my old original one . . . *a cry against corruption*.'[32] The second kick off was initially expressed through parodies in the *New Age*, in the stories she wrote for the magazine that were collected and published as *In a German Pension*, and eventually through the sophisticated satire of such stories as '*Je ne parle pas français*', in which the macabre vision of the narrator constructs his favourite Parisian café as a haunt for the vampiric undead, for instance the waiter:

He is grey, flat-footed and withered, with long, brittle nails that set your nerves on edge while he scrapes up your two sous. When he is not smearing over the table or flicking at a dead fly or two, he stands with one hand on the back of a chair, in his far too long apron, and over his other arm the three-cornered dip of dirty napkin, waiting to be photographed in

[30] *CL* iii. 97–8.   [31] *CL* iv. 278.   [32] *CL* ii. 54.

connection with some wretched murder. 'Interior of Café where Body was Found.' You've seen him hundreds of times. (p. 143)

Mansfield's comedy pivots on disruption, here the disjunction between the common view of the hygiene desirable in cafés and the grisly spectacle offered by the ghoulish waiter. The comedy that stems from joy, on the other hand, reveals a sympathetic pleasure in idiosyncrasy, for instance at the timidity of the two sisters in 'The Daughters of the Late Colonel'. Their genteel vicar asks if they would like a consolatory 'little Communion', and the narrative perspective enacts the sisters' response:

But the idea of a little Communion terrified them. What! In the drawing-room by themselves—with no—no altar or anything! The piano would be much too high, thought Constantia, and Mr Farolles could not possibly lean over it with the chalice. And Kate would be sure to come bursting in and interrupt them, thought Josephine. And supposing the bell rang in the middle? It might be somebody important—about their mourning. Would they get up reverently and go out, or would they have to wait . . . in torture? (p. 235)

Here the disruption stems from the sisters' own sense that there is a place for everything: religion belongs in church and would be embarrassing if it invaded the drawing-room. Their conservatism is not mocked, but is part of a subtle revelation of their suppressed secret selves which come out of the shadows fleetingly, and temporarily, at the end of the story. The harsh comedy of '*Je ne parle pas français*', however, gives the reader an insight into the secret self of the narrator, Duquette, the gigolo and pimp who poses as a writer. Comedy pervades Mansfield's stories as it does her personal writing; not long before her death she wrote in her notebook: 'the sense of humour I have found true of every single occasion of my life'.[33] Virginia Woolf's husband, Leonard, said that Mansfield made him laugh more than anyone else in their brilliant set, and her wit flickered even over her own death: 'I told poor old L.M. [Ida Baker] yesterday that after I died to PROVE there was no immortality I would send her a coffin worm in a matchbox. She was gravely puzzled.'[34]

Roger Fry defines the Modernism of the Post-Impressionists in a

---

[33] *KM Notebooks*, ii. 329.   [34] *CL* iv. 100.

way that also applies to Mansfield's fiction: 'They do not seek to imitate form, but to create form; not to imitate life, but to find an equivalent for life'.[35] His stress is on their avoidance of realism and of imitating life, creating in their art an experience for the viewer or reader that is like living, that gives the readers a charge that is an event in their lives, not a mirror of reality. Mansfield's friend Virginia Woolf, who was also a close friend and biographer of Roger Fry, shared Mansfield's dissatisfaction with conventional realism in fiction, and expressed her frustration with it in a review essay which Mansfield admired, written in 1919, and called 'Modern Fiction' when it appeared in *The Common Reader*. In it Woolf attacks her contemporaries, not the great nineteenth-century realists, and says that writers like Arnold Bennett and John Galsworthy fill their novels with details about contexts and clothes but 'Life escapes'. She then asks the reader to think what it is like to inhabit 'an ordinary mind on an ordinary day':

The mind receives a myriad impressions—trivial, fantastic, evanescent, or engraved with the sharpness of steel. From all sides they come, an incessant shower of innumerable atoms; and as they fall, as they shape themselves into the life of Monday or Tuesday, the accent falls differently from of old; the moment of importance came not here but there ... Let us record the atoms as they fall upon the mind in the order in which they fall, let us trace the pattern, however disconnected and incoherent in appearance, which each sight or incident scores upon the consciousness. Let us not take it for granted that life exists more fully in what is commonly thought big than in what is commonly thought small.[36]

What this implies is that something small, such as a moment in a shop, might be more vivid to us than something more apparently significant, like an election or a battle; human consciousness does not respond according to an existing hierarchy of events. Similarly, our experience of an ordinary day will bring conflicting sensations; there is not a necessary order of significance. The seeing mind, and therefore the memory, do not notice every item of dress worn by companions; they will, for instance, register how a shirt enhances the colour of the wearer's eyes but not notice or remember what kind of shoes accompany it. Woolf requires a pared-down fiction, a

[35] Roger Fry, *Vision and Design* (Harmondsworth: Penguin, 1937), 195.

[36] Virginia Woolf, *The Common Reader* (London: Hogarth, 1962), i. 189–90.

simplified line that records the atoms as they fall and makes the ordinary life of Monday different from Tuesday.

In Mansfield's fiction the various kinds of disruption that signify disturbance are not as obvious formally as they are either in the fragmented *Waste Land*, or in the strange juxtaposition of the various parts of *To the Lighthouse*. None the less the pared-down line is there, requiring an observant reader who is not seduced by nostalgia into thinking that stories like 'The Garden Party' celebrate the lost colonial world of Mansfield's childhood. Pound's definition of Imagism, that the artist seeks out luminous detail without commenting on it, resembles what Mansfield writes after the war about ordinary things being intensified and illumined. She rejects realism: '<u>Art</u> is not an attempt to reconcile existence with his [the artist's] vision: it is an attempt to create his own world <u>in</u> this world. That which suggests the subject to the artist is the <u>unlikeness</u> of it to what we accept as reality. We single out, we bring into the light, we put up higher.'[37] Mansfield's stories focus on luminous details which resonate within the story and gain significance in the reader's mind in retrospect because they elude definition. The aloe in 'Prelude', the pear tree in 'Bliss', the little lamp in 'The Doll's House', the swan-headed umbrella in 'The Voyage', the signet ring in 'The Man Without a Temperament', the fur necklet in 'Miss Brill' are all brought into the light, but the light flickers as the object is seen from different angles, and no two readers interpret it in the same way. This nebulous but haunting symbolism has affinities with Woolf's rather than with D. H. Lawrence's writing practice. When Roger Fry first read *To the Lighthouse* he wrote to the author asking what the lighthouse symbolized. She replied tartly:

I meant *nothing* by The Lighthouse. One has to have a central line down the middle of the book to hold the design together. I saw that all sorts of feelings would accrue to this, but I refused to think them out, and trusted that people would make it the deposit for their own emotions—which they have done, one thinking it means one thing another another. I can't manage Symbolism except in this vague, generalised way. Whether its right or wrong I don't know, but directly I'm told what a thing means, it becomes hateful to me.[38]

[37] *KM Notebooks*, ii. 267.
[38] Nigel Nicholson and Joanne Trautmann (eds.), *The Letters of Virginia Woolf* (6 vols.; London: Chatto & Windus, 1980–3), iii. 385.

There must be the question put, as Mansfield said to Woolf of Chekhov's stories; both Woolf and Mansfield invite the reader to speculate about the luminous details in their fiction, but their texts resist definitive readings as Chekhov's do. For both writers it is the design of the novel or story which is crucial rather than plot or character.

Mansfield enacts in their form the disruption that is often the oblique focus of the stories. They frequently open abruptly, plunging readers into a situation about which they know nothing: 'Suddenly—dreadfully—she wakes up' (p. 74) and 'She is like St Anne' (p. 60) are equally disorientating opening sentences, their urgency intensified by the use of the present tense. Even more disconcertingly, stories sometimes begin apparently in the middle of a sentence, with a conjunction, as if the reader is coming in on a conversation: 'And then, after six years, she saw him again' (p. 135) or 'And after all the weather was ideal' (p. 336). Beneath the sharply observed detail and the shimmering grace of the prose there is constant pressure on readers to be more alert to the nuances of what they encounter. 'The Daughters of the Late Colonel' is one of what are sometimes called the 'twelve-cell' stories, meaning that the parts are organically connected, 'multi-cellular like living tissue'.[39] A logical reader might expect the separate parts to shift in time, or to focus on different characters, and the openings to the sections seem to indicate this. The second part begins 'Another thing which complicated matters', but there is no indication of what the first thing was. Sections begin 'But, after all', 'Well, at any rate', 'But at that moment', as if the reader is inhabiting the sisters' fuzzy debate that is never articulated. The sisters' inability to name what has happened is implied in the first sentence: 'The week after was one of the busiest weeks of their lives' (p. 230). After what? 'On the morning—well, on the last morning' (p. 232) is as close as we get to an answer, though we understand that the event is the death of the colonel. The title implies the daughters' subordination, as they are seen exclusively in relation to their father; they may be unable to think clearly because they are overcome with grief, but the comic disjunctions in the story hint at something else. They discuss the funeral arrangements with the vicar:

[39] See Ian Gordon (ed.), *Undiscovered Country: The New Zealand Stories of Katherine Mansfield* (London: Longman, 1974), p. xix.

'I should like it to be quite simple,' said Josephine firmly, 'and not too expensive. At the same time, I should like—'

'A good one that will last,' thought dreamy Constantia, as if Josephine were buying a night-gown. (p. 235)

Under their dutiful exterior, and apparently without knowing it themselves, the sisters want their old brute of a father safely and permanently underground, just as they want to embarrass their pompous brother who is in the colonial service. Josephine contemplates sending him their father's watch:

She even thought for a moment of hiding the watch in a narrow cardboard corset-box that she'd kept by her for a long time, waiting for it to come in for something. It was such beautiful firm cardboard. But, no, it wouldn't be appropriate for this occasion. It had lettering on it: *Medium Women's* 28. *Extra Firm Busks*. It would be almost too much of a surprise for Benny to open that and find father's watch inside. (p. 240)

The unanswered questions and ellipses suggest the sisters' indecision, and their wavering movement towards an epiphany, a moment of revelation which never arrives: 'She wanted to say something to Josephine, something frightfully important, about—about the future and what. . . .' (p. 249). The secret self is repressed, and the punctuation, as frequently occurs in Mansfield's stories, gestures towards what cannot be said because it is only subliminally known.

Disruption is a feature of Kezia's experience, as it is of her older counterpart, Laura in 'The Garden Party'; both characters and their families, the Burnells and the Sheridans, recur in the stories. The phrase 'after all' in the opening sentence of 'The Garden Party' is an example of the avoidance of the kind of detailed realistic description that Virginia Woolf found so tedious. Without spelling it out, it conveys to us that the family have been worrying about the weather for the garden party, and we can guess at their social status through the phrase 'if they had ordered it'. These people are used to ordering what they want; we see that when a florist arrives with trays full of canna lilies. In the first paragraph we are plunged into the story's situation and have to figure it out for ourselves; we cannot sit back and wait for it all to come to us. It is a bit like overhearing a conversation on a bus and trying to work out what is going on. The family giving the party have a gardener who does not just mow the lawns but sweeps them and takes out the daisy plants; these are wealthy perfectionists who want to impress. There is a shift in the passage from 'they' to 'you', altering the reader's position. The narrative voice in Mansfield's fiction is often polyphonic; it speaks with multiple voices, and the reader has to be alert to follow what is happening. The use of free indirect speech creates a flexible and mobile narrative perspective; the writer always wears a disguise or a mask. The move from 'they' to 'you' is the beginning, particularly in 'Hundreds, yes literally hundreds', of a voice that is identified later in the story when Mrs Sheridan says, ' "*Not* in the garden?" ' (p. 344). Readers can only know this when they have finished the story and think back to the beginning, a process that, like lyric poetry, Mansfield's fiction invites. We also have to work out where this story is taking place. It could be in the home counties of England, or in other places in Britain, but the mention of karaka trees, the veranda, and the juxtaposition of the big houses and lanes of little cottages all imply that this is not so, and that the story takes place in colonial Wellington. Perhaps that suggests a society that is mimicking another; it might remind us of royal garden parties in Buckingham Palace and Holyrood House. Another question that arises is, how old is Laura? Again, we are almost never told the ages of Mansfield's characters; we have to work it out. A lot is not said and the reader has to be active and draw inferences.

The story is a sharp-edged attack on New Zealand's myths of nationhood; a classless society is uncomfortably eroded by the narrative, which shows New Zealand dutifully mirroring British snobbery. The perspective in the passage asserting Laura's freedom from 'these absurd class distinctions' (p. 338) is obviously hers, and is undermined by her surprise that a working man takes pleasure in the smell of lavender, showing that she expects workmen to be coarse and insensitive. Since the narrative takes Laura's perspective, it is unreliable, but the reader is constantly reminded of class distinctions that Laura does not notice: there is an insistent contrast, for instance, between the working men in shirt-sleeves and Laura's father and Laurie brushing their hats to go to the office. The gardener has been up since dawn but Jose is still in her dressing-gown.

The reader's impression of the Sheridan household is one of opulence, canna lilies, whipped cream, and silver, and the prose moves to enact the excitement and self-indulgence in the house. The description of the lane where the carter's family live makes an interesting contrast with it; here the gardens grow sick hens and tomato cans. The voice of the opening paragraph returns in supercilious phrases such as: 'They were the greatest possible eyesore' and 'Children swarmed' (p. 343). We can hear Mrs Sheridan's horror of the poor breeding like rabbits as she worries about this kind of squalor in her backyard, lowering the real estate value of her house. So, like the colonel's daughters, Laura seems to be heading for a moment of epiphany or self-revelation, when she will recognize fully that the poor are human too, and dissociate herself from her family. However, that is not quite what happens.

The pivotal crisis occurs, significantly, in front of a mirror. Laura's mother knows the power of the image in her family, and she uses it to counter Laura's horror at the callousness of giving a garden party next door to a bereaved family. She pops her new hat on Laura's head. This is a clever anticipation of the duckling-into-swan moment; Laura responds to the seductive glamour of being transformed, as we see when her thoughts echo her mother's register: 'quite the best plan' (p. 345). At the moment when Laura sees a charming girl in the mirror she is a stranger to herself: 'the first thing she saw was this charming girl in the mirror, in her black hat trimmed with gold daisies, and a long black velvet ribbon' (p. 345). Her bourgeois Wellington persona is not integrated into the secret self that wants to rebel, but her clear image of the carter's suffering family recedes to become part of the social world, 'unreal, like a picture in the newspaper'. Laura and her day then blossom like the roses that impress people at garden parties; we read that 'the perfect afternoon slowly ripened, slowly faded, slowly its petals closed' (p. 346). The hat becomes the embodiment of Sheridan materialism; Laura wears it as she carries cream puffs to people wearing tweed caps or shawls. The clothes have a heightened symbolic function, rather than filling in realistic detail. The garden party itself is described in less than half a page, which, considering the title of the story, is disorientating to the reader.

The moment of disruption comes when one picture meets another. Before the Sheridans' party, Mrs Sheridan tells Laura, '"I have never seen you look such a picture"' (p. 344), and other guests and her family confirm this with the reiterated word 'look' (p. 345). When Laura gets to the carter's house, wanting to leave the basket and flee, the carter's sister-in-law offers her another picture, in a different but equally ritualized social situation: ' "You'd like a look at 'im, wouldn't you?" said Em's sister . . . "'e looks a picture" '. (p. 349). What Laura is learning is that the working class, so despised by her family, have their own formalities, that these strangers are not alien to her, and that the dead young man has a temporary iconic status in his world as she had in hers. The language of her encounter with her first corpse is complex. She sentimentalizes the moment, turning the carter into a kind of male Sleeping Beauty, but she ends by sobbing ' "Forgive my hat" ' (p. 349). Though she avoids an understanding of the terminal significance of the death for the carter's family, she recognizes that she has betrayed the carter and herself by repressing her secret self, which knows that the party should have been cancelled, and by becoming the young woman in the mirror who looked a picture. It is a moment of epiphany which needs to be articulated; she is on the edge of learning something. The final paragraph of the story could be seen as Laura's moment of disruption, when she escapes from the boundaries of her mother's class-bound bourgeois view of the world, but the familiar voice suggests otherwise. Laura resembles the daughters of the colonel in being unable to articulate what she partly knows; the punctuation indicates her incoherence: ' "Isn't life," she stammered, "isn't life—" ' Laura's confidence that Laurie 'quite understood' is thrown into question for the reader by his: ' "*Isn't* it, darling?" ' (p. 349), which sounds just like Mrs Sheridan, not wanting to hear Laura's disturbed and disturbing account of what she has seen. What Mansfield herself wrote about the story shows her perception that the order which the colonial world and early twentieth-century realistic fiction wanted to impose was liable to disruption, and that the atoms fall in unruly ways:

[Laura] feels things ought to happen differently. First one and then another. But life isn't like that. We haven't the ordering of it. Laura says, 'But all these things must not happen at once.' And Life answers, 'Why not? How are they divided from each other.' And they *do* all happen, it is inevitable.[40]

'The Garden Party' gives the reader an equivalent for life in that it requires us to pick up hints and oblique suggestions instead of describing characters in realistic detail. Laura's attempt to explore

[40] *The Letters of Katherine Mansfield*, ii. 196.

the deep structures of the self are implied when she leaves the silver and cream puff world and enters the 'smoky and dark' arena of the lane to meet her own equivalent, the young man who looks a picture and whom she partly recognizes as herself, the stranger within. It is an odd doubling, revealing that difference between classes is a myth, and at the same time recognizing how profoundly Laura has internalized class-consciousness. Particularly because of her gender, she needs to articulate her experience of disruption, but she resorts to the semiotic: she sobs and embraces her brother, but allows him to speak for her and to misrepresent what she knows. This female disempowerment in the face of patriarchal intervention is a characteristic motif in Mansfield's fiction, as it is in Woolf's early novel *The Voyage Out*.

Selections from Mansfield's Stories: New Zealand and Europe

All selections from Mansfield's stories include 'Prelude', 'At the Bay', and 'The Garden Party'; the stories most frequently anthologized are 'The Garden Party', 'The Daughters of the Late Colonel', and 'The Fly'. Mansfield's New Zealand stories and fragments were collected and arranged by subject rather than date by Ian Gordon in the volume *Undiscovered Country* (1974); the chronology is provided by the characters and ranges from the lives of children to those of old people. The editor's view that Mansfield's mature New Zealand stories create 'a romantic dream-world . . . an Arcadian country' with people who are 'idealised, happy, encapsulated in a world that never was'[41] is belied by the disruption that is characteristic of them. What the empire city is shown in the mirror held up by Mansfield's stories is not a realistic reflection, but disjunctive images that comment on each other. She is like her own Kezia, holding the dirty calico cat up to the mirror: '"Now look at yourself," said she sternly' (p. 120). Various pictures coexist that are not simply binary opposites, as they do in Cubist portraits: in 'Prelude' Linda Burnell both loves and hates her husband; Mrs Fairfield both comforts the little girls and is complicit with patriarchy; Kezia is imaginative but haunted. Vincent O'Sullivan's selection, *Katherine Mansfield: New Zealand Stories* (1997), places twenty-five of Mansfield's New Zealand stories

---

[41] Gordon (ed.), *Undiscovered Country*, p. xviii.

in the order in which they were written; only nine of those were included in the volumes that Mansfield herself compiled for publication. This collection invites a reading that recognizes Mansfield's critique of the remembered world of childhood:

There are times when the reading of Mansfield in her own country has meant fairly persistent simplifying. The almost innate belief in most New Zealanders that theirs is a classless community, that the social hierarchies of an older world, if not quite shucked off, are certainly less constraining, has perhaps led to odd distortions. 'The Garden Party', understandably a classroom favourite, is usually read as a story about growing up, one in which there might indeed be an element of social criticism, but where most of all we see a 17-year-old girl face the impenetrable reality of death and mature before its disturbing wonder. The story is read too in terms of its lingering colonial charm . . . The text defies such an easy assumption.[42]

Mansfield herself, in some of her plans for volumes of her stories, thought of alternating New Zealand and European stories though she did not carry this out. Though the stories set in Europe often focus on lonely, displaced women, many of the New Zealand stories give a different twist to a similar theme, in that their characters suddenly feel themselves to be in danger where they thought they were safest, in the supposedly known world of home. The moment of insecurity and terror is caught in sharply defined clarity, often through an object which gains symbolic significance such as Laura's hat, Linda's wallpaper, the window of the washhouse, or the aloe.

Disruption is as characteristic of Mansfield's European stories as of her New Zealand ones. The opening paragraph of 'The Man Without a Temperament' enacts through the rhythm of its sentences the action of its protagonist: 'He pursed his lips—he might have been going to whistle—but he did not whistle—only turned the ring—turned the ring on his pink, freshly washed hands' (p. 201). The reader hears, rhythmically, the ring being turned through the punctuation of the passage; part of the pared-down quality of Mansfield's prose is the crafting of the lines. She said of rhythm: 'In Miss Brill I chose not only the length of every sentence, but even the sound of every sentence—I chose the rise and fall of every paragraph to fit her . . . After Id written it I read it aloud—numbers of times—

---

just as one would *play over* a musical composition.'[43] The man's consciousness is never revealed by his speech, but by unexplained disjunctions in the text that are signalled by an ellipsis and a line space:

On the hedges on the other side of the road there were grapes small as berries, growing wild, growing among the stones. He leaned against a wall, filled his pipe, put a match to it. . . .

Leaned across a gate, turned up the collar of his mackintosh. It was going to rain. It didn't matter, he was prepared for it. You didn't expect anything else in November. He looked over the bare field. (p. 208)

The reader experiences the disruption, and realizes that the man who is dutifully caring for his invalid wife is in-between, in that he is imagining himself to be far from the Provençal countryside, and at home in England; if he were portrayed only through his speech and behaviour he could seem a conventionally patriarchal figure. A portfolio of pictures of him emerges from the story apart from the privileged insight into his consciousness: some guests see him as an ox rather than a man, some are contemptuous of him, to the staff he is autocratic, to his wife he is 'bread and wine', to three little local girls he seems a potential child molester. The question about him is posed but not answered by the story; its final line, with its 'penetrating, punning bitterness',[44] is ' "Rot!" he whispers' (p. 212). He may be dismissing her anxieties as he tucks her in, he may be longing for her to decay, he may be describing how he feels about his own situation; the reader can only speculate. The story is sharply etched but not tidily wrapped up with a narrative twist that provides a conclusive ending.

The man is aware of the stranger within, but represses his yearning for that otherness and mimics a model husband. Mansfield's youthful experience of the empire city's mimicry of the metropolitan centre, and of its repression of guilt, prepared her to recognize the potential of experimental Modernism for her own fiction: she quickly registered how she could adapt a Fauvist aesthetic to her writing, by paring down her stories to luminous detail and cogent design in order to put a question. What her contemporary, the artist Paul Klee, said in 1920 suggests her achievement: 'Art does not reproduce the visible but makes visible.'

[43] *CL* iv. 165.   [44] *CL* iii, p. xi.

NOTE ON THE TEXT

Many of the stories included here were first published in such magazines as the *New Age*, *Rhythm*, or the *Athenaeum*. Information about the stories' first appearance, for which I am indebted to B. J. Kirkpatrick's comprehensive *A Bibliography of Katherine Mansfield*, is given in the Explanatory Notes at the end of the book. Most of Mansfield's stories were included in volumes published either by her in her lifetime or immediately after her death by her husband, John Middleton Murry. In 1984 Antony Alpers, author of the most comprehensive biography of Mansfield, published *The Stories of Katherine Mansfield*. He omitted some of the stories included in the Constable volume edited by John Middleton Murry in 1945, and included some early work which had not previously appeared in book form. He also returned to the manuscripts of the stories if they still existed; to the first editions of the three books that appeared in Mansfield's lifetime, which she had checked or amended in proof; and to magazine versions of the stories for which she usually had no access to the proofs. The text of the stories here is taken from that edition (punctuation slightly amended occasionally), with the exception of 'A Cup of Tea', not included by Alpers, and taken from the Constable edition. The extensive 'Commentary' at the end of Alpers's edition of the stories is invaluable; I have used it in the notes on individual stories. The most significant difference between the Constable edition and this one occurs in '*Je ne parle pas français*'; Michael Sadleir insisted that Mansfield should bowdlerize the story if Constable was to publish it. She did so, though the original version appeared as the second publication of the Murrys' own Heron Press and is reinstated here as it is in Alpers's edition of the stories.

The notes to individual stories include Mansfield's comments on them, where they are relevant; the stories are in the chronological order offered by Alpers. Some of her early stories, written for *Rhythm* or the *Blue Review*, which were not part of Dan Davin's previous World's Classics selection, are included here: 'The Woman at the Store', 'Millie', and 'How Pearl Button Was Kidnapped'. Mansfield herself refused to allow 'The Woman at the Store', for example, to be reprinted during her lifetime. Its conventional form, with the narrative twist at the end, was a structure she subsequently rejected, but it evokes the ironic in-between situation of the protagonist whose womanhood has been her destruction and whose store is empty. These are early examples of Mansfield's brilliant probing of what she called, as a girl, women's 'self fashioned chains of slavery': that is, girls' and women's complicity with patriarchy. The only story set in Europe that is added, 'Frau Brechenmacher Attends a Wedding', originally appeared in the *New Age* and is the most complex of the satirical stories about Bavaria in *In a German Pension*. It anticipates the nuanced narrative perspective that Mansfield was later to develop with such subtlety, suggesting the young Frau's secret self through the way in which she perceives the bride's and her own situation: 'she in a white dress trimmed with stripes and bows of coloured ribbon, giving her the appearance of an iced cake all ready to be cut and served in neat little pieces to the bridegroom beside her' (p. 5). 'The Wind Blows' is included partly because it was admired by Mansfield's contemporaries, including Virginia Woolf and Lytton Strachey, but also for its surreal and almost cinematic conclusion. It is not included in the selections of Mansfield's stories edited by Elizabeth Bowen and by Claire Tomalin, but Tomalin includes 'A Married Man's Story', which is also added here. It is comparable with '*Je ne parle pas français*' in that the male narrators of both stories are writers telling their own macabre stories. The sinister married man tells 'the plain truth, as only a liar can tell it' (p. 328); the story is unfinished but that intensifies its malign suggestiveness.

I have indicated in the notes for 'An Indiscreet Journey' that an account of an incident which is directly comparable with the story is given in Mansfield's notebooks. Otherwise I have generally avoided biographical speculation, in spite of the possible correlations that can be made between the life and the stories. As Mansfield wrote in a notebook that was mainly concerned with her reading of Shakespeare: 'That which suggests the subject to the artist is the <u>unlikeness</u> of it to what we accept as reality. We single out, we bring into the light, we put up higher' (*KM Notebooks*, ii. 267).

SELECT BIBLIOGRAPHY

Works by Katherine Mansfield

Works published in Mansfield's lifetime:

In a German Pension (London: Stephen Swift, 1911; New York: Knopf, 1926).

Prelude (Richmond: Hogarth Press, 1918).

Je ne parle pas français (Hampstead: Heron Press, 1920).

Bliss and Other Stories (London: Constable, 1920; New York: Knopf, 1921).

The Garden Party and Other Stories (London: Constable, 1922; New York: Knopf, 1922).

Works published since Mansfield's death:

The Dove's Nest and Other Stories (London: Constable, 1923).

Poems (London: Constable, 1923).

Something Childish and Other Stories (London: Constable, 1924).

The Aloe (London: Constable, 1930).

The Collected Short Stories (London: Constable, 1945).

The Collected Short Stories (Harmondsworth: Penguin, 1981).

Alpers, Antony (ed.), *The Stories of Katherine Mansfield* (Auckland: Oxford University Press, 1984).

Gordon, Ian (ed.), *Undiscovered Country: The New Zealand Stories of Katherine Mansfield* (London: Longman, 1974).

—— (ed.), *Katherine Mansfield: The Urewera Notebook* (Auckland: Oxford University Press, 1978).

Hankin, Cherry A. (ed.), *Letters Between Katherine Mansfield and John Middleton Murry* (London: Virago, 1988).

Hanson, Clare (ed.), *The Critical Writings of Katherine Mansfield* (London: Macmillan, 1987).

Murry, John Middleton (ed.), *The Journal of Katherine Mansfield*, Definitive Edition (London: Constable, 1954).

—— (ed.), *The Letters of Katherine Mansfield* (2 vols.; London: Constable, 1928).

—— (ed.), *Novels and Novelists* (London: Constable, 1930).

O'Sullivan, Vincent (ed.), *The Aloe with Prelude* (Wellington: Port Nicholson, 1982).

—— (ed.), *The Aloe* (London: Virago, 1985).

—— (ed.), *Katherine Mansfield: New Zealand Stories* (Auckland: Oxford University Press, 1997).

O'Sullivan, Vincent (ed.), *Poems of Katherine Mansfield* (Oxford: Oxford University Press, 1988).

—— and Scott, Margaret (eds.), *The Collected Letters of Katherine Mansfield* (4 vols.; Oxford: Clarendon Press, 1984–96).

Scott, Margaret (ed.), *The Katherine Mansfield Notebooks* (Canterbury and Wellington: Lincoln University Press and Daphne Brasell Assoc., 1997).

Biography, Bibliography, and Criticism

Alpers, Antony, *The Life of Katherine Mansfield* (New York: Viking, 1980).

[Baker, Ida], *Katherine Mansfield: The Memories of L.M.* (London: Michael Joseph, 1971).

Boddy, Gillian, *Katherine Mansfield: The Woman and the Writer* (Ringwood: Penguin, 1988).

Burgan, Mary, *Illness, Gender, and Writing* (London: Johns Hopkins University Press, 1994).

Dunbar, Pamela, *Radical Mansfield: Double Discourse in Katherine Mansfield's Short Stories* (London: Macmillan, 1997).

Fullbrook, Kate, *Katherine Mansfield* (Brighton: Harvester, 1986).

Hanson, Clare and Gurr, Andrew, *Katherine Mansfield* (London: Macmillan, 1981).

Kaplan, Sydney Janet, *Katherine Mansfield and the Origins of Modernist Fiction* (Ithaca, NY: Cornell University Press, 1991).

Kirkpatrick, B. J., *A Bibliography of Katherine Mansfield* (Oxford: Clarendon Press, 1989).

Moran, Patricia, *Word of Mouth: Body Language in Katherine Mansfield and Virginia Woolf* (London: University Press of Virginia, 1996).

O'Sullivan, Vincent, *Katherine Mansfield's New Zealand* (Auckland and Christchurch: Golden Press, 1974).

Pilditch, Jan (ed.), *The Critical Response to Katherine Mansfield* (Westport, Conn.: Greenwood, 1996).

Robinson, Roger (ed.), *Katherine Mansfield: In from the Margin* (Baton Rouge, La.: Louisiana State University, 1994).

Smith, Angela, *Katherine Mansfield and Virginia Woolf: A Public of Two* (Oxford: Clarendon Press, 1999).

—— *Katherine Mansfield: A Literary Life* (London: Palgrave, 2000).

Tomalin, Claire, *Katherine Mansfield: A Secret Life* (London: Viking, 1987).

Further Reading in Oxford World's Classics

Lawrence, D. H., *The Prussian Officer and Other Stories*, ed. Antony Atkins.

—— *The Rainbow*, ed. Kate Flint.

—— *Selected Critical Writings*, ed. Michael Herbert.

—— *Sons and Lovers*, ed. David Trotter.

—— *The White Peacock*, ed. David Bradshaw.

—— *Women in Love*, ed. David Bradshaw.

Woolf, Virginia, *Between the Acts*, ed. Frank Kermode.

—— *Flush*, ed. Kate Flint.

—— *Jacob's Room*, ed. Kate Flint.

—— *The Mark on the Wall and Other Short Fiction*, ed. David Bradshaw.

—— *Night and Day*, ed. Suzanne Raitt.

—— *Orlando: A Biography*, ed. Rachel Bowlby.

—— *A Room of One's Own/Three Guineas*, ed. Morag Schiach.

—— *To the Lighthouse*, ed. Margaret Drabble.

—— *The Voyage Out*, ed. Lorna Sage.

—— *The Waves*, ed. Gillian Beer.

—— *The Years*, ed. Hermione Lee.

A CHRONOLOGY OF
KATHERINE MANSFIELD

1888   Born Kathleen Mansfield Beauchamp on 14 October at 11 Tinakori Road, Wellington, New Zealand; third daughter of Harold and Annie Beauchamp. Two more sisters, one of whom died, born in 1890 and 1892.

1894   Brother Leslie born.

1895–1903   KM attends various schools in Karori and Wellington, showing literary and musical talent.

1903–6   KM and her two sisters enter Queen's College, Harley Street, London, travelling from New Zealand with their whole family. Her parents and younger brother and sister return after 10 months. KM befriends Ida Baker, whom she calls Lesley Moore or LM. She contributes to and eventually edits the school magazine, travels to Germany and Belgium, and meets the brothers Arnold and Garnet Trowell, whom she had known in Wellington. Returns with her family to Wellington in 1906; her Grandmother Dyer dies.

1907   Harold Beauchamp becomes Chairman of Directors of the Bank of New Zealand; the family moves to a large house, 47 Fitzherbert Terrace. KM longs to return to London; she has relationships with Maata Mahupuku and Edith Bendall. Some of her vignettes are published by the *Native Companion* in Melbourne. She goes on a caravan expedition in the North Island, during which she writes the diary that becomes *The Urewera Notebook*.

1908   KM persuades her father that she needs to develop her writing in London and arrives in August on an allowance of £100 per year. She falls in love with Garnet Trowell, and hopes to marry him. Visits Paris.

1909   Marries G. C. Bowden but leaves him almost immediately to join Garnet Trowell who is on tour with an opera company. KM becomes pregnant and is taken to Bavaria by her mother. Her mother leaves her and the baby miscarries. KM has a relationship with Florian Sobieniowski.

1910   KM returns to London and lives briefly with Bowden. She publishes her Bavarian sketches in the *New Age*. She has an operation which results in a febrile illness, which is diagnosed retrospectively, several years later, as gonococcal in origin.

1911   In December Stephen Swift publishes *In a German Pension*, and KM meets John Middleton Murry for the first time.

1912   Murry becomes KM's lodger and then her lover; she is named as assistant editor of *Rhythm*. Stephen Swift absconds, leaving Murry responsible for the magazine's debts. Edward Marsh, a patron of the arts, offers financial support so that *Rhythm* can continue. Hostility between Orage at the *New Age* and the *Rhythm* group. In December KM goes to Paris with Murry and meets the painters J. D. Fergusson (the art editor of *Rhythm*) and Anne Estelle Rice.

1913   *Rhythm* is reorganized as the *Blue Review* but ends after three issues. KM and Murry meet D. H. Lawrence and Frieda; in December they move to Paris where KM meets Francis Carco. Murry is pressed to repay *Rhythm*'s debts.

1914   Murry is declared bankrupt; he and KM return to London. Lawrence and Frieda marry; Frieda gives KM the wedding ring from her first marriage which KM wears for the rest of her life, and she is buried wearing it. Murry enlists at the outbreak of World War I but is given a medical exemption the next day.

1915   KM develops a persistent cough; her brother arrives in London to join up. KM leaves Murry and goes to Paris, then on to Gray to join Francis Carco in his quarters near the Western Front. Returning, KM is reconciled with Murry; Murry and Lawrence begin *Signature*. Leslie Beauchamp is killed in a training accident in France. Too distressed to stay in England, and troubled by her cough, KM leaves for the South of France accompanied by Murry; they settle at the Villa Pauline in Bandol.

1916   The months up until April are among KM's most productive; she grieves for her brother but also writes steadily, and is happier with Murry than ever before. They return to England in April, living in a cottage in Zennor, Cornwall, near the Lawrences, but the couples quarrel and KM and Murry move away. Murry gets a job in Military Intelligence; KM begins to visit Garsington, home of Lady Ottoline Morrell, a patron of the arts. Through the people she meets there she is introduced to Virginia Woolf, T. S. Eliot, Lytton Strachey, and Bertrand Russell.

1917   KM and Murry separate at the beginning of the year; KM
            begins to write again for the *New Age*. She refashions 'The
            Aloe' as 'Prelude' for the Woolfs' new Hogarth Press. She
            visits the Woolfs at their house in Sussex. In December she is
            ill and a doctor advises her to go abroad to protect her lungs.

1918   In January KM travels alone to Bandol, a strenuous journey
            through wartime France which makes her ill. She writes '*Je
            ne parle pas français*'. LM arrives uninvited to help her; KM
            has her first pulmonary haemorrhage in February. They try to
            travel back to Britain but are trapped for three weeks in Paris
            which is under bombardment. On 3 May KM and Murry are
            married; KM spends several weeks in Cornwall where Anne
            Estelle Rice paints her portrait. 'Prelude' and 'Bliss' are pub-
            lished. KM's mother dies in Wellington; the Murrys move to
            a house in Hampstead, and are reconciled with Lawrence.
            KM is advised to enter a sanatorium; she begins treatment
            with Dr Sorapure.

1919   Murry becomes the editor of the *Athenaeum*; KM reviews
            novels for it each week. KM sees Virginia Woolf regularly
            during the summer, but feels so ill that she leaves for the
            Italian Riviera, writing an informal will before she goes. She
            is visited by her Catholic cousin and her father; Murry
            spends Christmas with her, disturbed by her desolate
            letters.

1920   In January KM writes 'The Man Without a Temperament'
            and moves to Menton to stay with her cousin. Her father
            remarries as soon as he returns to Wellington. '*Je ne parle pas
            français*' is published by the Murrys' own Heron Press. KM
            receives a letter from Lawrence: 'You revolt me, stewing in
            your consumption.' KM and LM return to London in late
            April; KM publishes stories in the *Athenaeum*. In August KM
            has what proves to be her last meeting with Virginia Woolf;
            she leaves for Menton with LM in September. In December
            Bliss and Other Stories is published by Constable; KM finishes
            'The Daughters of the Late Colonel' and writes her last
            review for the *Athenaeum*.

1921   KM leaves for Switzerland with LM in May; she settles with
            Murry, who has given up the editorship of the *Athenaeum* to
            be with her, in a chalet at Montana-sur-Sierre. She begins a
            frenetic period of activity, writing 'At the Bay', 'The Voyage',
            'A Married Man's Story', 'The Garden Party', and 'The

Doll's House' by the end of October. She begins to corre-
spond with Dr Manoukhin.

1922   In January KM leaves for Paris to consult Manoukhin, and
decides to begin his very expensive treatment; Murry joins
her. *The Garden Party and Other Stories* is published by Con-
stable. The Murrys have tea with James Joyce in Paris; the
Manoukhin treatment is unsuccessful and KM returns to
Switzerland with Murry. She finishes her last complete story,
'The Canary', in July, and returns to London in August with
LM and Murry, having made a formal will. She sees her
father in London, and discusses Gurdjieff's treatment with
Orage. In October she leaves for Gurdjieff's Institute at
Fontainebleau. She lives there in spartan conditions.

1923   KM writes to Murry inviting him to visit her in Fontainebleau. He arrives on 9 January; that evening she has a
haemorrhage and dies.

SELECTED STORIES

FRAU BRECHENMACHER ATTENDS
A WEDDING

Getting ready was a terrible business. After supper Frau Brechen-macher packed four of the five babies to bed, allowing Rosa to stay with her and help to polish the buttons of Herr Brechenmacher's uniform. Then she ran over his best shirt with a hot iron, polished his boots, and put a stitch or two into his black satin necktie.

'Rosa,' she said, 'fetch my dress and hang it in front of the stove to get the creases out. Now, mind, you must look after the children and not sit up later than half-past eight, and not touch the lamp—you know what will happen if you do.'

'Yes, mamma,' said Rosa, who was nine and felt old enough to manage a thousand lamps. 'But let me stay up—the "Bub"* may wake and want some milk.'

'Half-past eight!' said the Frau. 'I'll make the father tell you, too.'

Rosa drew down both corners of her mouth.

'But . . . but . . . .'

'Here comes the father. You go into the bedroom and fetch my blue silk handkerchief. You can wear my black shawl while I'm out—there now!'

Rosa dragged it off her mother's shoulders and wound it carefully round her own, tying the two ends in a knot at the back. After all, she reflected, if she had to go to bed at half-past eight she would keep the shawl on. Which resolution comforted her absolutely.

'Now, then, where are my clothes?' cried Herr Brechenmacher, hanging his empty letter-bag behind the door and stamping the snow out of his boots. 'Nothing ready, of course, and everybody at the wedding by this time. I heard the music as I passed. What are you doing? You're not dressed. You can't go like that.'

'Here they are—all ready for you on the table, and some warm water in the tin basin. Dip your head in. Rosa, give your father the towel. Everything ready except the trousers. I haven't had time to shorten them. You must tuck the ends into your boots until we get there.'

'Nu,'* said the Herr, 'there isn't room to turn. I want the light. You go and dress in the passage.'

Dressing in the dark was nothing to Frau Brechenmacher. She hooked her skirt and bodice, fastened her handkerchief round her neck with a beautiful brooch that had four medals to the Virgin dangling from it, and then drew on her cloak and hood.

'Here, come and fasten this buckle,' called Herr Brechenmacher. He stood in the kitchen puffing himself out, the buttons on his blue uniform shining with an enthusiasm which nothing but official buttons could possibly possess. 'How do I look?'

'Wonderful,' replied the little Frau, straining at the waist buckle and giving him a little pull here, a little tug there. 'Rosa, come and look at your father.'

Herr Brechenmacher strode up and down the kitchen, was helped on with his coat, then waited while the Frau lighted the lantern.

'Now, then—finished at last! Come along.'

'The lamp, Rosa,' warned the Frau, slamming the front door behind them.

Snow had not fallen all day; the frozen ground was slippery as an ice-pond. She had not been out of the house for weeks past, and the day had so flurried her that she felt muddled and stupid—felt that Rosa had pushed her out of the house and her man was running away from her.

'Wait, wait!' she cried.

'No. I'll get my feet damp—you hurry.'

It was easier when they came into the village. There were fences to cling to, and leading from the railway station to the Gasthaus* a little path of cinders had been strewn for the benefit of the wedding guests.

The Gasthaus was very festive. Lights shone out from every window, wreaths of fir twigs hung from the ledges. Branches decorated the front doors, which swung open, and in the hall the landlord voiced his superiority by bullying the waitresses, who ran about continually with glasses of beer, trays of cups and saucers, and bottles of wine.

'Up the stairs—up the stairs!' boomed the landlord. 'Leave your coats on the landing.'

Herr Brechenmacher, completely overawed by this grand manner, so far forgot his rights as a husband as to beg his wife's pardon for jostling her against the banisters in his efforts to get ahead of everybody else.

Herr Brechenmacher's colleagues greeted him with acclamation as he entered the door of the Festsaal,* and the Frau straightened her brooch and folded her hands, assuming the air of dignity becoming to the wife of a postman and the mother of five children. Beautiful indeed was the Festsaal. Three long tables were grouped at one end, the remainder of the floor space cleared for dancing. Oil lamps, hanging from the ceiling, shed a warm, bright light on the walls decorated with paper flowers and garlands; shed a warmer, brighter light on the red faces of the guests in their best clothes.

At the head of the centre table sat the bride and bridegroom, she in a white dress trimmed with stripes and bows of coloured ribbon, giving her the appearance of an iced cake all ready to be cut and served in neat little pieces to the bridegroom beside her, who wore a suit of white clothes much too large for him and a white silk tie that rose half way up his collar. Grouped about them, with a fine regard for dignity and precedence, sat their parents and relations; and perched on a stool at the bride's right hand a little girl in a crumpled muslin dress with a wreath of forget-me-nots hanging over one ear. Everybody was laughing and talking, shaking hands, clinking glasses, stamping on the floor—a stench of beer and perspiration filled the air.

Frau Brechenmacher, following her man down the room after greeting the bridal party, knew that she was going to enjoy herself. She seemed to fill out and become rosy and warm as she sniffed that familiar, festive smell. Somebody pulled at her skirt, and, looking down, she saw Frau Rupp, the butcher's wife, who pulled out an empty chair and begged her to sit beside her.

'Fritz will get you some beer,' she said. 'My dear, your skirt is open at the back. We could not help laughing as you walked up the room with the white tape of your petticoat showing!'

'But how frightful!' said Frau Brechenmacher, collapsing into her chair and biting her lip.

'Na,* it's over now,' said Frau Rupp, stretching her fat hands over the table and regarding her three mourning rings* with intense enjoyment; 'but one must be careful, especially at a wedding.'

'And such a wedding as this,' cried Frau Ledermann, who sat on the other side of Frau Brechenmacher. 'Fancy Theresa bringing that child with her. It's her own child, you know, my dear and it's going to live with them. That's what I call a sin against the Church for a free-born* child to attend its own mother's wedding.'

The three women sat and stared at the bride, who remained very still, with a little vacant smile on her lips, only her eyes shifting uneasily from side to side.

'Beer they've given it, too,' whispered Frau Rupp, 'and white wine and an ice. It never did have a stomach; she ought to have left it at home.'

Frau Brechenmacher turned round and looked towards the bride's mother. She never took her eyes off her daughter, but wrinkled her brown forehead like an old monkey, and nodded now and again very solemnly. Her hands shook as she raised her beer mug, and when she had drunk she spat on the floor and savagely wiped her mouth with her sleeve. Then the music started and she followed Theresa with her eyes, looking suspiciously at each man who danced with her.

'Cheer up, old woman,' shouted her husband, digging her in the ribs; 'this isn't Theresa's funeral.' He winked at the guests, who broke into loud laughter.

'I *am* cheerful,' mumbled the old woman, and beat upon the table with her fist, keeping time to the music, proving she was not out of the festivities.

'She can't forget how wild Theresa has been,' said Frau Ledermann. 'Who could—with the child there? I heard that last Sunday evening Theresa had hysterics and said that she would not marry this man. They had to get the priest to her.'

'Where is the other one?' asked Frau Brechenmacher. 'Why didn't he marry her?'

The woman shrugged her shoulders.

'Gone—disappeared. He was a traveller, and only stayed at their house two nights. He was selling shirt buttons—I bought some myself, and they were beautiful shirt buttons—but what a pig of a fellow! I can't think what he saw in such a plain girl—but you never know. Her mother says she's been like fire ever since she was sixteen!'

Frau Brechenmacher looked down at her beer and blew a little hole in the froth.

'That's not how a wedding should be,' she said; 'it's not religion to love two men.'

'Nice time she'll have with this one,' Frau Rupp exclaimed. 'He was lodging with me last summer and I had to get rid of him.

He never changed his clothes once in two months, and when I spoke to him of the smell in his room he told me he was sure it floated up from the shop. Ah, every wife has her cross. Isn't that true, my dear?'

Frau Brechenmacher saw her husband among his colleagues at the next table. He was drinking far too much, she knew—gesticulating wildly, the saliva spluttering out of his mouth as he talked.

'Yes,' she assented, 'that's true. Girls have a lot to learn.'

Wedged in between these two fat old women, the Frau had no hope of being asked to dance. She watched the couples going round and round; she forgot her five babies and her man and felt almost like a girl again. The music sounded sad and sweet. Her roughened hands clasped and unclasped themselves in the folds of her skirt. While the music went on she was afraid to look anybody in the face, and she smiled with a little nervous tremor round the mouth.

'But, my God,' Frau Rupp cried, 'they've given that child of Theresa's a piece of sausage. It's to keep her quiet. There's going to be a presentation now—your man has to speak.'

Frau Brechenmacher sat up stiffly. The music ceased, and the dancers took their places again at the tables.

Herr Brechenmacher alone remained standing—he held in his hands a big silver coffee-pot. Everybody laughed at his speech, except the Frau; everybody roared at his grimaces, and at the way he carried the coffee-pot to the bridal pair, as if it were a baby he was holding.

She lifted the lid, peeped in, then shut it down with a little scream and sat biting her lips. The bridegroom wrenched the pot away from her and drew forth a baby's bottle and two little cradles holding china dolls. As he dandled these treasures before Theresa the hot room seemed to heave and sway with laughter.

Frau Brechenmacher did not think it funny. She stared round at the laughing faces, and suddenly they all seemed strange to her. She wanted to go home and never come out again. She imagined that all these people were laughing at her, more people than there were in the room even—all laughing at her because they were so much stronger than she was.

*   *   *

They walked home in silence. Herr Brechenmacher strode ahead, she stumbled after him. White and forsaken lay the road from the railway station to their house—a cold rush of wind blew her hood from her face, and suddenly she remembered how they had come home together the first night. Now they had five babies and twice as much money; *but*—

'Na, what is it all for?' she muttered, and not until she had reached home, and prepared a little supper of meat and bread for her man did she stop asking herself that silly question.

Herr Brechenmacher broke the bread into his plate, smeared it round with his fork, and chewed greedily.

'Good?' she asked, leaning her arms on the table and pillowing her breast against them.

'But fine!'

He took a piece of the crumb, wiped it round his plate edge, and held it up to her mouth. She shook her head.

'Not hungry,' she said.

'But it is one of the best pieces, and full of the fat.'

He cleared the plate; then pulled off his boots and flung them into a corner.

'Not much of a wedding,' he said, stretching out his feet and wriggling his toes in the worsted* socks.

'N—no,' she replied, taking up the discarded boots and placing them on the oven to dry.

Herr Brechenmacher yawned and stretched himself, and then looked up at her, grinning.

'Remember the night that we came home? You were an innocent one, you were.'

'Get along! Such a time ago I forget.' Well she remembered.

'Such a clout on the ear as you gave me. . . . But I soon taught you.'

'Oh, don't start talking. You've too much beer. Come to bed.'

He tilted back in his chair, chuckling with laughter.

'That's not what you said to me that night. God, the trouble you gave me!'

But the little Frau seized the candle and went into the next room. The children were all soundly sleeping. She stripped the mattress off the baby's bed to see if he was still dry, then began unfastening her blouse and skirt.

'Always the same,' she said—'all over the world the same; but, God in heaven—but *stupid*.'

Then even the memory of the wedding faded quite. She lay down on the bed and put her arm across her face like a child who expected to be hurt as Herr Brechenmacher lurched in.

THE WOMAN AT THE STORE

All that day the heat was terrible. The wind blew close to the ground—it rooted among the tussock grass—slithered along the road, so that the white pumice dust swirled in our faces—settled and sifted over us and was like a dry-skin itching for growth on our bodies. The horses stumbled along, coughing and chuffing. The pack horse* was sick—with a big, open sore rubbed under the belly. Now and again she stopped short, threw back her head, looked at us as though she were going to cry, and whinnied. Hundreds of larks shrilled—the sky was slate colour, and the sound of the larks reminded me of slate pencils scraping over its surface. There was nothing to be seen but wave after wave of tussock grass—patched with purple orchids and manuka* bushes covered with thick spider webs.

Jo rode ahead. He wore a blue galatea* shirt, corduroy trousers and riding boots. A white handkerchief, spotted with red—it looked as though his nose had been bleeding on it—knotted round his throat. Wisps of white hair straggled from under his wideawake*—his moustache and eyebrows were called white—he slouched in the saddle—grunting. Not once that day had he sung 'I don't care, for don't you see, my wife's mother was in front of me!' . . . It was the first day we had been without it for a month, and now there seemed something uncanny in his silence. Hin rode beside me—white as a clown, his black eyes glittered, and he kept shooting out his tongue and moistening his lips. He was dressed in a Jaeger* vest—a pair of blue duck* trousers, fastened round the waist with a plaited leather belt. We had hardly spoken since dawn. At noon we had lunched off fly biscuits* and apricots by the side of a swampy creek.

'My stomach feels like the crop of a hen,' said Jo. 'Now then, Hin, you're the bright boy of the party—where's this 'ere store you kep' on talking about. "Oh, yes," you says, "I know a fine store, with a paddock for the horses an' a creek runnin' through, owned by a friend of mine who'll give yer a bottle of whisky before 'e shakes hands with yer." I'd like ter see that place—merely as a matter of curiosity—not that I'd ever doubt yer word—as yer know very well—*but*. . . .'

Hin laughed. 'Don't forget there's a woman too, Jo, with blue eyes and yellow hair, who'll promise you something else before she shakes hands with you. Put that in your pipe and smoke it.'

'The heat's making you balmy,' said Jo. But he dug his knees into his horse. We shambled on. I half fell asleep, and had a sort of uneasy dream that the horses were not moving forward at all—then that I was on a rocking-horse, and my old mother was scolding me for raising such a fearful dust from the drawing-room carpet. 'You've entirely worn off the pattern of the carpet,' I heard her saying, and she gave the reins a tug. I snivelled and woke to find Hin leaning over me, maliciously smiling.

'That was a case of all but,' said he, 'I just caught you. What's up, been bye-bye?'

'No!' I raised my head. 'Thank the Lord we're arriving somewhere.'

We were on the brow of the hill, and below us there was a whare* roofed in with corrugated iron. It stood in a garden, rather far back from the road—a big paddock opposite, and a creek and a clump of young willow trees. A thin line of blue smoke stood up straight from the chimney of the whare, and as I looked, a woman came out, followed by a child and a sheep dog—the woman carrying what appeared to me a black stick. She made frantic gestures at us. The horses put on a final spurt, Jo took off his wideawake, shouted, threw out his chest, and began singing, 'I don't care, for don't you see . . . .' The sun pushed through the pale clouds and shed a vivid light over the scene. It gleamed on the woman's yellow hair, over her flapping pinafore and the rifle she was carrying. The child hid behind her, and the yellow dog, a mangy beast, scuttled back into the whare, his tail between his legs. We drew rein and dismounted.

'Hallo,' screamed the woman. 'I thought you was three 'awks. My kid comes runnin' in ter me. "Mumma," says she, "there's three brown things comin' over the 'ill," says she. An' I comes out smart, I can tell yer. They'll be 'awks, I says to her. Oh, the 'awks about 'ere, yer wouldn't believe.'

The 'kid' gave us the benefit of one eye from behind the woman's pinafore—then retired again.

'Where's your old man,' asked Hin.

The woman blinked rapidly, screwing up her face.

'Away shearin'. Bin away a month. I suppose yer not goin' to stop, are yer? There's a storm comin' up.'

'You bet we are,' said Jo. 'So you're on your lonely, missis?'

She stood, pleating the frills of her pinafore, and glancing from one to the other of us, like a hungry bird. I smiled at the thought of how Hin had pulled Jo's leg about her. Certainly her eyes were blue, and what hair she had was yellow, but ugly. She was a figure of fun. Looking at her, you felt there was nothing but sticks and wires under that pinafore—her front teeth were knocked out, she had red pulpy hands, and she wore on her feet a pair of dirty 'Bluchers'.*

'I'll go and turn out the horses,' said Hin. 'Got any embrocation? Poi's rubbed herself to hell!'

'Arf a mo!' The woman stood silent a moment, her nostrils expanding as she breathed. Then she shouted violently, 'I'd rather you didn't stop—you *can't* and there's the end of it. I don't let out that paddock any more. You'll have to go on; I ain't got nothing!'

'Well, I'm blest!' said Jo, heavily. He pulled me aside. 'Gone a bit off 'er dot,' he whispered, 'too much alone, *you know*,' very significantly. 'Turn the sympathetic tap on 'er, she'll come round all right.'

But there was no need—she had come round by herself.

'Stop if yer like!' she muttered, shrugging her shoulders. To me— 'I'll give yer the embrocation if yer come along.'

'Right-o, I'll take it down to them.' We walked together up the garden path. It was planted on both sides with cabbages. They smelled like stale dishwater. Of flowers there were double poppies and sweet-williams. One little patch was divided off by pawa* shells— presumably it belonged to the child—for she ran from her mother and began to grub in it with a broken clothes peg. The yellow dog lay across the doorstep, biting fleas; the woman kicked him away.

'Gar-r, get away, you beast . . . the place ain't tidy. I 'aven't 'ad time ter fix things to-day—been ironing. Come right in.'

It was a large room, the walls plastered with old pages of English periodicals. Queen Victoria's Jubilee* appeared to be the most recent number—a table with an ironing board and wash tub on it—some wooden forms—a black horsehair sofa, and some broken cane chairs pushed against the walls. The mantelpiece above the stove was draped in pink paper, further ornamented with dried grasses and ferns and a coloured print of Richard Seddon.* There were four doors—one, judging from the smell, let into the 'Store', one on to the 'back yard', through the third I saw the bedroom. Flies buzzed in circles round the ceiling, and treacle papers* and bundles of dried clover were pinned to the window curtains. I was alone in the room—she had gone into the store for the embrocation. I heard her stamping about and muttering to herself: 'I got some, now where did I put that bottle? . . . It's behind the pickles . . . no, it ain't.' I cleared a place on the table and sat there, swinging my legs. Down in the paddock I could hear Jo singing and the sound of hammer strokes as Hin drove in the tent poles. It was sunset. There is no twilight to our New Zealand days, but a curious half-hour when everything appears grotesque—it frightens—as though the savage spirit of the country walked abroad and sneered at what it saw. Sitting alone in the hideous room I grew afraid. The woman next door was a long time finding that stuff. What was she doing in there? Once I thought I heard her bang her hands down on the counter, and once she half moaned, turning it into a cough and clearing her throat. I wanted to shout 'Buck up,' but I kept silent.

'Good Lord, what a life!' I thought. 'Imagine being here day in, day out, with that rat of a child and a mangy dog. Imagine bothering about ironing—*mad*, of course she's mad! Wonder how long she's been here—wonder if I could get her to talk.'

At that moment she poked her head round the door.

'Wot was it yer wanted,' she asked.

'Embrocation.'

'Oh, I forgot. I got it, it was in front of the pickle jars.'

She handed me the bottle.

'My, you do look tired, you do! Shall I knock yer up a few scones for supper? There's some tongue in the store, too, and I'll cook yer a cabbage if you fancy it.'

'Right-o.' I smiled at her. 'Come down to the paddock and bring the kid for tea.'

She shook her head, pursing up her mouth.

'Oh no. I don't fancy it. I'll send the kid down with the things and a billy of milk. Shall I knock up a few extry scones to take with you ter-morrow?'

'Thanks.'

She came and stood by the door.

'How old is the kid?'

'Six—come next Christmas. I 'ad a bit of trouble with 'er one way

an' another. I 'adn't any milk till a month after she was born and she
sickened like a cow.'

'She's not like you—takes after her father?' Just as the woman had
shouted her refusal at us before, she shouted at me then.

'No, she don't; she's the dead spit of me. Any fool could see that.
Come on in now, Els,* you stop messing in the dirt.'

I met Jo climbing over the paddock fence.

'What's the old bitch got in the store?' he asked.

'Don't know—didn't look.'

'Well, of all the fools. Hin's slanging you. What have you been
doing all the time?'

'She couldn't find this stuff. Oh, my shakes, you are smart!'

Jo had washed, combed his wet hair in a line across his forehead,
and buttoned a coat over his shirt. He grinned.

Hin snatched the embrocation from me. I went to the end of the
paddock where the willows grew and bathed in the creek. The water
was clear and soft as oil. Along the edges held by the grass and
rushes, white foam tumbled and bubbled. I lay in the water and
looked up at the trees that were still a moment, then quivered
lightly, and again were still. The air smelt of rain. I forgot about the
woman and the kid until I came back to the tent. Hin lay by the fire,
watching the billy boil.

I asked where Jo was and if the kid had brought our supper.

'Pooh,' said Hin, rolling over and looking up at the sky. 'Didn't
you see how Jo had been tittivating*—he said to me before he went up
to the whare, "Dang it! she'll look better by night light—at any rate,
my buck, she's female flesh!"'

'You had Jo about her looks—you had me, too.'

'No—look here. I can't make it out. It's four years since I came
past this way, and I stopped here two days. The husband was a pal of
mine once, down the West Coast—a fine, big chap, with a voice on
him like a trombone. She'd been barmaid down the Coast—as pretty
as a wax doll. The coach used to come this way then once a fortnight,
that was before they opened the railway up Napier* way, and she had
no end of a time! Told me once in a confidential moment that she
knew one hundred and twenty-five different ways of kissing!'

'Oh, go on, Hin! She isn't the same woman!'

'Course she is. . . . I can't make it out. What I think is the old
man's cleared out and left her: that's all my eye about shearing.

Sweet life! The only people who come through now are Maoris and sundowners!'*

Through the dark we saw the gleam of the kid's pinafore. She trailed over to us with a basket in her hand, the milk billy* in the other. I unpacked the basket, the child standing by.

'Come over here,' said Hin, snapping his fingers at her.

She went, the lamp from the inside of the tent cast a bright light over her. A mean, undersized brat, with whitish hair, and weak eyes. She stood, legs wide apart and her stomach protruding.

'What do you do all day?' asked Hin.

She scraped out one ear with her little finger, looked at the result and said—'Draw.'

'Huh! What do you draw?—leave your ears alone.'

'Pictures.'

'What on?'

'Bits of butter paper an' a pencil of my Mumma's.'

'Boh! What a lot of words at one time!' Hin rolled his eyes at her. 'Baa-lambs and moo-cows?'

'No, everything. I'll draw all of you when you're gone, and your horses and the tent, and that one'—she pointed to me—'with no clothes on in the creek. I looked at her where she wouldn't see me from.'*

'Thanks very much! How ripping of you,' said Hin. 'Where's Dad?'

The kid pouted. 'I won't tell you because I don't like yer face!' She started operations on the other ear.

'Here,' I said. 'Take the basket, get along home and tell the other man supper's ready.'

'I don't want to.'

'I'll give you a box on the ear if you don't,' said Hin, savagely.

'Hie! I'll tell Mumma. I'll tell Mumma'—the kid fled.

We ate until we were full and had arrived at the smoke stage before Jo came back, very flushed and jaunty, a whisky bottle in his hand.

''Ave a drink—you two!' he shouted, carrying off matters with a high hand. ''Ere, shove along the cups.'

'One hundred and twenty-five different ways,' I murmured to Hin.

'What's that? Oh! stow it!' said Jo. 'Why 'ave you always got your knife into me. You gas like a kid at a Sunday School beano. She wants us to go up there to-night, and have a comfortable chat. I'—he waved his hand airily—'I got 'er round.'

'Trust you for that,' laughed Hin. 'But did she tell you where the old man's got to?'

Jo looked up. 'Shearing! You 'eard 'er, you fool!'

The woman had fixed up the room, even to a light bouquet of sweet-williams on the table. She and I sat one side of the table, Jo and Hin the other. An oil lamp was set between us, the whisky bottle and glasses, and a jug of water. The kid knelt against one of the forms, drawing on butter paper. I wondered, grimly, if she was attempting the creek episode. But Jo had been right about night time. The woman's hair was tumbled—two red spots burned in her cheeks— her eyes shone—and we knew that they were kissing feet under the table. She had changed the blue pinafore for a white calico* dressing jacket and a black skirt—the kid was decorated to the extent of a blue sateen* hair ribbon. In the stifling room with the flies buzzing against the ceiling and dropping on to the table—we got slowly drunk.

'Now listen to me,' shouted the woman, banging her fist on the table. 'It's six years since I was married, and four miscarriages. I says to 'im, I says, what do you think I'm doin' up 'ere? If you was back at the Coast, I'd 'ave you lynched for child murder. Over and over I tells 'im—you've broken my spirit and spoiled my looks, and wot for—that's wot I'm driving at.' She clutched her head with her hands and stared round at us. Speaking rapidly, 'Oh, some days—an' months of them I 'ear them two words knockin' inside me all the time—"Wot for," but sometimes I'll be cooking the spuds* an' I lifts the lid off to give 'em a prong and I 'ears, quite sudden again, "Wot for." Oh! I don't mean only the spuds and the kid—I mean—I mean,' she hiccoughed—'you know what I mean, Mr Jo.'

'I know,' said Jo, scratching his head.

'Trouble with me is,' she leaned across the table, 'he left me too much alone. When the coach stopped coming, sometimes he'd go away days, sometimes he'd go away weeks, and leave me ter look after the store. Back 'e'd come—pleased as Punch. "Oh, 'allo," 'e'd say. "Ow are you gettin' on. Come and give us a kiss." Sometimes I'd turn a bit nasty, and then 'e'd go off again, and if I took it all right, 'e'd wait till 'e could twist me round 'is finger, then 'e'd say, "Well, so long, I'm off," and do you think I could keep 'im?—not me!'

'Mumma,' bleated the kid, 'I made a picture of them on the 'ill, an' you an' me, an' the dog down below.'

'Shut your mouth,' said the woman.

A vivid flash of lightning played over the room—we heard the mutter of thunder.

'Good thing that's broke loose,' said Jo. 'I've 'ad it in me 'ead for three days.'

'Where's your old man now?' asked Hin slowly.

The woman blubbered and dropped her head on to the table. 'Hin, 'e's gone shearin' and left me alone again,' she wailed.

' 'Ere, look out for the glasses,' said Jo. 'Cheer-o, 'ave another drop. No good cryin' over spilt 'usbands! You Hin, you blasted cuckoo!'

'Mr Jo,' said the woman, drying her eyes on her jacket frill, 'you're a gent, an' if I was a secret woman, I'd place any confidence in your 'ands. I don't mind if I do 'ave a glass on that.'

Every moment the lightning grew more vivid and the thunder sounded nearer. Hin and I were silent—the kid never moved from her bench. She poked her tongue out and blew on it as she drew.

'It's the loneliness,' said the woman, addressing Jo—he made sheep's eyes at her—'and bein' shut up 'ere like a broody 'en.' He reached his hand across the table and held hers, and though the position looked most uncomfortable when they wanted to pass the water and whisky, their hands stuck together as though glued. I pushed back my chair and went over to the kid, who immediately sat flat down on her artistic achievements and made a face at me.

'You're not to look,' said she.

'Oh, come on, don't be so nasty!' Hin came over to us, and we were just drunk enough to wheedle the kid into showing us. And those drawings of hers were extraordinary and repulsively vulgar. The creations of a lunatic with a lunatic's cleverness. There was no doubt about it, the kid's mind was diseased. While she showed them to us, she worked herself up into a mad excitement, laughing and trembling, and shooting out her arms.

'Mumma,' she yelled. 'Now I'm going to draw them what you told me I never was to—now I am.'

The woman rushed from the table and beat the child's head with the flat of her hand.

'I'll smack you with yer clothes turned up if yer dare say that again,' she bawled.

Jo was too drunk to notice, but Hin caught her by the arm. The kid did not utter a cry. She drifted over to the window and began picking flies from the treacle paper.

We returned to the table—Hin and I sitting one side, the woman and Jo, touching shoulders, the other. We listened to the thunder, saying stupidly, 'That was a near one,' 'There it goes again,' and Jo, with a heavy hit, 'Now we're off,' 'Steady on the brake,' until rain began to fall, sharp as cannon shot on the iron roof.

'You'd better doss here for the night,' said the woman.

'That's right,' assented Jo, evidently in the know about this move.

'Bring up yer things from the tent. You two can doss in the store along with the kid—she's used to sleep in there and won't mind you.'

'O, Mumma, I never did,' interrupted the kid.

'Shut yer lies! An' Mr Jo can 'ave this room.'

It sounded a ridiculous arrangement, but it was useless to attempt to cross them, they were too far gone. While the woman sketched the plan of action, Jo sat, abnormally solemn and red, his eyes bulging, and pulled at his moustache.

'Give us a lantern,' said Hin. 'I'll go down to the paddock.' We two went together. Rain whipped in our faces, the land was as light as though a bush fire was raging—we behaved like two children let loose in the thick of an adventure—laughed and shouted to each other, and came back to the whare to find the kid already bedded in the counter of the store. The woman brought us a lamp. Jo took his bundle from Hin, the door was shut.

'Good-night all,' shouted Jo.

Hin and I sat on two sacks of potatoes. For the life of us we could not stop laughing. Strings of onions and half-hams dangled from the ceiling—wherever we looked there were advertisements for 'Camp Coffee'* and tinned meats. We pointed at them, tried to read them aloud—overcome with laughter and hiccoughs. The kid in the counter stared at us. She threw off her blanket and scrambled to the floor where she stood in her grey flannel night gown, rubbing one leg against the other. We paid no attention to her.

'Wot are you laughing at,' she said, uneasily.

'You!' shouted Hin, 'the red tribe of you, my child.'

She flew into a rage and beat herself with her hands. 'I won't be laughed at, you curs—you.' He swooped down upon the child and swung her on to the counter.

'Go to sleep, Miss Smarty—or make a drawing—here's a pencil—you can use Mumma's account book.'

Through the rain we heard Jo creak over the boarding of the next room—the sound of a door being opened—then shut to.

'It's the loneliness,' whispered Hin.

'One hundred and twenty-five different ways—alas! my poor brother!'

The kid tore out a page and flung it at me.

'There you are,' she said. 'Now I done it ter spite Mumma for shutting me up 'ere with you two. I done the one she told me I never ought to. I done the one she told me she'd shoot me if I did. Don't care! Don't care!'

The kid had drawn the picture of the woman shooting at a man with a rook rifle and then digging a hole to bury him in.

She jumped off the counter and squirmed about on the floor biting her nails.

Hin and I sat till dawn with the drawing beside us. The rain ceased, the little kid fell asleep, breathing loudly. We got up, stole out of the whare, down into the paddock. White clouds floated over a pink sky—a chill wind blew; the air smelled of wet grass. Just as we swung into the saddle, Jo came out of the whare—he motioned to us to ride on.

'I'll pick you up later,' he shouted.

A bend in the road, and the whole place disappeared.

HOW PEARL BUTTON WAS KIDNAPPED

Pearl Button swung on the little gate in front of the House of Boxes.
It was the early afternoon of a sunshiny day with little winds playing
hide-and-seek in it. They blew Pearl Button's pinafore frill into her
mouth and they blew the street dust all over the House of Boxes.
Pearl watched it—like a cloud—like when mother peppered her fish
and the top of the pepper-pot came off. She swung on the little gate,
all alone, and she sang a small song. Two big women came walking
down the street. One was dressed in red and the other was dressed in
yellow and green. They had pink handkerchiefs over their heads, and
both of them carried a big flax basket of ferns.* They had no shoes
and stockings on and they came walking along, slowly, because they
were so fat, and talking to each other and always smiling. Pearl
stopped swinging and when they saw her they stopped walking.
They looked and looked at her and then they talked to each other
waving their arms and clapping their hands together. Pearl began to
laugh. The two women came up to her, keeping close to the hedge
and looking in a frightened way towards the House of Boxes. 'Hallo,
little girl!' said one. Pearl said, 'Hallo!' 'You all alone by yourself?'
Pearl nodded. 'Where's your mother?' 'In the kitching, ironing-
because-its-Tuesday.' The women smiled at her and Pearl smiled
back. 'Oh,' she said, 'haven't you got very white teeth indeed! Do it
again.' The dark women laughed and again they talked to each other
with funny words and wavings of the hands. 'What's your name?'
they asked her. 'Pearl Button.' 'You coming with us, Pearl Button?
We got beautiful things to show you,' whispered one of the women.
So Pearl got down from the gate and she slipped out into the road.
And she walked between the two dark women down the windy road,
taking little running steps to keep up and wondering what they had
in their House of Boxes.

They walked a long way. 'You tired?' asked one of the women,
bending down to Pearl. Pearl shook her head. They walked much
further. 'You not tired?' asked the other woman. And Pearl shook her
head again, but tears shook from her eyes at the same time and her
lips trembled. One of the women gave over her flax basket of ferns
and caught Pearl Button up in her arms and walked with Pearl

Button's head against her shoulder and her dusty little legs dangling. She was softer than a bed and she had a nice smell—a smell that made you bury your head and breathe and breathe it. . . . They set Pearl Button down in a long room full of other people the same colour as they were—and all these people came close to her and looked at her, nodding and laughing and throwing up their eyes. The woman who had carried Pearl took off her hair ribbon and shook her curls loose. There was a cry from the other women and they crowded close and some of them ran a finger through Pearl's yellow curls, very gently, and one of them, a young one, lifted all Pearl's hair and kissed the back of her little white neck. Pearl felt shy but happy at the same time. There were some men on the floor, smoking, with rugs and feather mats* round their shoulders. One of them made a funny face at her and he pulled a great big peach out of his pocket and set it on the floor, and flicked it with his finger as though it were a marble. It rolled right over to her. Pearl picked it up. 'Please can I eat it?' she asked. At that they all laughed and clapped their hands and the man with the funny face made another at her and pulled a pear out of his pocket and sent it bobbling over the floor. Pearl laughed. The women sat on the floor and Pearl sat down too. The floor was very dusty. She carefully pulled up her pinafore and dress and sat on her petticoat as she had been taught to sit in dusty places, and she ate the fruit, the juice running all down her front. 'Oh,' she said, in a very frightened voice to one of the women, 'I've spilt all the juice!' 'That doesn't matter at all,' said the woman, patting her cheek. A man came into the room with a long whip in his hand. He shouted something. They all got up, shouting, laughing, wrapping themselves up in rugs and blankets and feather mats. Pearl was carried again, this time into a great cart, and she sat on the lap of one of her women with the driver beside her. It was a green cart with a red pony and a black pony. It went very fast out of the town. The driver stood up and waved the whip round his head. Pearl peered over the shoulder of her woman. Other carts were behind like a procession. She waved at them. Then the country came. First fields of short grass with sheep on them and little bushes of white flowers and pink briar rose baskets—then big trees on both sides of the road—and nothing to be seen except big trees. Pearl tried to look through them but it was quite dark. Birds were singing. She nestled closer in the big lap. The woman was warm as a cat and she moved up and down when she breathed, just like purring. Pearl played with a green ornament* round her neck and the woman took the little hand and kissed each of her fingers and then turned it over and kissed the dimples. Pearl had never been happy like this before. On the top of a big hill they stopped. The driving man turned to Pearl and said 'Look, look!' and pointed with his whip. And down at the bottom of the hill was something perfectly different—a great big piece of blue water was creeping over the land. She screamed and clutched at the big woman. 'What is it, what is it?' 'Why,' said the woman, 'it's the sea.' 'Will it hurt us—is it coming?' 'Ai-e, no, it doesn't come to us. It's very beautiful. You look again.' Pearl looked. 'You're sure it can't come,' she said. 'Ai-e, no. It stays in its place,' said the big woman. Waves with white tops came leaping over the blue. Pearl watched them break on a long piece of land covered with garden-path shells. They drove round a corner. There were some little houses down close to the sea, with wood fences round them and gardens inside. They comforted her. Pink and red and blue washing hung over the fences and as they came near more people came out and five yellow dogs with long thin tails. All the people were fat and laughing, with little naked babies holding on to them or rolling about in the gardens like puppies. Pearl was lifted down and taken into a tiny house with only one room and a veranda. There was a girl there with two pieces of black hair* down to her feet. She was setting the dinner on the floor. 'It *is* a funny place,' said Pearl, watching the pretty girl while the woman unbuttoned her little drawers for her. She was very hungry. She ate meat and vegetables and fruit and the woman gave her milk out of a green cup. And it was quite silent except for the sea outside and the laughs of the two women watching her. 'Haven't you got any Houses in Boxes?' she said. 'Don't you all live in a row? Don't the men go to offices? Aren't there any nasty things?'

They took off her shoes and stockings, her pinafore and dress. She walked about in her petticoat and then she walked outside with the grass pushing between her toes. The two women came out with different sorts of baskets. They took her hands. Over a little paddock, through a fence, and then on warm sand with brown grass in it they went down to the sea. Pearl held back when the sand grew wet, but the women coaxed. 'Nothing to hurt, very beautiful. You come.' They dug in the sand and found some shells which they threw into the baskets. The sand was wet as mud pies. Pearl forgot her fright and began digging too. She got hot and wet and suddenly over her feet broke a little line of foam. 'Oo, oo!' she shrieked, dabbling with her feet, 'Lovely, lovely!' She paddled in the shallow water. It was warm. She made a cup of her hands and caught some of it. But it stopped being blue in her hands. She was so excited that she rushed over to her woman and flung her little thin arms round the woman's neck, hugging her, kissing. . . . Suddenly the girl gave a frightful scream. The woman raised herself and Pearl slipped down on the sand and looked towards the land. Little men in blue coats—little blue men came running, running towards her with shouts and whistlings—a crowd of little blue men to carry her back to the House of Boxes.

MILLIE

Millie stood leaning against the verandah until the men were out of sight. When they were far down the road Willie Cox turned round on his horse and waved. But she didn't wave back. She nodded her head a little and made a grimace. Not a bad young fellow, Willie Cox, but a bit too free and easy for her taste. Oh, my word! it was hot. Enough to fry your hair! Millie put her handkerchief over her head and shaded her eyes with her hand. In the distance along the dusty road she could see the horses—like brown spots dancing up and down, and when she looked away from them and over the burnt paddocks she could see them still—just before her eyes, jumping like mosquitoes. It was half-past two in the afternoon. The sun hung in the faded blue sky like a burning mirror, and away beyond the paddocks the blue mountains quivered and leapt like sea. Sid wouldn't be back until half-past ten. He had ridden over to the township with four of the boys to help hunt down the young fellow who'd murdered Mr Williamson. Such a dreadful thing! And Mrs Williamson left all alone with all those kids. Funny! she couldn't think of Mr Williamson being dead! He was such a one for a joke. Always having a lark. Willie Cox said they found him in the barn, shot bang through the head, and the young English 'johnny'* who'd been on the station learning farming—disappeared. Funny! she wouldn't think of anyone shooting Mr Williamson, and him so popular and all. My word! when they caught that young man! Well—you couldn't be sorry for a young fellow like that. As Sid said, if he wasn't strung up* where would they all be? A man like that doesn't stop at one go. There was blood all over the barn. And Willie Cox said he was that knocked out he picked a cigarette up out of the blood and smoked it. My word! he must have been half dotty.

Millie went back into the kitchen. She put some ashes on the stove and sprinkled them with water. Languidly, the sweat pouring down her face, and dropping off her nose and chin, she cleared away the dinner, and going into the bedroom, stared at herself in the fly-specked mirror, and wiped her face and neck with a towel. She didn't know what was the matter with herself that afternoon. She could have had a good cry—just for nothing—and then change her blouse and have a good cup of tea. Yes, she felt like that! She flopped down on the side of the bed and stared at the coloured print on the wall opposite, 'Garden Party at Windsor Castle'. In the foreground emerald lawns planted with immense oak trees, and in their grateful shade, a muddle of ladies and gentlemen and parasols and little tables. The background was filled with the towers of Windsor Castle, flying three Union Jacks, and in the middle of the picture the old Queen, like a tea cosy with a head on top of it. 'I wonder if it really looked like that.' Millie stared at the flowery ladies, who simpered back at her. 'I wouldn't care for that sort of thing. Too much side. What with the Queen an' one thing an' another.' Over the packing case dressing-table there was a large photograph of her and Sid, taken on their wedding day. Nice picture that—if you *do* like. She was sitting down in a basket chair, in her cream cashmere and satin ribbons, and Sid, standing with one hand on her shoulder, looking at her bouquet. And behind them there were some fern trees, and a waterfall, and Mount Cook* in the distance, covered with snow. She had almost forgotten her wedding day; time did pass so, and if you hadn't any one to talk things over with, they soon dropped out of your mind. 'I wunner why we never had no kids . . . .' She shrugged her shoulders—gave it up. 'Well, *I've* never missed them. I wouldn't be surprised if Sid had, though. He's softer than me.'

And then she sat, quiet, thinking of nothing at all, her red swollen hands rolled in her apron, her feet stuck out in front of her, her little head with the thick screw of dark hair, drooped on her chest. 'Tick-tick' went the kitchen clock, the ashes clinked in the grate, and the venetian blind knocked against the kitchen window. Quite suddenly Millie felt frightened. A queer trembling started inside her—in her stomach—and then spread all over to her knees and hands. 'There's somebody about.' She tiptoed to the door and peered into the kitchen. Nobody there; the verandah doors were closed, the blinds were down, and in the dusky light the white face of the clock shone, and the furniture seemed to bulge and breathe . . . and listen, too. The clock—the ashes—and the venetian—and then again—something else—like steps in the back yard. 'Go an' see what it is, Millie Evans.' She started to the back door, opened it, and at the same moment someone ducked behind the wood pile. 'Who's that,' she cried in a loud, bold voice. 'Come out o' that. I seen yer. I know where you are. I got my gun. Come out from behind of that wood stack.' She was not frightened any more. She was furiously angry. Her heart banged like a drum. 'I'll teach you to play tricks with a woman,' she yelled, and she took a gun from the kitchen corner, and dashed down the verandah steps, across the glaring yard to the other side of the wood stack. A young man lay there, on his stomach, one arm across his face. 'Get up! You're shamming!' Still holding the gun she kicked him in the shoulders. He gave no sign. 'Oh, my God, I believe he's dead.' She knelt down, seized hold of him, and turned him over on his back. He rolled like a sack. She crouched back on her haunches, staring, her lips and nostrils fluttered with horror.

He was not much more than a boy, with fair hair, and a growth of fair down on his lips and chin. His eyes were open, rolled up, showing the whites, and his face was patched with dust caked with sweat. He wore a cotton shirt and trousers with sandshoes on his feet. One of the trousers stuck to his leg with a patch of dark blood. 'I *can't*,' said Millie, and then, 'You've got to.' She bent over and felt his heart. 'Wait a minute,' she stammered, 'wait a minute,' and she ran into the house for brandy and a pail of water. 'What are you going to do, Millie Evans? Oh, I don't know. I never seen anyone in a dead faint before.' She knelt down, put her arm under the boy's head and poured some brandy between his lips. It spilled down both sides of his mouth. She dipped a corner of her apron in the water and wiped his face, and his hair and his throat, with fingers that trembled. Under the dust and sweat his face gleamed, white as her apron, and thin, and puckered in little lines. A strange dreadful feeling gripped Millie Evans' bosom—some seed that had never flourished there, unfolded, and struck deep roots and burst into painful leaf. 'Are yer coming round? Feeling all right again?' The boy breathed sharply, half choked, his eyelids quivered, and he moved his head from side to side. 'You're better,' said Millie, smoothing his hair. 'Feeling fine now again, ain't you?' The pain in her bosom half suffocated her. 'It's no good you crying, Millie Evans. You got to keep your head.' Quite suddenly he sat up and leaned against the wood pile, away from her, staring on the ground. 'There now!' cried Millie Evans, in a strange, shaking voice. The boy turned and looked at her, still not speaking, but his eyes were so full of pain and terror that she had to shut her teeth and clench her hand to stop from crying. After a long pause he said in the little voice of a child talking in his sleep, 'I'm hungry.' His lips quivered. She scrambled to her feet and stood over him. 'You come right into the house and have a set down meal,' she said. 'Can you walk?' 'Yes,' he whispered, and swaying he followed her across the glaring yard to the verandah. At the bottom step he paused, looking at her again. 'I'm not coming in,' he said. He sat on the verandah step in the little pool of shade that lay round the house. Millie watched him. 'When did yer last 'ave anythink to eat?' He shook his head. She cut a chunk off the greasy corned beef and a round of bread plastered with butter; but when she brought it he was standing up, glancing round him, and paid no attention to the plate of food. 'When are they coming back?' he stammered.

At the moment she knew. She stood, holding the plate, staring. He was Harrison. He was the English johnny who'd killed Mr Williamson. 'I know who you are,' she said, very slowly, 'yer can't fox me. That's who you are. I must have been blind in me two eyes not to 'ave known from the first.' He made a movement with his hands as though that was all nothing. 'When are they coming back?' And she meant to say, 'Any minute. They're on their way now.' Instead she said to the dreadful, frightened face, 'Not till 'arf past ten.' He sat down, leaning against one of the verandah poles. His face broke up into little quivers. He shut his eyes and tears streamed down his cheeks. 'Nothing but a kid. An' all them fellows after 'im. 'E don't stand any more of a chance than a kid would.' 'Try a bit of beef,' said Millie. 'It's the food you want. Something to steady your stomach.' She moved across the verandah and sat down beside him, the plate on her knees. ''Ere—try a bit.' She broke the bread and butter into little pieces, and she thought, 'They won't ketch 'im. Not if I can 'elp it. Men is all beasts. I don't care wot 'e's done, or wot 'e 'asn't done. See 'im through, Millie Evans. 'E's nothink but a sick kid.'

*   *   *

Millie lay on her back, her eyes wide open, listening. Sid turned over, hunched the quilt round his shoulders, muttered 'Good night, ole girl.' She heard Willie Cox and the other chap drop their clothes on to the kitchen floor, and then their voices, and Willie Cox saying, 'Lie down, Gumboil. Lie down, yer little devil,' to his dog. The house dropped quiet. She lay and listened. Little pulses tapped in her body, listening, too. It was hot. She was frightened to move because of Sid. ''E must get off. 'E must. I don' care anythink about justice an' all the rot they've bin spouting to-night,' she thought, savagely. ''Ow are yer to know what anythink's like till yer *do* know. It's all rot.' She strained to the silence. He ought to be moving. . . . Before there was a sound from outside Willie Cox's Gumboil got up and padded sharply across the kitchen floor and sniffed at the back door. Terror started up in Millie. 'What's that dog doing? Uh! What a fool that young fellow is with a dog 'anging about. Why don't 'e lie down an' sleep.' The dog stopped, but she knew it was listening. Suddenly, with a sound that made her cry out in horror the dog started barking and rushing to and fro. 'What's that? What's up?' Sid flung out of bed. 'It ain't nothink. It's only Gumboil. Sid, Sid.' She clutched his arm, but he shook her off. 'My Christ, there's something up. My God.' Sid flung into his trousers. Willie Cox opened the back door. Gumboil in a fury darted out into the yard, round the corner of the house. 'Sid, there's someone in the paddock,' roared the other chap. 'What's it—what's that?' Sid dashed out on to the front verandah. 'Here, Millie, take the lantin. Willie, some skunk's* got 'old of one of the 'orses.' The three men bolted out of the house and at the same moment Millie saw Harrison dash across the paddock on Sid's horse and down the road. 'Millie, bring that blasted lantin.' She ran in her bare feet, her nightdress flicking her legs. They were after him in a flash. And at the sight of Harrison in the distance, and the three men hot after, a strange mad joy smothered everything else. She rushed into the road—she laughed and shrieked and danced in the dust, jigging the lantern. 'A—ah! Arter 'im, Sid! A—a—a—h! ketch 'im, Willie. Go it! Go it! A—ah, Sid! Shoot 'im down. Shoot 'im!'

SOMETHING CHILDISH BUT
VERY NATURAL

Whether he had forgotten what it felt like, or his head had really grown bigger since the summer before, Henry could not decide. But his straw hat hurt him: it pinched his forehead and started a dull ache in the two bones just over the temples. So he chose a corner seat in a third-class 'smoker', took off his hat and put it in the rack with his large black cardboard portfolio and his Aunt B's Christmas-present gloves. The carriage smelt horribly of wet india-rubber and soot. There were ten minutes to spare before the train went, so Henry decided to go and have a look at the book-stall. Sunlight darted through the glass roof of the station in long beams of blue and gold; a little boy ran up and down carrying a tray of primroses; there was something about the people—about the women especially— something idle and yet eager. The most thrilling day of the year, the first real day of Spring had unclosed its warm delicious beauty even to London eyes. It had put a spangle in every colour and a new tone in every voice, and city folks walked as though they carried real live bodies under their clothes with real live hearts pumping the stiff blood through.

Henry was a great fellow for books. He did not read many nor did he possess above half-a-dozen. He looked at all in the Charing Cross Road* during lunch-time and at any odd time in London; the quantity with which he was on nodding terms was amazing. By his clean neat handling of them and by his nice choice of phrase when discussing them with one or another bookseller you would have thought that he had taken his pap with a tome propped before his nurse's bosom. But you would have been quite wrong. That was only Henry's way with everything he touched or said. That afternoon it was an anthology of English poetry, and he turned over the pages until a title struck his eye—*Something Childish but very Natural*

> Had I but two little wings,*
> And were a little feathery bird,
> To you I'd fly, my dear,
> But thoughts like these are idle things,
> And I stay here.

But in my sleep to you I fly,
I'm always with you in my sleep,
The world is all one's own,
But then one wakes and where am I?
All, all alone.

Sleep stays not though a monarch bids,
So I love to wake at break of day,
For though my sleep be gone,
Yet while 'tis dark one shuts one's lids,
And so, dreams on.

He could not have done with the little poem. It was not the words
so much as the whole air of it that charmed him! He might have
written it lying in bed, very early in the morning, and watching the
sun dance on the ceiling. 'It is *still*, like that,' thought Henry. 'I am
sure he wrote it when he was half-awake some time, for it's got a
smile of a dream on it.' He stared at the poem and then looked away
and repeated it by heart, missed a word in the third verse and
looked again, and again until he became conscious of shouting and
shuffling, and he looked up to see the train moving slowly.

'God's thunder!' Henry dashed forward. A man with a flag and a
whistle had his hand on a door. He clutched Henry somehow. . . .
Henry was inside with the door slammed, in a carriage that wasn't a
'smoker', that had not a trace of his straw hat or the black portfolio
or his Aunt B's Christmas-present gloves. Instead, in the opposite
corner, close against the wall, there sat a girl. Henry did not dare to
look at her, but he felt certain she was staring at him. 'She must think
I'm mad,' he thought, 'dashing into a train without even a hat, and in
the evening, too.' He felt so funny. He didn't know how to sit or
sprawl. He put his hands in his pockets and tried to appear quite
indifferent and frown at a large photograph of Bolton Abbey.* But
feeling her eyes on him he gave her just the tiniest glance. Quick she
looked away out of the window, and then Henry, careful of her
slightest movement, went on looking. She sat pressed against the
window, her cheek and shoulder half hidden by a long wave of
marigold-coloured hair. One little hand in a grey cotton glove held a
leather case on her lap with the initials E. M. on it. The other hand
she had slipped through the window-strap, and Henry noticed a
silver bangle on the wrist with a Swiss cow-bell and a silver shoe and
fish. She wore a green coat and a hat with a wreath round it. All this

Henry saw while the title of the new poem persisted in his brain—
Something Childish but very Natural. 'I suppose she goes to some
school in London,' thought Henry. 'She might be in an office. Oh,
no, she is too young. Besides she'd have her hair up* if she was. It isn't
even down her back.' He could not keep his eyes off that beautiful
waving hair. '"My eyes are like two drunken bees. . . . " Now, I
wonder if I read that or made it up?'

That moment the girl turned round and, catching his glance, she
blushed. She bent her head to hide the red colour that flew in her
cheeks, and Henry, terribly embarrassed, blushed too. 'I shall have to
speak—have to—have to!' He started putting up his hand to raise
the hat that wasn't there. He thought that funny; it gave him
confidence.

'I'm—I'm most awfully sorry,' he said, smiling at the girl's hat.
'But I can't go on sitting in the same carriage with you and not
explaining why I dashed in like that, without my hat even. I'm sure I
gave you a fright, and just now I was staring at you—but that's only
an awful fault of mine; I'm a terrible starer! If you'd like me to
explain—how I got in here—not about the staring, of course,'—he
gave a little laugh—'I will.'

For a minute she said nothing, then in a low, shy voice—'It doesn't
matter.'

The train had flung behind the roofs and chimneys. They were
swinging into the country, past little black woods and fading fields
and pools of water shining under an apricot evening sky. Henry's
heart began to thump and beat to the beat of the train. He couldn't
leave it like that. She sat so quiet, hidden in her fallen hair. He felt
that it was absolutely necessary that she should look up and understand him—understand him at least. He leant forward and clasped
his hands round his knees.

'You see I'd just put all my things—a portfolio—into a third-class
"smoker" and was having a look at the book-stall,' he explained.

As he told the story she raised her head. He saw her grey eyes
under the shadow of her hat and her eyebrows like two gold feathers.
Her lips were faintly parted. Almost unconsciously he seemed to
absorb the fact that she was wearing a bunch of primroses and that
her throat was white—the shape of her face wonderfully delicate
against all that burning hair. 'How beautiful she is! How simply
beautiful she is!' sang Henry's heart, and swelled with the words,

bigger and bigger and trembling like a marvellous bubble—so that he was afraid to breathe for fear of breaking it.

'I hope there was nothing valuable in the portfolio,' said she, very grave.

'Oh, only some silly drawings that I was taking back from the office,' answered Henry, airily. 'And—I was rather glad to lose my hat. It had been hurting me all day.'

'Yes,' she said, 'it's left a mark,' and she nearly smiled.

Why on earth should those words have made Henry feel so free suddenly and so happy and so madly excited? What was happening between them? They said nothing, but to Henry their silence was alive and warm. It covered him from his head to his feet in a trembling wave. Her marvellous words, 'It's made a mark,' had in some mysterious fashion established a bond between them. They could not be utter strangers to each other if she spoke so simply and so naturally. And now she was really smiling. The smile danced in her eyes, crept over her cheeks to her lips and stayed there. He leant back. The words flew from him.—'Isn't life wonderful!'

At that moment the train dashed into a tunnel. He heard her voice raised against the noise. She leant forward.

'I don't think so. But then I've been a fatalist for a long time now'—a pause—'months.'

They were shattering through the dark. 'Why?' called Henry.

'Oh. . . .'

Then she shrugged, and smiled and shook her head, meaning she could not speak against the noise. He nodded and leant back. They came out of the tunnel into a sprinkle of lights and houses. He waited for her to explain. But she got up and buttoned her coat and put her hands to her hat, swaying a little. 'I get out here,' she said. That seemed quite impossible to Henry.

The train slowed down and the lights outside grew brighter. She moved towards his end of the carriage.

'Look here!' he stammered. 'Shan't I see you again?' He got up, too, and leant against the rack with one hand. 'I *must* see you again.' The train was stopping.

She said breathlessly, 'I come down from London every evening.'

'You—you—you do—really?' His eagerness frightened her. He was quick to curb it. Shall we or shall we not shake hands? raced through his brain. One hand was on the door-handle, the other held the little bag. The train stopped. Without another word or glance she was gone.

*   *   *

Then came Saturday—a half day at the office—and Sunday between. By Monday evening Henry was quite exhausted. He was at the station far too early, with a pack of silly thoughts at his heels as it were driving him up and down. 'She didn't say she came by this train!' 'And supposing I go up and she cuts me.' 'There may be somebody with her.' 'Why do you suppose she's ever thought of you again?' 'What are you going to say if you do see her?' He even prayed, 'Lord if it be Thy will, let us meet.'

But nothing helped. White smoke floated against the roof of the station—dissolved and came again in swaying wreaths. Of a sudden, as he watched it, so delicate and so silent, moving with such mysterious grace above the crowd and the scuffle, he grew calm. He felt very tired—he only wanted to sit down and shut his eyes—she was not coming—a forlorn relief breathed in the words. And then he saw her quite near to him walking towards the train with the same little leather case in her hand. Henry waited. He knew, somehow, that she had seen him, but he did not move until she came close to him and said in her low, shy voice—'Did you get them again?'

'Oh, yes, thank you, I got them again,' and with a funny half gesture he showed her the portfolio and the gloves. They walked side by side to the train and into an empty carriage. They sat down opposite to each other, smiling timidly but not speaking, while the train moved slowly, and slowly gathered speed and smoothness. Henry spoke first.

'It's so silly,' he said, 'not knowing your name.' She put back a big piece of hair that had fallen on her shoulder, and he saw how her hand in the grey glove was shaking. Then he noticed that she was sitting very stiffly with her knees pressed together—and he was, too—both of them trying not to tremble so. She said 'My name is Edna.'

'And mine is Henry.'

In the pause they took possession of each other's names and turned them over and put them away, a shade less frightened after that.

'I want to ask you something else now,' said Henry. He looked at Edna, his head a little on one side. 'How old are you?'

'Over sixteen,' she said, 'and you?'

'I'm nearly eighteen. . . .'

'Isn't it hot?' she said suddenly, and pulled off her grey gloves and put her hands to her cheeks and kept them there. Their eyes were not frightened—they looked at each other with a sort of desperate calmness. If only their bodies would not tremble so stupidly! Still half hidden by her hair, Edna said:

'Have you ever been in love before?'

'No never! Have you?'

'Oh, never in all my life.' She shook her head. 'I never even thought it possible.'

His next words came in a rush. 'Whatever have you been doing since last Friday evening? Whatever did you do all Saturday and all Sunday and to-day?'

But she did not answer—only shook her head and smiled and said, 'No, you tell *me*.'

'I?' cried Henry—and then he found he couldn't tell her either. He couldn't climb back to those mountains of days, and he had to shake his head, too.

'But it's been agony,' he said, smiling brilliantly—'agony.' At that she took away her hands and started laughing, and Henry joined her. They laughed until they were tired.

'It's so—so extraordinary,' she said. 'So suddenly, you know, and I feel as if I'd known you for years.'

'So do I . . . .' said Henry. 'I believe it must be the Spring. I believe I've swallowed a butterfly—and it's fanning its wings just here.' He put his hand on his heart.

'And the really extraordinary thing is,' said Edna, 'that I had made up my mind that I didn't care for—men at all. I mean all the girls at College—'

'Were you at College?'

She nodded. 'A training college, learning to be a secretary.' She sounded scornful.

'I'm in an office,' said Henry. 'An architect's office—such a funny little place up one hundred and thirty stairs. We ought to be building nests instead of houses, I always think.'

'Do you like it?'

'No, of course I don't. I don't want to do anything, do you?'

'No, I hate it. . . . And,' she said, 'my mother is a Hungarian—I believe that makes me hate it even more.'

That seemed to Henry quite natural. 'It would,' he said.

'Mother and I are exactly alike. I haven't a thing in common with my father; he's just . . . a little man in the City—but mother has got wild blood in her and she's given it to me. She hates our life just as much as I do.' She paused and frowned. 'All the same, we don't get on a bit together—that's funny—isn't it? But I'm absolutely alone at home.'

Henry was listening—in a way he was listening, but there was something else he wanted to ask her. He said, very shyly, 'Would you—would you take off your hat?'

She looked startled. 'Take off my hat?'

'Yes—it's your hair. I'd give anything to see your hair properly.'

She protested. 'It isn't really . . . .'

'Oh, it *is*,' cried Henry, and then, as she took off the hat and gave her head a little toss, 'Oh, Edna! it's the loveliest thing in the world.'

'Do you like it?' she said, smiling and very pleased. She pulled it round her shoulders like a cape of gold. 'People generally laugh at it. It's such an absurd colour.' But Henry would not believe that. She leaned her elbows on her knees and cupped her chin in her hands. 'That's how I often sit when I'm angry and then I feel it burning me up. . . . Silly?'

'No, no, not a bit,' said Henry. 'I knew you did. It's your sort of weapon against all the dull horrid things.'

'However did you know that? Yes, that's just it. But however did you know?'

'Just knew,' smiled Henry. 'My God!' he cried, 'what fools people are! All the little pollies* that you know and that I know. Just look at you and me. Here we are—that's all there is to be said. I know about you and you know about me—we've just found each other—quite simply—just by being natural. That's all life is—something childish and very natural. Isn't it?'

'Yes—yes,' she said eagerly. 'That's what I've always thought.'

'It's people that make things so—silly. As long as you can keep away from them you're safe and you're happy.'

'Oh, I've thought that for a long time.'

'Then you're just like me,' said Henry. The wonder of that was so great that he almost wanted to cry. Instead he said very solemnly: 'I believe we're the only two people alive who think as we do. In fact, I'm sure of it. Nobody understands me. I feel as though I were living in a world of strange beings—do you?'

'Always.'

'We'll be in that loathsome tunnel again in a minute,' said Henry. 'Edna! can I—just touch your hair?'

She drew back quickly. 'Oh, no, please don't,' and as they were going into the dark she moved a little away from him.

*   *   *

'Edna! I've bought the tickets. The man at the concert hall didn't seem at all surprised that I had the money. Meet me outside the gallery doors at three, and wear that cream blouse and the corals—will you? I love you. I don't like sending these letters to the shop. I always feel those people with "Letters received" in their window keep a kettle in their back parlour that would steam open an elephant's ear of an envelope. But it really doesn't matter, does it, darling? Can you get away on Sunday? Pretend you are going to spend the day with one of the girls from the office, and let's meet at some little place and walk or find a field where we can watch the daisies uncurling. I do love you, Edna. But Sundays without you are simply impossible. Don't get run over before Saturday, and don't eat anything out of a tin or drink anything from a public fountain.* That's all, darling.'

'My dearest, yes, I'll be there on Saturday—and I've arranged about Sunday, too. That is one great blessing. I'm quite free at home. I have just come in from the garden. It's such a lovely evening. Oh, Henry, I could sit and cry, I love you so to-night. Silly—isn't it? I either feel so happy I can hardly stop laughing or else so sad I can hardly stop crying and both for the same reason. But we are so young to have found each other, aren't we? I am sending you a violet. It is quite warm. I wish you were here now, just for a minute even. Good-night, darling. I am Edna.'

*   *   *

'Safe,' said Edna, 'safe! And excellent places, aren't they, Henry?'

She stood up to take off her coat and Henry made a movement

to help her. 'No—no—it's off.' She tucked it under the seat. She sat down beside him. 'Oh, Henry, what have you got there? Flowers?'

'Only two tiny little roses.' He laid them in her lap.

'Did you get my letter all right?' asked Edna, unpinning the paper.

'Yes,' he said, 'and the violet is growing beautifully. You should see my room. I planted a little piece of it in every corner and one on my pillow and one in the pocket of my pyjama jacket.'

She shook her hair at him. 'Henry, give me the programme.'

'Here it is—you can read it with me. I'll hold it for you.'

'No, let me have it.'

'Well, then, I'll read it for you.'

'No, you can have it after.'

'Edna,' he whispered.

'Oh, please don't,' she pleaded. 'Not here—the people.'

Why did he want to touch her so much and why did she mind? Whenever he was with her he wanted to hold her hand or take her arm when they walked together, or lean against her—not hard—just lean lightly so that his shoulder should touch her shoulder—and she wouldn't even have that. All the time that he was away from her he was hungry, he craved the nearness of her. There seemed to be comfort and warmth breathing from Edna that he needed to keep him calm. Yes, that was it. He couldn't get calm with her because she wouldn't let him touch her. But she loved him. He knew that. Why did she feel so curiously about it? Every time he tried to or even asked for her hand she shrank back and looked at him with pleading frightened eyes as though he wanted to hurt her. They could say anything to each other. And there wasn't any question of their belonging to each other. And yet he couldn't touch her. Why, he couldn't even help her off with her coat. Her voice dropped into his thoughts.

'Henry!' He leaned to listen, setting his lips. 'I want to explain something to you. I will—I will—I promise—after the concert.'

'All right.' He was still hurt.

'You're not sad, are you?' she said.

He shook his head.

'Yes, you are, Henry.'

'No, really not.' He looked at the roses lying in her hands.

'Well, are you happy?'

'Yes. Here comes the orchestra.'

It was twilight when they came out of the hall. A blue net of light hung over the streets and houses, and pink clouds floated in a pale sky. As they walked away from the hall Henry felt they were very little and alone. For the first time since he had known Edna his heart was heavy.

'Henry!' She stopped suddenly and stared at him. 'Henry, I'm not coming to the station with you. Don't—don't wait for me. Please, please leave me.'

'My God!' cried Henry, and started, 'what's the matter—Edna—darling—Edna, what have I done?'

'Oh, nothing—go away,' and she turned and ran across the street into a square and leaned up against the square railings—and hid her face in her hands.

'Edna—Edna—my little love—you're crying. Edna, my baby girl!'

She leaned her arms along the railings and sobbed distractedly.

'Edna—stop—it's all my fault. I'm a fool—I'm a thundering idiot. I've spoiled your afternoon. I've tortured you with my idiotic mad bloody clumsiness. That's it. Isn't it, Edna? For God's sake.'

'Oh,' she sobbed, 'I do hate hurting you so. Every time you ask me to let—let you hold my hand or—or kiss me I could kill myself for not doing it—for not letting you. I don't know why I don't even.' She said wildly, 'It's not that I'm frightened of you—it's not that—it's only a feeling, Henry, that I can't understand myself even. Give me your handkerchief, darling.' He pulled it from his pocket. 'All through the concert I've been haunted by this, and every time we meet I know it's bound to come up. Somehow I feel if once we did that—you know—held each other's hands and kissed it would be all changed—and I feel we wouldn't be free like we are—we'd be doing something secret. We wouldn't be children any more . . . silly, isn't it? I'd feel awkward with you, Henry, and I'd feel shy, and I do so feel that just because you and I are you and I, we don't need that sort of thing.' She turned and looked at him, pressing her hands to her cheeks in the way he knew so well, and behind her as in a dream he saw the sky and half a white moon and the trees of the square with their unbroken buds. He kept twisting, twisting up in his hands the concert programme. 'Henry! You do understand me—don't you?'

'Yes, I think I do. But you're not going to be frightened any more, are you?' He tried to smile. 'We'll forget, Edna. I'll never mention it again. We'll bury the bogy in this square—now—you and I—won't we?'

'But,' she said, searching his face—'will it make you love me less?'

'Oh, no,' he said. 'Nothing could—nothing on earth could do that.'

*   *   *

London became their play-ground. On Saturday afternoons they explored. They found their own shops where they bought cigarettes and sweets for Edna—and their own tea-shop with their own table— their own streets—and one night when Edna was supposed to be at a lecture at the Polytechnic* they found their own village. It was the name that made them go there. 'There's white geese in that name,' said Henry, telling it to Edna. 'And a river and little low houses with old men sitting outside them—old sea captains with wooden legs winding up their watches, and there are little shops with lamps in the windows.'

It was too late for them to see the geese or the old men, but the river was there and the houses and even the shops with lamps. In one a woman sat working a sewing-machine on the counter. They heard the whirring hum and they saw her big shadow filling the shop. 'Too full for a single customer,' said Henry. 'It is a perfect place.'

The houses were small and covered with creepers and ivy. Some of them had worn wooden steps leading up to the doors. You had to go down a little flight of steps to enter some of the others; and just across the road—to be seen from every window—was the river, with a walk beside it and some high poplar trees.

'This is the place for us to live in,' said Henry. 'There's a house to let, too. I wonder if it would wait if we asked it. I'm sure it would.'

'Yes, I would like to live there,' said Edna. They crossed the road and she leaned against the trunk of a tree and looked up at the empty house, with a dreamy smile.

'There is a little garden at the back, dear,' said Henry, 'a lawn with one tree on it and some daisy bushes round the wall. At night the stars shine in the tree like tiny candles. And inside there are two rooms downstairs and a big room with folding doors upstairs and above that an attic. And there are eight stairs to the kitchen—very dark, Edna. You are rather frightened of them, you know. "Henry, dear, would you mind bringing the lamp? I just want to make sure that Euphemia has raked out the fire before we go to bed."'

'Yes,' said Edna. 'Our bedroom is at the very top—that room with the two square windows. When it is quiet we can hear the river flowing and the sound of the poplar trees far, far away, rustling and flowing in our dreams, darling.'

'You're not cold—are you?' he said, suddenly.

'No—no, only happy.'

'The room with the folding doors is yours.' Henry laughed. 'It's a mixture—it isn't a room at all. It's full of your toys and there's a big blue chair in it where you sit curled up in front of the fire with the flames in your curls—because though we're married you refuse to put your hair up and only tuck it inside your coat for the church service. And there's a rug on the floor for me to lie on, because I'm so lazy. Euphemia—that's our servant—only comes in the day. After she's gone we go down to the kitchen and sit on the table and eat an apple, or perhaps we make some tea, just for the sake of hearing the kettle sing. That's not joking. If you listen to a kettle right through it's like an early morning in Spring.'

'Yes, I know,' she said. 'All the different kinds of birds.'

A little cat came through the railings of the empty house and into the road. Edna called it and bent down and held out her hands— 'Kitty! Kitty!' The little cat ran to her and rubbed against her knees.

'If we're going for a walk just take the cat and put it inside the front door,' said Henry, still pretending. 'I've got the key.'

They walked across the road and Edna stood stroking the cat in her arms while Henry went up the steps and pretended to open the door.

He came down again quickly. 'Let's go away at once. It's going to turn into a dream.'

The night was dark and warm. They did not want to go home. 'What I feel so certain of is,' said Henry, 'that we ought to be living there, now. We oughtn't to wait for things. What's age? You're as old as you'll ever be and so am I. You know,' he said, 'I have a feeling often and often that it's dangerous to wait for things—that if you wait for things they only go further and further away.'

'But, Henry,—money! You see we haven't any money.'

'Oh, well,—perhaps if I disguised myself as an old man we could get a job as caretakers in some large house—that would be rather fun. I'd make up a terrific history of the house if anyone came to look over it and you could dress up and be the ghost moaning and wringing your hands in the deserted picture gallery, to frighten them off. Don't you ever feel that money is more or less accidental—that if one really wants things it's either there or it doesn't matter?'

She did not answer that—she looked up at the sky and said, 'Oh dear, I don't want to go home.'

'Exactly—that's the whole trouble—and we oughtn't to go home. We ought to be going back to the house and find an odd saucer to give the cat the dregs of the milk-jug in. I'm not really laughing— I'm not even happy. I'm lonely for you, Edna—I would give anything to lie down and cry' . . . and he added limply, 'with my head in your lap and your darling cheek in my hair.'

'But, Henry,' she said, coming closer, 'you have faith, haven't you? I mean you are absolutely certain that we shall have a house like that and everything we want—aren't you?'

'Not enough—that's not enough. I want to be sitting on those very stairs and taking off these very boots this very minute. Don't you? Is faith enough for you?'

'If only we weren't so young . . . .' she said miserably. 'And yet,' she sighed, 'I'm sure I don't feel very young—I feel twenty at least.'

*　　*　　*

Henry lay on his back in the little wood. When he moved the dead leaves rustled beneath him, and above his head the new leaves quivered like fountains of green water steeped in sunlight. Some-where out of sight Edna was gathering primroses. He had been so full of dreams that morning that he could not keep pace with her delight in the flowers. 'Yes, love, you go and come back for me. I'm too lazy.' She had thrown off her hat and knelt down beside him, and by and by her voice and her footsteps had grown fainter. Now the wood was silent except for the leaves, but he knew that she was not far away and he moved so that the tips of his fingers touched her pink jacket. Ever since waking he had felt so strangely that he was not really awake at all, but just dreaming. The time before, Edna was a dream and now he and she were dreaming together and somewhere in some dark place another dream waited for him. 'No, that can't be true because I can't ever imagine the world without us. I feel that we two together mean something that's got to be there just as naturally as trees or birds or clouds.' He tried to remember what it had felt like without Edna, but he could not get back to those days. They were hidden by her; Edna, with the marigold hair and strange, dreamy smile filled him up to the brim. He breathed her; he ate and drank her. He walked about with a shining ring of Edna keeping the world away or touching whatever it lighted on with its own beauty. 'Long after you have stopped laughing,' he told her, 'I can hear your laugh running up and down my veins—and yet—are we a dream?' And suddenly he saw himself and Edna as two very small children walking through the streets, looking through windows, buying things and playing with them, talking to each other, smiling—he saw even their gestures and the way they stood, so often, quite still, face to face—and then he rolled over and pressed his face in the leaves—faint with longing. He wanted to kiss Edna, and to put his arms round her and press her to him and feel her cheek hot against his kiss and kiss her until he'd no breath left and so stifle the dream.

'No, I can't go on being hungry like this,' said Henry, and jumped up and began to run in the direction she had gone. She had wandered a long way. Down in a green hollow he saw her kneeling, and when she saw him she waved and said—'Oh, Henry—such beauties! I've never seen such beauties. Come and look.' By the time he had reached her he would have cut off his hand rather than spoil her happiness. How strange Edna was that day! All the time she talked to Henry her eyes laughed; they were sweet and mocking. Two little spots of colour like strawberries glowed on her cheeks and 'I wish I could feel tired,' she kept saying. 'I want to walk over the whole world until I die. Henry—come along. Walk faster—Henry! If I start flying suddenly, you'll promise to catch hold of my feet, won't you? Otherwise I'll never come down.' And 'Oh,' she cried, 'I am so happy. I'm so frightfully happy!' They came to a weird place, covered with heather. It was early afternoon and the sun streamed down upon the purple.

'Let's rest here a little,' said Edna, and she waded into the heather and lay down. 'Oh, Henry, it's so lovely. I can't see anything except the little bells and the sky.'

Henry knelt down by her and took some primroses out of her basket and made a long chain to go round her throat. 'I could almost fall asleep,' said Edna. She crept over to his knees and lay hidden in her hair just beside him. 'It's like being under the sea, isn't it, dearest, so sweet and so still?'

'Yes,' said Henry, in a strange husky voice. 'Now I'll make you one of violets.' But Edna sat up. 'Let's go in,' she said.

They came back to the road and walked a long way. Edna said, 'No, I couldn't walk over the world—I'm tired now.' She trailed on the grass edge of the road. 'You and I are tired, Henry! How much further is it?'

'I don't know—not very far,' said Henry, peering into the distance. Then they walked in silence.

'Oh,' she said at last, 'it really is too far, Henry, I'm tired and I'm hungry. Carry my silly basket of primroses.' He took them without looking at her.

At last they came to a village and a cottage with a notice 'Teas Provided'.

'This is the place,' said Henry. 'I've often been here. You sit on the little bench and I'll go and order the tea.' She sat down on the bench, in the pretty garden all white and yellow with spring flowers. A woman came to the door and leaned against it watching them eat. Henry was very nice to her, but Edna did not say a word. 'You haven't been here for a long spell,' said the woman.

'No—the garden's looking wonderful.'

'Fair,' said she. 'Is the young lady your sister?' Henry nodded Yes, and took some jam.

'There's a likeness,' said the woman. She came down into the garden and picked a head of white jonquils and handed it to Edna. 'I suppose you don't happen to know anyone who wants a cottage,' said she. 'My sister's taken ill and she left me hers. I want to let it.'

'For a long time?' asked Henry, politely.

'Oh,' said the woman vaguely, 'that depends.'

Said Henry, 'Well—I might know of somebody—could we go and look at it?'

'Yes, it's just a step down the road, the little one with the apple trees in front—I'll fetch you the key.'

While she was away Henry turned to Edna and said, 'Will you come?' She nodded.

They walked down the road and in through the gate and up the grassy path between the pink and white trees. It was a tiny place— two rooms downstairs and two rooms upstairs. Edna leaned out of the top window, and Henry stood at the doorway. 'Do you like it?' he asked.

'Yes,' she called, and then made a place for him at the window. 'Come and look. It's so sweet.'

He came and leant out of the window. Below them were the apple trees tossing in a faint wind that blew a long piece of Edna's hair across his eyes. They did not move. It was evening—the pale green sky was sprinkled with stars. 'Look!' she said—'stars, Henry.'

'There will be a moon in two T's,'* said Henry.

She did not seem to move and yet she was leaning against Henry's shoulder; he put his arm round her—'Are all those trees down there—apple?' she asked in a shaky voice.

'No, darling,' said Henry. 'Some of them are full of angels and some of them are full of sugar almonds—but evening light is awfully deceptive.' She sighed. 'Henry—we mustn't stay here any longer.'

He let her go and she stood up in the dusky room and touched her hair. 'What has been the matter with you all day?' she said—and then did not wait for an answer but ran to him and put her arms round his neck, and pressed his head into the hollow of her shoulder. 'Oh,' she breathed, 'I do love you. Hold me, Henry.' He put his arms round her, and she leaned against him and looked into his eyes. 'Hasn't it been terrible, all to-day?' said Edna. 'I knew what was the matter and I've tried every way I could to tell you that I wanted you to kiss me— that I'd quite got over the feeling.'

'You're perfect, perfect, perfect,' said Henry.

*   *   *

'The thing is,' said Henry, 'how am I going to wait until evening?' He took his watch out of his pocket, went into the cottage and popped it into a china jar on the mantelpiece. He'd looked at it seven times in one hour, and now he couldn't remember what time it was. Well, he'd look once again. Half-past four. Her train arrived at seven. He'd have to start for the station at half-past six. Two hours more to wait. He went through the cottage again—downstairs and upstairs. 'It looks lovely,' he said. He went into the garden and picked a round bunch of white pinks* and put them in a vase on the little table by Edna's bed. 'I don't believe this,' thought Henry. 'I don't believe this for a minute. It's too much. She'll be here in two hours and we'll walk home, and then I'll take that white jug off the kitchen table and go across to Mrs Biddie's and get the milk, and then come back, and when I come back she'll have lighted the lamp in the kitchen and I'll look through the window and see her moving about in the pool of lamplight. And then we shall have supper, and after supper (Bags I washing up!) I shall put some wood on the fire and we'll sit on the hearth-rug and watch it burning. There won't be a sound except the wood and perhaps the wind will creep round the house once. . . . And then we shall change our candles and she will go up first with her shadow on the wall beside her, and she will call out, Good-night, Henry—and I shall answer—Good-night, Edna. And then I shall dash upstairs and jump into bed and watch the tiny bar of light from her room brush my door, and the moment it disappears will shut my eyes and sleep until morning. Then we'll have all to-morrow and to-morrow and to-morrow* night. Is she thinking all this, too? Edna, come quickly!

> Had I two little wings,
> And were a little feathery bird,
> To you I'd fly, my dear—

No, no, dearest. . . . Because the waiting is a sort of Heaven, too, darling. If you can understand that. Did you ever know a cottage could stand on tip-toe. This one is doing it now.'

He was downstairs and sat on the doorstep with his hands clasped round his knees. That night when they found the village—and Edna said, 'Haven't you faith, Henry?' 'I hadn't then. Now I have,' he said, 'I feel just like God.'

He leaned his head against the lintel. He could hardly keep his eyes open, not that he was sleepy, but . . . for some reason . . . and a long time passed.

Henry thought he saw a big white moth flying down the road. It perched on the gate. No, it wasn't a moth. It was a little girl in a pinafore. What a nice little girl, and he smiled in his sleep, and she smiled, too, and turned in her toes as she walked. 'But she can't be living here,' thought Henry. 'Because this is ours. Here she comes.'

When she was quite close to him she took her hand from under her pinafore and gave him a telegram* and smiled and went away. There's a funny present! thought Henry, staring at it. 'Perhaps it's only a make-believe one, and it's got one of those snakes inside it that fly up at you.' He laughed gently in the dream and opened it very carefully. 'It's just a folded paper.' He took it out and spread it open.

The garden became full of shadows—they span a web of darkness over the cottage and the trees and Henry and the telegram. But Henry did not move.

THE LITTLE GOVERNESS

Oh dear, how she wished that it wasn't night-time. She'd have much rather travelled by day, much much rather. But the lady at the Governess Bureau* had said: 'You had better take an evening boat and then if you get into a compartment for "Ladies Only" in the train you will be far safer than sleeping in a foreign hotel. Don't go out of the carriage; don't walk about the corridors and *be sure* to lock the lavatory door if you go there. The train arrives at Munich at eight o'clock, and Frau Arnholdt says that the Hotel Grünewald is only one minute away. A porter can take you there. She will arrive at six the same evening, so you will have a nice quiet day to rest after the journey and rub up your German. And when you want anything to eat I would advise you to pop into the nearest baker's and get a bun and some coffee. You haven't been abroad before, have you?' 'No.' 'Well, I always tell my girls that it's better to mistrust people at first rather than trust them, and it's safer to suspect people of evil intentions rather than good ones. . . . It sounds rather hard but we've got to be women of the world, haven't we?'

It had been nice in the Ladies' Cabin.* The stewardess was so kind and changed her money for her and tucked up her feet. She lay on one of the hard pink-sprigged couches and watched the other passengers, friendly and natural, pinning their hats to the bolsters, taking off their boots and skirts, opening dressing-cases and arranging mysterious rustling little packages, tying their heads up in veils before lying down. *Thud, thud, thud*, went the steady screw of the steamer. The stewardess pulled a green shade over the light and sat down by the stove, her skirt turned back over her knees, a long piece of knitting on her lap. On a shelf above her head there was a water-bottle with a tight bunch of flowers stuck in it. 'I like travelling very much,' thought the little governess. She smiled and yielded to the warm rocking.

But when the boat stopped and she went up on deck, her dress-basket* in one hand, her rug and umbrella in the other, a cold, strange wind flew under her hat. She looked up at the masts and spars of the ship black against a green glittering sky and down to the dark landing stage where strange muffled figures lounged, waiting; she moved forward with the sleepy flock, all knowing where to go to and what to do except her, and she felt afraid. Just a little—just enough to wish—oh, to wish that it was daytime and that one of those women who had smiled at her in the glass, when they both did their hair in the Ladies' Cabin, was somewhere near now. 'Tickets, please. Show your tickets. Have your tickets ready.' She went down the gangway balancing herself carefully on her heels. Then a man in a black leather cap came forward and touched her on the arm. 'Where for, Miss?' He spoke English—he must be a guard or a stationmaster with a cap like that. She had scarcely answered when he pounced on her dress-basket. 'This way,' he shouted, in a rude, determined voice, and elbowing his way he strode past the people. 'But I don't want a porter.' What a horrible man! 'I don't want a porter. I want to carry it myself.' She had to run to keep up with him, and her anger, far stronger than she, ran before her and snatched the bag out of the wretch's hand. He paid no attention at all, but swung on down the long dark platform, and across a railway line. 'He is a robber.' She was sure he was a robber as she stepped between the silvery rails and felt the cinders crunch under her shoes. On the other side—oh, thank goodness!—there was a train with Munich written on it. The man stopped by the huge lighted carriages. 'Second class?' asked the insolent voice. 'Yes, a Ladies' compartment.' She was quite out of breath. She opened her little purse to find something small enough to give this horrible man while he tossed her dress-basket into the rack of an empty carriage that had a ticket, *Dames Seules*,* gummed on the window. She got into the train and handed him twenty centimes. 'What's this?' shouted the man, glaring at the money and then at her, holding it up to his nose, sniffing at it as though he had never in his life seen, much less held, such a sum. 'It's a franc. You know that, don't you? It's a franc. That's my fare!' A franc! Did he imagine that she was going to give him a franc for playing a trick like that just because she was a girl and travelling alone at night? Never, never! She squeezed her purse in her hand and simply did not see him—she looked at a view of St Malo on the wall opposite and simply did not hear him. 'Ah, no. Ah, no. Four sous. You make a mistake. Here, take it. It's a franc I want.' He leapt on to the step of the train and threw the money on to her lap. Trembling with terror she screwed herself tight, tight, and put out an icy hand and took the money—stowed it away in her hand. 'That's all you're going to get,' she said.

For a minute or two she felt his sharp eyes pricking her all over, while he nodded slowly, pulling down his mouth: 'Ve-ry well. *Trrrès bien.*'* He shrugged his shoulders and disappeared into the dark. Oh, the relief! How simply terrible that had been! As she stood up to feel if the dress-basket was firm she caught sight of herself in the mirror, quite white, with big round eyes. She untied her 'motor veil'* and unbuttoned her green cape. 'But it's all over now,' she said to the mirror face, feeling in some way that it was more frightened than she.

People began to assemble on the platform. They stood together in little groups talking; a strange light from the station lamps painted their faces almost green. A little boy in red clattered up with a huge tea wagon and leaned against it, whistling and flicking his boots with a serviette. A woman in a black alpaca* apron pushed a barrow with pillows for hire. Dreamy and vacant she looked—like a woman wheeling a perambulator—up and down, up and down—with a sleeping baby inside it. Wreaths of white smoke floated up from somewhere and hung below the roof like misty vines. 'How strange it all is,' thought the little governess, 'and the middle of the night, too.' She looked out from her safe corner, frightened no longer but proud that she had not given that franc. 'I can look after myself—of course I can. The great thing is not to—' Suddenly from the corridor there came a stamping of feet and men's voices, high and broken with snatches of loud laughter. They were coming her way. The little governess shrank into her corner as four young men in bowler hats passed, staring through the door and window. One of them, bursting with the joke, pointed to the notice *Dames Seules* and the four bent down the better to see the one little girl in the corner. Oh dear, they were in the carriage next door. She heard them tramping about and then a sudden hush followed by a tall thin fellow with a tiny black moustache who flung her door open. 'If mademoiselle cares to come in with us,' he said, in French. She saw the others crowding behind him, peeping under his arm and over his shoulder, and she sat very straight and still. 'If mademoiselle will do us the honour,' mocked the tall man. One of them could be quiet no longer; his laughter went off in a loud crack. 'Mademoiselle is serious,' persisted the young man, bowing and grimacing. He took off his hat with a flourish, and she was alone again.

'*En voiture.** *En voi-ture!*' Some one ran up and down beside the train. 'I wish it wasn't night-time. I wish there was another woman in the carriage. I'm frightened of the men next door.' The little governess looked out to see her porter coming back again—the same man making for her carriage with his arms full of luggage. But—but what *was* he doing? He put his thumb nail under the label *Dames Seules* and tore it right off and then stood aside squinting at her while an old man wrapped in a plaid cape climbed up the high step. 'But this is a ladies' compartment.' 'Oh, no, Mademoiselle, you make a mistake. No, no, I assure you. Merci, Monsieur.' '*En voi-turre!*' A shrill whistle. The porter stepped off triumphant and the train started. For a moment or two big tears brimmed her eyes and through them she saw the old man unwinding a scarf from his neck and untying the flaps of his Jaeger cap. He looked very old. Ninety at least. He had a white moustache and big gold-rimmed spectacles with little blue eyes behind them and pink wrinkled cheeks. A nice face—and charming the way he bent forward and said in halting French: 'Do I disturb you, Mademoiselle? Would you rather I took all these things out of the rack and found another carriage?' What! that old man have to move all those heavy things just because she . . . . 'No, it's quite all right. You don't disturb me at all.' 'Ah, a thousand thanks.' He sat down opposite her and unbuttoned the cape of his enormous coat and flung it off his shoulders.

The train seemed glad to have left the station. With a long leap it sprang into the dark. She rubbed a place in the window with her glove but she could see nothing—just a tree outspread like a black fan or a scatter of lights, or the line of a hill, solemn and huge. In the carriage next door the young men started singing '*Un, deux, trois.*'* They sang the same song over and over at the tops of their voices.

'I never could have dared to go to sleep if I had been alone,' she decided. '*I couldn't* have put my feet up or even taken off my hat.' The singing gave her a queer little tremble in her stomach and, hugging herself to stop it, with her arms crossed under her cape, she felt really glad to have the old man in the carriage with her. Careful to see that he was not looking she peeped at him through her long lashes. He sat extremely upright, the chest thrown out, the chin well in, knees pressed together, reading a German paper. That was why he spoke French so funnily. He was a German. Something in the army, she supposed—a Colonel or a General—once, of course, not now; he was too old for that now. How spick and span he looked for an old man. He wore a pearl pin stuck in his black tie and a ring with a dark red stone on his little finger; the tip of a white silk handkerchief showed in the pocket of his double-breasted jacket. Somehow, altogether, he was really nice to look at. Most old men were so horrid. She couldn't bear them doddery—or they had a disgusting cough or something. But not having a beard—that made all the difference—and then his cheeks were so pink and his moustache so very white. Down went the German paper and the old man leaned forward with the same delightful courtesy: 'Do you speak German, Mademoiselle?' '*Ja, ein wenig, mehr als Französisch,*'* said the little governess, blushing a deep pink colour that spread slowly over her cheeks and made her blue eyes look almost black. 'Ach, so!' The old man bowed graciously. 'Then perhaps you would care to look at some illustrated papers.' He slipped a rubber band from a little roll of them and handed them across. 'Thank you very much.' She was very fond of looking at pictures, but first she would take off her hat and gloves. So she stood up, unpinned the brown straw and put it neatly in the rack beside the dress-basket, stripped off her brown kid gloves, paired them in a tight roll and put them in the crown of the hat for safety, and then sat down again, more comfortably this time, her feet crossed, the papers on her lap. How kindly the old man in the corner watched her bare little hand turning over the big white pages, watched her lips moving as she pronounced the long words to herself, rested upon her hair that fairly blazed under the light. Alas! how tragic for a little governess to possess hair that made one think of tangerines and marigolds, of apricots and tortoiseshell cats and champagne! Perhaps that was what the old man was thinking as he gazed and gazed, and that not even the dark ugly clothes could disguise her soft beauty. Perhaps the flush that licked his cheeks and lips was a flush of rage that anyone so young and tender should have to travel alone and unprotected through the night. Who knows he was not murmuring in his sentimental German fashion: '*Ja, es ist eine Tragœdie!*'* Would to God I were the child's grandpapa!'

'Thank you very much. They were very interesting.' She smiled prettily handing back the papers. 'But you speak German extremely well,' said the old man. 'You have been in Germany before, of course?' 'Oh no, this is the first time'—a little pause, then—'this is the first time that I have ever been abroad at all.' 'Really! I am surprised. You gave me the impression, if I may say so, that you were accustomed to travelling.' 'Oh, well—I have been about a good deal in England, and to Scotland, once.' 'So. I myself have been in England once, but I could not learn English.' He raised one hand and shook his head, laughing. 'No, it was too difficult for me. . . . "Ow-do-you-do. Please vich is ze vay to Leicestaire Squaare."' She laughed too. 'Foreigners always say . . . .' They had quite a little talk about it. 'But you will like Munich,' said the old man. 'Munich is a wonderful city. Museums, pictures, galleries, fine buildings and shops, concerts, theatres, restaurants—all are in Munich. I have travelled all over Europe many, many times in my life, but it is always to Munich that I return. You will enjoy yourself there.' 'I am not going to *stay* in Munich,' said the little governess, and she added shyly, 'I am going to a post as governess to a doctor's family in Augsburg.' Ah, that was it. Augsburg he knew. Augsburg—well—was not beautiful. A solid manufacturing town. But if Germany was new to her he hoped she would find something interesting there too. 'I am sure I shall.' 'But what a pity not to see Munich before you go. You ought to take a little holiday on your way'—he smiled—'and store up some pleasant memories.' 'I am afraid I could not do *that*,' said the little governess, shaking her head, suddenly important and serious. 'And also, if one is alone . . . .' He quite understood. He bowed, serious too. They were silent after that. The train shattered on, baring its dark, flaming breast to the hills and to the valleys. It was warm in the carriage. She seemed to lean against the dark rushing and to be carried away and away. Little sounds made themselves heard; steps in the corridor, doors opening and shutting—a murmur of voices—whistling. . . . Then the window was pricked with long needles of rain. . . . But it did not matter . . . it was outside . . . and she had her umbrella . . . she pouted, sighed, opened and shut her hands once and fell fast asleep.

'Pardon! Pardon!' The sliding back of the carriage door woke her with a start. What had happened? Some one had come in and gone out again. The old man sat in his corner, more upright than ever, his hands in the pockets of his coat, frowning heavily. 'Ha! ha! ha!' came from the carriage next door. Still half asleep, she put her hands to her hair to make sure it wasn't dream. 'Disgraceful!' muttered the old man more to himself than to her. 'Common, vulgar fellows! I am afraid they disturbed you, gracious Fräulein, blundering in here like that.' No, not really. She was just going to wake up, and she took out her silver watch to look at the time. Half-past four. A cold blue light filled the window panes. Now when she rubbed a place she could see bright patches of fields, a clump of white houses like mushrooms, a road 'like a picture' with poplar trees on either side, a thread of river. How pretty it was! How pretty and how different! Even those pink clouds in the sky looked foreign. It was cold, but she pretended that it was far colder and rubbed her hands together and shivered, pulling at the collar of her coat because she was so happy.

The train began to slow down. The engine gave a long shrill whistle. They were coming to a town. Taller houses, pink and yellow, glided by, fast asleep behind their green eyelids, and guarded by the poplar trees that quivered in the blue air as if on tiptoe, listening. In one house a woman opened the shutters, flung a red and white mattress across the window frame and stood staring at the train. A pale woman with black hair and a white woollen shawl over her shoulders. More women appeared at the doors and at the windows of the sleeping houses. There came a flock of sheep. The shepherd wore a blue blouse and pointed wooden shoes. Look! look what flowers—and by the railway station too! Standard roses* like bridesmaids' bouquets, white geraniums, waxy pink ones that you would *never* see out of a greenhouse at home. Slower and slower. A man with a watering-can was spraying the platform. 'A-a-a-ah!' Somebody came running and waving his arms. A huge fat woman waddled through the glass doors of the station with a tray of strawberries. Oh, she was thirsty! She was very thirsty! 'A-a-a-ah!' The same somebody ran back again. The train stopped.

The old man pulled his coat round him and got up, smiling at her. He murmured something she didn't quite catch, but she smiled back at him as he left the carriage. While he was away the little governess looked at herself again in the glass, shook and patted herself with the precise practical care of a girl who is old enough to travel by herself and has nobody else to assure her that she is 'quite all right behind'. Thirsty and thirsty! The air tasted of water. She let down the window and the fat woman with the strawberries passed as if on purpose; holding up the tray to her. '*Nein, danke*,'* said the little governess, looking at the big berries on their gleaming leaves. '*Wie viel?*'* she asked as the fat woman moved away. 'Two marks fifty, Fraülein.' 'Good gracious!' She came in from the window and sat down in the corner, very sobered for a minute. Half a crown! 'H-o-o-o-o-o-e-e-e!' shrieked the train, gathering itself together to be off again. She hoped the old man wouldn't be left behind. Oh, it was daylight—everything was lovely if only she hadn't been so thirsty. Where *was* the old man—oh, here he was—she dimpled at him as though he were an old accepted friend as he closed the door and, turning, took from under his cape a basket of the strawberries. 'If Fräulein would honour me by accepting these . . . .' 'What for me?' But she drew back and raised her hands as though he were about to put a wild little kitten on her lap.

'Certainly, for you,' said the old man. 'For myself it is twenty years since I was brave enough to eat strawberries.' 'Oh, thank you very much. *Danke bestens*,' she stammered, '*sie sind so sehr schön!*'* 'Eat them and see,' said the old man looking pleased and friendly. 'You won't have even one?' 'No, no, no.' Timidly and charmingly her hand hovered. They were so big and juicy she had to take two bites to them—the juice ran all down her fingers—and it was while she munched the berries that she first thought of the old man as a grandfather. What a perfect grandfather he would make! Just like one out of a book!

The sun came out, the pink clouds in the sky, the strawberry clouds were eaten by the blue. 'Are they good?' asked the old man. 'As good as they look?'

When she had eaten them she felt she had known him for years. She told him about Frau Arnholdt and how she had got the place. Did he know the Hotel Grünewald? Frau Arnholdt would not arrive until the evening. He listened, listened until he knew as much about the affair as she did, until he said—not looking at her—but smoothing the palms of his brown suède gloves together: 'I wonder if you would let me show you a little of Munich to-day. Nothing much—but just perhaps a picture gallery and the Englischer Garten.* It seems such a pity that you should have to spend the day at the hotel, and also a little uncomfortable . . . in a strange place. *Nicht wahr?** You would be back there by the early afternoon or whenever you wish, of course, and you would give an old man a great deal of pleasure.'

It was not until long after she had said 'Yes'—because the moment she had said it and he had thanked her he began telling her about his travels in Turkey and attar of roses—that she wondered whether she had done wrong. After all, she really did not know him. But he was so old and he had been so very kind—not to mention the strawberries . . . . And she couldn't have explained the reason why she said 'No,' and it was her *last* day in a way, her last day to really enjoy herself in. 'Was I wrong? Was I?' A drop of sunlight fell into her hands and lay there, warm and quivering. 'If I might accompany you as far as the hotel,' he suggested, 'and call for you again at about ten o'clock.' He took out his pocket-book and handed her a card. 'Herr Regierungsrat. . . .'* He had a title! Well, it was *bound* to be all right! So after that the little governess gave herself up to the excitement of being really abroad, to looking out and reading the foreign advertisement signs, to being told about the places they came to—having her attention and enjoyment looked after by the charming old grandfather—until they reached Munich and the Hauptbahnhof.* 'Porter! Porter!' He found her a porter, disposed of his own luggage in a few words, guided her through the bewildering crowd out of the station down the clean white steps into the white road to the hotel. He explained who she was to the manager as though all this had been bound to happen, and then for one moment her little hand lost itself in the big brown suède ones. 'I will call for you at ten o'clock.' He was gone.

'This way, Fräulein,' said a waiter, who had been dodging behind the manager's back, all eyes and ears for the strange couple. She followed him up two flights of stairs into a dark bedroom. He dashed down her dress-basket and pulled up a clattering, dusty blind. Ugh! what an ugly, cold room—what enormous furniture! Fancy spending the day in here! 'Is this the room Frau Arnholdt ordered?' asked the little governess. The waiter had a curious way of staring as if there was something *funny* about her. He pursed up his lips about to whistle, and then changed his mind. '*Gewiss*,'* he said. Well, why didn't he go? Why did he stare so? '*Gehen Sie*,'* said the little governess, with frigid English simplicity. His little eyes, like currants, nearly popped out of his doughy cheeks. '*Gehen Sie sofort*,'* she repeated icily. At the door he turned. 'And the gentleman,' said he, 'shall I show the gentleman upstairs when he comes?'

Over the white streets big white clouds fringed with silver—and sunshine everywhere. Fat, fat coachmen driving fat cabs; funny women with little round hats cleaning the tramway lines; people laughing and pushing against one another; trees on both sides of the streets and everywhere you looked almost, immense fountains; a noise of laughing from the footpaths or the middle of the streets or the open windows. And beside her, more beautifully brushed than ever, with a rolled umbrella in one hand and yellow gloves instead of brown ones, her grandfather who had asked her to spend the day. She wanted to run, she wanted to hang on his arm, she wanted to cry every minute, 'Oh, I am so frightfully happy!' He guided her across the roads, stood still while she 'looked', and his kind eyes beamed on her and he said 'just whatever you wish'. She ate two white sausages and two little rolls of fresh bread at eleven o'clock in the morning and she drank some beer, which he told her wasn't intoxicating, wasn't at all like English beer, out of a glass like a flower vase. And then they took a cab and really she must have seen thousands and thousands of wonderful classical pictures in about a quarter of an hour! 'I shall have to think them over when I am alone.' . . . But when they came out of the picture gallery it was raining. The grandfather unfurled his umbrella and held it over the little governess. They started to walk to the restaurant for lunch. She, very close beside him so that he should have some of the umbrella, too. 'It goes easier,' he remarked in a detached way, 'if you take my arm, Fräulein. And besides it is the custom in Germany.' So she took his arm and walked beside him while he pointed out the famous statues, so interested that he quite forgot to put down the umbrella even when the rain was long over.

After lunch they went to a café to hear a gipsy band, but she did not like that at all. Ugh! such horrible men were there with heads like eggs and cuts on their faces, so she turned her chair and cupped her burning cheeks in her hands and watched her old friend instead. . . . Then they went to the Englischer Garten.

'I wonder what the time is,' asked the little governess. 'My watch has stopped. I forgot to wind it in the train last night. We've seen such a lot of things that I feel it must be quite late.' 'Late!' He stopped in front of her laughing and shaking his head in a way she had begun to know. 'Then you have not really enjoyed yourself. Late! Why, we have not had any ice cream yet!' 'Oh, but I have enjoyed myself,' she cried, distressed, 'more than I can possibly say. It has been wonderful! Only Frau Arnholdt is to be at the hotel at six and I ought to be there by five.' 'So you shall. After the ice cream I shall put you into a cab and you can go there comfortably.' She was happy again. The chocolate ice cream melted—melted in little sips a long way down. The shadows of the trees danced on the table cloths, and she sat with her back safely turned to the ornamental clock that pointed to twenty-five minutes to seven. 'Really and truly,' said the little governess earnestly, 'this has been the happiest day of my life. I've never even imagined such a day.' In spite of the ice cream her grateful baby heart glowed with love for the fairy grandfather.

So they walked out of the garden down a long alley. The day was nearly over. 'You see those big buildings opposite,' said the old man. 'The third storey—that is where I live. I and the old housekeeper who looks after me.' She was very interested. 'Now just before I find a cab for you, will you come and see my little "home" and let me give you a bottle of the attar of roses I told you about in the train? For remembrance?' She would love to. 'I've never seen a bachelor's flat in my life,' laughed the little governess.

The passage was quite dark. 'Ah, I suppose my old woman has gone out to buy me a chicken. One moment.' He opened a door and stood aside for her to pass, a little shy but curious, into a strange room. She did not know quite what to say. It wasn't pretty. In a way it was very ugly—but neat, and, she supposed, comfortable for such an old man. 'Well, what do you think of it?' He knelt down and took from a cupboard a round tray with two pink glasses and a tall pink bottle. 'Two little bedrooms beyond,' he said gaily, 'and a kitchen. It's enough, eh?' 'Oh, quite enough.' 'And if ever you should be in Munich and care to spend a day or two—why there is always a little nest—a wing of a chicken, and a salad, and an old man delighted to be your host once more and many many times, dear little Fräulein!' He took the stopper out of the bottle and poured some wine into the two pink glasses. His hand shook and the wine spilled over the tray. It was very quiet in the room. She said: 'I think I ought to go now.' 'But you will have a tiny glass of wine with me—just one before you go?' said the old man. 'No, really no. I never drink wine. I—I have promised never to touch wine or anything like that.' And though he pleaded and though she felt dreadfully rude, especially when he seemed to take it to heart so, she was quite determined. 'No, *really*, please.' 'Well, will you just sit down on the sofa for five minutes and let me drink your health?' The little governess sat down on the edge of the red velvet couch and he sat down beside her and drank her health at a gulp. 'Have you really been happy to-day?' asked the old man, turning round, so close beside her that she felt his knee twitching against hers. Before she could answer he held her hands. 'And are you going to give me one little kiss before you go?' he asked, drawing her closer still.

It was a dream! It wasn't true! It wasn't the same old man at all. Ah, how horrible! The little governess stared at him in terror. 'No, no, no!' she stammered, struggling out of his hands. 'One little kiss. A kiss. What is it? Just a kiss, dear little Fräulein. A kiss,' He pushed his face forward, his lips smiling broadly; and how his little blue eyes gleamed behind the spectacles! 'Never—never. How can you!' She sprang up, but he was too quick and he held her against the wall, pressed against her his hard old body and his twitching knee and, though she shook her head from side to side, distracted, kissed her on the mouth. On the mouth! Where not a soul who wasn't a near relation had ever kissed her before. . . .

She ran, ran down the street until she found a broad road with tram lines and a policeman standing in the middle like a clockwork doll. 'I want to get a tram to the Hauptbahnhof,' sobbed the little governess. 'Fräulein?' She wrung her hands at him. 'The Hauptbahnhof. There—there's one now,' and while he watched very much surprised, the little girl with her hat on one side, crying without a handkerchief, sprang on to the tram—not seeing the conductor's eyebrows, nor hearing the *hochwohlgebildete Dame** talking her over with a scandalized friend. She rocked herself and cried out loud and said 'Ah, ah!' pressing her hands to her mouth. 'She has been to the dentist,' shrilled a fat old woman, too stupid to be uncharitable. '*Na, sagen Sie 'mal*,* what toothache! The child hasn't one left in her mouth.' While the tram swung and jangled through a world full of old men with twitching knees.

When the little governess reached the hall of the Hotel Grünewald the same waiter who had come into her room in the morning was standing by a table, polishing a tray of glasses. The sight of the little governess seemed to fill him out with some inexplicable important content. He was ready for her question; his answer came pat and suave. 'Yes, Fräulein, the lady has been here. I told her that you had arrived and gone out again immediately with a gentleman. She asked me when you were coming back again—but of course I could not say.

And then she went to the manager.' He took up a glass from the table, held it up to the light, looked at it with one eye closed, and started polishing it with a corner of his apron. '. . . ?' 'Pardon, Fräulein? Ach, no, Fräulein. The manager could tell her nothing— nothing.' He shook his head and smiled at the brilliant glass. 'Where is the lady now?' asked the little governess, shuddering so violently that she had to hold her handkerchief up to her mouth. 'How should I know?' cried the waiter, and as he swooped past her to pounce upon a new arrival his heart beat so hard against his ribs that he nearly chuckled aloud. 'That's it! that's it!' he thought. 'That will show her.' And as he swung the new arrival's box on to his shoulders— hoop!—as though he were a giant and the box a feather, he minced over again the little governess's words, '*Gehen Sie. Gehen Sie sofort.* Shall I! Shall I!' he shouted to himself.

AN INDISCREET JOURNEY

She is like St Anne.* Yes, the concierge is the image of St Anne, with that black cloth over her head, the wisps of grey hair hanging, and the tiny smoking lamp in her hand. Really very beautiful, I thought, smiling at St Anne, who said severely: 'Six o'clock. You have only just got time. There is a bowl of milk on the writing table.' I jumped out of my pyjamas and into a basin of cold water like any English lady in any French novel. The concierge, persuaded that I was on my way to prison cells and death by bayonets, opened the shutters and the cold clear light came through. A little steamer hooted on the river; a cart with two horses at a gallop flung past. The rapid swirling water; the tall black trees on the far side, grouped together like negroes conversing. Sinister, very, I thought, as I buttoned on my age-old Burberry.* (That Burberry was very significant. It did not belong to me. I had borrowed it from a friend. My eye lighted upon it hanging in her little dark hall. The very thing! The perfect and adequate disguise—an old Burberry. Lions have been faced in a Burberry. Ladies have been rescued from open boats in mountainous seas wrapped in nothing else. An old Burberry seems to me the sign and the token of the undisputed venerable traveller, I decided, leaving my purple peg-top* with the real seal collar and cuffs in exchange.)

'You will never get there,' said the concierge, watching me turn up the collar. 'Never! Never!' I ran down the echoing stairs—strange they sounded, like a piano flicked by a sleepy housemaid—and on to the Quai. 'Why so fast, *ma mignonne*?'* said a lovely little boy in coloured socks, dancing in front of the electric lotus buds* that curve over the entrance to the Métro. Alas! there was not even time to blow him a kiss. When I arrived at the big station I had only four minutes to spare, and the platform entrance was crowded and packed with soldiers, their yellow papers in one hand and big untidy bundles. The Commissaire of Police stood on one side, a Nameless Official on the other. Will he let me pass? Will he? He was an old man with a fat swollen face covered with big warts. Horn-rimmed spectacles squatted on his nose. Trembling, I made an effort. I conjured up my sweetest early-morning smile and handed it with the papers. But the delicate thing fluttered against the horn spectacles and fell. Nevertheless, he let me pass, and I ran, ran in and out among the soldiers and up the high steps into the yellow-painted carriage.

'Does one go direct to X?' I asked the collector who dug at my ticket with a pair of forceps and handed it back again. 'No, Mademoiselle, you must change at X.Y.Z.'

'At—?'

'X.Y.Z.'

Again I had not heard. 'At what time do we arrive there if you please?'

'One o'clock.' But that was no good to me. I hadn't a watch. Oh, well—later.

Ah! the train had begun to move. The train was on my side. It swung out of the station, and soon we were passing the vegetable gardens, passing the tall blind houses to let, passing the servants beating carpets. Up already and walking in the fields, rosy from the rivers and the red-fringed pools, the sun lighted upon the swinging train and stroked my muff and told me to take off that Burberry. I was not alone in the carriage. An old woman sat opposite, her skirt turned back over her knees, a bonnet of black lace on her head. In her fat hands, adorned with a wedding and two mourning rings,* she held a letter. Slowly, slowly she sipped a sentence, and then looked up and out of the window, her lips trembling a little, and then another sentence, and again the old face turned to the light, tasting it . . . . Two soldiers leaned out of the window, their heads nearly touching—one of them was whistling, the other had his coat fastened with some rusty safety-pins. And now there were soldiers everywhere working on the railway line, leaning against trucks or standing hands on hips, eyes fixed on the train as though they expected at least one camera at every window. And now we were passing big wooden sheds* like rigged-up dancing halls or seaside pavilions, each flying a flag. In and out of them walked the Red Cross men; the wounded sat against the walls sunning themselves. At all the bridges, the crossings, the stations, a *petit soldat*,* all boots and bayonet. Forlorn and desolate he looked,—like a little comic picture waiting for the joke to be written underneath. Is there really such a thing as war? Are all these laughing voices really going to the war? These dark woods lighted so mysteriously by the white stems of the birch and the ash—these watery fields with the big birds flying over—these rivers green and blue in the light—have battles been fought in places like these?

What beautiful cemeteries we are passing! They flash gay in the sun. They seem to be full of cornflowers and poppies and daisies. How can there be so many flowers at this time of the year? But they are not flowers at all. They are bunches of ribbons tied on to the soldiers' graves.

I glanced up and caught the old woman's eye. She smiled and folded the letter. 'It is from my son—the first we have had since October. I am taking it to my daughter-in-law.'

'. . . .?'

'Yes, very good,' said the old woman, shaking down her skirt and putting her arm through the handle of her basket. 'He wants me to send him some handkerchieves and a piece of stout string.'

What is the name of the station where I have to change? Perhaps I shall never know. I got up and leaned my arms across the window rail, my feet crossed. One cheek burned as in infancy on the way to the sea-side. When the war is over I shall have a barge and drift along these rivers with a white cat and a pot of mignonette to bear me company.

Down the side of the hill filed the troops, winking red and blue in the light. Far away, but plainly to be seen, some more flew by on bicycles. But really, *ma France adorée*,* this uniform is ridiculous. Your soldiers are stamped upon your bosom like bright irreverent transfers.

The train slowed down, stopped. . . . Everybody was getting out except me. A big boy, his sabots* tied to his back with a piece of string, the inside of his tin wine cup stained a lovely impossible pink, looked very friendly. Does one change here perhaps for X? Another whose képi* had come out of a wet paper cracker swung my suit-case to earth. What darlings soldiers are! 'Merci bien, Monsieur, vous êtes tout à fait aimable . . . .'* 'Not this way,' said a bayonet. 'Nor this,' said another. So I followed the crowd. 'Your passport, Mademoiselle . . . .' *'We, Sir Edward Grey . . . .'* I ran through the muddy square and into the buffet.

A green room with a stove jutting out and tables on each side. On the counter, beautiful with coloured bottles, a woman leans, her breasts in her folded arms. Through an open door I can see a kitchen, and the cook in a white coat breaking eggs into a bowl and tossing the shells into a corner. The blue and red coats of the men who are eating hang upon the walls. Their short swords and belts are piled upon chairs. Heavens! what a noise. The sunny air seemed all broken up and trembling with it. A little boy, very pale, swung from table to table, taking the orders, and poured me out a glass of purple coffee. *Ssssh*, came from the eggs. They were in a pan. The woman rushed from behind the counter and began to help the boy. *Toute de suite,* * *tout' suite!* she chirruped to the loud impatient voices. There came a clatter of plates and the pop-pop of corks being drawn.

Suddenly in the doorway I saw someone with a pail of fish— brown speckled fish, like the fish one sees in a glass case, swimming through forests of beautiful pressed sea-weed. He was an old man in a tattered jacket, standing humbly, waiting for someone to attend to him. A thin beard fell over his chest, his eyes under the tufted eyebrows were bent on the pail he carried. He looked as though he had escaped from some holy picture, and was entreating the soldiers' pardon for being there at all . . . .

But what could I have done? I could not arrive at X with two fishes hanging on a straw; and I am sure it is a penal offence in France to throw fish out of railway-carriage windows, I thought, miserably climbing into a smaller, shabbier train. Perhaps I might have taken them to—*ah, mon Dieu**—I had forgotten the name of my uncle and aunt again! Buffard, Buffon—what was it? Again I read the unfamiliar letter in the familiar handwriting.

'My dear niece,

'Now that the weather is more settled, your uncle and I would be charmed if you would pay us a little visit. Telegraph me when you are coming. I shall meet you outside the station if I am free. Otherwise our good friend, Madame Grinçon, who lives in the little tollhouse by the bridge, *juste en face de la gare,** will conduct you to our home. *Je vous embrasse bien tendrement,** JULIE BOIFFARD.'

A visiting card* was enclosed: *M. Paul Boiffard.*

Boiffard—of course that was the name. *Ma tante Julie et mon oncle Paul*—suddenly they were there with me, more real, more solid than any relations I had ever known. I saw *tante Julie* bridling, with the soup-tureen in her hands, and *oncle Paul* sitting at the table, with a red and white napkin tied round his neck. Boiffard—Boiffard—I must remember the name. Supposing the Commissaire Militaire should ask me who the relations were I was going to and I muddled the name—Oh, how fatal! Buffard—no, Boiffard. And then for the first time, folding Aunt Julie's letter, I saw scrawled in a corner of the empty back page: *Venez vite, vite.** Strange impulsive woman! My heart began to beat . . . .

'Ah, we are not far off now,' said the lady opposite. 'You are going to X, Mademoiselle?'

'Oui,* Madame.'

'I also. . . . You have been there before?'

'No, Madame. This is the first time.'

'Really, it is a strange time for a visit.'

I smiled faintly, and tried to keep my eyes off her hat. She was quite an ordinary little woman, but she wore a black velvet toque, with an incredibly surprised looking sea-gull camped on the very top of it. Its round eyes, fixed on me so inquiringly, were almost too much to bear. I had a dreadful impulse to shoo it away, or to lean forward and inform her of its presence . . . .

'*Excusez-moi, madame*, but perhaps you have not remarked there is an *espèce de* sea-gull *couché sur votre chapeau.*'*

Could the bird be there on purpose? I must not laugh . . . . I must not laugh. Had she ever looked at herself in a glass with that bird on her head?

'It is very difficult to get into X at present, to pass the station,' she said, and she shook her head with the sea-gull at me. 'Ah, such an affair. One must sign one's name and state one's business.'

'Really, is it as bad as all that?'

'But naturally. You see the whole place is in the hands of the military, and'—she shrugged—'they have to be strict. Many people do not get beyond the station at all. They arrive. They are put in the waiting-room, and there they remain.'

Did I or did I not detect in her voice a strange, insulting relish?

'I suppose such strictness is absolutely necessary,' I said coldly, stroking my muff.

'Necessary,' she cried. 'I should think so. Why, *mademoiselle*, you cannot imagine what it would be like otherwise! You know what women are like about soldiers'—she raised a final hand—'mad, completely mad. But—' and she gave a little laugh of triumph—'they could not get into X. *Mon Dieu*, no! There is no question about that.'

'I don't suppose they even try,' said I.

'Don't you?' said the sea-gull.

Madame said nothing for a moment. 'Of course the authorities are very hard on the men. It means instant imprisonment, and then—off to the firing-line without a word.'*

'What are *you* going to X for?' said the sea-gull. 'What on earth are *you* doing here?'

'Are you making a long stay in X, *mademoiselle*?'

She had won, she had won. I was terrified. A lamp-post swam past the train with the fatal name upon it. I could hardly breathe—the train had stopped. I smiled gaily at Madame and danced down the steps to the platform . . . .

It was a hot little room completely furnished with two colonels seated at two tables. They were large grey-whiskered men with a touch of burnt red on their cheeks. Sumptuous and omnipotent they looked. One smoked what ladies love to call a heavy Egyptian cigarette, with a long creamy ash, the other toyed with a gilded pen. Their heads rolled on their tight collars, like big over-ripe fruits. I had a terrible feeling, as I handed my passport and ticket, that a soldier would step forward and tell me to kneel. I would have knelt without question.

'What's this?' said God I., querulously. He did not like my passport at all. The very sight of it seemed to annoy him. He waved a dissenting hand at it, with a '*Non, je ne peux pas manger ça*'* air.

'But it won't do. It won't do at all, you know. Look,—read for yourself,' and he glanced with extreme distaste at my photograph, and then with even greater distaste his pebble eyes looked at me.

'Of course the photograph is deplorable,' I said, scarcely breathing with terror, 'but it has been viséd* and viséd.'

He raised his big bulk and went over to God II.

'Courage!' I said to my muff and held it firmly, 'Courage!'

God II. held up a finger to me, and I produced Aunt Julie's letter and her card. But he did not seem to feel the slightest interest in her. He stamped my passport idly, scribbled a word on my ticket, and I was on the platform again.

'That way—you pass out that way.'

Terribly pale, with a faint smile on his lips, his hand at salute, stood the little corporal. I gave no sign, I am sure I gave no sign. He stepped behind me.

'And then follow me as though you do not see me,' I heard him half whisper, half sing.

How fast he went, through the slippery mud towards a bridge. He had a postman's bag on his back, a paper parcel and the *Matin** in his hand. We seemed to dodge through a maze of policemen, and I could not keep up at all with the little corporal who began to whistle. From the toll-house 'our good friend, Madame Grinçon', her hands wrapped in a shawl, watched our coming, and against the toll-house there leaned a tiny faded cab. *Montez vite,** *vite!* said the little corporal, hurling my suit-case, the postman's bag, the paper parcel and the *Matin* on to the floor.

'A-ie! A-ie! Do not be so mad. Do not ride yourself. You will be seen,' wailed 'our good friend, Madame Grinçon'.

'Ah, je m'en f . . . .'* said the little corporal.

The driver jerked into activity. He lashed the bony horse and away we flew, both doors, which were the complete sides of the cab, flapping and banging.

'Bon jour, mon amie.'*

'Bon jour, mon ami.'

And then he swooped down and clutched at the banging doors. They would not keep shut. They were fools of doors.

'Lean back, let me do it!' I cried. 'Policemen are as thick as violets everywhere.'

At the barracks the horse reared up and stopped. A crowd of laughing faces blotted the window.

'Prends ça, mon vieux,'* said the little corporal, handing the paper parcel.

'It's all right,' called someone.

We waved, we were off again. By a river, down a strange white street, with little houses on either side, gay in the late sunlight.

'Jump out as soon as he stops again. The door will be open. Run straight inside. I will follow. The man is already paid. I know you will like the house. It is quite white, and the room is white, too, and the people are—'

'White as snow.'

We looked at each other. We began to laugh. 'Now,' said the little corporal.

Out I flew and in at the door. There stood, presumably, my aunt

Julie. There in the background hovered, I supposed, my uncle Paul.

'Bon jour, madame!' 'Bon jour, monsieur!'

'It is all right, you are safe,' said my aunt Julie. Heavens, how I loved her! And she opened the door of the white room and shut it upon us. Down went the suit-case, the postman's bag, the *Matin*. I threw my passport up into the air, and the little corporal caught it.

*   *   *

What an extraordinary thing. We had been there to lunch and to dinner each day; but now in the dusk and alone I could not find it. I clop-clopped in my borrowed *sabots* through the greasy mud, right to the end of the village, and there was not a sign of it. I could not even remember what it looked like, or if there was a name painted on the outside, or any bottles or tables showing at the window. Already the village houses were sealed for the night behind big wooden shutters. Strange and mysterious they looked in the ragged drifting light and thin rain, like a company of beggars perched on the hill-side, their bosoms full of rich unlawful gold. There was nobody about but the soldiers. A group of wounded stood under a lamp-post, petting a mangy, shivering dog. Up the street came four big boys singing:

Dodo, mon homme, fais vit' dodo . . .*

and swung off down the hill to their sheds behind the railway station. They seemed to take the last breath of the day with them. I began to walk slowly back.

'It must have been one of these houses. I remember it stood far back from the road—and there were no steps, not even a porch—one seemed to walk right through the window.' And then quite suddenly the waiting-boy came out of just such a place. He saw me and grinned cheerfully, and began to whistle through his teeth.

'Bon soir, mon petit.'

'Bon soir, madame.' And he followed me up the café to our special table, right at the far end by the window, and marked by a bunch of violets that I had left in a glass there yesterday.

'You are two?' asked the waiting-boy, flicking the table with a red and white cloth. His long swinging steps echoed over the bare floor. He disappeared into the kitchen and came back to light the lamp that hung from the ceiling under a spreading shade, like a haymaker's hat. Warm light shone on the empty place that was really a barn, set out with dilapidated tables and chairs. Into the middle of the room a black stove jutted. At one side of it there was a table with a row of bottles on it, behind which Madame sat and took the money and made entries in a red book. Opposite her desk a door led into the kitchen. The walls were covered with a creamy paper patterned all over with green and swollen trees—hundreds and hundreds of trees reared their mushroom heads to the ceiling. I began to wonder who had chosen the paper and why. Did Madame think it was beautiful, or that it was a gay and lovely thing to eat one's dinner at all seasons in the middle of a forest . . . . On either side of the clock there hung a picture: one, a young gentleman in black tights wooing a pear-shaped lady in yellow over the back of a garden seat, *Premier Rencontre;** two, the black and yellow in amorous confusion. *Triomphe d'Amour.**

The clock ticked to a soothing lilt, *C'est ça,** *C'est ça*. In the kitchen the waiting-boy was washing up. I heard the ghostly chatter of the dishes.

And years passed. Perhaps the war is long since over—there is no village outside at all—the streets are quiet under the grass. I have an idea this is the sort of thing one will do on the very last day of all— sit in an empty café and listen to a clock ticking until—.

Madame came through the kitchen door, nodded to me and took her seat behind the table, her plump hands folded on the red book. *Ping* went the door. A handful of soldiers came in, took off their coats and began to play cards, chaffing and poking fun at the pretty waiting-boy, who threw up his little round head, rubbed his thick fringe out of his eyes and checked them back in his broken voice. Sometimes his voice boomed up from his throat, deep and harsh, and then in the middle of a sentence it broke and scattered in a funny squeaking. He seemed to enjoy it himself. You would not have been surprised if he had walked into the kitchen on his hands and brought back your dinner turning a catherine-wheel.

Ping went the door again. Two more men came in. They sat at the table nearest Madame, and she leaned to them with a birdlike move- ment, her head on one side. Oh, they had a grievance! The Lieuten- ant was a fool—nosing about—springing out at them—and they'd only been sewing on buttons. Yes, that was all—sewing on buttons, and up comes this young spark. 'Now then, what are you up to?' They mimicked the idiotic voice. Madame drew down her mouth, nodding sympathy. The waiting-boy served them with glasses. He took a bottle of some orange-coloured stuff and put it on the table-edge. A shout from the card-players made him turn sharply, and crash! over went the bottle, spilling on the table, the floor—smash! to tinkling atoms. An amazed silence. Through it the drip-drip of the wine from the table on to the floor. It looked very strange dropping so slowly, as though the table were crying. Then there came a roar from the card-players. 'You'll catch it, my lad! That's the style! Now you've done it! . . . Sept, huit, neuf.'* They started playing again. The waiting-boy never said a word. He stood, his head bent, his hands spread out, and then he knelt and gathered up the glass, piece by piece, and soaked the wine up with a cloth. Only when Madame cried cheerfully, 'You wait until *he* finds out,' did he raise his head.

'He can't say anything, if I pay for it,' he muttered, his face jerking, and he marched off into the kitchen with the soaking cloth.

'*Il pleure de colère*,'* said Madame delightedly, patting her hair with her plump hands.

The café slowly filled. It grew very warm. Blue smoke mounted from the tables and hung about the haymaker's hat in misty wreaths. There was a suffocating smell of onion soup and boots and damp cloth. In the din the door sounded again. It opened to let in a weed of a fellow, who stood with his back against it, one hand shading his eyes.

'Hullo! you've got the bandage off?'

'How does it feel, *mon vieux*?'

'Let's have a look at them.'

But he made no reply. He shrugged and walked unsteadily to a table, sat down and leant against the wall. Slowly his hand fell. In his white face his eyes showed, pink as a rabbit's. They brimmed and spilled, brimmed and spilled. He dragged a white cloth out of his pocket and wiped them.

'It's the smoke,' said someone. 'It's the smoke tickles them up for you.'

His comrades watched him a bit, watched his eyes fill again, again brim over. The water ran down his face, off his chin on to the table. He rubbed the place with his coat-sleeve, and then, as though forget-ful, went on rubbing, rubbing with his hand across the table, staring in front of him. And then he started shaking his head to the move-ment of his hand. He gave a loud strange groan and dragged out the cloth again.

'*Huit, neuf, dix,*' said the card-players.

'*P'tit,* some more bread.'

'Two coffees.'

'*Un Picon!*'*

The waiting-boy, quite recovered, but with scarlet cheeks, ran to and fro. A tremendous quarrel flared up among the card-players, raged for two minutes, and died in flickering laughter. 'Ooof!' groaned the man with the eyes, rocking and mopping. But nobody paid any attention to him except Madame. She made a little grimace at her two soldiers.

'*Mais vous savez, c'est un peu dégoûtant, ça,*'* she said severely.

'*Ah, oui, Madame,*' answered the soldiers, watching her bent head and pretty hands, as she arranged for the hundredth time a frill of lace on her lifted bosom.

'*V'là monsieur!*'* cawed the waiting-boy over his shoulder to me. For some silly reason I pretended not to hear, and I leaned over the table smelling the violets, until the little corporal's hand closed over mine.

'Shall we have *un peu de charcuterie** to begin with?' he asked tenderly.

*   *   *

'In England,' said the blue-eyed soldier, 'you drink whiskey with your meals. *N'est-ce pas,** *mademoiselle?* A little glass of whiskey neat before eating. Whiskey and soda with your *bifteks,** and after, more whiskey with hot water and lemon.'

'Is it true, that?' asked his great friend who sat opposite, a big red-faced chap with a black beard and large moist eyes and hair that looked as though it had been cut with a sewing-machine.

'Well, not quite true,' said I.

'*Si, si,*'* cried the blue-eyed soldier. 'I ought to know. I'm in business. English travellers come to my place, and it's always the same thing.'

'Bah, I can't stand whiskey,' said the little corporal. 'It's too disgusting the morning after. Do you remember, *ma fille,** the whiskey in that little bar at Montmartre?'

'*Souvenir tendre,*'* sighed Blackbeard, putting two fingers in the breast of his coat and letting his head fall. He was very drunk.

'But I know something that you've never tasted,' said the

blue-eyed soldier pointing a finger at me; 'something really good.' *Cluck* he went with his tongue. '*É-pa-tant!** And the curious thing is that you'd hardly know it from whiskey except that it's'—he felt with his hand for the word—'finer, sweeter perhaps, not so sharp, and it leaves you feeling gay as a rabbit next morning.'

'What is it called?'

'Mirabelle!'* He rolled the word round his mouth, under his tongue. 'Ah-ha, that's the stuff.'

'I could eat another mushroom,' said Blackbeard. 'I would like another mushroom very much. I am sure I could eat another mushroom if Mademoiselle gave it to me out of her hand.'

'You ought to try it,' said the blue-eyed soldier, leaning both hands on the table and speaking so seriously that I began to wonder how much more sober he was than Blackbeard. 'You ought to try it, and to-night. I would like you to tell me if you don't think it's like whiskey.'

'Perhaps they've got it here,' said the little corporal, and he called the waiting-boy. '*P'tit!*'

'*Non, monsieur*,' said the boy, who never stopped smiling. He served us with dessert plates painted with blue parrots and horned beetles.

'What is the name for this in English?' said Blackbeard, pointing. I told him 'Parrot'.

'Ah, *mon Dieu!* . . . Pair-rot.' He put his arms round his plate. 'I love you, *ma petite* pair-rot. You are sweet, you are blonde, you are English. You do not know the difference between whiskey and mirabelle.'

The little corporal and I looked at each other, laughing. He squeezed up his eyes when he laughed, so that you saw nothing but the long curly lashes.

'Well, I know a place where they do keep it,' said the blue-eyed soldier. '*Café des Amis*.* We'll go there—I'll pay—I'll pay for the whole lot of us.' His gesture embraced thousands of pounds.

But with a loud whirring noise the clock on the wall struck half-past eight; and no soldier is allowed in a café after eight o'clock at night.

'It is fast,' said the blue-eyed soldier. The little corporal's watch said the same. So did the immense turnip that Blackbeard produced, and carefully deposited on the head of one of the horned beetles.

'Ah, well, we'll take the risk,' said the blue-eyed soldier, and he thrust his arms into his immense cardboard coat. 'It's worth it,' he said. 'It's worth it. You just wait.'

Outside, stars shone between wispy clouds, and the moon fluttered like a candle flame over a pointed spire. The shadows of the dark plume-like trees waved on the white houses. Not a soul to be seen. No sound to be heard but the *Hsh! Hsh!* of a far-away train, like a big beast shuffling in its sleep.

'You are cold,' whispered the little corporal. 'You are cold, *ma fille.*'

'No, really not.'

'But you are trembling.'

'Yes, but I'm not cold.'

'What are the women like in England?' asked Blackbeard. 'After the war is over I shall go to England. I shall find a little English woman and marry her—and her pair-rot.' He gave a loud choking laugh.

'Fool!' said the blue-eyed soldier, shaking him; and he leant over to me. 'It is only after the second glass that you really taste it,' he whispered. 'The second little glass and then—ah!—then you know.'

Café des Amis gleamed in the moonlight. We glanced quickly up and down the road. We ran up the four wooden steps, and opened the ringing glass door into a low room lighted with a hanging lamp, where about ten people were dining. They were seated on two benches at a narrow table.

'Soldiers!' screamed a woman, leaping up from behind a white soup-tureen—a scrag of a woman in a black shawl. 'Soldiers! At this hour! Look at that clock, look at it.' And she pointed to the clock with the dripping ladle.

'It's fast,' said the blue-eyed soldier. 'It's fast, Madame. And don't make so much noise, I beg of you. We will drink and we will go.'

'Will you?' she cried, running round the table and planting herself in front of us. 'That's just what you won't do. Coming into an honest woman's house this hour of the night—making a scene—getting the police after you. Ah, no! Ah, no! It's a disgrace, that's what it is.'

'Sh!' said the little corporal, holding up his hand. Dead silence. In the silence we heard steps passing.

'The police,' whispered Blackbeard, winking at a pretty girl with rings in her ears, who smiled back at him, saucy. 'Sh!'

The faces lifted, listening. 'How beautiful they are!' I thought. 'They are like a family party having supper in the New Testament. . . . ' The steps died away.

'Serve you very well right if you had been caught,' scolded the angry woman. 'I'm sorry on your account that the police didn't come. You deserve it—you deserve it.'

'A little glass of mirabelle and we will go,' persisted the blue-eyed soldier.

Still scolding and muttering she took four glasses from the cupboard and a big bottle. 'But you're not going to drink in here. Don't you believe it.' The little corporal ran into the kitchen. 'Not there! Not there! Idiot!' she cried. 'Can't you see there's a window there, and a wall opposite where the police come every evening to. . . .'

'Sh!' Another scare.

'You are mad and you will end in prison,—all four of you,' said the woman. She flounced out of the room. We tiptoed after her into a dark smelling scullery, full of pans of greasy water, of salad leaves and meat-bones.

'There now,' she said, putting down the glasses. 'Drink and go!'

'Ah, at last!' The blue-eyed soldier's happy voice trickled through the dark. 'What do you think? Isn't it just as I said? Hasn't it got a taste of excellent—*ex-cellent* whiskey?'

THE WIND BLOWS

Suddenly—dreadfully—she wakes up. What has happened? Something dreadful has happened. No—nothing has happened. It is only the wind shaking the house, rattling the windows, banging a piece of iron on the roof and making her bed tremble. Leaves flutter past the window, up and away; down in the avenue a whole newspaper wags in the air like a lost kite and falls, spiked on a pine tree. It is cold. Summer is over—it is autumn—everything is ugly. The carts rattle by, swinging from side to side; two Chinamen lollop along under their wooden yokes with the straining vegetable baskets—their pigtails and blue blouses fly out in the wind. A white dog on three legs yelps past the gate. It is all over! What is? Oh, everything! And she begins to plait her hair with shaking fingers, not daring to look in the glass. Mother is talking to grandmother in the hall.

'A perfect idiot! Imagine leaving anything out on the line in weather like this. . . . Now my best little Teneriffe-work teacloth is simply in ribbons. *What* is that extraordinary smell? It's the porridge burning. Oh, heavens—this wind!'

She has a music lesson at ten o'clock. At the thought the minor movement of the Beethoven begins to play in her head, the trills long and terrible like little rolling drums. . . . Marie Swainson runs into the garden next door to pick the 'chrysanths' before they are ruined. Her skirt flies up above her waist; she tries to beat it down, to tuck it between her legs while she stoops, but it is no use—up it flies. All the trees and bushes beat about her. She picks as quickly as she can, but she is quite distracted. She doesn't mind what she does—she pulls the plants up by the roots and bends and twists them, stamping her foot and swearing.

'For heaven's sake keep the front door shut! Go round to the back,' shouts someone. And then she hears Bogey:

'Mother, you're wanted on the telephone. Telephone, Mother. It's the butcher.'

How hideous life is—revolting, simply revolting. . . . And now her hat-elastic's* snapped. Of course it would. She'll wear her old tam* and slip out the back way. But Mother has seen.

'Matilda. Matilda. Come back im-me-diately! What on earth have you got on your head? It looks like a tea cosy. And why have you got that mane of hair on your forehead.'

'I can't come back, Mother. I'll be late for my lesson.'

'Come back immediately!'

She won't. She won't. She hates Mother. 'Go to hell,' she shouts, running down the road.

In waves, in clouds, in big round whirls the dust comes stinging, and with it little bits of straw and chaff and manure. There is a loud roaring sound from the trees in the gardens, and standing at the bottom of the road outside Mr Bullen's gate she can hear the sea sob: 'Ah! . . . Ah! . . . Ah-h!' But Mr Bullen's drawing-room is as quiet as a cave. The windows are closed, the blinds half pulled, and she is not late. The-girl-before-her has just started playing MacDowell's* 'To an Iceberg'. Mr Bullen looks over at her and half smiles.

'Sit down,' he says. 'Sit over there in the sofa corner, little lady.'

How funny he is. He doesn't exactly laugh at you . . . but there is just something. . . . Oh, how peaceful it is here. She likes this room. It smells of art serge and stale smoke and chrysanthemums . . . there is a big vase of them on the mantelpiece behind the pale photograph of Rubinstein* . . . *à mon ami Robert Bullen*. . . . Over the black glittering piano hangs 'Solitude'—a dark tragic woman draped in white, sitting on a rock, her knees crossed, her chin on her hands.

'No, no!' says Mr Bullen, and he leans over the other girl, puts his arms over her shoulders and plays the passage for her. The stupid— she's blushing! How ridiculous!

Now the-girl-before-her has gone; the front door slams. Mr Bullen comes back and walks up and down, very softly, waiting for her. What an extraordinary thing. Her fingers tremble so that she can't undo the knot in the music satchel. It's the wind. . . . And her heart beats so hard she feels it must lift her blouse up and down. Mr Bullen does not say a word. The shabby red piano seat is long enough for two people to sit side by side. Mr Bullen sits down by her.

'Shall I begin with scales,' she asks, squeezing her hands together. 'I had some arpeggios, too.'

But he does not answer. She doesn't believe he even hears . . . and then suddenly his fresh hand with the ring on it reaches over and opens Beethoven.

'Let's have a little of the old master,' he says.

But why does he speak so kindly—so awfully kindly—and as
though they had known each other for years and years and knew
everything about each other.

He turns the page slowly. She watches his hand—it is a very nice
hand and always looks as though it had just been washed.

'Here we are,' says Mr Bullen.

Oh, that kind voice—Oh, that minor movement. Here come the
little drums. . . .

'Shall I take the repeat?'

'Yes, dear child.'

His voice is far, far too kind. The crotchets and quavers are dancing up and down the stave* like little black boys on a fence. Why is he
so . . . She will not cry—she has nothing to cry about. . . .

'What is it, dear child?'

Mr Bullen takes her hands. His shoulder is there—just by her
head. She leans on it ever so little, her cheek against the springy
tweed.

'Life is so dreadful,' she murmurs, but she does not feel it's
dreadful at all. He says something about 'waiting' and 'marking
time' and 'that rare thing, a woman', but she does not hear. It is so
comfortable . . . for ever . . . .

Suddenly the door opens and in pops Marie Swainson, hours
before her time.

'Take the allegretto* a little faster,' says Mr Bullen, and gets up
and begins to walk up and down again.

'Sit in the sofa corner, little lady,' he says to Marie.

The wind, the wind. It's frightening to be here in her room by
herself. The bed, the mirror, the white jug and basin gleam like the
sky outside. It's the bed that is frightening. There it lies, sound
asleep. . . . Does Mother imagine for one moment that she is going to
darn all those stockings knotted up on the quilt like a coil of snakes?
She's not. No, Mother. I do not see why I should. . . . The wind—
the wind! There's a funny smell of soot blowing down the chimney.
Hasn't anyone written poems to the wind? . . . 'I bring fresh flowers
to the leaves and showers.'* . . . What nonsense.

'Is that you, Bogey?'*

'Come for a walk round the esplanade, Matilda. I can't stand this
any longer.'

'Right-o. I'll put on my ulster.* Isn't it an awful day!' Bogey's ulster is just like hers. Hooking the collar she looks at herself in the glass. Her face is white, they have the same excited eyes and hot lips. Ah, they know those two in the glass. Good-bye, dears; we shall be back soon.

'This is better, isn't it?'

'Hook on,' says Bogey.

They cannot walk fast enough. Their heads bent, their legs just touching, they stride like one eager person through the town, down the asphalt zigzag where the fennel grows wild and on to the esplanade. It is dusky—just getting dusky. The wind is so strong that they have to fight their way through it, rocking like two old drunkards. All the poor little pahutukawas* on the esplanade are bent to the ground.

'Come on! Come on! Let's get near.'

Over by the breakwater the sea is very high. They pull off their hats and her hair blows across her mouth, tasting of salt. The sea is so high that the waves do not break at all; they thump against the rough stone wall and suck up the weedy, dripping steps. A fine spray skims from the water right across the esplanade. They are covered with drops; the inside of her mouth tastes wet and cold.

Bogey's voice is breaking. When he speaks he rushes up and down the scale. It's funny—it makes you laugh—and yet it just suits the day. The wind carries their voices—away fly the sentences like the narrow ribbons.

'Quicker! Quicker!'

It is getting very dark. In the harbour the coal hulks show two lights—one high on a mast, and one from the stern.

'Look, Bogey. Look over there.'

A big black steamer with a long loop of smoke streaming, with the portholes lighted, with lights everywhere, is putting out to sea. The wind does not stop her; she cuts through the waves, making for the open gate between the pointed rocks that leads to. . . . It's the light that makes her look so awfully beautiful and mysterious. . . . *They* are on board leaning over the rail arm in arm.

'. . . Who are they?'

'. . . Brother and sister.'

'Look, Bogey, there's the town. Doesn't it look small? There's the post office clock chiming for the last time. There's the esplanade where we walked that windy day. Do you remember? I cried at my music lesson that day—how many years ago! Good-bye, little island, good-bye. . . .'

Now the dark stretches a wing over the tumbling water. They can't see those two any more. Good-bye, good-bye. Don't forget. . . . But the ship is gone, now.

The wind—the wind.

PRELUDE

I

There was not an inch of room for Lottie and Kezia in the buggy.*
When Pat swung them on top of the luggage they wobbled; the
grandmother's lap was full and Linda Burnell could not possibly
have held a lump of a child on hers for any distance. Isabel, very
superior, was perched beside the new handy-man on the driver's
seat. Hold-alls, bags and boxes were piled upon the floor. 'These are
absolute necessities that I will not let out of my sight for one instant,'
said Linda Burnell, her voice trembling with fatigue and excitement.

Lottie and Kezia stood on the patch of lawn just inside the gate all
ready for the fray in their coats with brass anchor buttons and little
round caps with battleship ribbons. Hand in hand, they stared with
round solemn eyes first at the absolute necessities and then at their
mother.

'We shall simply have to leave them. That is all. We shall simply
have to cast them off,' said Linda Burnell. A strange little laugh flew
from her lips; she leaned back against the buttoned leather cushions
and shut her eyes, her lips trembling with laughter. Happily at that
moment Mrs Samuel Josephs, who had been watching the scene
from behind her drawing-room blind, waddled down the garden
path.

'Why nod leave the chudren with be for the afterdoon, Brs Burnell? They could go on the dray with the storeban when he comes in
the eveding. Those thigs on the path have to go, dod't they?'

'Yes, everything outside the house is supposed to go,' said Linda
Burnell, and she waved a white hand at the tables and chairs standing
on their heads on the front lawn. How absurd they looked! Either
they ought to be the other way up, or Lottie and Kezia ought to
stand on their heads, too. And she longed to say: 'Stand on your
heads, children, and wait for the storeman.' It seemed to her that
would be so exquisitely funny that she could not attend to Mrs
Samuel Josephs.

The fat creaking body leaned across the gate, and the big jelly of a
face smiled. 'Dod't you worry, Brs Burnell. Loddie and Kezia can

have tea with by chudren in the dursery, and I'll see theb on the dray afterwards.'

The grandmother considered. 'Yes, it really is quite the best plan. We are very obliged to you, Mrs Samuel Josephs. Children, say "thank you" to Mrs Samuel Josephs.'

Two subdued chirrups: 'Thank you, Mrs Samuel Josephs.'

'And be good little girls, and—come closer—' they advanced, 'don't forget to tell Mrs Samuel Josephs when you want to. . . .'

'No, granma.'

'Dod't worry, Brs Burnell.'

At the last moment Kezia let go Lottie's hand and darted towards the buggy.

'I want to kiss my granma good-bye again.'

But she was too late. The buggy rolled off up the road, Isabel bursting with pride, her nose turned up at all the world, Linda Burnell prostrated, and the grandmother rummaging among the very curious oddments she had put in her black silk reticule* at the last moment, for something to give her daughter. The buggy twinkled away in the sunlight and fine golden dust up the hill and over. Kezia bit her lip, but Lottie, carefully finding her handkerchief first, set up a wail.

'Mother! Granma!'

Mrs Samuel Josephs, like a huge warm black silk tea cosy, enveloped her.

'It's all right, by dear. Be a brave child. You come and blay in the dursery!'

She put her arm round weeping Lottie and led her away. Kezia followed, making a face at Mrs Samuel Josephs' placket, which was undone as usual, with two long pink corset laces hanging out of it. . . .

Lottie's weeping died down as she mounted the stairs, but the sight of her at the nursery door with swollen eyes and a blob of a nose gave great satisfaction to the S. J.'s, who sat on two benches before a long table covered with American cloth and set out with immense plates of bread and dripping and two brown jugs that faintly steamed.

'Hullo! You've been crying!'

'Ooh! Your eyes have gone right in.'

'Doesn't her nose look funny.'

'You're all red-and-patchy.'

Lottie was quite a success. She felt it and swelled, smiling timidly.

'Go and sit by Zaidee, ducky,' said Mrs Samuel Josephs, 'and Kezia, you sid ad the end by Boses.'

Moses grinned and gave her a nip as she sat down; but she pretended not to notice. She did hate boys.

'Which will you have?' asked Stanley, leaning across the table very politely, and smiling at her. 'Which will you have to begin with— strawberries and cream or bread and dripping?'*

'Strawberries and cream, please,' said she.

'Ah-h-h-h.' How they all laughed and beat the table with their tea-spoons. Wasn't that a take in! Wasn't it now! Didn't he fox her! Good old Stan!

'Ma! She thought it was real.'

Even Mrs Samuel Josephs, pouring out the milk and water, could not help smiling. 'You bustn't tease theb on their last day,' she wheezed.

But Kezia bit a big piece out of her bread and dripping, and then stood the piece up on her plate. With the bite out it made a dear little sort of a gate. Pooh! She didn't care! A tear rolled down her cheek, but she wasn't crying. She couldn't have cried in front of those awful Samuel Josephs. She sat with her head bent, and as the tear dripped slowly down, she caught it with a neat little whisk of her tongue and ate it before any of them had seen.

II

After tea Kezia wandered back to their own house. Slowly she walked up the back steps, and through the scullery* into the kitchen. Nothing was left in it but a lump of gritty yellow soap in one corner of the kitchen window sill and a piece of flannel stained with a blue bag in another. The fireplace was choked up with rubbish. She poked among it but found nothing except a hair-tidy with a heart painted on it that had belonged to the servant girl. Even that she left lying, and she trailed through the narrow passage into the drawing-room. The Venetian blind was pulled down but not drawn close. Long pencil rays of sunlight shone through and the wavy shadow of a bush outside danced on the gold lines. Now it was still, now it began to flutter again, and now it came almost as far as her feet. Zoom! Zoom! a blue-bottle knocked against the ceiling; the carpet-tacks had little bits of red fluff sticking to them.

The dining-room window had a square of coloured glass at each corner. One was blue and one was yellow. Kezia bent down to have one more look at a blue lawn with blue arum lilies growing at the gate, and then at a yellow lawn with yellow lilies and a yellow fence. As she looked a little Chinese Lottie came out on to the lawn and began to dust the tables and chairs with a corner of her pinafore. Was that really Lottie? Kezia was not quite sure until she had looked through the ordinary window.

Upstairs in her father's and mother's room she found a pill box black and shiny outside and red in, holding a blob of cotton wool.

'I could keep a bird's egg in that,' she decided.

In the servant girl's room there was a stay-button* stuck in a crack of the floor, and in another crack some beads and a long needle. She knew there was nothing in her grandmother's room; she had watched her pack. She went over to the window and leaned against it, pressing her hands against the pane.

Kezia liked to stand so before the window. She liked the feeling of the cold shining glass against her hot palms, and she liked to watch the funny white tops that came on her fingers when she pressed them hard against the pane. As she stood there, the day flickered out and dark came. With the dark crept the wind snuffling and howling. The windows of the empty house shook, a creaking came from the walls and floors, a piece of loose iron* on the roof banged forlornly. Kezia was suddenly quite, quite still, with wide open eyes and knees pressed together. She was frightened. She wanted to call Lottie and to go on calling all the while she ran downstairs and out of the house. But IT was just behind her, waiting at the door, at the head of the stairs, at the bottom of the stairs, hiding in the passage, ready to dart out at the back door. But Lottie was at the back door, too.

'Kezia!' she called cheerfully. 'The storeman's here. Everything is on the dray* and three horses, Kezia. Mrs Samuel Josephs has given us a big shawl to wear round us, and she says to button up your coat. She won't come out because of asthma.'

Lottie was very important.

'Now then, you kids,' called the storeman. He hooked his big thumbs under their arms and up they swung. Lottie arranged the shawl 'most beautifully' and the storeman tucked up their feet in a piece of old blanket.

'Lift up. Easy does it.'

They might have been a couple of young ponies. The storeman felt over the cords holding his load, unhooked the brakechain from the wheel, and whistling, he swung up beside them.

'Keep close to me,' said Lottie, 'because otherwise you pull the shawl away from my side, Kezia.'

But Kezia edged up to the storeman. He towered beside her big as a giant and he smelled of nuts and new wooden boxes.

III

It was the first time that Lottie and Kezia had ever been out so late. Everything looked different—the painted wooden houses far smaller than they did by day, the gardens far bigger and wilder. Bright stars speckled the sky and the moon hung over the harbour dabbling the waves with gold. They could see the lighthouse shining on Quarantine Island,* and the green lights on the old coal hulks.*

'There comes the Picton boat,'* said the storeman, pointing to a little steamer all hung with bright beads.

But when they reached the top of the hill and began to go down the other side the harbour disappeared, and although they were still in the town they were quite lost. Other carts rattled past. Everybody knew the storeman.

'Night, Fred.'

'Night O,' he shouted.

Kezia liked very much to hear him. Whenever a cart appeared in the distance she looked up and waited for his voice. He was an old friend; and she and her grandmother had often been to his place to buy grapes. The storeman lived alone in a cottage that had a glass-house against one wall built by himself. All the glasshouse was spanned and arched over with one beautiful vine. He took her brown basket from her, lined it with three large leaves, and then he felt in his belt for a little horn knife, reached up and snapped off a big blue cluster and laid it on the leaves so tenderly that Kezia held her breath to watch. He was a very big man. He wore brown velvet trousers, and he had a long brown beard. But he never wore a collar, not even on Sunday. The back of his neck was burnt bright red.

'Where are we now?' Every few minutes one of the children asked him the question.

'Why, this is Hawk Street, or Charlotte Crescent.'

'Of course it is,' Lottie pricked up her ears at the last name; she always felt that Charlotte Crescent belonged specially to her. Very few people had streets with the same name as theirs.

'Look, Kezia, there is Charlotte Crescent. Doesn't it look different?' Now everything familiar was left behind. Now the big dray rattled into unknown country, along new roads* with high clay banks on either side, up steep, steep hills, down into bushy valleys, through wide shallow rivers. Further and further. Lottie's head wagged; she drooped, she slipped half into Kezia's lap and lay there. But Kezia could not open her eyes wide enough. The wind blew and she shivered; but her cheeks and ears burned.

'Do stars ever blow about?' she asked.

'Not to notice,' said the storeman.

'We've got a nuncle and a naunt living near our new house,' said Kezia. 'They have got two children, Pip, the eldest is called, and the youngest's name is Rags. He's got a ram. He has to feed it with a nenamuel teapot and a glove top over the spout. He's going to show us. What is the difference between a ram and a sheep?'

'Well, a ram has horns and runs for you.'

Kezia considered. 'I don't want to see it frightfully,' she said. 'I hate rushing animals like dogs and parrots. I often dream that animals rush at me—even camels—and while they are rushing, their heads swell e-enormous.'

The storeman said nothing. Kezia peered up at him, screwing up her eyes. Then she put her finger out and stroked his sleeve; it felt hairy. 'Are we near?' she asked.

'Not far off, now,' answered the storeman. 'Getting tired?'

'Well, I'm not an atom bit sleepy,' said Kezia. 'But my eyes keep curling up in such a funny sort of way.' She gave a long sigh, and to stop her eyes from curling she shut them. . . . When she opened them again they were clanking through a drive that cut through the garden like a whip lash, looping suddenly an island of green, and behind the island, but out of sight until you came upon it, was the house. It was long and low built, with a pillared verandah and balcony all the way round. The soft white bulk of it lay stretched upon the green garden like a sleeping beast. And now one and now another of the windows leaped into light. Someone was walking through the empty rooms carrying a lamp. From a window downstairs the light of a fire flickered. A strange beautiful excitement seemed to stream from the house in quivering ripples.

'Where are we?' said Lottie, sitting up. Her reefer* cap was all on one side and on her cheek there was the print of an anchor button she had pressed against while sleeping. Tenderly the storeman lifted her, set her cap straight, and pulled down her crumpled clothes. She stood blinking on the lowest verandah step watching Kezia who seemed to come flying through the air to her feet.

'Ooh!' cried Kezia, flinging up her arms. The grandmother came out of the dark hall carrying a little lamp. She was smiling.

'You found your way in the dark?' said she.

'Perfectly well.'

But Lottie staggered on the lowest verandah step like a bird fallen out of the nest. If she stood still for a moment she fell asleep, if she leaned against anything her eyes closed. She could not walk another step.

'Kezia,' said the grandmother, 'can I trust you to carry the lamp?'

'Yes, my granma.'

The old woman bent down and gave the bright breathing thing into her hands and then she caught up drunken Lottie. 'This way.'

Through a square hall filled with bales and hundreds of parrots (but the parrots were only on the wall-paper) down a narrow passage where the parrots persisted in flying past Kezia with her lamp.

'Be very quiet,' warned the grandmother, putting down Lottie and opening the dining-room door. 'Poor little mother has got such a headache.'

Linda Burnell, in a long cane chair, with her feet on a hassock,* and a plaid over her knees, lay before a crackling fire. Burnell and Beryl sat at the table in the middle of the room eating a dish of fried chops and drinking tea out of a brown china teapot. Over the back of her mother's chair leaned Isabel. She had a comb in her fingers and in a gentle absorbed fashion she was combing the curls from her mother's forehead. Outside the pool of lamp and firelight the room stretched dark and bare to the hollow windows.

'Are those the children?' But Linda did not really care; she did not even open her eyes to see.

'Put down the lamp, Kezia,' said Aunt Beryl, 'or we shall have the house on fire before we are out of the packing cases. More tea, Stanley?'

'Well, you might just give me five-eighths of a cup,' said Burnell, leaning across the table. 'Have another chop, Beryl. Tip-top meat, isn't it? Not too lean and not too fat.' He turned to his wife. 'You're sure you won't change your mind, Linda darling?'

'The very thought of it is enough.' She raised one eyebrow in the way she had. The grandmother brought the children bread and milk and they sat up to the table, flushed and sleepy behind the wavy steam.

'I had meat for my supper,' said Isabel, still combing gently.

'I had a whole chop for my supper, the bone and all and Worcester Sauce. Didn't I, father?'

'Oh, don't boast, Isabel,' said Aunt Beryl.

Isabel looked astounded. 'I wasn't boasting, was I, Mummy? I never thought of boasting. I thought they would like to know. I only meant to tell them.'

'Very well. That's enough,' said Burnell. He pushed back his plate, took a tooth-pick out of his pocket and began picking his strong white teeth.

'You might see that Fred has a bite of something in the kitchen before he goes, will you, mother?'

'Yes, Stanley.' The old woman turned to go.

'Oh, hold on half a jiffy. I suppose nobody knows where my slippers were put? I suppose I shall not be able to get at them for a month or two—what?'

'Yes,' came from Linda. 'In the top of the canvas hold-all marked "urgent necessities".'

'Well you might get them for me will you, mother?'

'Yes, Stanley.'

Burnell got up, stretched himself, and going over to the fire he turned his back to it and lifted up his coat tails.

'By Jove, this is a pretty pickle. Eh, Beryl?'

Beryl, sipping tea, her elbows on the table, smiled over the cup at him. She wore an unfamiliar pink pinafore; the sleeves of her blouse were rolled up to her shoulders showing her lovely freckled arms, and she had let her hair fall down her back in a long pig-tail.

'How long do you think it will take to get straight—couple of weeks—eh?' he chaffed.

'Good heavens, no,' said Beryl airily. 'The worst is over already. The servant girl and I have simply slaved all day, and ever since mother came she has worked like a horse, too. We have never sat down for a moment. We have had a day.'

Stanley scented a rebuke.

'Well, I suppose you did not expect me to rush away from the office and nail carpets—did you?'

'Certainly not,' laughed Beryl. She put down her cup and ran out of the dining-room.

'What the hell does she expect us to do?' asked Stanley. 'Sit down and fan herself with a palm leaf fan while I have a gang of professionals to do the job? By Jove, if she can't do a hand's turn occasionally without shouting about it in return for . . . .'

And he gloomed as the chops began to fight the tea in his sensitive stomach. But Linda put up a hand and dragged him down to the side of her long chair.

'This is a wretched time for you, old boy,' she said. Her cheeks were very white but she smiled and curled her fingers into the big red hand she held. Burnell became quiet. Suddenly he began to whistle 'Pure as a lily, joyous and free'*—a good sign.

'Think you're going to like it?' he asked.

'I don't want to tell you, but I think I ought to, mother,' said Isabel. 'Kezia is drinking tea out of Aunt Beryl's cup.'

IV

They were taken off to bed by the grandmother. She went first with a candle; the stairs rang to their climbing feet. Isabel and Lottie lay in a room to themselves, Kezia curled in her grandmother's soft bed.

'Aren't there going to be any sheets, my granma?'

'No, not to-night.'

'It's tickly,' said Kezia, 'but it's like Indians.' She dragged her grandmother down to her and kissed her under the chin. 'Come to bed soon and be my Indian brave.'

'What a silly you are,' said the old woman, tucking her in as she loved to be tucked.

'Aren't you going to leave me a candle?'

'No. Sh-h. Go to sleep.'

'Well, can I have the door left open?'

She rolled herself up into a round but she did not go to sleep. From all over the house came the sound of steps. The house itself creaked and popped. Loud whispering voices came from downstairs. Once she heard Aunt Beryl's rush of high laughter, and once she heard a loud trumpeting from Burnell blowing his nose. Outside the window hundreds of black cats with yellow eyes sat in the sky watching her—but she was not frightened. Lottie was saying to Isabel:

'I'm going to say my prayers in bed to-night.'

'No you can't, Lottie.' Isabel was very firm. 'God only excuses you saying your prayers in bed if you've got a temperature.' So Lottie yielded:

> Gentle Jesus meek anmile,
> Look pon a little chile.
> Pity me, simple Lizzie
> Suffer me to come to thee.*

And then they lay down back to back, their little behinds just touching, and fell asleep.

Standing in a pool of moonlight Beryl Fairfield undressed herself. She was tired, but she pretended to be more tired than she really was—letting her clothes fall, pushing back with a languid gesture her warm, heavy hair.

'Oh, how tired I am—very tired.'

She shut her eyes a moment, but her lips smiled. Her breath rose and fell in her breast like two fanning wings. The window was wide open; it was warm, and somewhere out there in the garden a young man, dark and slender, with mocking eyes, tip-toed among the bushes, and gathered the flowers into a big bouquet, and slipped under her window and held it up to her. She saw herself bending forward. He thrust his head among the bright waxy flowers, sly and laughing. 'No, no,' said Beryl. She turned from the window and dropped her nightgown over her head.

'How frightfully unreasonable Stanley is sometimes,' she thought, buttoning. And then, as she lay down, there came the old thought, the cruel thought—ah, if only she had money of her own.

A young man, immensely rich, has just arrived from England. He meets her quite by chance. . . . The new governor is unmarried. . . . There is a ball at Government house. . . . Who is that exquisite creature in *eau de nil** satin? Beryl Fairfield. . . .

'The thing that pleases me,' said Stanley, leaning against the side of the bed and giving himself a good scratch on his shoulders and back before turning in, 'is that I've got the place dirt cheap, Linda. I was talking about it to little Wally Bell to-day and he said he simply could not understand why they had accepted my figure. You see land about here is bound to become more and more valuable . . . in about ten years' time . . . of course we shall have to go very slow and cut down expenses as fine as possible. Not asleep—are you?'

'No, dear, I've heard every word,' said Linda. He sprang into bed, leaned over her and blew out the candle.

'Good night, Mr Business Man,' said she, and she took hold of his head by the ears and gave him a quick kiss. Her faint far-away voice seemed to come from a deep well.

'Good night, darling.' He slipped his arm under her neck and drew her to him.

'Yes, clasp me,' said the faint voice from the deep well.

Pat the handy man sprawled in his little room behind the kitchen. His sponge-bag, coat and trousers hung from the door-peg like a hanged man. From the edge of the blanket his twisted toes protruded, and on the floor beside him there was an empty cane bird-cage. He looked like a comic picture.

'Honk, honk,' came from the servant girl. She had adenoids.*

Last to go to bed was the grandmother.

'What. Not asleep yet?'

'No, I'm waiting for you,' said Kezia. The old woman sighed and lay down beside her. Kezia thrust her head under the grandmother's arm and gave a little squeak. But the old woman only pressed her faintly, and sighed again, took out her teeth, and put them in a glass of water beside her on the floor.

In the garden some tiny owls, perched on the branches of a lace-bark tree, called: 'More pork; more pork.' And far away in the bush there sounded a harsh rapid chatter: 'Ha-ha-ha . . . Ha-ha-ha.'

V

Dawn came sharp and chill with red clouds on a faint green sky and drops of water on every leaf and blade. A breeze blew over the garden, dropping dew and dropping petals, shivered over the drenched paddocks, and was lost in the sombre bush. In the sky some tiny stars floated for a moment and then they were gone—they were dissolved like bubbles. And plain to be heard in the early quiet was the sound of the creek in the paddock running over the brown stones, running in and out of the sandy hollows, hiding under clumps of dark berry bushes, spilling into a swamp of yellow water flowers and cresses.

And then at the first beam of sun the birds began. Big cheeky birds, starlings and mynahs, whistled on the lawns, the little birds, the goldfinches and linnets and fantails* flicked from bough to bough. A lovely kingfisher perched on the paddock fence preening his rich beauty, and a *tui** sang his three notes and laughed and sang them again.

'How loud the birds are,' said Linda in her dream. She was walking with her father through a green paddock sprinkled with daisies. Suddenly he bent down and parted the grasses and showed her a tiny ball of fluff just at her feet. 'Oh, Papa, the darling.' She made a cup of her hands and caught the tiny bird and stroked its head with her finger. It was quite tame. But a funny thing happened. As she stroked it began to swell, it ruffled and pouched, it grew bigger and bigger and its round eyes seemed to smile knowingly at her. Now her arms were hardly wide enough to hold it and she dropped it into her apron. It had become a baby with a big naked head and a gaping bird-mouth, opening and shutting. Her father broke into a loud clattering laugh and she woke to see Burnell standing by the windows rattling the Venetian blind up to the very top.

'Hullo,' he said. 'Didn't wake you, did I? Nothing much wrong with the weather this morning.'

He was enormously pleased. Weather like this set a final seal on his bargain. He felt, somehow, that he had bought the lovely day, too—got it chucked in dirt cheap with the house and ground. He dashed off to his bath and Linda turned over and raised herself on one elbow to see the room by daylight. All the furniture had found a place—all the old paraphernalia—as she expressed it. Even the photographs were on the mantelpiece and the medicine bottles on the shelf above the wash-stand. Her clothes lay across a chair—her outdoor things, a purple cape and a round hat with a plume in it. Looking at them she wished that she was going away from this house, too. And she saw herself driving away from them all in a little buggy, driving away from everybody and not even waving.

Back came Stanley girt with a towel, glowing and slapping his thighs. He pitched the wet towel on top of her hat and cape, and standing firm in the exact centre of a square of sunlight he began to do his exercises. Deep breathing, bending and squatting like a frog and shooting out his legs. He was so delighted with his firm, obedient body that he hit himself on the chest and gave a loud 'Ah.' But this amazing vigour seemed to set him worlds away from Linda. She lay on the white tumbled bed and watched him as if from the clouds.

'Oh, damn! Oh, blast!' said Stanley, who had butted into a crisp white shirt only to find that some idiot had fastened the neck-band and he was caught. He stalked over to Linda waving his arms.

'You look like a big fat turkey,' said she.

'Fat. I like that,' said Stanley. 'I haven't a square inch of fat on me. Feel that.'

'It's rock—it's iron,' mocked she.

'You'd be surprised,' said Stanley, as though this were intensely interesting, 'at the number of chaps at the club who have got a corporation.* Young chaps, you know—men of my age.' He began parting his bushy ginger hair, his blue eyes fixed and round in the glass, his knees bent, because the dressing table was always— confound it—a bit too low for him. 'Little Wally Bell, for instance,' and he straightened, describing upon himself an enormous curve with the hairbrush. 'I must say I've a perfect horror . . . .'

'My dear, don't worry. You'll never be fat. You are far too energetic.'

'Yes, yes, I suppose that's true,' said he, comforted for the hundredth time, and taking a pearl pen-knife out of his pocket he began to pare his nails.

'Breakfast, Stanley.' Beryl was at the door. 'Oh, Linda, mother says you are not to get up yet.' She popped her head in at the door. She had a big piece of syringa stuck through her hair.

'Everything we left on the verandah last night is simply sopping this morning. You should see poor dear mother wringing out the tables and the chairs. However, there is no harm done—' this with the faintest glance at Stanley.

'Have you told Pat to have the buggy round in time? It's a good six and a half miles to the office.'

'I can imagine what this early start for the office will be like,' thought Linda. 'It will be very high pressure indeed.'

'Pat, Pat.' She heard the servant girl calling. But Pat was evidently hard to find; the silly voice went baa-baaing through the garden.

Linda did not rest again until the final slam of the front door told her that Stanley was really gone.

Later she heard her children playing in the garden. Lottie's stolid, compact little voice cried: 'Ke—zia. Isa—bel.' She was always getting lost or losing people only to find them again, to her great surprise, round the next tree or the next corner. 'Oh, there you are after all.' They had been turned out after breakfast and told not to come back to the house until they were called. Isabel wheeled a neat pramload of prim dolls and Lottie was allowed for a great treat to walk beside her holding the doll's parasol over the face of the wax one.

'Where are you going to, Kezia?' asked Isabel, who longed to find some light and menial duty that Kezia might perform and so be roped in under her government.

'Oh, just away,' said Kezia. . . .

Then she did not hear them any more. What a glare there was in the room. She hated blinds pulled up to the top at any time, but in the morning it was intolerable. She turned over to the wall and idly, with one finger, she traced a poppy on the wall-paper with a leaf and a stem and a fat bursting bud. In the quiet, and under her tracing finger, the poppy seemed to come alive. She could feel the sticky, silky petals, the stem, hairy like a gooseberry skin, the rough leaf and the tight glazed bud. Things had a habit of coming alive like that. Not only large substantial things like furniture but curtains and the patterns of stuffs and the fringes of quilts and cushions. How often she had seen the tassel fringe of her quilt change into a funny procession of dancers with priests attending. . . . For there were some tassels that did not dance at all but walked stately, bent forward as if praying or chanting. How often the medicine bottles had turned into a row of little men with brown top-hats on; and the washstand jug had a way of sitting in the basin like a fat bird in a round nest.

'I dreamed about birds last night,' thought Linda. What was it? She had forgotten. But the strangest part of this coming alive of things was what they did. They listened, they seemed to swell out with some mysterious important content, and when they were full she felt that they smiled. But it was not for her, only, their sly secret smile; they were members of a secret society and they smiled among themselves. Sometimes, when she had fallen asleep in the daytime, she woke and could not lift a finger, could not even turn her eyes to left or right because THEY were there; sometimes when she went out of a room and left it empty, she knew as she clicked the door to that THEY were filling it. And there were times in the evenings when she was upstairs, perhaps, and everybody else was down, when she could hardly escape from them. Then she could not hurry, she could not hum a tune; if she tried to say ever so carelessly—'Bother that old thimble'—THEY were not deceived. THEY knew how frightened she was; THEY saw how she turned her head away as she passed the mirror. What Linda always felt was that THEY wanted something of her, and she knew that if she gave herself up and was quiet, more than quiet, silent, motionless, something would really happen.

'It's very quiet now,' she thought. She opened her eyes wide, and she heard the silence spinning its soft endless web. How lightly she breathed; she scarcely had to breathe at all.

Yes, everything had come alive down to the minutest, tiniest particle, and she did not feel her bed, she floated, held up in the air. Only she seemed to be listening with her wide open watchful eyes, waiting for someone to come who just did not come, watching for something to happen that just did not happen.

VI

In the kitchen at the long deal table under the two windows old Mrs Fairfield was washing the breakfast dishes. The kitchen window looked out on to a big grass patch that led down to the vegetable garden and the rhubarb beds. On one side the grass patch was bordered by the scullery and wash-house* and over this whitewashed lean-to there grew a knotted vine. She had noticed yesterday that a few tiny corkscrew tendrils had come right through some cracks in the scullery ceiling and all the windows of the lean-to had a thick frill of ruffled green.

'I am very fond of a grape vine,' declared Mrs Fairfield, 'but I do not think that the grapes will ripen here. It takes Australian sun.' And she remembered how Beryl when she was a baby had been picking some white grapes from the vine on the back verandah of their Tasmanian house and she had been stung on the leg by a huge red ant. She saw Beryl in a little plaid dress with red ribbon tie-ups on the shoulders screaming so dreadfully that half the street rushed in. And how the child's leg had swelled! 'T—t—t—t!' Mrs Fairfield caught her breath remembering. 'Poor child, how terrifying it was.' And she set her lips tight and went over to the stove for some more hot water. The water frothed up in the big soapy bowl with pink and blue bubbles on top of the foam. Old Mrs Fairfield's arms were bare to the elbow and stained a bright pink. She wore a grey foulard* dress patterned with large purple pansies, a white linen apron and a high cap shaped like a jelly mould of white muslin. At her throat there was a silver crescent moon with five little owls seated on it, and round her neck she wore a watch-guard* made of black beads.

It was hard to believe that she had not been in that kitchen for years; she was so much a part of it. She put the crocks away with a sure, precise touch, moving leisurely and ample from the stove to the dresser, looking into the pantry and the larder as though there were not an unfamiliar corner. When she had finished, everything in the kitchen had become part of a series of patterns. She stood in the middle of the room wiping her hands on a check cloth; a smile beamed on her lips; she thought it looked very nice, very satisfactory.

'Mother! Mother! Are you there?' called Beryl.

'Yes, dear. Do you want me?'

'No. I'm coming,' and Beryl rushed in, very flushed, dragging with her two big pictures.

'Mother, whatever can I do with these awful hideous Chinese paintings that Chung Wah gave Stanley when he went bankrupt? It's absurd to say that they are valuable, because they were hanging in Chung Wah's fruit shop for months before. I can't make out why Stanley wants them kept. I'm sure he thinks them just as hideous as we do, but it's because of the frames,' she said spitefully. 'I suppose he thinks the frames might fetch something some day or other.'

'Why don't you hang them in the passage?' suggested Mrs Fairfield; 'they would not be much seen there.'

'I can't. There is no room. I've hung all the photographs of his office there before and after building, and the signed photos of his business friends, and that awful enlargement of Isabel lying on the mat in her singlet.' Her angry glance swept the placid kitchen. 'I know what I'll do. I'll hang them here. I will tell Stanley they got a little damp in the moving so I have put them in here for the time being.'

She dragged a chair forward, jumped on it, took a hammer and a big nail out of her pinafore pocket and banged away.

'There! That is enough! Hand me the picture, mother.'

'One moment, child.' Her mother was wiping over the carved ebony frame.

'Oh, mother, really you need not dust them. It would take years to dust all those little holes.' And she frowned at the top of her mother's head and bit her lip with impatience. Mother's deliberate way of doing things was simply maddening. It was old age, she supposed, loftily.

At last the two pictures were hung side by side. She jumped off the chair, stowing away the little hammer.

'They don't look so bad there, do they?' said she. 'And at any rate nobody need gaze at them except Pat and the servant girl—have I got a spider's web on my face, mother? I've been poking into that cupboard under the stairs and now something keeps tickling my nose.'

But before Mrs Fairfield had time to look Beryl had turned away. Someone tapped on the window: Linda was there, nodding and smiling. They heard the latch of the scullery door lift and she came in. She had no hat on; her hair stood up on her head in curling rings and she was wrapped up in an old cashmere shawl.

'I'm so hungry,' said Linda: 'where can I get something to eat, mother? This is the first time I've been in the kitchen. It says "mother" all over; everything is in pairs.'

'I will make you some tea,' said Mrs Fairfield, spreading a clean napkin over a corner of the table, 'and Beryl can have a cup with you.'

'Beryl, do you want half my gingerbread?' Linda waved the knife at her. 'Beryl, do you like the house now that we are here?'

'Oh yes, I like the house immensely and the garden is beautiful, but it feels very far away from everything to me. I can't imagine people coming out from town to see us in that dreadful jolting bus, and I am sure there is not anyone here to come and call. Of course it does not matter to you because——'

'But there's the buggy,' said Linda. 'Pat can drive you into town whenever you like.'

That was a consolation, certainly, but there was something at the back of Beryl's mind, something she did not even put into words for herself.

'Oh, well, at any rate it won't kill us,' she said dryly, putting down her empty cup and standing up and stretching. 'I am going to hang curtains.' And she ran away singing:

> How many thousand birds I see
> That sing aloud from every tree . . .

'. . . birds I see That sing aloud from every tree. . . .' But when she reached the dining-room she stopped singing, her face changed; it became gloomy and sullen.

'One may as well rot here as anywhere else,' she muttered savagely, digging the stiff brass safety-pins into the red serge curtains.

The two left in the kitchen were quiet for a little. Linda leaned her cheek on her fingers and watched her mother. She thought her mother looked wonderfully beautiful with her back to the leafy window. There was something comforting in the sight of her that Linda felt she could never do without. She needed the sweet smell of her flesh, and the soft feel of her cheeks and her arms and shoulders still softer. She loved the way her hair curled, silver at her forehead, lighter at her neck, and bright brown still in the big coil under the muslin cap. Exquisite were her mother's hands, and the two rings she wore seemed to melt into her creamy skin. And she was always so fresh, so delicious. The old woman could bear nothing but linen next to her body and she bathed in cold water winter and summer.

'Isn't there anything for me to do?' asked Linda.

'No, darling. I wish you would go into the garden and give an eye to your children; but that I know you will not do.'

'Of course I will, but you know Isabel is much more grown up than any of us.'

'Yes, but Kezia is not,' said Mrs Fairfield.

'Oh, Kezia has been tossed by a bull hours ago,' said Linda, winding herself up in her shawl again.

But no, Kezia had seen a bull through a hole in a knot of wood in the paling that separated the tennis lawn from the paddock. But she had not liked the bull frightfully, so she had walked away back through the orchard, up the grassy slope, along the path by the lace bark tree and so into the spread tangled garden. She did not believe that she would ever not get lost in this garden. Twice she had found her way back to the big iron gates they had driven through the night before, and then had turned to walk up the drive that led to the house, but there were so many little paths on either side. On one side they all led into a tangle of tall dark trees and strange bushes with flat velvet leaves and feathery cream flowers that buzzed with flies when you shook them—this was the frightening side, and no garden at all. The little paths here were wet and clayey with tree roots spanned across them like the marks of big fowls' feet.

But on the other side of the drive there was a high box* border and the paths had box edges and all of them led into a deeper and deeper tangle of flowers. The camellias were in bloom, white and crimson and pink and white striped with flashing leaves. You could not see a leaf on the syringa bushes for the white clusters. The roses were in flower—gentlemen's button-hole roses, little white ones, but far too full of insects to hold under anyone's nose, pink monthly roses with a ring of fallen petals round the bushes, cabbage roses on thick stalks, moss roses, always in bud, pink smooth beauties opening curl on curl, red ones so dark they seemed to turn black as they fell, and a certain exquisite cream kind with a slender red stem and bright scarlet leaves.

There were clumps of fairy bells, and all kinds of geraniums, and there were little trees of verbena and bluish lavender bushes and a bed of pelagoniums with velvet eyes and leaves like moths' wings. There was a bed of nothing but mignonette and another of nothing but pansies—borders of double and single daisies and all kinds of little tufty plants she had never seen before.

The red-hot pokers were taller than she; the Japanese sunflowers grew in a tiny jungle. She sat down on one of the box borders. By pressing hard at first it made a nice seat. But how dusty it was inside! Kezia bent down to look and sneezed and rubbed her nose.

And then she found herself at the top of the rolling grassy slope that led down to the orchard. . . . She looked down at the slope a moment; then she lay down on her back, gave a squeak and rolled over and over into the thick flowery orchard grass. As she lay waiting for things to stop spinning, she decided to go up to the house and ask the servant girl for an empty match-box. She wanted to make a surprise for the grandmother. . . . First she would put a leaf inside with a big violet lying on it, then she would put a very small white picotee,* perhaps, on each side of the violet, and then she would sprinkle some lavender on the top, but not to cover their heads.

She often made these surprises for the grandmother, and they were always most successful.

'Do you want a match, my granny?'

'Why, yes, child, I believe a match is just what I'm looking for.'

The grandmother slowly opened the box and came upon the picture inside.

'Good gracious, child! How you astonished me!'

'I can make her one every day here,' she thought, scrambling up the grass on her slippery shoes.

But on her way back to the house she came to that island that lay in the middle of the drive, dividing the drive into two arms that met in front of the house. The island was made of grass banked up high. Nothing grew on the top except one huge plant with thick, grey-green, thorny leaves, and out of the middle there sprang up a tall stout stem. Some of the leaves of the plant were so old that they curled up in the air no longer; they turned back, they were split and broken; some of them lay flat and withered on the ground.

Whatever could it be? She had never seen anything like it before. She stood and stared. And then she saw her mother coming down the path.

'Mother, what is it?' asked Kezia.

Linda looked up at the fat swelling plant with its cruel leaves and fleshy stem. High above them, as though becalmed in the air, and yet holding so fast to the earth it grew from, it might have had claws instead of roots. The curving leaves seemed to be hiding something; the blind stem cut into the air as if no wind could ever shake it.

'That is an aloe, Kezia,' said her mother.

'Does it ever have any flowers?'

'Yes, Kezia,' and Linda smiled down at her, and half shut her eyes. 'Once every hundred years.'

VII

On his way home from the office Stanley Burnell stopped the buggy at the Bodega,* got out and bought a large bottle of oysters. At the Chinaman's shop next door he bought a pineapple in the pink of condition, and noticing a basket of fresh black cherries he told John to put him a pound of those as well. The oysters and the pine he stowed away in the box under the front seat, but the cherries he kept in his hand.

Pat, the handy-man, leapt off the box and tucked him up again in the brown rug.

'Lift yer feet, Mr Burnell, while I give yer a fold under,' said he.

'Right! Right! First-rate!' said Stanley. 'You can make straight for home now.'

Pat gave the grey mare a touch and the buggy sprang forward.

'I believe this man is a first-rate chap,' thought Stanley. He liked the look of him sitting up there in his neat brown coat and brown bowler. He liked the way Pat had tucked him in, and he liked his eyes. There was nothing servile about him—and if there was one thing he hated more than another it was servility. And he looked as if he was pleased with his job, happy and contented already.

The grey mare went very well; Burnell was impatient to be out of the town. He wanted to be home. Ah, it was splendid to live in the country—to get right out of that hole of a town once the office was closed; and this drive in the fresh warm air, knowing all the while that his own house was at the other end, with its garden and pad-docks, its three tip-top cows and enough fowls and ducks to keep them in poultry, was splendid too.

As they left the town finally and bowled away up the deserted road his heart beat hard for joy. He rooted in the bag and began to eat the cherries, three or four at a time, chucking the stones over the side of the buggy. They were delicious, so plump and cold, without a spot or a bruise on them.

Look at those two, now—black one side and white the other— perfect! A perfect little pair of Siamese twins. And he stuck them in his button-hole. . . . By Jove, he wouldn't mind giving that chap up there a handful—but no, better not. Better wait until he had been with him a bit longer.

He began to plan what he would do with his Saturday afternoon and his Sundays. He wouldn't go to the club for lunch on Saturday. No, cut away from the office as soon as possible and get them to give him a couple of slices of cold meat and half a lettuce when he got home. And then he'd get a few chaps out from town to play tennis in the afternoon. Not too many—three at most. Beryl was a good player, too. . . . He stretched out his right arm and slowly bent it, feeling the muscle. . . . A bath, a good rub-down, a cigar on the verandah after dinner. . . .

On Sunday morning they would go to church—children and all. Which reminded him that he must hire a pew,* in the sun if possible and well forward so as to be out of the draught from the door. In fancy he heard himself intoning extremely well: 'When thou did overcome the *Sharp*ness of Death Thou didst open the *King*dom of Heaven to *all* Believers.'* And he saw the neat brass-edged card on the corner of the pew—Mr Stanley Burnell and family. . . . The rest of the day he'd loaf about with Linda. . . . Now they were walking about the garden; she was on his arm, and he was explaining to her at length what he intended doing at the office the week following. He heard her saying: 'My dear, I think that is most wise.' . . . Talking things over with Linda was a wonderful help even though they were apt to drift away from the point.

Hang it all! They weren't getting along very fast. Pat had put the brake on again. Ugh! What a brute of a thing it was. He could feel it in the pit of his stomach.

A sort of panic overtook Burnell whenever he approached near home. Before he was well inside the gate he would shout to anyone within sight: 'Is everything all right?' And then he did not believe it was until he heard Linda say: 'Hullo! Are you home again?' That was the worst of living in the country—it took the deuce of a long time to get back. . . . But now they weren't far off. They were on the top of the last hill; it was a gentle slope all the way now and not more than half a mile.

Pat trailed the whip over the mare's back and he coaxed her: 'Goop now. Goop now.'

It wanted a few minutes to sunset. Everything stood motionless bathed in bright, metallic light and from the paddocks on either side there streamed the milky scent of ripe grass. The iron gates were open. They dashed through and up the drive and round the island, stopping at the exact middle of the verandah.

'Did she satisfy yer, Sir?' said Pat, getting off the box and grinning at his master.

'Very well indeed, Pat,' said Stanley.

Linda came out of the glass door; her voice rang in the shadowy quiet. 'Hullo! Are you home again?'

At the sound of her his heart beat so hard that he could hardly stop himself dashing up the steps and catching her in his arms.

'Yes, I'm home again. Is everything all right?'

Pat began to lead the buggy round to the side gate that opened into the courtyard.

'Here, half a moment,' said Burnell. 'Hand me those two parcels.' And he said to Linda, 'I've brought you back a bottle of oysters and a pineapple,' as though he had brought her back all the harvest of the earth.

They went into the hall; Linda carried the oysters in one hand and the pineapple in the other. Burnell shut the glass door, threw his hat down, put his arms round her and strained her to him, kissing the top of her head, her ears, her lips, her eyes.

'Oh, dear! Oh, dear!' said she. 'Wait a moment. Let me put down these silly things,' and she put the bottle of oysters and the pine on a little carved chair. 'What have you got in your buttonhole— cherries?' She took them out and hung them over his ear.

'Don't do that, darling. They are for you.'

So she took them off his ear again. 'You don't mind if I save them. They'd spoil my appetite for dinner. Come and see your children. They are having tea.'

The lamp was lighted on the nursery table. Mrs Fairfield was cutting and spreading bread and butter. The three little girls sat up to table wearing large bibs embroidered with their names. They wiped their mouths as their father came in ready to be kissed. The windows were open; a jar of wild flowers stood on the mantelpiece, and the lamp made a big soft bubble of light on the ceiling.

'You seem pretty snug, mother,' said Burnell, blinking at the light. Isabel and Lottie sat one on either side of the table, Kezia at the bottom—the place at the top was empty.

'That's where my boy ought to sit,' thought Stanley. He tightened his arm round Linda's shoulder. By God, he was a perfect fool to feel as happy as this!

'We are, Stanley. We are very snug,' said Mrs Fairfield, cutting Kezia's bread into fingers.

'Like it better than town—eh, children?' asked Burnell.

'Oh, yes,' said the three little girls, and Isabel added as an after-thought: 'Thank you very much indeed, father dear.'

'Come upstairs,' said Linda. 'I'll bring your slippers.'

But the stairs were too narrow for them to go up arm in arm. It was quite dark in the room. He heard her ring tapping on the marble mantelpiece as she felt for the matches.

'I've got some, darling. I'll light the candles.'

But instead he came up behind her and again he put his arms round her and pressed her head into his shoulder.

'I'm so confoundedly happy,' he said.

'Are you?' She turned and put her hands on his breast and looked up at him.

'I don't know what has come over me,' he protested.

It was quite dark outside now and heavy dew was falling. When Linda shut the window the cold dew touched her finger tips. Far away a dog barked. 'I believe there is going to be a moon,' she said.

At the words, and with the cold wet dew on her fingers, she felt as though the moon had risen—that she was being strangely discovered in a flood of cold light. She shivered; she came away from the window and sat down upon the box ottoman* beside Stanley.

*   *   *

In the dining-room, by the flicker of a wood fire, Beryl sat on a hassock playing the guitar. She had bathed and changed all her clothes. Now she wore a white muslin dress with black spots on it and in her hair she had pinned a black silk rose.

> Nature has gone to her rest, love,
>   See, we are alone.
> Give me your hand to press, love,
>   Lightly within my own.

She played and sang half to herself, for she was watching herself playing and singing. The firelight gleamed on her shoes, on the ruddy belly of the guitar, and on her white fingers. . . .

'If I were outside the window and looked in and saw myself I really would be rather struck,' thought she. Still more softly she played the accompaniment—not singing now but listening.

... 'The first time that I ever saw you, little girl—oh, you had no idea that you were not alone—you were sitting with your little feet upon a hassock, playing the guitar. God, I can never forget. . . .' Beryl flung up her head and began to sing again:

Even the moon is aweary . . .

But there came a loud bang at the door. The servant girl's crimson face popped through.

'Please, Miss Beryl, I've got to come and lay.'

'Certainly, Alice,' said Beryl, in a voice of ice. She put the guitar in a corner. Alice lunged in with a heavy black iron tray.

'Well, I have had a job with that oving,' said she. 'I can't get nothing to brown.'

'Really!' said Beryl.

But no, she could not stand that fool of a girl. She ran into the dark drawing-room and began walking up and down. . . . Oh, she was restless, restless. There was a mirror over the mantel. She leaned her arms along and looked at her pale shadow in it. How beautiful she looked, but there was nobody to see, nobody.

'Why must you suffer so?' said the face in the mirror. 'You were not made for suffering. . . . Smile!'

Beryl smiled, and really her smile *was* so adorable that she smiled again—but this time because she could not help it.

VIII

'Good morning, Mrs Jones.'

'Oh, good morning, Mrs Smith. I'm so glad to see you. Have you brought your children?'

'Yes, I've brought both my twins. I have had another baby since I saw you last, but she came so suddenly that I haven't had time to make her any clothes, yet. So I left her. . . . How is your husband?'

'Oh, he is very well, thank you. At least he had a nawful cold but Queen Victoria—she's my godmother, you know—sent him a case of pineapples and that cured it im-mediately. Is that your new servant?'

'Yes, her name's Gwen. I've only had her two days. Oh, Gwen, this is my friend, Mrs Smith.'

'Good morning, Mrs Smith. Dinner won't be ready for about ten minutes.'

'I don't think you ought to introduce me to the servant. I think I ought to just begin talking to her.'

'Well, she's more of a lady-help than a servant and you do introduce lady-helps, I know, because Mrs Samuel Josephs had one.'

'Oh, well, it doesn't matter,' said the servant, carelessly, beating up a chocolate custard with half a broken clothes peg. The dinner was baking beautifully on a concrete step. She began to lay the cloth on a pink garden seat. In front of each person she put two geranium leaf plates, a pine needle fork and a twig knife. There were three daisy heads on a laurel leaf for poached eggs, some slices of fuchsia petal cold beef, some lovely little rissoles* made of earth and water and dandelion seeds, and the chocolate custard which she had decided to serve in the pawa shell she had cooked it in.

'You needn't trouble about my children,' said Mrs Smith graciously. 'If you'll just take this bottle and fill it at the tap—I mean at the dairy.'

'Oh, all right,' said Gwen, and she whispered to Mrs Jones: 'Shall I go and ask Alice for a little bit of real milk?'

But someone called from the front of the house and the luncheon party melted away, leaving the charming table, leaving the rissoles and the poached eggs to the ants and to an old snail who pushed his quivering horns over the edge of the garden seat and began to nibble a geranium plate.

'Come round to the front, children. Pip and Rags have come.'

The Trout boys were the cousins Kezia had mentioned to the storeman. They lived about a mile away in a house called Monkey Tree Cottage. Pip was tall for his age, with lank black hair and a white face, but Rags was very small and so thin that when he was undressed his shoulder blades stuck out like two little wings. They had a mongrel dog with pale blue eyes and a long tail turned up at the end who followed them everywhere; he was called Snooker. They spent half their time combing and brushing Snooker and dosing him with various awful mixtures concocted by Pip, and kept secretly by him in a broken jug covered with an old kettle lid. Even faithful little Rags was not allowed to know the full secret of these mixtures. . . . Take some carbolic tooth powder and a pinch of sulphur powdered up fine, and perhaps a bit of starch to stiffen up Snooker's coat. . . . But that was not all; Rags privately thought that the rest was gunpowder. . . . And he never was allowed to help with the mixing because of the danger. . . . 'Why if a spot of this flew in your eye, you would be blinded for life,' Pip would say, stirring the mixture with an iron spoon. 'And there's always the chance—just the chance, mind you—of it exploding if you whack it hard enough. . . . Two spoons of this in a kerosene* tin will be enough to kill thousands of fleas.' But Snooker spent all his spare time biting and snuffling, and he stank abominably.

'It's because he is such a grand fighting dog,' Pip would say. 'All fighting dogs smell.'

The Trout boys had often spent the day with the Burnells in town, but now that they lived in this fine house and boncer* garden they were inclined to be very friendly. Besides, both of them liked playing with girls—Pip, because he could fox them so, and because Lottie was so easily frightened, and Rags for a shameful reason. He adored dolls. How he would look at a doll as it lay asleep, speaking in a whisper and smiling timidly, and what a treat it was to him to be allowed to hold one. . . .

'Curve your arms round her. Don't keep them stiff like that. You'll drop her,' Isabel would say sternly.

Now they were standing on the verandah and holding back Snooker who wanted to go into the house but wasn't allowed to because Aunt Linda hated decent dogs.

'We came over in the bus with Mum,' they said, 'and we're going to spend the afternoon with you. We brought over a batch of our gingerbread for Aunt Linda. Our Minnie made it. It's all over nuts.'

'I skinned the almonds,' said Pip. 'I just stuck my hand into a saucepan of boiling water and grabbed them out and gave them a kind of pinch and the nuts flew out of the skins, some of them as high as the ceiling. Didn't they, Rags?'

Rags nodded. 'When they make cakes at our place,' said Pip, 'we always stay in the kitchen, Rags and me, and I get the bowl and he gets the spoon and the egg beater. Sponge cake's best. It's all frothy stuff, then.'

He ran down the verandah steps to the lawn, planted his hands on the grass, bent forward, and just did not stand on his head.

'That lawn's all bumpy,' he said. 'You have to have a flat place for standing on your head. I can walk round the monkey tree on my head at our place. Can't I, Rags?'

'Nearly,' said Rags faintly.

'Stand on your head on the verandah. That's quite flat,' said Kezia.

'No, smarty,' said Pip. 'You have to do it on something soft. Because if you give a jerk and fall over, something in your neck goes click, and it breaks off. Dad told me.'

'Oh, do let's play something,' said Kezia.

'Very well,' said Isabel quickly, 'we'll play hospitals. I will be the nurse and Pip can be the doctor and you and Lottie and Rags can be the sick people.'

Lottie didn't want to play that, because last time Pip had squeezed something down her throat and it hurt awfully.

'Pooh,' scoffed Pip. 'It was only the juice out of a bit of mandarin peel.'

'Well, let's play ladies,' said Isabel. 'Pip can be the father and you can be all our dear little children.'

'I hate playing ladies,' said Kezia. 'You always make us go to church hand in hand and come home and go to bed.'

Suddenly Pip took a filthy handkerchief out of his pocket. 'Snooker! Here, sir,' he called. But Snooker, as usual, tried to sneak away, his tail between his legs. Pip leapt on top of him, and pressed him between his knees.

'Keep his head firm, Rags,' he said, and he tied the handkerchief round Snooker's head with a funny knot sticking up at the top.

'Whatever is that for?' asked Lottie.

'It's to train his ears to grow more close to his head—see?' said Pip. 'All fighting dogs have ears that lie back. But Snooker's ears are a bit too soft.'

'I know,' said Kezia. 'They are always turning inside out. I hate that.'

Snooker lay down, made one feeble effort with his paw to get the handkerchief off, but finding he could not, trailed after the children, shivering with misery.

IX

Pat came swinging along; in his hand he held a little tomahawk that winked in the sun.

'Come with me,' he said to the children, 'and I'll show you how the kings of Ireland chop the head off a duck.'

They drew back—they didn't believe him, and besides, the Trout boys had never seen Pat before.

'Come on now,' he coaxed, smiling and holding out his hand to Kezia.

'Is it a real duck's head? One from the paddock?'

'It is,' said Pat. She put her hand in his hard dry one, and he stuck the tomahawk in his belt and held out the other to Rags. He loved little children.

'I'd better keep hold of Snooker's head if there's going to be any blood about,' said Pip, 'because the sight of blood makes him awfully wild.' He ran ahead dragging Snooker by the handkerchief.

'Do you think we ought to go?' whispered Isabel. 'We haven't asked or anything. Have we?'

At the bottom of the orchard a gate was set in the paling fence. On the other side a steep bank led down to a bridge that spanned the creek, and once up the bank on the other side you were on the fringe of the paddocks. A little old stable in the first paddock had been turned into a fowl house. The fowls had strayed far away across the paddock down to a dumping ground, in a hollow, but the ducks kept close to that part of the creek that flowed under the bridge.

Tall bushes overhung the stream with red leaves and yellow flowers and clusters of blackberries. At some places the stream was wide and shallow, but at others it tumbled into deep little pools with foam at the edges and quivering bubbles. It was in these pools that the big white ducks had made themselves at home, swimming and guzzling along the weedy banks.

Up and down they swam, preening their dazzling breasts, and other ducks with the same dazzling breasts and yellow bills swam upside down with them.

'There is the little Irish navy,' said Pat, 'and look at the old
admiral there with the green neck and the grand little flagstaff on
his tail.'

He pulled a handful of grain from his pocket and began to walk
towards the fowl-house, lazy, his straw hat with the broken crown
pulled over his eyes.

'Lid. Lid—lid—lid—lid——' he called.

'Qua. Qua—qua—qua—qua——' answered the ducks, making
for land, and flapping and scrambling up the bank they streamed
after him in a long waddling line. He coaxed them, pretending to
throw the grain, shaking it in his hands and calling to them until they
swept round him in a white ring.

From far away the fowls heard the clamour and they too came
running across the paddock, their heads thrust forward, their wings
spread, turning in their feet in the silly way fowls run and scolding as
they came.

Then Pat scattered the grain and the greedy ducks began to
gobble. Quickly he stooped, seized two, one under each arm, and
strode across to the children. Their darting heads and round eyes
frightened the children—all except Pip.

'Come on, sillies,' he cried, 'they can't bite. They haven't any
teeth. They've only got those two little holes in their beaks for
breathing through.'

'Will you hold one while I finish with the other?' asked Pat. Pip let
go of Snooker. 'Won't I? Won't I? Give us one. I don't mind how
much he kicks.'

He nearly sobbed with delight when Pat gave the white lump into
his arms.

There was an old stump beside the door of the fowl-house. Pat
grabbed the duck by the legs, laid it flat across the stump, and almost
at the same moment down came the little tomahawk and the duck's
head flew off the stump. Up the blood spurted over the white feathers and over his hand.

When the children saw the blood they were frightened no longer.
They crowded round him and began to scream. Even Isabel leaped
about crying: 'The blood! The blood!' Pip forgot all about his duck.
He simply threw it away from him and shouted, 'I saw it. I saw it,'
and jumped round the wood block.

Rags, with cheeks as white as paper, ran up to the little head, put out a finger as if he wanted to touch it, shrank back again and then again put out a finger. He was shivering all over.

Even Lottie, frightened little Lottie, began to laugh and pointed at the duck and shrieked: 'Look, Kezia, look.'

'Watch it!' shouted Pat. He put down the body and it began to waddle—with only a long spurt of blood where the head had been; it began to pad away without a sound towards the steep bank that led to the stream. . . . That was the crowning wonder.

'Do you see that? Do you see that?' yelled Pip. He ran among the little girls tugging at their pinafores.

'It's like a little engine. It's like a funny little railway engine,' squealed Isabel.

But Kezia suddenly rushed at Pat and flung her arms round his legs and butted her head as hard as she could against his knees.

'Put head back! Put head back!' she screamed.

When he stooped to move her she would not let go or take her head away. She held on as hard as she could and sobbed: 'Head back! Head back!' until it sounded like a loud strange hiccup.

'It's stopped. It's tumbled over. It's dead,' said Pip.

Pat dragged Kezia up into his arms. Her sun-bonnet had fallen back, but she would not let him look at her face. No, she pressed her face into a bone in his shoulder and clasped her arms round his neck.

The children stopped screaming as suddenly as they had begun. They stood round the dead duck. Rags was not frightened of the head any more. He knelt down and stroked it, now.

'I don't think the head is quite dead yet,' he said. 'Do you think it would keep alive if I gave it something to drink?'

But Pip got very cross: 'Bah! You baby.' He whistled to Snooker and went off.

When Isabel went up to Lottie, Lottie snatched away.

'What are you always touching me for, Isabel?'

'There now,' said Pat to Kezia. 'There's the grand little girl.'

She put up her hands and touched his ears. She felt something. Slowly she raised her quivering face and looked. Pat wore little round gold ear-rings. She never knew that men wore ear-rings. She was very much surprised.

'Do they come on and off?' she asked huskily.

X

Up in the house, in the warm tidy kitchen, Alice, the servant girl, was getting the afternoon tea. She was 'dressed'. She had on a black stuff* dress that smelt under the arms, a white apron like a large sheet of paper, and a lace bow pinned on to her hair with two jetty* pins. Also her comfortable carpet slippers were changed for a pair of black leather ones that pinched her corn on her little toe something dreadful. . . .

It was warm in the kitchen. A blow-fly buzzed, a fan of whity steam came out of the kettle, and the lid kept up a rattling jig as the water bubbled. The clock ticked in the warm air, slow and deliberate, like the click of an old woman's knitting needle, and sometimes—for no reason at all, for there wasn't any breeze—the blind swung out and back, tapping the window.

Alice was making water-cress sandwiches. She had a lump of butter on the table, a barracouta* loaf, and the cresses tumbled in a white cloth.

But propped against the butter dish there was a dirty, greasy little book, half unstitched, with curled edges, and while she mashed the butter she read:

'To dream of black-beetles drawing a hearse is bad. Signifies death of one you hold near or dear, either father, husband, brother, son, or intended. If beetles crawl backwards as you watch them it means death from fire or from great height such as flight of stairs, scaffolding, etc.

'Spiders. To dream of spiders creeping over you is good. Signifies large sum of money in near future. Should party be in family way an easy confinement may be expected. But care should be taken in sixth month to avoid eating of probable present of shell fish. . . .'

How many thousand birds I see.

Oh, life. There was Miss Beryl. Alice dropped the knife and slipped the *Dream Book* under the butter dish. But she hadn't time to hide it quite, for Beryl ran into the kitchen and up to the table, and the first thing her eye lighted on were those greasy edges. Alice saw Miss Beryl's meaning little smile and the way she raised her eye-

brows and screwed up her eyes as though she were not quite sure
what that could be. She decided to answer if Miss Beryl should ask
her: 'Nothing as belongs to you, Miss.' But she knew Miss Beryl
would not ask her.

Alice was a mild creature in reality, but she had the most marvellous retorts ready for questions that she knew would never be put
to her. The composing of them and the turning of them over and
over in her mind comforted her just as much as if they'd been
expressed. Really, they kept her alive in places where she'd been
that chivvied she'd been afraid to go to bed at night with a box of
matches on the chair in case she bit the tops off in her sleep, as you
might say.

'Oh, Alice,' said Miss Beryl. 'There's one extra to tea, so heat a
plate of yesterday's scones, please. And put on the Victoria sandwich
as well as the coffee cake. And don't forget to put little doyleys* under
the plates—will you? You did yesterday, you know, and the tea
looked so ugly and common. And, Alice, don't put that dreadful old
pink and green cosy on the afternoon teapot again. That is only for
the mornings. Really, I think it ought to be kept for the kitchen—it's
so shabby, and quite smelly. Put on the Japanese one. You quite
understand, don't you?'

Miss Beryl had finished.

That sing aloud from every tree . . .

she sang as she left the kitchen, very pleased with her firm handling
of Alice.

Oh, Alice was wild. She wasn't one to mind being told, but there
was something in the way Miss Beryl had of speaking to her that she
couldn't stand. Oh, that she couldn't. It made her curl up inside, as
you might say, and she fair trembled. But what Alice really hated
Miss Beryl for was that she made her feel low. She talked to Alice in a
special voice as though she wasn't quite all there; and she never lost
her temper with her—never. Even when Alice dropped anything or
forgot anything important Miss Beryl seemed to have expected it to
happen.

'If you please, Mrs Burnell,' said an imaginary Alice, as she
buttered the scones, 'I'd rather not take my orders from Miss
Beryl. I may be only a common servant girl as doesn't know how to
play the guitar, but . . . .'

This last thrust pleased her so much that she quite recovered her temper.

'The only thing to do,' she heard, as she opened the dining-room door, 'is to cut the sleeves out entirely and just have a broad band of black velvet over the shoulders instead. . . .'

XI

The white duck did not look as if it had ever had a head when Alice placed it in front of Stanley Burnell that night. It lay, in beautifully basted resignation, on a blue dish—its legs tied together with a piece of string and a wreath of little balls of stuffing round it.

It was hard to say which of the two, Alice or the duck, looked the better basted; they were both such a rich colour and they both had the same air of gloss and strain. But Alice was fiery red and the duck a Spanish mahogany.

Burnell ran his eye along the edge of the carving knife. He prided himself very much upon his carving, upon making a first-class job of it. He hated seeing a woman carve; they were always too slow and they never seemed to care what the meat looked like afterwards. Now he did; he took a real pride in cutting delicate shaves of cold beef, little wads of mutton, just the right thickness, and in dividing a chicken or a duck with nice precision. . . .

'Is this the first of the home products?' he asked, knowing perfectly well that it was.

'Yes, the butcher did not come. We have found out that he only calls twice a week.'

But there was no need to apologise. It was a superb bird. It wasn't meat at all, but a kind of very superior jelly. 'My father would say,' said Burnell, 'this must have been one of those birds whose mother played to it in infancy upon the German flute. And the sweet strains of the dulcet instrument acted with such effect upon the infant mind. . . . Have some more, Beryl? You and I are the only ones in this house with a real feeling for food. I'm perfectly willing to state, in a court of law, if necessary, that I love good food.'

Tea was served in the drawing-room, and Beryl, who for some reason had been very charming to Stanley ever since he came home, suggested a game of crib.* They sat at a little table near one of the open windows. Mrs Fairfield disappeared, and Linda lay in a rocking-chair, her arms above her head, rocking to and fro.

'You don't want the light—do you, Linda?' said Beryl. She moved the tall lamp so that she sat under its soft light.

How remote they looked, those two, from where Linda sat and rocked. The green table, the polished cards, Stanley's big hands and Beryl's tiny ones, all seemed to be part of one mysterious movement. Stanley himself, big and solid, in his dark suit, took his ease, and Beryl tossed her bright head and pouted. Round her throat she wore an unfamiliar velvet ribbon. It changed her, somehow—altered the shape of her face—but it was charming, Linda decided. The room smelled of lilies; there were two big jars of arums in the fire-place.

'Fifteen two—fifteen four—and a pair is six and a run of three is nine,' said Stanley, so deliberately, he might have been counting sheep.

'I've nothing but two pairs,' said Beryl, exaggerating her woe because she knew how he loved winning.

The cribbage pegs were like two little people going up the road together, turning round the sharp corner, and coming down the road again. They were pursuing each other. They did not so much want to get ahead as to keep near enough to talk—to keep near, perhaps that was all.

But no, there was always one who was impatient and hopped away as the other came up, and would not listen. Perhaps the white peg was frightened of the red one, or perhaps he was cruel and would not give the red one a chance to speak. . . .

In the front of her dress Beryl wore a bunch of pansies, and once when the little pegs were side by side, she bent over and the pansies dropped out and covered them.

'What a shame,' said she, picking up the pansies. 'Just as they had a chance to fly into each other's arms.'

'Farewell, my girl,' laughed Stanley, and away the red peg hopped.

The drawing-room was long and narrow with glass doors that gave on to the verandah. It had a cream paper with a pattern of gilt roses, and the furniture, which had belonged to old Mrs Fairfield, was dark and plain. A little piano stood against the wall with yellow pleated silk let into the carved front. Above it hung an oil painting by Beryl of a large cluster of surprised looking clematis. Each flower was the size of a small saucer, with a centre like an astonished eye fringed in black. But the room was not finished yet. Stanley had set his heart on a Chesterfield* and two decent chairs. Linda liked it best as it was. . . .

Two big moths flew in through the window and round and round the circle of lamplight.

'Fly away before it is too late. Fly out again.'

Round and round they flew; they seemed to bring the silence and the moonlight in with them on their silent wings. . . .

'I've two kings,' said Stanley. 'Any good?'

'Quite good,' said Beryl.

Linda stopped rocking and got up. Stanley looked across. 'Anything the matter, darling?'

'No, nothing. I'm going to find mother.'

She went out of the room and standing at the foot of the stairs she called, but her mother's voice answered her from the verandah.

The moon that Lottie and Kezia had seen from the storeman's wagon was full, and the house, the garden, the old woman and Linda—all were bathed in dazzling light.

'I have been looking at the aloe,' said Mrs Fairfield. 'I believe it is going to flower this year. Look at the top there. Are those buds, or is it only an effect of light?'

As they stood on the steps, the high grassy bank on which the aloe rested rose up like a wave, and the aloe seemed to ride upon it like a ship with the oars lifted. Bright moonlight hung upon the lifted oars like water, and on the green wave glittered the dew.

'Do you feel it, too,' said Linda, and she spoke to her mother with the special voice that women use at night to each other as though they spoke in their sleep or from some hollow cave—'Don't you feel that it is coming towards us?'

She dreamed that she was caught up out of the cold water into the ship with the lifted oars and the budding mast. Now the oars fell striking quickly, quickly. They rowed far away over the top of the garden trees, the paddocks and the dark bush beyond. Ah, she heard herself cry: 'Faster! Faster!' to those who were rowing.

How much more real this dream was than that they should go back to the house where the sleeping children lay and where Stanley and Beryl played cribbage.

'I believe those are buds,' said she. 'Let us go down into the garden, mother. I like that aloe. I like it more than anything here.

And I am sure I shall remember it long after I've forgotten all the other things.'

She put her hand on her mother's arm and they walked down the steps, round the island and on to the main drive that led to the front gates.

Looking at it from below she could see the long sharp thorns that edged the aloe leaves, and at the sight of them her heart grew hard. . . . She particularly liked the long sharp thorns. . . . Nobody would dare to come near the ship or to follow after.

'Not even my Newfoundland dog,' thought she, 'that I'm so fond of in the daytime.'

For she really was fond of him; she loved and admired and respected him tremendously. Oh, better than anyone else in the world. She knew him through and through. He was the soul of truth and decency, and for all his practical experience he was awfully simple, easily pleased and easily hurt. . . .

If only he wouldn't jump at her so, and bark so loudly, and watch her with such eager, loving eyes. He was too strong for her; she had always hated things that rush at her, from a child. There were times when he was frightening—really frightening. When she just had not screamed at the top of her voice: 'You are killing me.' And at those times she had longed to say the most coarse, hateful things. . . .

'You know I'm very delicate. You know as well as I do that my heart is affected, and the doctor has told you I may die any moment. I have had three great lumps of children already. . . .'

Yes, yes, it was true. Linda snatched her hand from mother's arm. For all her love and respect and admiration she hated him. And how tender he always was after times like those, how submissive, how thoughtful. He would do anything for her; he longed to serve her. . . . Linda heard herself saying in a weak voice:

'Stanley, would you light a candle?'

And she heard his joyful voice answer: 'Of course I will, my darling,' and he leapt out of bed as though he were going to leap at the moon for her.

It had never been so plain to her as it was at this moment. There were all her feelings for him, sharp and defined, one as true as the other. And there was this other, this hatred, just as real as the rest. She could have done her feelings up in little packets and given them to Stanley. She longed to hand him that last one, for a surprise. She could see his eyes as he opened that. . . .

She hugged her folded arms and began to laugh silently. How absurd life was—it was laughable, simply laughable. And why this mania of hers to keep alive at all? For it really was a mania, she thought, mocking and laughing.

'What am I guarding myself for so preciously? I shall go on having children and Stanley will go on making money and the children and the gardens will grow bigger and bigger, with whole fleets of aloes in them for me to choose from.'

She had been walking with her head bent, looking at nothing. Now she looked up and about her. They were standing by the red and white camellia trees. Beautiful were the rich dark leaves spangled with light and the round flowers that perch among them like red and white birds. Linda pulled a piece of verbena and crumpled it, and held her hands to her mother.

'Delicious,' said the old woman. 'Are you cold, child? Are you trembling? Yes, your hands are cold. We had better go back to the house.'

'What have you been thinking about?' said Linda. 'Tell me.'

'I haven't really been thinking of anything. I wondered as we passed the orchard what the fruit trees were like and whether we should be able to make much jam this autumn. There are splendid healthy currant bushes in the vegetable garden. I noticed them to-day. I should like to see those pantry shelves thoroughly well stocked with our own jam. . . .'

XII

'My Darling Nan,

Don't think me a piggy wig because I haven't written before. I haven't had a moment, dear, and even now I feel so exhausted that I can hardly hold a pen.

Well, the dreadful deed is done. We have actually left the giddy whirl of town, and I can't see how we shall ever go back again, for my brother-in-law has bought this house 'lock, stock and barrel',* to use his own words.

In a way, of course, it is an awful relief, for he has been threatening to take a place in the country ever since I've lived with them—and I must say the house and garden are awfully nice—a million times better than that awful cubby-hole in town.

But buried, my dear. Buried isn't the word.

We have got neighbours, but they are only farmers—big louts of boys who seem to be milking all day, and two dreadful females with rabbit teeth who brought us some scones when we were moving and said they would be pleased to help. But my sister who lives a mile away doesn't know a soul here, so I am sure we never shall. It's pretty certain nobody will ever come out from town to see us, because though there is a bus it's an awful old rattling thing with black leather sides that any decent person would rather die than ride in for six miles.

Such is life. It's a sad ending for poor little B. I'll get to be a most awful frump in a year or two and come and see you in a mackintosh and a sailor hat tied on with a white china silk motor veil. So pretty.

Stanley says that now we are settled—for after the most awful week of my life we really are settled—he is going to bring out a couple of men from the club on Saturday afternoons for tennis. In fact, two are promised as a great treat to-day. But, my dear, if you could see Stanley's men from the club . . . rather fattish, the type who look frightfully indecent without waistcoats—always with toes that turn in rather—so conspicuous when you are walking about a court in white shoes. And they are pulling up their trousers every minute—don't you know—and whacking at imaginary things with their rackets.

I used to play with them at the club last summer, and I am sure you will know the type when I tell you that after I'd been there about three times they all called me Miss Beryl. It's a weary world. Of course mother simply loves the place, but then I suppose when I am mother's age I shall be content to sit in the sun and shell peas into a basin. But I'm not–not–not.

What Linda thinks about the whole affair, per usual, I haven't the slightest idea. Mysterious as ever. . . .

My dear, you know that white satin dress of mine. I have taken the sleeves out entirely, put bands of black velvet across the shoulders and two big red poppies off my dear sister's *chapeau*.* It is a great success, though when I shall wear it I do not know.'

Beryl sat writing this letter at a little table in her room. In a way, of course, it was all perfectly true, but in another way it was all the greatest rubbish and she didn't believe a word of it. No, that wasn't true. She felt all those things, but she didn't really feel them like that.

It was her other self who had written that letter. It not only bored, it rather disgusted her real self.

'Flippant and silly,' said her real self. Yet she knew that she'd send it and she'd always write that kind of twaddle to Nan Pym. In fact, it was a very mild example of the kind of letter she generally wrote.

Beryl leaned her elbows on the table and read it through again. The voice of the letter seemed to come up to her from the page. It was faint already, like a voice heard over the telephone, high, gushing, with something bitter in the sound. Oh, she detested it to-day.

'You've always got so much animation,' said Nan Pym. 'That's why men are so keen on you.' And she had added, rather mournfully, for men were not at all keen on Nan, who was a solid kind of girl, with fat hips and a high colour—'I can't understand how you can keep it up. But it is your nature, I suppose.'

What rot. What nonsense. It wasn't her nature at all. Good heavens, if she had ever been her real self with Nan Pym, Nannie would have jumped out of the window with surprise. . . . My dear, you know that white satin of mine. . . . Beryl slammed the letter-case to.

She jumped up and half unconsciously, half consciously she drifted over to the looking-glass.

There stood a slim girl in white—a white serge* skirt, a white silk blouse, and a leather belt drawn in very tightly at her tiny waist.

Her face was heart-shaped, wide at the brows and with a pointed chin—but not too pointed. Her eyes, her eyes were perhaps her best feature; they were such a strange uncommon colour—greeny blue with little gold points in them.

She had fine black eyebrows and long lashes—so long, that when they lay on her cheeks you positively caught the light in them, someone or other had told her.

Her mouth was rather large. Too large? No, not really. Her under-lip protruded a little; she had a way of sucking it in that somebody else had told her was awfully fascinating.

Her nose was her least satisfactory feature. Not that it was really ugly. But it was not half as fine as Linda's. Linda really had a perfect little nose. Hers spread rather—not badly. And in all probability she exaggerated the spreadiness of it just because it was her nose, and she was so awfully critical of herself. She pinched it with a thumb and first finger and made a little face. . . .

Lovely, lovely hair. And such a mass of it. It had the colour of fresh fallen leaves, brown and red with a glint of yellow. When she did it in a long plait she felt it on her backbone like a long snake. She loved to feel the weight of it dragging her head back, and she loved to feel it loose, covering her bare arms. 'Yes, my dear, there is no doubt about it, you really are a lovely little thing.'

At the words her bosom lifted; she took a long breath of delight, half closing her eyes.

But even as she looked the smile faded from her lips and eyes. Oh God, there she was, back again, playing the same old game. False—false as ever. False as when she'd written to Nan Pym. False even when she was alone with herself, now.

What had that creature in the glass to do with her, and why was she staring? She dropped down to one side of her bed and buried her face in her arms.

'Oh,' she cried, 'I am so miserable—so frightfully miserable. I know that I'm silly and spiteful and vain; I'm always acting a part. I'm never my real self for a moment.' And plainly, plainly, she saw her false self running up and down the stairs, laughing a special trilling laugh if they had visitors, standing under the lamp if a man came to dinner, so that he should see the light on her hair, pouting and pretending to be a little girl when she was asked to play the guitar. Why? She even kept it up for Stanley's benefit. Only last night when he was reading the paper her false self had stood beside him and leaned against his shoulder on purpose. Hadn't she put her hand over his, pointing out something so that he should see how white her hand was beside his brown one.

How despicable! Despicable! Her heart was cold with rage. 'It's marvellous how you keep it up,' said she to the false self. But then it was only because she was so miserable—so miserable. If she had been happy and leading her own life, her false life would cease to be. She saw the real Beryl—a shadow . . . a shadow. Faint and unsubstantial she shone. What was there of her except the radiance? And for what tiny moments she was really she. Beryl could almost remember every one of them. At those times she had felt: 'Life is rich and mysterious and good, and I am rich and mysterious and good, too.' Shall I ever be that Beryl for ever? Shall I? How can I? And was there ever a time when I did not have a false self? . . . But just as she had got that far she heard the sound of little steps running along the passage; the door handle rattled. Kezia came in.

'Aunt Beryl, mother says will you please come down? Father is home with a man and lunch is ready.'

Botheration! How she had crumpled her skirt, kneeling in that idiotic way.

'Very well, Kezia.' She went over to the dressing table and powdered her nose.

Kezia crossed too, and unscrewed a little pot of cream and sniffed it. Under her arm she carried a very dirty calico cat.

When Aunt Beryl ran out of the room she sat the cat up on the dressing table and stuck the top of the cream jar over its ear.

'Now look at yourself,' said she sternly.

The calico cat was so overcome by the sight that it toppled over backwards and bumped and bumped on to the floor. And the top of the cream jar flew through the air and rolled like a penny in a round on the linoleum—and did not break.

But for Kezia it had broken the moment it flew through the air, and she picked it up, hot all over, and put it back on the dressing table.

Then she tip-toed away, far too quickly and airily. . . .

MR REGINALD PEACOCK'S DAY

If there was one thing that he hated more than another it was the way she had of waking him in the morning. She did it on purpose, of course. It was her way of establishing her grievance for the day, and he was not going to let her know how successful it was. But really, really, to wake a sensitive person like that was positively dangerous! It took him hours to get over it—simply hours. She came into the room buttoned up in an overall, with a handkerchief over her head— thereby proving that she had been up herself and slaving since dawn—and called in a low, warning voice: 'Reginald!'

'Eh! What! What's that? What's the matter?'

'It's time to get up; it's half-past eight.' And out she went, shutting the door quietly after her, to gloat over her triumph, he supposed.

He rolled over in the big bed, his heart still beating in quick, dull throbs, and with every throb he felt his energy escaping him, his— his inspiration for the day stifling under those thudding blows. It seemed that she took a malicious delight in making life more difficult for him than—Heaven knows—it was, by denying him his rights as an artist, by trying to drag him down to her level. What was the matter with her? What the hell did she want? Hadn't he three times as many pupils now as when they were first married, earned three times as much, paid for every stick and stone that they possessed, and now had begun to shell out for Adrian's kindergarten? . . . And had he ever reproached her for not having a penny to her name? Never a word—never a sign! The truth was that once you married a woman she became insatiable, and the truth was that nothing was more fatal for an artist than marriage, at any rate until he was well over forty. . . . Why had he married her? He asked himself this question on an average about three times a day, but he never could answer it satisfactorily. She had caught him at a weak moment, when the first plunge into reality had bewildered and overwhelmed him for a time. Looking back, he saw a pathetic, youthful creature, half child, half wild untamed bird, totally incompetent to cope with bills and creditors and all the sordid details of existence. Well—she had done her best to clip his wings, if that was any satisfaction for her, and she could congratulate herself on the success of this early morning trick. One ought to wake exquisitely, reluctantly, he thought, slipping down in the warm bed. He began to imagine a series of enchanting scenes which ended with his latest, most charming pupil putting her bare, scented arms round his neck, and covering him with her long, perfumed hair. 'Awake, my love!' . . .

As was his daily habit, while the bath water ran, Reginald Peacock tried his voice.

> When her mother tends her before the laughing mirror,
> Looping up her laces, tying up her hair,

he sang, softly at first, listening to the quality, nursing his voice until he came to the third line:

> Often she thinks, were this wild thing wedded . . .*

and upon the word 'wedded' he burst into such a shout of triumph that the tooth-glass on the bathroom shelf trembled and even the bath tap seemed to gush stormy applause. . . .

Well, there was nothing wrong with his voice, he thought, leaping into the bath and soaping his soft, pink body all over with a loofah shaped like a fish. He could fill Covent Garden* with it! '*Wedded*,' he shouted again, seizing the towel with a magnificent operatic gesture, and went on singing while he rubbed as though he had been Lohengrin tipped out by an unwary Swan and drying himself in the greatest haste before that tiresome Elsa* came along. . . .

Back in his bedroom, he pulled the blind up with a jerk, and standing upon the pale square of sunlight that lay upon the carpet like a sheet of cream blotting-paper, he began to do his exercises—deep breathing, bending forward and back, squatting like a frog and shooting out his legs—for if there was one thing he had a horror of it was of getting fat, and men in his profession had a dreadful tendency that way. However, there was no sign of it at present. He was, he decided, just right, just in good proportion. In fact, he could not help a thrill of satisfaction when he saw himself in the glass, dressed in a morning coat, dark grey trousers, grey socks and a black tie with a silver thread in it. Not that he was vain—he couldn't stand vain men—no; the sight of himself gave him a thrill of purely artistic satisfaction. '*Voilà tout!*'* said he, passing his hand over his sleek hair.

That little, easy French phrase blown so lightly from his lips, like a whiff of smoke, reminded him that someone had asked him again, the evening before, if he was English. People seemed to find it impossible to believe that he hadn't some Southern blood. True, there was an emotional quality in his singing that had nothing of the John Bull* in it. . . . The door-handle rattled and turned round and round. Adrian's head popped through.

'Please, father, mother says breakfast is quite ready, please.'

'Very well,' said Reginald. Then, just as Adrian disappeared: 'Adrian!'

'Yes, father.'

'You haven't said "good morning".'

A few months ago Reginald had spent a weekend in a very aristo-cratic family, where the father received his little sons in the morning and shook hands with them. Reginald thought the practice charm-ing, and introduced it immediately, but Adrian felt dreadfully silly at having to shake hands with his own father every morning. And why did his father always sort of sing to him instead of talk? . . .

In excellent temper, Reginald walked into the dining-room and sat down before a pile of letters, a copy of *The Times*, and a little covered dish. He glanced at the letters and then at his breakfast. There were two thin slices of bacon and one egg.

'Don't you want any bacon?' he asked.

'No, I prefer a cold baked apple. I don't feel the need of bacon every morning.'

Now, did she mean that there was no need for him to have bacon every morning, either, and that she grudged having to cook it for him?

'If you don't want to cook the breakfast,' said he, 'why don't you keep a servant? You know we can afford one, and you know how I loathe to see my wife doing the work. Simply because all the women we have had in the past have been failures, and utterly upset my regime, and made it almost impossible for me to have any pupils here, you've given up trying to find a decent woman. It's not impossible to train a servant—is it? I mean, it doesn't require genius?'

'But I prefer to do the work myself; it makes life so much more peaceful. . . . Run along, Adrian darling, and get ready for school.'

'Oh no, that's not it!' Reginald pretended to smile. 'You do the work yourself, because, for some extraordinary reason, you love to humiliate me. Objectively, you may not know that, but, subjectively, it's the case.' This last remark so delighted him that he cut open an envelope as gracefully as if he had been on the stage. . . .

'Dear Mr Peacock,

I feel I cannot go to sleep until I have thanked you again for the wonderful joy your singing gave me this evening. Quite unforgettable. You make me wonder, as I have not wondered since I was a girl, if this is *all*. I mean, if this ordinary world is *all*. If there is not, perhaps, for those of us who understand, divine beauty and richness awaiting us if we only have the *courage* to see it. And to make it ours. . . . The house is so quiet. I wish you were here now that I might thank you in person. You are doing a great thing. You are teaching the world to escape from life!

Yours, most sincerely,

ÆNONE FELL.

P.S.—I am in every afternoon this week. . . .'

The letter was scrawled in violet ink on thick, handmade paper. Vanity, that bright bird, lifted its wings again, lifted them until he felt his breast would break.

'Oh well, don't let us quarrel,' said he, and actually flung out a hand to his wife.

But she was not great enough to respond.

'I must hurry and take Adrian to school,' said she. 'Your room is quite ready for you.'

Very well—very well—let there be open war between them! But he was hanged if he'd be the first to make it up again!

He walked up and down his room, and was not calm again until he heard the outer door close upon Adrian and his wife. Of course, if this went on, he would have to make some other arrangement. That was obvious. Tied and bound like this, how could he help the world to escape from life? He opened the piano and looked up his pupils for the morning. Miss Betty Brittle, the Countess Wilkowska and Miss Marian Morrow. They were charming, all three.

Punctually at half-past ten the door-bell rang. He went to the door. Miss Betty Brittle was there, dressed in white, with her music in a blue silk case.

'I'm afraid I'm early,' she said, blushing and shy, and she opened her big blue eyes very wide. 'Am I?'

'Not at all, dear lady. I am only too charmed,' said Reginald. 'Won't you come in?'

'It's such a heavenly morning,' said Miss Brittle. 'I walked across the Park. The flowers were too marvellous.'

'Well, think about them while you sing your exercises,' said Reginald, sitting down at the piano. 'It will give your voice colour and warmth.'

Oh, what an enchanting idea! What a *genius* Mr Peacock was. She parted her pretty lips, and began to sing like a pansy.

'Very good, very good, indeed,' said Reginald, playing chords that would waft a hardened criminal to heaven. 'Make the notes round. Don't be afraid. Linger over them, breathe them like a perfume.'

How pretty she looked, standing there in her white frock, her little blonde head tilted, showing her milky throat.

'Do you ever practise before a glass?' asked Reginald. 'You ought to, you know; it makes the lips more flexible. Come over here.'

They went over to the mirror and stood side by side.

'Now sing moo-e-koo-e-oo-e-a!'

But she broke down, and blushed more brightly than ever.

'Oh,' she cried, 'I can't. It makes me feel so silly. It makes me want to laugh. I do look so absurd!'

'No, you don't. Don't be afraid,' said Reginald, but laughed, too, very kindly. 'Now, try again!'

The lesson simply flew, and Betty Brittle quite got over her shyness.

'When can I come again?' she asked, tying the music up again in the blue silk case. 'I want to take as many lessons as I can just now. Oh, Mr. Peacock, I *do* enjoy them so much. May I come the day after to-morrow?'

'Dear lady, I shall be only too charmed,' said Reginald, bowing her out.

Glorious girl! And when they had stood in front of the mirror, her white sleeve had just touched his black one. He could feel—yes, he could actually feel a warm glowing spot, and he stroked it. She loved her lessons. His wife came in.

'Reginald, can you let me have some money? I must pay the dairy. And will you be in for dinner to-night?'

'Yes, you know I'm singing at Lord Timbuck's at half-past nine. Can you make me some clear soup, with an egg in it?'

'Yes. And the money, Reginald. It's eight and sixpence.'

'Surely that's very heavy—isn't it?'

'No, it's just what it ought to be. And Adrian must have milk.'

There she was—off again. Now she was standing up for Adrian against him.

'I have not the slightest desire to deny my child a proper amount of milk,' said he. 'Here is ten shillings.'

The door-bell rang. He went to the door.

'Oh,' said the Countess Wilkowska, 'the stairs. I have not a breath.' And she put her hand over her heart as she followed him into the music-room. She was all in black, with a little black hat with a floating veil—violets in her bosom.

'Do not make me sing exercises, to-day,' she cried, throwing out her hands in her delightful foreign way. 'No, to-day, I want only to sing songs. . . . And may I take off my violets? They fade so soon.'

'They fade so soon—they fade so soon,' played Reginald on the piano.

'May I put them here?' asked the Countess, dropping them in a little vase that stood in front of one of Reginald's photographs.

'Dear lady, I should be only too charmed!'

She began to sing, and all was well until she came to the phrase: 'You love me. Yes, I *know* you love me!' Down dropped his hands from the keyboard, he wheeled round, facing her.

'No, no; that's not good enough. You can do better than that,' cried Reginald ardently. 'You must sing as if you were in love. Listen; let me try and show you.' And he sang.

'Oh, yes, yes. I see what you mean,' stammered the little Countess. 'May I try it again?'

'Certainly. Do not be afraid. Let yourself go. Confess yourself. Make proud surrender!' he called above the music. And she sang.

'Yes; better that time. But I still feel you are capable of more. Try it with me. There must be a kind of exultant defiance as well— don't you feel?' And they sang together. Ah! now she was sure she understood. 'May I try once again?'

'You love me. Yes, I *know* you love me.'

The lesson was over before that phrase was quite perfect. The little foreign hands trembled as they put the music together.

'And you are forgetting your violets,' said Reginald softly.

'Yes, I think I will forget them,' said the Countess, biting her underlip. What fascinating ways these foreign women have!

'And you will come to my house on Sunday and make music?' she asked.

'Dear lady, I shall be only too charmed!' said Reginald.

> Weep ye no more, sad fountains
> Why need ye flow so fast?*

sang Miss Marian Morrow, but her eyes filled with tears and her chin trembled.

'Don't sing just now,' said Reginald. 'Let me play it for you.' He played so softly.

'Is there anything the matter?' asked Reginald. 'You're not quite happy this morning.'

No, she wasn't; she was awfully miserable.

'You don't care to tell me what it is?'

It really was nothing particular. She had those moods sometimes when life seemed almost unbearable.

'Ah, I know,' he said; 'if I could only help!'

'But you do; you do! Oh, if it were not for my lessons I don't feel I could go on.'

'Sit down in the arm-chair and smell the violets and let me sing to you. It will do you just as much good as a lesson.'

Why weren't all men like Mr Peacock?

'I wrote a poem after the concert last night—just about what I felt. Of course, it wasn't *personal*. May I send it to you?'

'Dear lady, I should be only too charmed!'

By the end of the afternoon he was quite tired and lay down on a sofa to rest his voice before dressing. The door of his room was open. He could hear Adrian and his wife talking in the dining-room.

'Do you know what that teapot reminds me of, Mummy? It reminds me of a little sitting-down kitten.'

'Does it, Mr Absurdity?'

Reginald dozed. The telephone bell woke him.

'Ænone Fell is speaking. Mr Peacock, I have just heard that you are singing at Lord Timbuck's to-night. Will you dine with me, and we can go on together afterwards?' And the words of his reply dropped like flowers down the telephone.

'Dear lady, I should be only too charmed.'

What a triumphant evening! The little dinner *tête-à-tête* with Ænone Fell, the drive to Lord Timbuck's in her white motor-car, when she thanked him again for the unforgettable joy. Triumph upon triumph! And Lord Timbuck's champagne simply flowed.

'Have some more champagne, Peacock,' said Lord Timbuck. Peacock, you notice—not Mr Peacock—but Peacock, as if he were one of them. And wasn't he? He was an artist. He could sway them all. And wasn't he teaching them all to escape from life? How he sang! And as he sang, as in a dream he saw their feathers and their flowers and their fans, offered to him, laid before him, like a huge bouquet.

'Have another glass of wine, Peacock.'

'I could have any one I liked by lifting a finger,' thought Peacock, positively staggering home.

But as he let himself into the dark flat his marvellous sense of elation began to ebb away. He turned up the light in the bedroom. His wife lay asleep, squeezed over to her side of the bed. He remembered suddenly how she had said when he had told her he was going out to dinner: 'You might have let me know before!' And how he had answered: 'Can't you possibly speak to me without offending against even good manners?' It was incredible, he thought, that she cared so little for him—incredible that she wasn't interested in the slightest in his triumphs and his artistic career. When so many women in her place would have given their eyes. . . . Yes, he knew it. . . . Why not acknowledge it? . . . And there she lay, an enemy, even in her sleep. . . . Must it ever be thus? he thought, the champagne still working. Ah, if we only were friends, how much I could tell her now! About this evening; even about Timbuck's manner to me, and all that they said to me and so on and so on. If only I felt that she was here to come back to—that I could confide in her—and so on and so on.

In his emotion he pulled off his evening boot and simply hurled it in the corner. The noise woke his wife with a terrible start. She sat up, pushing back her hair. And he suddenly decided to have one more try to treat her as a friend, to tell her everything, to win her. Down he sat on the side of the bed, and seized one of her hands. But of all those splendid things he had to say, not one could he utter. For some fiendish reason, the only words he could get out were: 'Dear lady, I should be so charmed—so charmed!'

FEUILLE D'ALBUM

He really was an impossible person. Too shy altogether. With absolutely nothing to say for himself. And such a weight. Once he was in your studio he never knew when to go, but would sit on and on until you nearly screamed, and burned to throw something enormous after him when he did finally blush his way out—something like the tortoise stove.* The strange thing was that at first sight he looked most interesting. Everybody agreed about that. You would drift into the café one evening and there you would see, sitting in a corner, with a glass of coffee in front of him, a thin, dark boy, wearing a blue jersey with a little grey flannel jacket buttoned over it. And somehow that blue jersey and the grey jacket with the sleeves that were too short gave him the air of a boy that has made up his mind to run away to sea. Who has run away, in fact, and will get up in a moment and sling a knotted handkerchief containing his nightshirt and his mother's picture on the end of a stick, and walk out into the night and be drowned. . . . Stumble over the wharf edge on his way to the ship, even. . . . He had black close-cropped hair, grey eyes with long lashes, white cheeks and a mouth pouting as though he were determined not to cry. . . . How could one resist him? Oh, one's heart was wrung at sight. And, as if that were not enough, there was his trick of blushing. . . . Whenever the waiter came near him he turned crimson—he might have been just out of prison and the waiter in the know. . . .

'Who is he, my dear? Do you know?'

'Yes. His name is Ian French. Painter. Awfully clever, they say. Someone started by giving him a mother's tender care. She asked him how often he heard from home, whether he had enough blankets on his bed, how much milk he drank a day. But when she went round to his studio to give an eye to his socks, she rang and rang, and though she could have sworn she heard someone breathing inside, the door was not answered. . . . Hopeless!'

Someone else decided that he ought to fall in love. She summoned him to her side, called him 'boy', leaned over him so that he might smell the enchanting perfume of her hair, took his arm, told him how marvellous life could be if one only had the courage, and went round to his studio one evening and rang and rang. . . . Hopeless.

'What the poor boy really wants is thoroughly rousing,' said a third. So off they went to cafés and cabarets, little dances, places where you drank something that tasted like tinned apricot juice, but cost twenty-seven shillings a bottle and was called champagne, other places, too thrilling for words, where you sat in the most awful gloom, and where some one had always been shot the night before. But he did not turn a hair. Only once he got very drunk, but instead of blossoming forth, there he sat, stony, with two spots of red on his cheeks, like, my dear, yes, the dead image of that rag-time thing they were playing, like a 'Broken Doll'. But when she took him back to his studio he had quite recovered, and said 'good night' to her in the street below, as though they had walked home from church together. . . . Hopeless.

After heaven knows how many more attempts—for the spirit of kindness dies very hard in women—they gave him up. Of course, they were still perfectly charming, and asked him to their shows, and spoke to him in the café, but that was all. When one is an artist one has no time simply for people who won't respond. Has one?

'And besides I really think there must be something rather fishy somewhere . . . don't you? It can't all be as innocent as it looks! Why come to Paris if you want to be a daisy in the field? No, I'm not suspicious. But—'

He lived at the top of a tall mournful building overlooking the river. One of those buildings that look so romantic on rainy nights and moonlight nights, when the shutters are shut, and the heavy door, and the sign advertising 'a little apartment to let immediately' gleams forlorn beyond words. One of those buildings that smell so unromantic all the year round, and where the concierge lives in a glass cage on the ground floor, wrapped up in a filthy shawl, stirring something in a saucepan and ladling out tit-bits to the swollen old dog lolling on a bead cushion. . . . Perched up in the air the studio had a wonderful view. The two big windows faced the water; he could see the boats and the barges swinging up and down, and the fringe of an island planted with trees, like a round bouquet. The side window looked across to another house, shabbier still and smaller, and down below there was a flower market. You could see the tops of huge umbrellas, with frills of bright flowers escaping from them, booths covered with striped awning where they sold plants in boxes and clumps of wet gleaming palms in terra-cotta jars. Among the flowers the old women scuttled from side to side, like crabs. Really there was no need for him to go out. If he sat at the window until his white beard fell over the sill he still would have found something to draw. . . .

How surprised those tender women would have been if they had managed to force the door. For he kept his studio as neat as a pin.* Everything was arranged to form a pattern, a little 'still life' as it were—the saucepans with their lids on the wall behind the gas stove, the bowl of eggs, milk jug and teapot on the shelf, the books and the lamp with the crinkly paper shade on the table. An Indian curtain that had a fringe of red leopards marching round it covered his bed by day, and on the wall beside the bed on a level with your eyes when you were lying down there was a small neatly printed notice: GET UP AT ONCE.

Every day was much the same. While the light was good he slaved at his painting, then cooked his meals and tidied up the place. And in the evenings he went off to the café, or sat at home reading or making out the most complicated list of expenses headed: 'What I ought to be able to do it on', and ending with a sworn statement . . . 'I swear not to exceed this amount for next month. Signed, Ian French.'

Nothing very fishy about this; but those far-seeing women were quite right. It wasn't all.

One evening he was sitting at the side window eating some prunes and throwing the stones on to the tops of the huge umbrellas in the deserted flower market. It had been raining—the first real spring rain of the year had fallen—a bright spangle hung on everything, and the air smelled of buds and moist earth. Many voices sounding languid and content rang out in the dusky air, and the people who had come to close their windows and fasten the shutters leaned out instead. Down below in the market the trees were peppered with new green. What kind of trees were they? he wondered. And now came the lamplighter.* He stared at the house across the way, the small, shabby house, and suddenly, as if in answer to his gaze, two wings of windows opened and a girl came out on to the tiny balcony carrying a pot of daffodils. She was a strangely thin girl in a dark pinafore, with a pink handkerchief tied over her hair. Her sleeves were rolled up almost to her shoulders and her slender arms shone against the dark stuff.

'Yes, it is quite warm enough. It will do them good,' she said, putting down the pot and turning to some one in the room inside. As she turned she put her hands up to the handkerchief and tucked away some wisps of hair. She looked down at the deserted market and up at the sky, but where he sat there might have been a hollow in the air. She simply did not see the house opposite. And then she disappeared.

His heart fell out of the side window of his studio, and down to the balcony of the house opposite—buried itself in the pot of daffodils under the half-opened buds and spears of green. . . . That room with the balcony was the sitting-room, and the one next door to it was the kitchen. He heard the clatter of the dishes as she washed up after supper, and then she came to the window, knocked a little mop against the ledge, and hung it on a nail to dry. She never sang or unbraided her hair, or held out her arms to the moon as young girls are supposed to do. And she always wore the same dark pinafore and the pink handkerchief over her hair. . . . Whom did she live with? Nobody else came to those two windows, and yet she was always talking to some one in the room. Her mother, he decided, was an invalid. They took in sewing. The father was dead. . . . He had been a journalist—very pale, with long moustaches, and a piece of black hair falling over his forehead.

By working all day they just made enough money to live on, but they never went out and they had no friends. Now when he sat down at his table he had to make an entirely new set of sworn state-ment. . . . Not to go to the side window before a certain hour: signed, Ian French. Not to think about her until he had put away his painting things for the day: signed, Ian French.

It was quite simple. She was the only person he really wanted to know, because she was, he decided, the only other person alive who was just his age. He couldn't stand giggling girls, and he had no use for grown-up women. . . . She was his age, she was—well, just like him. He sat in his dusky studio, tired, with one arm hanging over the back of his chair, staring in at her window and seeing himself in there with her. She had a violent temper; they quarrelled terribly at times, he and she. She had a way of stamping her foot and twisting her hands in her pinafore . . . furious. And she very rarely laughed. Only when she told him about an absurd little kitten she once had who used to roar and pretend to be a lion when it was given meat to eat. Things like that made her laugh. . . . But as a rule they sat together very quietly; he, just as he was sitting now, and she with her hands folded in her lap and her feet tucked under, talking in low tones, or silent and tired after the day's work. Of course, she never asked him about his pictures, and of course he made the most wonderful drawings of her which she hated, because he made her so thin and so dark. . . . But how could he get to know her? This might go on for years. . . .

Then he discovered that once a week, in the evenings, she went out shopping. On two successive Thursdays she came to the window wearing an old-fashioned cape over the pinafore, and carrying a basket. From where he sat he could not see the door of her house, but on the next Thursday evening at the same time he snatched up his cap and ran down the stairs. There was a lovely pink light over everything. He saw it glowing in the river, and the people walking towards him had pink faces and pink hands.

He leaned against the side of his house waiting for her and he had no idea of what he was going to do or say. 'Here she comes,' said a voice in his head. She walked very quickly, with small, light steps; with one hand she carried the basket, with the other she kept the cape together. . . . What could he do? He could only follow. . . . First she went into the grocer's and spent a long time in there, and then she went into the butcher's where she had to wait her turn. Then she was an age at the draper's matching something, and then she went to the fruit shop and bought a lemon. As he watched her he knew more surely than ever he must get to know her now. Her composure, her seriousness and her loneliness, the very way she walked as though she was eager to be done with this world of grown-ups all was so natural to him and so inevitable.

'Yes, she is always like that,' he thought proudly. 'We have nothing to do with these people.'

But now she was on her way home and he was as far off as ever. . . . She suddenly turned into the dairy and he saw her through the window buying an egg. She picked it out of the basket with such care—a brown one, a beautifully shaped one, the one he would have chosen. And when she came out of the dairy he went in after her. In a moment he was out again, and following her past his house across the flower market, dodging among the huge umbrellas and treading on the fallen flowers and the round marks where the pots had stood. . . . Through her door he crept, and up the stairs after, taking care to tread in time with her so that she should not notice. Finally, she stopped on the landing, and took the key out of her purse. As she put it into the door he ran up and faced her.

Blushing more crimson than ever, but looking at her severely he said, almost angrily: 'Excuse me, Mademoiselle, you dropped this.'

And he handed her an egg.

A DILL PICKLE

And then, after six years, she saw him again. He was seated at one of those little bamboo tables decorated with a Japanese vase of paper daffodils. There was a tall plate of fruit in front of him, and very carefully, in a way she recognized immediately as his 'special' way, he was peeling an orange.

He must have felt that shock of recognition in her for he looked up and met her eyes. Incredible! He didn't know her! She smiled; he frowned. She came towards him. He closed his eyes an instant, but opening them his face lit up as though he had struck a match in a dark room. He laid down the orange and pushed back his chair, and she took her little warm hand out of her muff and gave it to him.

'Vera!' he exclaimed. 'How strange. Really, for a moment I didn't know you. Won't you sit down? You've had lunch? Won't you have some coffee?'

She hesitated, but of course she meant to.

'Yes, I'd like some coffee.' And she sat down opposite him.

'You've changed. You've changed very much,' he said, staring at her with that eager, lighted look. 'You look so well. I've never seen you look so well before.'

'Really?' She raised her veil* and unbuttoned her high fur collar. 'I don't feel very well. I can't bear this weather, you know.'

'Ah, no. You hate the cold. . . .'

'Loathe it.' She shuddered. 'And the worst of it is that the older one grows . . . .'

He interrupted her. 'Excuse me,' and tapped on the table for the waitress. 'Please bring some coffee and cream.' To her: 'You are sure you won't eat anything? Some fruit, perhaps. The fruit here is very good.'

'No, thanks. Nothing.'

'Then that's settled.' And smiling just a hint too broadly he took up the orange again. 'You were saying—the older one grows—'

'The colder,' she laughed. But she was thinking how well she remembered that trick of his—the trick of interrupting her—and of how it used to exasperate her six years ago. She used to feel then as though he, quite suddenly, in the middle of what she was saying, put his hand over her lips, turned from her, attended to something different, and then took his hand away, and with just the same slightly too broad smile, gave her his attention again. . . . Now we are ready. That is settled.

'The colder!' He echoed her words, laughing too. 'Ah, ah. You still say the same things. And there is another thing about you that is not changed at all—your beautiful voice—your beautiful way of speaking.' Now he was very grave; he leaned towards her, and she smelled the warm, stinging scent of the orange peel. 'You have only to say one word and I would know your voice among all other voices. I don't know what it is—I've often wondered—that makes your voice such a—haunting memory. . . . Do you remember that first afternoon we spent together at Kew Gardens?* You were so surprised because I did not know the names of any flowers. I am still just as ignorant for all your telling me. But whenever it is very fine and warm, and I see some bright colours—it's awfully strange—I hear your voice saying: "Geranium, marigold and verbena." And I feel those three words are all I recall of some forgotten, heavenly language. . . . You remember that afternoon?'

'Oh, yes, very well.' She drew a long, soft breath, as though the paper daffodils between them were almost too sweet to bear. Yet, what had remained in her mind of that particular afternoon was an absurd scene over the tea table. A great many people taking tea in a Chinese pagoda, and he behaving like a maniac about the wasps— waving them away, flapping at them with his straw hat, serious and infuriated out of all proportion to the occasion. How delighted the sniggering tea drinkers had been. And how she had suffered.

But now, as he spoke, that memory faded. His was the truer. Yes, it had been a wonderful afternoon, full of geranium and marigold and verbena, and—warm sunshine. Her thoughts lingered over the last two words as though she sang them.

In the warmth, as it were, another memory unfolded. She saw herself sitting on a lawn. He lay beside her, and suddenly, after a long silence, he rolled over and put his head in her lap.

'I wish,' he said, in a low, troubled voice, 'I wish that I had taken poison and were about to die—here now!'

At that moment a little girl in a white dress, holding a long, dripping water lily, dodged from behind a bush, stared at them, and dodged back again. But he did not see. She leaned over him.

'Ah, why do you say that? I could not say that.'

But he gave a kind of soft moan, and taking her hand he held it to his cheek.

'Because I know I am going to love you too much—far too much. And I shall suffer so terribly, Vera, because you never, never will love me.'

He was certainly far better looking now than he had been then. He had lost all that dreamy vagueness and indecision. Now he had the air of a man who has found his place in life, and fills it with a confidence and an assurance which was, to say the least, impressive. He must have made money, too. His clothes were admirable, and at that moment he pulled a Russian cigarette case out of his pocket.

'Won't you smoke?'

'Yes, I will.' She hovered over them. 'They look very good.'

'I think they are. I get them made for me by a little man in St James's Street. I don't smoke very much. I'm not like you—but when I do, they must be delicious, very fresh cigarettes. Smoking isn't a habit with me; it's a luxury—like perfume. Are you still so fond of perfumes? Ah, when I was in Russia . . . .'

She broke in: 'You've really been to Russia?'

'Oh, yes. I was there for over a year. Have you forgotten how we used to talk of going there?'

'No, I've not forgotten.'

He gave a strange half laugh and leaned back in his chair. 'Isn't it curious. I have really carried out all those journeys that we planned. Yes, I have been to all those places that we talked of, and stayed in them long enough to—as you used to say, "air oneself" in them. In fact, I have spent the last three years of my life travelling all the time. Spain, Corsica, Siberia, Russia, Egypt. The only country left is China, and I mean to go there, too, when the war is over.'

As he spoke, so lightly, tapping the end of his cigarette against the ash-tray, she felt the strange beast that had slumbered so long within her bosom stir, stretch itself, yawn, prick up its ears, and suddenly bound to its feet, and fix its longing, hungry stare upon those far away places. But all she said was, smiling gently: 'How I envy you.'

He accepted that. 'It has been,' he said, 'very wonderful—especially Russia. Russia was all that we had imagined, and far, far more. I even spent some days on a river boat on the Volga. Do you remember that boatman's song* that you used to play?'

'Yes.' It began to play in her mind as she spoke.

'Do you ever play it now?'

'No, I've no piano.'

He was amazed at that. 'But what has become of your beautiful piano?'

She made a little grimace. 'Sold. Ages ago.'

'But you were so fond of music,' he wondered.

'I've no time for it now,' said she.

He let it go at that. 'That river life,' he went on, 'is something quite special. After a day or two you cannot realize that you have ever known another. And it is not necessary to know the language—the life of the boat creates a bond between you and the people that's more than sufficient. You eat with them, pass the day with them, and in the evening there is that endless singing.'

She shivered, hearing the boatman's song break out again loud and tragic, and seeing the boat floating on the darkening river with melancholy trees on either side. . . . 'Yes, I should like that,' said she, stroking her muff.

'You'd like almost everything about Russian life,' he said warmly. 'It's so informal, so impulsive, so free without question. And then the peasants are so splendid. They are such human beings—yes, that is it. Even the man who drives your carriage has—has some real part in what is happening. I remember the evening a party of us, two friends of mine and the wife of one of them, went for a picnic by the Black Sea. We took supper and champagne and ate and drank on the grass. And while we were eating the coachman came up. "Have a dill pickle," he said. He wanted to share with us. That seemed to me so right, so—you know what I mean?'

And she seemed at that moment to be sitting on the grass beside the mysteriously Black Sea, black as velvet, and rippling against the banks in silent, velvet waves. She saw the carriage drawn up to one side of the road, and the little group on the grass, their faces and hands white in the moonlight. She saw the pale dress of the woman outspread and her folded parasol, lying on the grass like a huge pearl crochet hook.* Apart from them, with his supper in a cloth on his knees, sat the coachman. 'Have a dill pickle,' said he, and although she was not certain what a dill pickle was, she saw the greenish glass jar with a red chili like a parrot's beak glimmering through. She sucked in her cheeks; the dill pickle was terribly sour. . . .

'Yes, I know perfectly what you mean,' she said.

In the pause that followed they looked at each other. In the past when they had looked at each other like that they had felt such a boundless understanding between them that their souls had, as it were, put their arms round each other and dropped into the same sea, content to be drowned, like mournful lovers. But now, the surprising thing was that it was he who held back. He who said:

'What a marvellous listener you are. When you look at me with those wild eyes I feel that I could tell you things that I would never breathe to another human being.'

Was there just a hint of mockery in his voice or was it her fancy? She could not be sure.

'Before I met you,' he said, 'I had never spoken of myself to anybody. How well I remember one night, the night that I brought you the little Christmas tree, telling you all about my childhood. And of how I was so miserable that I ran away and lived under a cart in our yard for two days without being discovered. And you listened, and your eyes shone, and I felt that you had even made the little Christmas tree listen too, as in a fairy story.'

But of that evening she had remembered a little pot of caviare. It had cost seven and sixpence. He could not get over it. Think of it—a tiny jar like that costing seven and sixpence. While she ate it he watched her, delighted and shocked.

'No, really, that *is* eating money. You could not get seven shillings into a little pot that size. Only think of the profit they must make. . . .' And he had begun some immensely complicated calculations. . . . But now good-bye to the caviare. The Christmas tree was on the table, and the little boy lay under the cart with his head pillowed on the yard dog.

'The dog was called Bosun,' she cried delightedly.

But he did not follow. 'Which dog? Had you a dog? I don't remember a dog at all.'

'No, no. I mean the yard dog when you were a little boy.' He laughed and snapped the cigarette case to.

'Was he? Do you know I had forgotten that. It seems such ages ago. I cannot believe that it is only six years. After I had recognized you to-day—I had to take such a leap—I had to take a leap over my whole life to get back to that time. I was such a kid then.' He drummed on the table. 'I've often thought how I must have bored

you. And now I understand so perfectly why you wrote to me as you
did—although at the time that letter nearly finished my life. I found
it again the other day, and I couldn't help laughing as I read it. It was
so clever—such a true picture of me.' He glanced up. 'You're not
going?'

She had buttoned her collar again and drawn down her veil.

'Yes, I am afraid I must,' she said, and managed a smile. Now she
knew that he had been mocking.

'Ah, no, please,' he pleaded. 'Don't go just for a moment,' and he
caught up one of her gloves from the table and clutched at it as if that
would hold her. 'I see so few people to talk to nowadays, that I have
turned into a sort of barbarian,' he said. 'Have I said something to
hurt you?'

'Not a bit,' she lied. But as she watched him draw her glove
through his fingers, gently, gently, her anger really did die down, and
besides, at the moment he looked more like himself of six years
ago. . . .

'What I really wanted then,' he said softly, 'was to be a sort of
carpet—to make myself into a sort of carpet for you to walk on so
that you need not be hurt by the sharp stones and the mud that you
hated so. It was nothing more positive than that—nothing more
selfish. Only I did desire, eventually, to turn into a magic carpet and
carry you away to all those lands you longed to see.'

As he spoke she lifted her head as though she drank something;
the strange beast in her bosom began to purr. . . .

'I felt that you were more lonely than anybody else in the world,'
he went on, 'and yet, perhaps, that you were the only person in the
world who was really, truly alive. Born out of your time,' he
murmured, stroking the glove, 'fated.'

Ah, God! What had she done! How had she dared to throw away
her happiness like this. This was the only man who had ever understood her. Was it too late? Could it be too late? *She* was that glove
that he held in his fingers. . . .

'And then the fact that you had no friends and never had made
friends with people. How I understood that, for neither had I. Is it
just the same now?'

'Yes,' she breathed. 'Just the same. I am as alone as ever.'

'So am I,' he laughed gently, 'just the same.'

Suddenly with a quick gesture he handed her back the glove and scraped his chair on the floor. 'But what seemed to me so mysterious then is perfectly plain to me now. And to you, too, of course. . . . It simply was that we were such egoists, so self-engrossed, so wrapped up in ourselves that we hadn't a corner in our hearts for anybody else. Do you know,' he cried, naive and hearty, and dreadfully like another side of that old self again, 'I began studying a Mind System when I was in Russia, and I found that we were not peculiar at all. It's quite a well known form of . . . .'

She had gone. He sat there, thunder-struck, astounded beyond words. . . . And then he asked the waitress for his bill.

'But the cream has not been touched,' he said. 'Please do not charge me for it.'

JE NE PARLE PAS FRANÇAIS

I do not know why I have such a fancy for this little café. It's dirty and sad, sad. It's not as if it had anything to distinguish it from a hundred others—it hasn't; or as if the same strange types came here every day, whom one could watch from one's corner and recognise and more or less (with a strong accent on the less) get the hang of.

But pray don't imagine that those brackets are a confession of my humility before the mystery of the human soul. Not at all; I don't believe in the human soul. I never have. I believe that people are like portmanteaux*—packed with certain things, started going, thrown about, tossed away, dumped down, lost and found, half emptied suddenly, or squeezed fatter than ever, until finally the Ultimate Porter swings them on to the Ultimate Train and away they rattle. . . .

Not but what these portmanteaux can be very fascinating. Oh, but very! I see myself standing in front of them, don't you know, like a Customs official.

'Have you anything to declare? Any wines, spirits, cigars, perfumes, silks?'

And the moment of hesitation as to whether I am going to be fooled just before I chalk that squiggle, and then the other moment of hesitation just after, as to whether I have been, are perhaps the two most thrilling instants in life. Yes, they are, to me.

But before I started that long and rather far-fetched and not frightfully original digression, what I meant to say quite simply was that there are no portmanteaux to be examined here because the clientele of this café, ladies and gentlemen, does not sit down. No, it stands at the counter, and it consists of a handful of workmen who come up from the river, all powdered over with white flour, lime or something, and a few soldiers, bringing with them thin, dark girls with silver rings in their ears and market baskets on their arms.

Madame is thin and dark, too, with white cheeks and white hands. In certain lights she looks quite transparent, shining out of her black shawl with an extraordinary effect. When she is not serving she sits on a stool with her face turned, always, to the window. Her dark-ringed eyes search among and follow after the people passing, but not as if she was looking for somebody. Perhaps, fifteen years ago, she was; but now the pose has become a habit. You can tell from her air of fatigue and hopelessness that she must have given them up for the last ten years, at least. . . .

And then there is the waiter. Not pathetic—decidedly not comic. Never making one of those perfectly insignificant remarks which amaze you so coming from a waiter (as though the poor wretch were a sort of cross between a coffee-pot and a wine bottle and not expected to hold so much as a drop of anything else). He is grey, flat-footed and withered, with long, brittle nails that set your nerves on edge while he scrapes up your two sous.* When he is not smearing over the table or flicking at a dead fly or two, he stands with one hand on the back of a chair, in his far too long apron, and over his other arm the three-cornered dip of dirty napkin, waiting to be photographed in connection with some wretched murder. 'Interior of Café where Body was Found.' You've seen him hundreds of times.

Do you believe that every place has its hour of the day when it really does come alive? That's not exactly what I mean. It's more like this. There does seem to be a moment when you realize that, quite by accident, you happen to have come on to the stage at exactly the moment you were expected. Everything is arranged for you—waiting for you. Ah, master of the situation! You fill with important breath. And at the same time you smile, secretly, slyly, because Life seems to be opposed to granting you these entrances, seems indeed to be engaged in snatching them from you and making them impossible, keeping you in the wings until it is too late, in fact. . . . Just for once you've beaten the old hag.

I enjoyed one of these moments the first time I ever came in here. That's why I keep coming back, I suppose. Revisiting the scene of my triumph, or the scene of the crime where I had the old bitch by the throat for once and did what I pleased with her.

Query: Why am I so bitter against Life? And why do I see her as a rag-picker on the American cinema, shuffling along wrapped in a filthy shawl with her old claws crooked over a stick?

Answer: The direct result of the American cinema acting upon a weak mind.

Anyhow, the 'short winter afternoon was drawing to a close', as they say, and I was drifting along, either going home or not going home, when I found myself in here, walking over to this seat in the corner.

I hung up my English overcoat and grey felt hat on that same peg behind me, and after I had allowed the waiter time for at least twenty photographers to snap their fill of him, I ordered a coffee.

He poured me out a glass of the familiar, purplish stuff with a green wandering light playing over it, and shuffled off, and I sat pressing my hands against the glass because it was bitterly cold outside.

Suddenly I realized that quite apart from myself, I was smiling. Slowly I raised my head and saw myself in the mirror opposite. Yes, there I sat, leaning on the table, smiling my deep, sly smile, the glass of coffee with its vague plume of steam before me and beside it the ring of white saucer with two pieces of sugar.

I opened my eyes very wide. There I had been for all eternity, as it were, and now at last I was coming to life. . . .

It was very quiet in the café. Outside, one could just see through the dusk that it had begun to snow. One could just see the shapes of horses and carts and people, soft and white, moving through the feathery air. The waiter disappeared and reappeared with an armful of straw. He strewed it over the floor from the door to the counter and round about the stove with humble, almost adoring gestures. One would not have been surprised if the door had opened and the Virgin Mary had come in, riding upon an ass, her meek hands folded over her big belly. . . .

That's rather nice, don't you think, that bit about the Virgin? It comes from the pen so gently; it has such a 'dying fall'.* I thought so at the time and decided to make a note of it. One never knows when a little tag like that may come in useful to round off a paragraph. So, taking care to move as little as possible because the 'spell' was still unbroken (you know that?), I reached over to the next table for a writing pad.

No paper or envelopes, of course. Only a morsel of pink blotting-paper, incredibly soft and limp and almost moist, like the tongue of a little dead kitten, which I've never felt.

I sat—but always underneath, in this state of expectation, rolling the little dead kitten's tongue round my finger and rolling the soft phrase round my mind while my eyes took in the girls' names and dirty jokes and drawings of bottles and cups that would not sit in the saucers, scattered over the writing pad.

They are always the same, you know. The girls always have the same names, the cups never sit in the saucers; all the hearts are stuck and tied up with ribbons.

But then, quite suddenly, at the bottom of the page, written in green ink, I fell on to that stupid, stale little phrase: *Je ne parle pas français*.

There! it had come—the moment—the *geste*!* And although I was so ready, it caught me, it tumbled me over; I was simply overwhelmed. And the physical feeling was so curious, so particular. It was as if all of me, except my head and arms, all of me that was under the table, had simply dissolved, melted, turned into water. Just my head remained and two sticks of arms pressing on to the table. But, ah! the agony of that moment! How can I describe it? I didn't think of anything. I didn't even cry out to myself. Just for one moment I was not. I was Agony, Agony, Agony.

Then it passed, and the very second after I was thinking: 'Good God! Am I capable of feeling as strongly as that? But I was absolutely unconscious! I hadn't a phrase to meet it with! I was overcome! I was swept off my feet! I didn't even try, in the dimmest way, to put it down!'

And up I puffed and puffed, blowing off finally with: 'After all I must be first-rate. No second-rate mind could have experienced such an intensity of feeling so . . . purely.'

The waiter has touched a spill* at the red stove and lighted a bubble of gas* under a spreading shade. It is no use looking out of the window, Madame; it is quite dark now. Your white hands hover over your dark shawl. They are like two birds that have come home to roost. They are restless, restless. . . . You tuck them, finally, under your warm little armpits.

Now the waiter has taken a long pole and clashed the curtains together. 'All gone', as children say.

And besides, I've no patience with people who can't let go of things, who will follow after and cry out. When a thing's gone, it's gone. It's over and done with. Let it go then! Ignore it, and comfort yourself, if you do want comforting, with the thought that you never do recover the same thing that you lose. It's always a new thing. The moment it leaves you it's changed. Why, that's even true of a hat you chase after; and I don't mean superficially—I mean profoundly speaking. . . . I have made it a rule of my life never to regret and never to look back. Regret is an appalling waste of energy, and no one who intends to be a writer can afford to indulge in it. You can't get it into shape; you can't build on it; it's only good for wallowing in. Looking back, of course, is equally fatal to Art. It's keeping yourself poor. Art can't and won't stand poverty.

Je ne parle pas français. Je ne parle pas français. All the while I wrote that last page my other self has been chasing up and down out in the dark there. It left me just when I began to analyse my grand moment, dashed off distracted, like a lost dog who thinks at last, at last, he hears the familiar step again.

'Mouse! Mouse! Where are you? Are you near? Is that you leaning from the high window and stretching out your arms for the wings of the shutters? Are you this soft bundle moving towards me through the feathery snow? Are you this little girl pressing through the swing-doors of the restaurant? Is that your dark shadow bending forward in the cab? Where are you? Where are you? Which way must I turn? Which way shall I run? And every moment I stand here hesitating you are farther away again. Mouse! Mouse!'

Now the poor dog has come back into the café, his tail between his legs, quite exhausted.

'It was a . . . false . . . alarm. She's nowhere . . . to . . . be seen.'

'Lie down then! Lie down! Lie down!'

My name is Raoul Duquette. I am twenty-six years old and a Parisian, a true Parisian. About my family—it really doesn't matter. I have no family; I don't want any. I never think about my childhood. I've forgotten it.

In fact, there's only one memory that stands out at all. That is rather interesting because it seems to me now so very significant as regards myself from the literary point of view. It is this.

When I was about ten our laundress was an African woman, very big, very dark, with a check handkerchief over her frizzy hair. When she came to our house she always took particular notice of me, and after the clothes had been taken out of the basket she would lift me up into it and give me a rock while I held tight to the handles and screamed for joy and fright. I was tiny for my age, and pale, with a lovely little half-open mouth—I feel sure of that.

One day when I was standing at the door, watching her go, she turned round and beckoned to me, nodding and smiling in a strange secret way. I never thought of not following. She took me into a little outhouse at the end of the passage, caught me up in her arms and began kissing me. Ah, those kisses! Especially those kisses inside my ears that nearly deafened me.

And then with a soft growl she tore open her bodice and put me to her. When she set me down she took from her pocket a little round fried cake covered with sugar and I reeled along the passage back to our door.

As this performance was repeated once a week it is no wonder that I remember it so vividly. Besides, from that very first afternoon, my childhood was, to put it prettily, 'kissed away'. I became very languid, very caressing, and greedy beyond measure. And so quickened, so sharpened, I seemed to understand everybody and be able to do what I liked with everybody.

I suppose I was in a state of more or less physical excitement, and that was what appealed to them. For all Parisians are more than half—oh, well, enough of that. And enough of my childhood, too. Bury it under a laundry basket instead of a shower of roses and *passons outre*.*

I date myself from the moment that I became the tenant of a small bachelor flat on the fifth floor of a tall, not too shabby house, in a street that might or might not be discreet. Very useful, that. . . . There I emerged, came out into the light and put out my two horns with a study and a bedroom and a kitchen on my back. And real furniture planted in the rooms. In the bedroom a wardrobe with a long glass, a big bed covered with a yellow puffed-up quilt, a bed table with a marbled top and a toilet set sprinkled with tiny apples. In my study—English writing table with drawers, writing chair with leather cushions, books, arm-chair, side table with paper-knife and lamp on it and some nude studies on the walls. I didn't use the kitchen except to throw old papers into.

Ah, I can see myself that first evening, after the furniture men had gone and I'd managed to get rid of my atrocious old concierge*— walking about on tip-toe, arranging and standing in front of the glass with my hands in my pockets and saying to that radiant vision: 'I am a young man who has his own flat. I write for two newspapers. I am going in for serious literature. I am starting a career. The book that I shall bring out will simply stagger the critics. I am going to write about things that have never been touched before. I am going to make a name for myself as a writer about the submerged world. But not as others have done before me. Oh, no! Very naively, with a sort of tender humour and from the inside, as though it were all quite simple, quite natural. I see my way quite perfectly. Nobody has ever done it as I shall do it because none of the others have lived my experiences. I'm rich—I'm rich.'

All the same I had no more money than I have now. It's extraordinary how one can live without money. . . . I have quantities of good clothes, silk underwear, two evening suits, four pairs of patent leather boots with light uppers, all sorts of little things, like gloves and powder boxes and a manicure set, perfumes, very good soap, and nothing is paid for. If I find myself in need of right-down cash— well, there's always an African laundress and an outhouse, and I am very frank and *bon enfant** about plenty of sugar on the little fried cake afterwards. . . .

And here I should like to put something on record. Not from any strutting conceit, but rather with a mild sense of wonder. I've never yet made the first advances to any woman. It isn't as though I've known only one class of woman—not by any means. But from little prostitutes and kept women and elderly widows and shop girls and wives of respectable men, and even advanced modern literary ladies at the most select dinners and soirées (I've been there), I've met invariably with not only the same readiness, but with the same positive invitation. It surprised me at first. I used to look across the table and think 'Is that very distinguished young lady, discussing *le Kipling** with the gentleman with the brown beard, really pressing my foot?' And I was never really certain until I had pressed hers.

Curious, isn't it? Why should I be able to have any woman I want? I don't look at all like a maiden's dream. . . .

I am little and light with an olive skin, black eyes with long lashes, black silky hair cut short, tiny square teeth that show when I smile. My hands are supple and small. A woman in a bread shop once said to me: 'You have the hands for making fine little pastries.' I confess, without my clothes I am rather charming. Plump, almost like a girl, with smooth shoulders, and I wear a thin gold bracelet above my left elbow.

But, wait! Isn't it strange I should have written all that about my body and so on? It's the result of my bad life, my submerged life. I am like a little woman in a café who has to introduce herself with a handful of photographs.* 'Me in my chemise, coming out of an egg-shell. . . . Me upside down in a swing, with a frilly behind like a cauliflower. . . .' You know the things.

If you think what I've written is merely superficial and impudent and cheap you're wrong. I'll admit it does sound so, but then it is not all. If it were, how could I have experienced what I did when I read that stale little phrase written in green ink, in the writing-pad? That proves there's more in me and that I really am important, doesn't it? Anything a fraction less than that moment of anguish I might have put on. But no! That was real.

'Waiter, a whisky.'

I hate whisky. Every time I take it into my mouth my stomach rises against it, and the stuff they keep here is sure to be particularly vile. I only ordered it because I am going to write about an Englishman. We French are incredibly old-fashioned and out of date still in some ways. I wonder I didn't ask him at the same time for a pair of tweed knickerbockers,* a pipe, some long teeth and a set of ginger whiskers.

'Thanks, *mon vieux*. You haven't got perhaps a set of ginger whiskers?'

'No, monsieur,' he answers sadly. 'We don't sell American drinks.'

And having smeared a corner of the table he goes back to have another couple of dozen taken by artificial light.

Ugh! The smell of it! And the sickly sensation when one's throat contracts.

'It's bad stuff to get drunk on,' says Dick Harmon, turning his little glass in his fingers and smiling his slow, dreaming smile. So he gets drunk on it slowly and dreamily and at a certain moment begins to sing very low, very low, about a man who walks up and down trying to find a place where he can get some dinner.

Ah! how I loved that song, and how I loved the way he sang it, slowly, slowly, in a dark, soft voice

> There was a man
> Walked up and down
> To get a dinner in the town . . .

It seemed to hold, in its gravity and muffled measure, all those tall grey buildings, those fogs, those endless streets, those sharp shadows of policemen that mean England.

And then—the subject! The lean, starved creature walking up and down with every house barred against him because he had no 'home'. How extraordinarily English that is. . . . I remember that it ended where he did at last 'find a place' and ordered a little cake of fish, but when he asked for bread the waiter cried contemptuously, in a loud voice: 'We don't serve bread with one fish ball.'

What more do you want? How profound those songs are! There is the whole psychology of a people; and how un-French—how un-French!

'Once more, Deeck, once more!' I would plead, clasping my hands and making a pretty mouth at him. He was perfectly content to sing it for ever.

There again. Even with Dick. It was he who made the first advances.

I met him at an evening party given by the editor of a new review. It was a very select, very fashionable affair. One or two of the older men were there and the ladies were extremely *comme il faut*.* They sat on cubist* sofas in full evening dress and allowed us to hand them thimbles of cherry brandy and to talk to them about their poetry. For, as far as I can remember, they were all poetesses.

It was impossible not to notice Dick. He was the only Englishman present, and instead of circulating gracefully round the room as we all did, he stayed in one place leaning against the wall, his hands in his pockets, that dreamy half smile on his lips, and replying in excellent French in his low, soft voice to anybody who spoke to him.

'Who is he?'

'An Englishman. From London. A writer. And he is making a special study of modern French literature.'

That was enough for me. My little book, *False Coins*, had just been published. I was a young, serious writer who was making a special study of modern English literature.

But I really had not time to fling my line before he said, giving himself a soft shake, coming right out of the water after the bait, as it were: 'Won't you come and see me at my hotel? Come about five o'clock and we can have a talk before going out to dinner.'

'Enchanted!'

I was so deeply, deeply flattered that I had to leave him then and there to preen and preen myself before the cubist sofas. What a catch! An Englishman, reserved, serious, making a special study of French literature. . . .

That same night a copy of *False Coins* with a carefully cordial inscription was posted off, and a day or two later we did dine together and spent the evening talking.

Talking—but not only of literature. I discovered to my relief that it wasn't necessary to keep to the tendency of the modern novel, the need of a new form, or the reason why our young men appeared to be just missing it. Now and again, as if by accident, I threw in a card that seemed to have nothing to do with the game, just to see how he'd take it. But each time he gathered it into his hands with his dreamy look and smile unchanged. Perhaps he murmured: 'That's very curious.' But not as if it were curious at all.

That calm acceptance went to my head at last. It fascinated me. It led me on and on till I threw every card that I possessed at him and sat back and watched him arrange them in his hand.

'Very curious and interesting. . . .'

By that time we were both fairly drunk, and he began to sing his song very soft, very low, about the man who walked up and down seeking his dinner.

But I was quite breathless at the thought of what I had done. I had shown somebody both sides of my life. Told him everything as sincerely and truthfully as I could. Taken immense pains to explain things about my submerged life that really were disgusting and never could possibly see the light of literary day. On the whole I had made myself out far worse than I was—more boastful, more cynical, more calculating.

And there sat the man I had confided in, singing to himself and smiling. . . . It moved me so that real tears came into my eyes. I saw them glittering on my long silky lashes—so charming.

After that I took Dick about with me everywhere, and he came to my flat, and sat in the arm-chair, very indolent, playing with the paper-knife. I cannot think why his indolence and dreaminess always gave me the impression he had been to sea. And all his leisurely slow ways seemed to be allowing for the movement of the ship. This impression was so strong that often when we were together and he got up and left a little woman just when she did not expect him to get up and leave her, but quite the contrary, I would explain: 'He can't help it, Baby. He has to go back to his ship.' And I believed it far more than she did.

All the while we were together Dick never went with a woman. I sometimes wondered whether he wasn't completely innocent. Why didn't I ask him? Because I never did ask him anything about himself. But late one night he took out his pocket-book and a photograph dropped out of it. I picked it up and glanced at it before I gave it to him. It was of a woman. Not quite young. Dark, handsome, wild-looking, but so full in every line of a kind of haggard pride that even if Dick had not stretched out so quickly I wouldn't have looked longer.

'Out of my sight, you little perfumed fox-terrier of a Frenchman,' said she. (In my very worst moments my nose reminds me of a fox-terrier's.)

'That is my Mother,' said Dick, putting up the pocket-book.

But if he had not been Dick I should have been tempted to cross myself, just for fun.

This is how we parted. As we stood outside his hotel one night waiting for the concierge to release the catch of the outer door, he said, looking up at the sky: 'I hope it will be fine to-morrow. I am leaving for England in the morning.'

'You're not serious.'

'Perfectly. I have to get back. I've some work to do that I can't manage here.'

'But—but have you made all your preparations?'

'Preparations?' He almost grinned. 'I've none to make.'

'But—*enfin*,* Dick, England is not the other side of the boulevard.'

'It isn't much farther off,' said he. 'Only a few hours, you know.' The door cracked open.

'Ah, I wish I'd known at the beginning of the evening!'

I felt hurt. I felt as a woman must feel when a man takes out his watch and remembers an appointment that cannot possibly concern her, except that its claim is the stronger. 'Why didn't you tell me?'

He put out his hand and stood, lightly swaying upon the step as though the whole hotel were his ship, and the anchor weighed.

'I forgot. Truly I did. But you'll write, won't you? Good night, old chap. I'll be over again one of these days.'

And then I stood on the shore alone, more like a little fox-terrier than ever. . . .

'But after all it was you who whistled to me, you who asked me to come! What a spectacle I've cut wagging my tail and leaping round you, only to be left like this while the boat sails off in its slow, dreamy way. . . . Curse these English! No, this is too insolent altogether. Who do you imagine I am? A little paid guide to the night pleasures of Paris? . . . No, monsieur. I am a young writer, very serious, and extremely interested in modern English literature. And I have been insulted—insulted.'

Two days after came a long, charming letter from him, written in French that was a shade too French, but saying how he missed me and counted on our friendship, on keeping in touch.

I read it standing in front of the (unpaid for) wardrobe mirror. It was early morning. I wore a blue kimono embroidered with white birds and my hair was still wet; it lay on my forehead, wet and gleaming.

'Portrait of Madame Butterfly,' said I, 'on hearing of the arrival of *ce cher Pinkerton.*'*

According to the books I should have felt immensely relieved and delighted. '. . . Going over to the window he drew apart the curtains and looked out at the Paris trees, just breaking into buds and green. . . . Dick! Dick! My English friend!'

I didn't. I merely felt a little sick. Having been up for my first ride in an aeroplane I didn't want to go up again, just now.

That passed, and months after, in the winter, Dick wrote that he was coming back to Paris to stay indefinitely. Would I take rooms for him? He was bringing a woman friend with him.

Of course I would. Away the little fox-terrier flew. It happened most usefully, too; for I owed much money at the hotel where I took my meals, and two English people requiring rooms for an indefinite time was an excellent sum on account.

Perhaps I did rather wonder, as I stood in the larger of the two rooms with Madame, saying 'Admirable,' what the woman friend would be like, but only vaguely. Either she would be very severe, flat back and front, or she would be tall, fair, dressed in mignonette green,* name—Daisy, and smelling of rather sweetish lavender water.

You see, by this time, according to my rule of not looking back, I had almost forgotten Dick. I even got the tune of his song about the unfortunate man a little bit wrong when I tried to hum it. . . .

I very nearly did not turn up at the station after all. I had arranged to, and had, in fact, dressed with particular care for the occasion. For I intended to take a new line with Dick this time. No more confidences and tears on eyelashes. No, thank you!

'Since you left Paris,' said I, knotting my black silver-spotted tie in the (also unpaid for) mirror over the mantelpiece, 'I have been very successful, you know. I have two more books in preparation, and then I have written a serial story, *Wrong Doors*, which is just on the point of publication and will bring me in a lot of money. And then my little book of poems,' I cried, seizing the clothes-brush and brushing the velvet collar of my new indigo-blue overcoat, 'my little book—*Left Umbrellas*—really did create,' and I laughed and waved the brush, 'an immense sensation!'

It was impossible not to believe this of the person who surveyed himself finally, from top to toe, drawing on his soft grey gloves. He was looking the part; he was the part.

That gave me an idea. I took out my notebook, and still in full view, jotted down a note or two. . . . How can one look the part and not be the part? Or be the part and not look it? Isn't looking—being? Or being—looking? At any rate who is to say that it is not? . . .

This seemed to me extraordinarily profound at the time, and quite new. But I confess that something did whisper as, smiling, I put up the notebook: 'You—literary? you look as though you've taken down a bet on a racecourse!' But I didn't listen. I went out, shutting the door of the flat with a soft, quick pull so as not to warn the concierge of my departure, and ran down the stairs quick as a rabbit for the same reason.

But ah! the old spider. She was too quick for me. She let me run down the last little ladder of the web and then she pounced. 'One moment. One little moment, Monsieur,' she whispered, odiously confidential. 'Come in. Come in.' And she beckoned with a dripping soup ladle. I went to the door, but that was not good enough. Right inside and the door shut before she would speak.

There are two ways of managing your concierge if you haven't any money. One is—to take the high hand, make her your enemy, bluster, refuse to discuss anything; the other is—to keep in with her, butter her up to the two knots of the black rag tying up her jaws, pretend to confide in her, and rely on her to arrange with the gas man and to put off the landlord.

I had tried the second. But both are equally detestable and unsuccessful. At any rate whichever you're trying is the worse, the impossible one.

It was the landlord this time. . . . Imitation of the landlord by the concierge threatening to toss me out. . . . Imitation of the concierge by the concierge taming the wild bull. . . . Imitation of the landlord rampant again, breathing in the concierge's face. I was the concierge. No, it was too nauseous. And all the while the black pot on the gas ring bubbling away, stewing out the hearts and livers of every tenant in the place.

'Ah!' I cried, staring at the clock on the mantelpiece, and then, realizing that it didn't go, striking my forehead as though the idea had nothing to do with it. 'Madame, I have a very important appointment with the director of my newspaper at nine-thirty. Perhaps to-morrow I shall be able to give you . . . .'

Out, out. And down the métro and squeezed into a full carriage. The more the better. Everybody was one bolster the more between me and the concierge. I was radiant.

'Ah! pardon, Monsieur!' said the tall charming creature in black with a big full bosom and a great bunch of violets dropping from it. As the train swayed it thrust the bouquet right into my eyes. 'Ah! pardon, Monsieur!'

But I looked up at her, smiling mischievously.

'There is nothing I love more, Madame, than flowers on a balcony.'

At the very moment of speaking I caught sight of the huge man in a fur coat against whom my charmer was leaning. He poked his head over her shoulder and he went white to the nose; in fact his nose stood out a sort of cheese green.

'What was that you said to my wife?'

Gare Saint Lazare* saved me. But you'll own that even as the author of *False Coins, Wrong Doors, Left Umbrellas*, and two in preparation, it was not too easy to go on my triumphant way.

*

At length, after countless trains had steamed into my mind, and countless Dick Harmons had come rolling towards me, the real train came. The little knot of us waiting at the barrier moved up close, craned forward, and broke into cries as though we were some kind of many-headed monster, and Paris behind us nothing but a great trap we had set to catch these sleepy innocents.

Into the trap they walked and were snatched and taken off to be devoured. Where was my prey?

'Good God!' My smile and my lifted hand fell together. For one terrible moment I thought this was the woman of the photograph, Dick's mother, walking towards me in Dick's coat and hat. In the effort—and you saw what an effort it was—to smile, his lips curled in just the same way and he made for me, haggard and wild and proud.

What had happened? What could have changed him like this? Should I mention it?

I waited for him and was even conscious of venturing a fox-terrier wag or two to see if he could possibly respond, in the way I said: 'Good evening, Dick! How are you, old chap? All right?'

'All right. All right.' He almost gasped. 'You've got the rooms?'

Twenty times, good God! I saw it all. Light broke on the dark waters and my sailor hadn't been drowned. I almost turned a somersault with amusement.

It was nervousness, of course. It was embarrassment. It was the famous English seriousness. What fun I was going to have! I could have hugged him.

'Yes, I've got the rooms,' I nearly shouted. 'But where is Madame?'

'She's been looking after the luggage,' he panted. 'Here she comes, now.'

Not this baby walking beside the old porter as though he were her nurse and had just lifted her out of her ugly perambulator while he trundled the boxes on it.

'And she's not Madame,' said Dick, drawling suddenly.

At that moment she caught sight of him and hailed him with her minute muff. She broke away from her nurse and ran up and said something, very quick, in English; but he replied in French: 'Oh, very well. I'll manage.'

But before he turned to the porter he indicated me with a vague wave and muttered something. We were introduced. She held out her hand in that strange boyish way Englishwomen do, and standing very straight in front of me with her chin raised and making—she too—the effort of her life to control her preposterous excitement, she said, wringing my hand (I'm sure she didn't know it was mine), *Je ne parle pas français.*

'But I'm sure you do,' I answered, so tender, so reassuring, I might have been a dentist about to draw her first little milk tooth.

'Of course she does.' Dick swerved back to us. 'Here, can't we get a cab or taxi or something? We don't want to stay in this cursed station all night. Do we?'

This was so rude that it took me a moment to recover; and he must have noticed, for he flung his arm round my shoulder in the old way, saying: 'Ah, forgive me, old chap. But we've had such a loathsome, hideous journey. We've taken years to come. Haven't we?' To her. But she did not answer. She bent her head and began stroking her grey muff; she walked beside us stroking her grey muff all the way.

'Have I been wrong?' thought I. 'Is this simply a case of frenzied impatience on their part? Are they merely "in need of a bed", as we say? Have they been suffering agonies on the journey? Sitting, perhaps, very close and warm under the same travelling rug?' and so on and so on while the driver strapped on the boxes. That done——

'Look here, Dick. I go home by métro. Here is the address of your hotel. Everything is arranged. Come and see me as soon as you can.'

Upon my life I thought he was going to faint. He went white to the lips.

'But you're coming back with us,' he cried. 'I thought it was all settled. Of course you're coming back. You're not going to leave us.' No, I gave it up. It was too difficult, too English for me.

'Certainly, certainly. Delighted. I only thought, perhaps . . . .'

'You must come!' said Dick to the little fox-terrier. And again he made that big awkward turn towards her.

'Get in, Mouse.'

And Mouse got in the black hole and sat stroking Mouse II and not saying a word.

Away we jolted and rattled like three little dice that life had decided to have a fling with.

I had insisted on taking the flap seat* facing them because I would not have missed for anything those occasional flashing glimpses I had as we broke through the white circles of lamplight.

They revealed Dick, sitting far back in his corner, his coat collar turned up, his hands thrust in his pockets, and his broad dark hat shading him as if it were a part of him—a sort of wing he hid under. They showed her, sitting up very straight, her lovely little face more like a drawing than a real face—every line was so full of meaning and so sharp cut against the swimming dark.

For Mouse was beautiful. She was exquisite, but so fragile and fine that each time I looked at her it was as if for the first time. She came upon you with the same kind of shock that you feel when you have been drinking tea out of a thin innocent cup and suddenly, at the bottom, you see a tiny creature, half butterfly, half woman, bowing to you with her hands in her sleeves.

As far as I could make out she had dark hair and blue or black eyes. Her long lashes and the two little feathers traced above were most important.

She wore a long dark cloak such as one sees in old-fashioned pictures of Englishwomen abroad. Where her arms came out of it there was grey fur—fur round her neck, too, and her close-fitting cap was furry.

'Carrying out the mouse idea,' I decided.

Ah, but how intriguing it was—how intriguing! Their excitement came nearer and nearer to me, while I ran out to meet it, bathed in it, flung myself far out of my depth, until at last I was as hard put to it to keep control as they.

But what I wanted to do was to behave in the most extraordinary fashion—like a clown. To start singing, with large extravagant gestures, to point out of the window and cry: 'We are now passing, ladies and gentlemen, one of the sights for which *notre Paris* is justly famous'; to jump out of the taxi while it was going, climb over the roof and dive in by another door; to hang out of the window and look for the hotel through the wrong end of a broken telescope, which was also a peculiarly ear-splitting trumpet.

I watched myself do all this, you understand, and even managed to applaud in a private way by putting my gloved hands gently together, while I said to Mouse: 'And is this your first visit to Paris?'

'Yes, I've not been here before.'

'Ah, then you have a great deal to see.'

And I was just going to touch lightly upon the objects of interest and the museums when we wrenched to a stop.

Do you know—it's very absurd—but as I pushed open the door for them and followed up the stairs to the bureau on the landing I felt somehow that this hotel was mine.

There was a vase of flowers on the window sill of the bureau and I even went so far as to re-arrange a bud or two and to stand off and note the effect while the manageress welcomed them. And when she turned to me and handed me the keys (the *garçon** was hauling up the boxes) and said: 'Monsieur Duquette will show you your rooms'—I had a longing to tap Dick on the arm with a key and say, very confidentially: 'Look here, old chap. As a friend of mine I'll be only too willing to make a slight reduction . . . .'

Up and up we climbed. Round and round. Past an occasional pair of boots* (why is it one never sees an attractive pair of boots outside a door?). Higher and higher.

'I'm afraid they're rather high up,' I murmured idiotically. 'But I chose them because . . . .'

They so obviously did not care why I chose them that I went no further. They accepted everything. They did not expect anything to be different. This was just part of what they were going through— that was how I analysed it.

'Arrived at last.' I ran from one side of the passage to the other, turning on the lights, explaining.

'This one I thought for you, Dick. The other is larger and it has a little dressing-room in the alcove.'

My 'proprietary' eye noted the clean towels and covers, and the bed linen embroidered in red cotton. I thought them rather charm-ing rooms, sloping, full of angles, just the sort of rooms one would expect to find if one had not been to Paris before.

Dick dashed his hat down on the bed.

'Oughtn't I to help that chap with the boxes?' he asked—nobody.

'Yes, you ought,' replied Mouse, 'they're dreadfully heavy.'

And she turned to me with the first glimmer of a smile: 'Books, you know.' Oh, he darted such a strange look at her before he rushed out. And he not only helped, he must have torn the box off the

garçon's back, for he staggered back, carrying one, dumped it down
and then fetched in the other.

'That's yours, Dick,' said she.

'Well, you don't mind it standing here for the present, do you?' he
asked, breathless, breathing hard (the box must have been tremendously heavy). He pulled out a handful of money. 'I suppose I ought
to pay this chap.'

The *garçon*, standing by, seemed to think so too.

'And will you require anything further, Monsieur?'

'No! No!' said Dick impatiently.

But at that Mouse stepped forward. She said, too deliberately, not
looking at Dick, with her quaint clipped English accent: 'Yes, I'd like
some tea. Tea for three.'

And suddenly she raised her muff as though her hands were
clasped inside it, and she was telling the pale, sweaty *garçon* by that
action that she was at the end of her resources, that she cried out to
him to save her with 'Tea. Immediately!'

This seemed to me so amazingly in the picture, so exactly the gesture
and cry that one would expect (though I couldn't have imagined it)
to be wrung out of an Englishwoman faced with a great crisis, that I
was almost tempted to hold up my hand and protest.

'No! No! Enough. Enough. Let us leave off there. At the word—
tea. For really, really, you've filled your greediest subscriber so full
that he will burst if he has to swallow another word.'

It even pulled Dick up. Like someone who has been unconscious
for a long long time he turned slowly to Mouse and slowly looked at
her with his tired, haggard eyes, and murmured with the echo of his
dreamy voice: 'Yes. That's a good idea.' And then: 'You must be
tired, Mouse. Sit down.'

She sat down in a chair with lace tabs on the arms; he leaned
against the bed, and I established myself on a straight-backed chair,
crossed my legs and brushed some imaginary dust off the knees of
my trousers. (The Parisian at his ease.)

There came a tiny pause. Then he said: 'Won't you take off your
coat, Mouse?'

'No, thanks. Not just now.'

Were they going to ask me? Or should I hold up my hand and call
out in a baby voice: 'It's my turn to be asked.'

No, I shouldn't. They didn't ask me.

The pause became a silence. A real silence.

'. . . Come, my Parisian fox-terrier! Amuse these sad English! It's no wonder they are such a nation for dogs.'

But, after all—why should I? It was not my 'job', as they would say. Nevertheless, I made a vivacious little bound at Mouse.

'What a pity it is that you did not arrive by daylight. There is such a charming view from these two windows. You know, the hotel is on a corner and each window looks down an immensely long, straight street.'

'Yes,' said she.

'Not that that sounds very charming,' I laughed. 'But there is so much animation—so many absurd little boys on bicycles and people hanging out of windows and—oh, well, you'll see for yourself in the morning. . . . Very amusing. Very animated.'

'Oh, yes,' said she.

If the pale, sweaty *garçon* had not come in at that moment, carrying the tea-tray high on one hand as if the cups were cannon-balls and he a heavy weight lifter on the cinema. . . .

He managed to lower it on to a round table.

'Bring the table over here,' said Mouse. The waiter seemed to be the only person she cared to speak to. She took her hands out of her muff, drew off her gloves and flung back the old-fashioned cape.

'Do you take milk and sugar?'

'No milk, thank you, and no sugar.'

I went over for mine like a little gentleman. She poured out another cup.

'That's for Dick.'

And the faithful fox-terrier carried it across to him and laid it at his feet, as it were.

'Oh, thanks,' said Dick.

And then I went back to my chair and she sank back in hers.

But Dick was off again. He stared wildly at the cup of tea for a moment, glanced round him, put it down on the bed-table, caught up his hat and stammered at full gallop: 'Oh, by the way, do you mind posting a letter for me? I want to get it off by to-night's post. I must. It's very urgent. . . .' Feeling her eyes on him, he flung: 'It's to my mother.' To me: 'I won't be long. I've got everything I want. But it must go off to-night. You don't mind? It . . . it won't take any time.'

'Of course I'll post it. Delighted.'

'Won't you drink your tea first?' suggested Mouse softly.

. . . Tea? Tea? Yes, of course. Tea. . . . A cup of tea on the bed-table. . . . In his racing dream he flashed the brightest, most charming smile at his little hostess.

'No, thanks. Not just now.'

And still hoping it would not be any trouble to me he went out of the room and closed the door, and we heard him cross the passage.

I scalded myself with mine in my hurry to take the cup back to the table and to say as I stood there: 'You must forgive me if I am impertinent . . . if I am too frank. But Dick hasn't tried to disguise it—has he? There is something the matter. Can I help?'

(Soft music. Mouse gets up, walks the stage for a moment or so before she returns to her chair and pours him out, oh, such a brimming, such a burning cup that the tears come into the friend's eyes while he sips—while he drains it to the bitter dregs. . . .)

I had time to do all this before she replied. First she looked in the teapot, filled it with hot water, and stirred it with a spoon.

'Yes, there is something the matter. No, I'm afraid you can't help, thank you.' Again I got that glimmer of a smile. 'I'm awfully sorry. It must be horrid for you.'

Horrid, indeed! Ah, why couldn't I tell her that it was months and months since I had been so entertained?

'But you are suffering,' I ventured softly, as though that was what I could not bear to see.

She didn't deny it. She nodded and bit her under-lip and I thought I saw her chin tremble.

'And there is really nothing I can do?' More softly still.

She shook her head, pushed back the table and jumped up.

'Oh, it will be all right soon,' she breathed, walking over to the dressing-table and standing with her back towards me. 'It will be all right. It can't go on like this.'

'But of course it can't.' I agreed, wondering whether it would look heartless if I lit a cigarette; I had a sudden longing to smoke.

In some way she saw my hand move to my breast pocket, half draw out my cigarette case and put it back again, for the next thing she said was: 'Matches . . . in . . . candlestick. I noticed them.'

And I heard from her voice that she was crying.

'Ah! thank you. Yes. Yes. I've found them.' I lighted my cigarette and walked up and down, smoking.

It was so quiet it might have been two o'clock in the morning. It was so quiet you heard the boards creak and pop as one does in a house in the country. I smoked the whole cigarette and stabbed the end into my saucer before Mouse turned round and came back to the table.

'Isn't Dick being rather a long time?'

'You are very tired. I expect you want to go to bed,' I said kindly. (And pray don't mind me if you do, said my mind.)

'But isn't he being a very long time?' she insisted.

I shrugged. 'He is, rather.'

Then I saw she looked at me strangely. She was listening.

'He's been gone ages,' she said, and she went with little light steps to the door, opened it, and crossed the passage into his room.

I waited. I listened too, now. I couldn't have borne to miss a word. She had left the door open. I stole across the room and looked after her. Dick's door was open, too. But—there wasn't a word to miss.

You know I had the mad idea that they were kissing in that quiet room—a long comfortable kiss. One of those kisses that not only puts one's grief to bed, but nurses it and warms it and tucks it up and keeps it fast enfolded until it is sleeping sound. Ah! how good that is.

It was over at last. I heard some one move and tip-toed away.

It was Mouse. She came back. She felt her way into the room carrying the letter for me. But it wasn't in an envelope; it was just a sheet of paper and she held it by the corner as though it was still wet.

Her head was bent so low—so tucked in her furry collar that I hadn't a notion—until she let the paper fall and almost fell herself on to the floor by the side of the bed, leaned her cheek against it, flung out her hands as though the last of her poor little weapons was gone and now she let herself be carried away, washed out into the deep water.

Flash! went my mind. Dick has shot himself, and then a succession of flashes while I rushed in, saw the body, head unharmed, small blue hole over temple, roused hotel, arranged funeral, attended funeral, closed cab, new morning coat. . . .*

I stooped down and picked up the paper and would you believe it—so ingrained is my Parisian sense of *comme il faut*—I murmured 'pardon' before I read it.

'Mouse, my little Mouse,

It's no good. It's impossible. I can't see it through. Oh, I do love you. I do love you, Mouse, but I can't hurt her. People have been hurting her all her life. I simply dare not give her this final blow. You see, though she's stronger than both of us, she's so frail and proud. It would kill her—kill her, Mouse. And, oh God, I can't kill my mother! Not even for you. Not even for us. You do see that—don't you.

It all seemed so possible when we talked and planned, but the very moment the train started it was all over. I felt her drag me back to her—calling. I can hear her now as I write. And she's alone and she doesn't know. A man would have to be a devil to tell her and I'm not a devil, Mouse. She mustn't know. Oh, Mouse, somewhere, somewhere in you don't you agree? It's all so unspeakably awful that I don't know if I want to go or not. Do I? Or is Mother just dragging me? I don't know. My head is too tired. Mouse, Mouse—what will you do? But I can't think of that, either. I dare not. I'd break down. And I must not break down. All I've got to do is—just to tell you this and go. I couldn't have gone off without telling you. You'd have been frightened. And you must not be frightened. You won't—will you? I can't bear—but no more of that. And don't write. I should not have the courage to answer your letters and the sight of your spidery handwriting——

Forgive me. Don't love me any more. Yes. Love me. Love me. Dick.'

What do you think of that? Wasn't that a rare find? My relief at his not having shot himself was mixed with a wonderful sense of elation. I was even—more than even with my 'that's very curious and interesting' Englishman. . . .

She wept so strangely. With her eyes shut, with her face quite calm except for the quivering eyelids. The tears pearled down her cheeks and she let them fall.

But feeling my glance upon her she opened her eyes and saw me holding the letter.

'You've read it?'

Her voice was quite calm, but it was not her voice any more. It was like the voice you might imagine coming out of a tiny, cold sea-shell swept high and dry at last by the salt tide. . . .

I nodded, quite overcome, you understand, and laid the letter down.

'It's incredible! incredible!' I whispered.

At that she got up from the floor, walked over to the wash-stand, dipped her handkerchief into the jug and sponged her eyes, saying: 'Oh, no. It's not incredible at all.' And still pressing the wet ball to her eyes she came back to me, to her chair with the lace tabs, and sank into it.

'I knew all along, of course,' said the cold, salty little voice. 'From the very moment that we started. I felt it all through me, but I still went on hoping—' and here she took the handkerchief down and gave me a final glimmer—'as one so stupidly does, you know.'

'As one does.'

Silence.

'But what will you do? You'll go back? You'll see him?'

That made her sit right up and stare across at me.

'What an extraordinary idea!' she said, more coldly than ever. 'Of course I shall not dream of seeing him. As for going back—that is quite out of the question. I can't go back.'

'But . . . .'

'It's impossible. For one thing all my friends think I am married.'

I put out my hand—'Ah, my poor little friend.'

But she shrank away. (False move.)

Of course there was one question that had been at the back of my mind all this time. I hated it.

'Have you any money?'

'Yes, I have twenty pounds—here,' and she put her hand on her breast. I bowed. It was a great deal more than I had expected.

'And what are your plans?'

Yes, I know. My question was the most clumsy, the most idiotic one I could have put. She had been so tame, so confiding, letting me, at any rate spiritually speaking, hold her tiny quivering body in one hand and stroke her furry head—and now, I'd thrown her away. Oh, I could have kicked myself.

She stood up. 'I have no plans. But—it's very late. You must go now, please.'

How could I get her back? I wanted her back, I swear I was not acting then.

'Do feel that I am your friend,' I cried. 'You will let me come to-morrow, early? You will let me look after you a little—take care of you a little? You'll use me just as you think fit?'

I succeeded. She came out of her hole . . . timid . . . but she came out.

'Yes, you're very kind. Yes. Do come to-morrow. I shall be glad. It makes things rather difficult because—' and again I clasped her boyish hand—'*je ne parle pas français.*'

Not until I was half-way down the boulevard did it come over me—the full force of it.

Why, they were suffering . . . those two . . . really suffering. I have seen two people suffer as I don't suppose I ever shall again . . . . And . . . . 'Good-night, my little cat,' said I, impudently, to the fattish old prostitute picking her way home through the slush . . . . I didn't give her time to reply.

Of course you know what to expect. You anticipate, fully, what I am going to write. It wouldn't be me, otherwise.

I never went near the place again.

Yes, I still owe that considerable amount for lunches and dinners, but that's beside the mark. It's vulgar to mention it in the same breath with the fact that I never saw Mouse again.

Naturally, I intended to. Started out—got to the door—wrote and tore up letters—did all those things. But I simply could not make the final effort.

Even now I don't fully understand why. Of course I knew that I couldn't have kept it up. That had a great deal to do with it. But you would have thought, putting it at its lowest, curiosity couldn't have kept my fox-terrier nose away . . . .

Je ne parle pas français. That was her swan song for me.

But how she makes me break my rule. Oh, you've seen for yourself, but I could give you countless examples.

. . . Evenings, when I sit in some gloomy café, and an automatic piano starts playing a 'mouse' tune (there are dozens of tunes that evoke just her) I begin to dream things like. . . .

A little house on the edge of the sea, somewhere far, far away. A girl outside in a frock rather like Red Indian women wear, hailing a light, bare-foot boy who runs up from the beach.

'What have you got?'

'A fish.' I smile and give it to her.

. . . The same girl, the same boy, different costumes—sitting at an open window, eating fruit and leaning out and laughing.

'All the wild strawberries are for you, Mouse. I won't touch one.'

. . . A wet night. They are going home together under an umbrella. They stop on the door to press their wet cheeks together.

And so on and so on until some dirty old gallant* comes up to my table and sits opposite and begins to grimace and yap. Until I hear myself saying: 'But I've got the little girl for you, *mon vieux*. So little . . . so tiny. And a virgin.' I kiss the tips of my fingers—'A virgin'—and lay them upon my heart. 'I give you my word of honour as a gentleman, a writer, serious, young, and extremely interested in modern English literature.'

I must go. I must go. I reach down my coat and hat. Madame knows me. 'You haven't dined yet?' she smiles.

'No, not yet, Madame.'

I'd rather like to dine with her. Even to sleep with her afterwards. Would she be pale like that all over?

But no. She'd have large moles. They go with that kind of skin. And I can't bear them. They remind me somehow, disgustingly, of mushrooms.

SUN AND MOON

In the afternoon the chairs came, a whole big cart full of little gold ones with their legs in the air. And then the flowers came. When you stared down from the balcony at the people carrying them the flower pots looked like funny awfully nice hats nodding up the path.

Moon thought they were hats. She said: 'Look. There's a man wearing a palm on his head.' But she never knew the difference between real things and not real ones.

There was nobody to look after Sun and Moon. Nurse was helping Annie alter Mother's dress which was much-too-long-and-tight-under-the-arms and Mother was running all over the house and telephoning Father to be sure not to forget things. She only had time to say: 'Out of my way, children!'

They kept out of her way—at any rate Sun did. He did so hate being sent stumping back to the nursery. It didn't matter about Moon. If she got tangled in people's legs they only threw her up and shook her till she squeaked. But Sun was too heavy for that. He was so heavy that the fat man who came to dinner on Sundays used to say: 'Now, young man, let's try to lift you.' And then he'd put his thumbs under Sun's arms and groan and try and give it up at last saying: 'He's a perfect little ton of bricks!'

Nearly all the furniture was taken out of the dining-room. The big piano was put in a corner and then there came a row of flower pots and then there came the goldy chairs. That was for the concert. When Sun looked in a white faced man sat at the piano—not play-ing, but banging at it and then looking inside. He had a bag of tools on the piano and he had stuck his hat on a statue against the wall. Sometimes he just started to play and then he jumped up again and looked inside. Sun hoped he wasn't the concert.

But of course the place to be in was the kitchen. There was a man helping in a cap like a blancmange, and their real cook, Minnie, was all red in the face and laughing. Not cross at all. She gave them each an almond finger and lifted them up on to the flour bin so that they could watch the wonderful things she and the man were making for supper. Cook brought in the things and he put them on dishes and trimmed them. Whole fishes, with their heads and eyes and tails still on, he sprinkled with red and green and yellow bits; he made squiggles all over the jellies, he stuck a collar on a ham and put a very thin sort of a fork in it; he dotted almonds and tiny round biscuits on the creams. And more and more things kept coming.

'Ah, but you haven't seen the ice pudding,' said Cook. 'Come along.' Why was she being so nice, thought Sun as she gave them each a hand. And they looked into the refrigerator.

Oh! Oh! Oh! It was a little house. It was a little pink house with white snow on the roof and green windows and a brown door and stuck in the door there was a nut for a handle.

When Sun saw the nut he felt quite tired and had to lean against Cook.

'Let me touch it. Just let me put my finger on the roof,' said Moon, dancing. She always wanted to touch all the food. Sun didn't.

'Now, my girl, look sharp with the table,' said Cook as the housemaid came in.

'It's a picture, Min,' said Nellie. 'Come along and have a look.' So they all went into the dining-room. Sun and Moon were almost frightened. They wouldn't go up to the table at first; they just stood at the door and made eyes at it.

It wasn't real night yet but the blinds were down in the dining-room and the lights turned on—and all the lights were red roses. Red ribbons and bunches of roses tied up the table at the corners. In the middle was a lake with rose petals floating on it.

'That's where the ice pudding is to be,' said Cook.

Two silver lions with wings had fruit on their backs, and the salt cellars were tiny birds drinking out of basins.

And all the winking glasses and shining plates and sparkling knives and forks—and all the food. And the little red table napkins made into roses. . . .

'Are people going to eat the food?' asked Sun.

'I should just think they were,' laughed Cook, laughing with Nellie. Moon laughed, too; she always did the same as other people. But Sun didn't want to laugh. Round and round he walked with his hands behind his back. Perhaps he never would have stopped if Nurse hadn't called suddenly: 'Now then, children. It's high time you were washed and dressed.' And they were marched off to the nursery.

While they were being unbuttoned Mother looked in with a white thing* over her shoulders; she was rubbing stuff on her face.

'I'll ring for them when I want them, Nurse, and then they can just come down and be seen and go back again,' said she.

Sun was undressed, first nearly to his skin, and dressed again in a white shirt with red and white daisies speckled on it, breeches with strings at the sides and braces that came over, white socks and red shoes.

'Now you're in your Russian costume,' said Nurse, flattening down his fringe.

'Am I?' said Sun.

'Yes. Sit quiet in that chair and watch your little sister.'

Moon took ages. When she had her socks put on she pretended to fall back on the bed and waved her legs at Nurse as she always did, and every time Nurse tried to make her curls with a finger and a wet brush she turned round and asked Nurse to show her the photo in her brooch or something like that. But at last she was finished too. Her dress stuck out, with fur on it, all white; there was even fluffy stuff on the legs of her drawers. Her shoes were white with big blobs on them.

'There you are, my lamb,' said Nurse. 'And you look like a sweet little cherub of a picture of a powder-puff.' Nurse rushed to the door. 'Ma'am, one moment.'

Mother came in again with half her hair down.

'Oh,' she cried. 'What a picture!'

'Isn't she,' said Nurse.

And Moon held out her skirts by the tips and dragged one of her feet. Sun didn't mind people not noticing him— much. . . .

After that they played clean tidy games up at the table while Nurse stood at the door, and when the carriages began to come and the sound of laughter and voices and soft rustlings came from down below she whispered: 'Now then, children, stay where you are.' Moon kept jerking the table cloth so that it all hung down her side and Sun hadn't any—and then she pretended she didn't do it on purpose.

At last the bell rang. Nurse pounced at them with the hair brush, flattened his fringe, made her bow stand on end and joined their hands together.

'Down you go!' she whispered.

And down they went. Sun did feel silly holding Moon's hand like that but Moon seemed to like it. She swung her arm and the bell on her coral bracelet jingled.

At the drawing-room door stood Mother fanning herself with a black fan. The drawing-room was full of sweet smelling, silky, rustling ladies and men in black with funny tails on their coats—like beetles. Father was among them, talking very loud, and rattling something in his pocket.

'What a picture!' cried the ladies. 'Oh, the ducks! Oh, the lambs! Oh, the sweets! Oh, the pets!'

All the people who couldn't get at Moon kissed Sun, and a skinny old lady with teeth that clicked said: 'Such a serious little poppet,' and rapped him on the head with something hard.

Sun looked to see if the same concert was there, but he was gone. Instead, a fat man with a pink head leaned over the piano talking to a girl who held a violin at her ear.

There was only one man that Sun really liked. He was a little grey man, with long grey whiskers, who walked about by himself. He came up to Sun and rolled his eyes in a very nice way and said: 'Hullo, my lad.' Then he went away. But soon he came back again and said: 'Fond of dogs?' Sun said: 'Yes.' But then he went away again, and though Sun looked for him everywhere he couldn't find him. He thought perhaps he'd gone outside to fetch in a puppy.

'Good night, my precious babies,' said Mother, folding them up in her bare arms. 'Fly up to your little nest.'

Then Moon went and made a silly of herself again. She put up her arms in front of everybody and said: 'My Daddy must carry me.'

But they seemed to like it, and Daddy swooped down and picked her up as he always did.

Nurse was in such a hurry to get them to bed that she even interrupted Sun over his prayers and said: 'Get on with them, child, *do*.' And the moment after they were in bed and in the dark except for the nightlight in its little saucer.

'Are you asleep?' asked Moon.

'No,' said Sun. 'Are you?'

'No,' said Moon.

A long while after Sun woke up again. There was a loud, loud noise of clapping from downstairs, like when it rains. He heard Moon turn over.

'Moon, are you awake?'

'Yes, are you?'

'Yes. Well, let's go and look over the stairs.'

They had just got settled on the top step when the drawing-room door opened and they heard the party cross over the hall into the dining-room. Then that door was shut; there was a noise of 'pops' and laughing. Then that stopped and Sun saw them all walking round and round the lovely table with their hands behind their backs like he had done. . . . Round and round they walked, looking and staring. The man with the grey whiskers liked the little house best. When he saw the nut for a handle he rolled his eyes like he did before and said to Sun: 'Seen the nut?'

'Don't nod your head like that, Moon.'

'I'm not nodding. It's you.'

'It is not. I never nod my head.'

'O-oh, you do. You're nodding it now.'

'I'm not. I'm only showing you how not to do it.'

When they woke up again they could only hear Father's voice very loud, and Mother, laughing away. Father came out of the dining-room, bounded up the stairs, and nearly fell over them.

'Hullo!' he said. 'By Jove, Kitty, come and look at this.'

Mother came out. 'Oh, you naughty children,' said she from the hall.

'Let's have 'em down and give 'em a bone,' said Father. Sun had never seen him so jolly.

'No, certainly not,' said Mother.

'Oh, my Daddy, do! Do have us down,' said Moon.

'I'm hanged if I won't,' cried Father. 'I won't be bullied. Kitty—way there.' And he caught them up, one under each arm.

Sun thought Mother would have been dreadfully cross. But she wasn't. She kept on laughing at Father.

'Oh, you dreadful boy!' said she. But she didn't mean Sun.

'Come on, kiddies. Come and have some pickings,' said this jolly Father. But Moon stopped a minute.

'Mother—your dress is right off one side.'

'Is it?' said Mother. And Father said 'Yes' and pretended to bite her white shoulder, but she pushed him away.

And so they went back to the beautiful dining-room.

But—oh! oh! what had happened? The ribbons and the roses were all pulled untied. The little red table napkins lay on the floor, all the shining plates were dirty and all the winking glasses. The lovely food that the man had trimmed was all thrown about, and there were bones and bits and fruit peels and shells everywhere. There was even a bottle lying down with stuff coming out of it on to the cloth and nobody stood it up again.

And the little pink house with the snow roof and the green windows was broken—broken—half melted away in the centre of the table.

'Come on, Sun,' said Father, pretending not to notice.

Moon lifted up her pyjama legs and shuffled up to the table and stood on a chair, squeaking away.

'Have a bit of this ice,' said Father, smashing in some more of the roof.

Mother took a little plate and held it for him; she put her other arm round his neck.

'Daddy! Daddy!' shrieked Moon. 'The little handle's left. The little nut. Kin I eat it?' And she reached across and picked it out of the door and scrunched it up, biting hard and blinking.

'Here, my lad,' said Father.

But Sun did not move from the door. Suddenly he put up his head and gave a loud wail.

'I think it's horrid—horrid—horrid!' he sobbed.

'There, you see!' said Mother. 'You see!'

'Off with you,' said Father, no longer jolly. 'This moment. Off you go!'

And wailing loudly, Sun stumped off to the nursery.

BLISS

Although Bertha Young was thirty she still had moments like this when she wanted to run instead of walk, to take dancing steps on and off the pavement, to bowl a hoop, to throw something up in the air and catch it again, or to stand still and laugh at—nothing—at nothing, simply.

What can you do if you are thirty and, turning the corner of your own street, you are overcome, suddenly, by a feeling of bliss—absolute bliss!—as though you'd suddenly swallowed a bright piece of that late afternoon sun and it burned in your bosom, sending out a little shower of sparks into every particle, into every finger and toe? . . .

Oh, is there no way you can express it without being 'drunk and disorderly'? How idiotic civilization is! Why be given a body if you have to keep it shut up in a case like a rare, rare fiddle?

'No, that about the fiddle is not quite what I mean,' she thought, running up the steps and feeling in her bag for the key—she'd forgotten it, as usual—and rattling the letter-box. 'It's not what I mean, because—Thank you, Mary'—she went into the hall. 'Is Nurse back?'

'Yes, M'm.'

'And has the fruit come?'

'Yes, M'm. Everything's come.'

'Bring the fruit up to the dining-room, will you? I'll arrange it before I go upstairs.'

It was dusky in the dining-room and quite chilly. But all the same Bertha threw off her coat; she could not bear the tight clasp of it another moment, and the cold air fell on her arms.

But in her bosom there was still that bright glowing place—that shower of little sparks coming from it. It was almost unbearable. She hardly dared to breathe for fear of fanning it higher, and yet she breathed deeply, deeply. She hardly dared to look into the cold mirror—but she did look, and it gave her back a woman, radiant, with smiling, trembling lips, with big, dark eyes and an air of listening, waiting for something . . . divine to happen . . . that she knew must happen . . . infallibly.

Mary brought in the fruit on a tray and with it a glass bowl, and a blue dish, very lovely, with a strange sheen on it as though it had been dipped in milk.

'Shall I turn on the light, M'm?'

'No, thank you. I can see quite well.'

There were tangerines and apples stained with strawberry pink. Some yellow pears, smooth as silk; some white grapes covered with a silver bloom and a big cluster of purple ones. These last she had bought to tone in with the new dining-room carpet. Yes, that did sound rather far-fetched and absurd, but it was really why she had bought them. She had thought in the shop: 'I must have some purple ones to bring the carpet up to the table.' And it had seemed quite sense at the time.

When she had finished with them and had made two pyramids of these bright round shapes, she stood away from the table to get the effect—and it really was most curious. For the dark table seemed to melt into the dusky light and the glass dish and the blue bowl to float in the air. This, of course in her present mood, was so incredibly beautiful. . . . She began to laugh.

'No, no. I'm getting hysterical.' And she seized her bag and coat and ran upstairs to the nursery.

Nurse sat at a low table giving Little B her supper after her bath. The baby had on a white flannel gown and a blue woollen jacket, and her dark, fine hair was brushed up into a funny little peak. She looked up when she saw her mother and began to jump.

'Now, my lovey, eat it up like a good girl,' said Nurse, setting her lips in a way that Bertha knew, and that meant she had come into the nursery at another wrong moment.

'Has she been good, Nanny?'

'She's been a little sweet all the afternoon,' whispered Nanny. 'We went to the park and I sat down on a chair and took her out of the pram and a big dog came along and put its head on my knee and she clutched its ear, tugged it. Oh, you should have seen her.'

Bertha wanted to ask if it wasn't rather dangerous to let her clutch at a strange dog's ear. But she did not dare to. She stood watching them, her hands by her side, like the poor little girl in front of the rich little girl with the doll.

The baby looked up at her again, stared, and then smiled so charmingly that Bertha couldn't help crying:

'Oh, Nanny, do let me finish giving her her supper while you put the bath things away.'

'Well, M'm, she oughtn't to be changed hands while she's eating,' said Nanny, still whispering. 'It unsettles her; it's very likely to upset her.'

How absurd it was. Why have a baby if it has to be kept—not in a case like a rare, rare fiddle—but in another woman's arms?

'Oh, I must!' said she.

Very offended, Nanny handed her over.

'Now, don't excite her after her supper. You know you do, M'm. And I have such a time with her after!'

Thank heaven! Nanny went out of the room with the bath towels.

'Now I've got you to myself, my little precious,' said Bertha, as the baby leaned against her.

She ate delightfully, holding up her lips for the spoon and then waving her hands. Sometimes she wouldn't let the spoon go; and sometimes, just as Bertha had filled it, she waved it away to the four winds.

When the soup was finished Bertha turned round to the fire.

'You're nice—you're very nice!' said she, kissing her warm baby. 'I'm fond of you. I like you.'

And, indeed, she loved Little B so much—her neck as she bent forward, her exquisite toes as they shone transparent in the firelight—that all her feeling of bliss came back again, and again she didn't know how to express it—what to do with it.

'You're wanted on the telephone,' said Nanny, coming back in triumph and seizing *her* Little B.

Down she flew. It was Harry.

'Oh, is that you, Ber? Look here. I'll be late. I'll take a taxi and come along as quickly as I can, but get dinner put back ten minutes—will you? All right?'

'Yes, perfectly. Oh, Harry!'

'Yes?'

What had she to say? She'd nothing to say. She only wanted to get in touch with him for a moment. She couldn't absurdly cry: 'Hasn't it been a divine day!'

'What is it?' rapped out the little voice.

'Nothing. *Entendu*,'* said Bertha, and hung up the receiver, thinking how more than idiotic civilization was.

They had people coming to dinner. The Norman Knights—a very sound couple—he was about to start a theatre, and she was awfully keen on interior decoration, a young man, Eddie Warren, who had just published a little book of poems and whom everybody was asking to dine, and a 'find' of Bertha's called Pearl Fulton. What Miss Fulton did, Bertha didn't know. They had met at the club and Bertha had fallen in love with her, as she always did fall in love with beautiful women who had something strange about them.

The provoking thing was that, though they had been about together and met a number of times and really talked, Bertha couldn't yet make her out. Up to a certain point Miss Fulton was rarely, wonderfully frank, but the certain point was there, and beyond that she would not go.

Was there anything beyond it? Harry said 'No.' Voted her dullish, and 'cold like all blond women, with a touch, perhaps, of anemia of the brain'. But Bertha wouldn't agree with him; not yet, at any rate.

'No, the way she has of sitting with her head a little on one side, and smiling, has something behind it, Harry, and I must find out what that something is.'

'Most likely it's a good stomach,' answered Harry.

He made a point of catching Bertha's heels with replies of that kind . . . 'liver frozen, my dear girl', or 'pure flatulence', or 'kidney disease', . . . and so on. For some strange reason Bertha liked this, and almost admired it in him very much.

She went into the drawing-room and lighted the fire; then, picking up the cushions, one by one, that Mary had disposed so carefully, she threw them back on to the chairs and the couches. That made all the difference; the room came alive at once. As she was about to throw the last one she surprised herself by suddenly hugging it to her, passionately, passionately. But it did not put out the fire in her bosom. Oh, on the contrary!

The windows of the drawing-room opened on to a balcony overlooking the garden. At the far end, against the wall, there was a tall, slender pear tree in fullest, richest bloom; it stood perfect, as though becalmed against the jade-green sky. Bertha couldn't help feeling, even from this distance, that it had not a single bud or a faded petal. Down below, in the garden beds, the red and yellow tulips, heavy with flowers, seemed to lean upon the dusk. A grey cat, dragging its belly, crept across the lawn, and a black one, its shadow, trailed after. The sight of them, so intent and so quick, gave Bertha a curious shiver.

'What creepy things cats are!' she stammered, and she turned away from the window and began walking up and down. . . .

How strong the jonquils smelled in the warm room. Too strong? Oh, no. And yet, as though overcome, she flung down on a couch and pressed her hands to her eyes.

'I'm too happy—too happy!' she murmured.

And she seemed to see on her eyelids the lovely pear tree with its wide open blossoms as a symbol of her own life.

Really—really—she had everything. She was young. Harry and she were as much in love as ever, and they got on together splendidly and were really good pals. She had an adorable baby. They didn't have to worry about money. They had this absolutely satisfactory house and garden. And friends—modern, thrilling friends, writers and painters and poets or people keen on social questions—just the kind of friends they wanted. And then there were books, and there was music, and she had found a wonderful little dressmaker, and they were going abroad in the summer, and their new cook made the most superb omelettes. . . .

'I'm absurd. Absurd!' She sat up; but she felt quite dizzy, quite drunk. It must have been the spring.

Yes, it was the spring. Now she was so tired she could not drag herself upstairs to dress.

A white dress, a string of jade beads, green shoes and stockings. It wasn't 'intentional'. She had thought of this scheme hours before she stood at the drawing-room window.

Her petals rustled softly into the hall, and she kissed Mrs Norman Knight, who was taking off the most amusing orange coat with a procession of black monkeys round the hem and up the fronts.

'. . . Why! Why! Why is the middle-class so stodgy—so utterly without a sense of humour! My dear, it's only by a fluke that I am here at all—Norman being the protective fluke. For my darling monkeys so upset the train that it rose to a man and simply ate me with its eyes. Didn't laugh—wasn't amused—that I should have loved. No, just stared—and bored me through and through.'

'But the cream of it was,' said Norman, pressing a large tortoiseshell-rimmed monocle* into his eye, 'you don't mind me telling this, Face, do you?' (In their home and among their friends they called each other Face and Mug.) 'The cream of it was when she, being full fed, turned to the woman beside her and said: "Haven't you ever seen a monkey before?"'

'Oh, yes!' Mrs Norman Knight joined in the laughter. 'Wasn't that too absolutely creamy?'

And a funnier thing still was that now her coat was off she did look like a very intelligent monkey—who had even made that yellow silk dress out of scraped banana skins. And her amber ear-rings; they were like little dangling nuts.

'This is a sad, sad fall!' said Mug, pausing in front of Little B's perambulator.* 'When the perambulator comes into the hall—' and he waved the rest of the quotation away.

The bell rang. It was lean, pale Eddie Warren (as usual) in a state of acute distress.

'It *is* the right house, *isn't* it?' he pleaded.

'Oh, I think so—I hope so,' said Bertha brightly.

'I have had such a *dreadful* experience with a taxi-man; he was *most* sinister. I couldn't get him to *stop*. The *more* I knocked and called the *faster* he went. And *in* the moonlight this *bizarre* figure with the *flattened* head *crouching* over the *lit-tle* wheel. . . .'

He shuddered, taking off an immense white silk scarf. Bertha noticed that his socks were white, too—most charming.

'But how dreadful!' she cried.

'Yes, it really was,' said Eddie, following her into the drawing-room. 'I saw myself *driving* through Eternity in a *timeless* taxi.'

He knew the Norman Knights. In fact, he was going to write a play for N. K. when the theatre scheme came off.

'Well, Warren, how's the play?' said Norman Knight, dropping his monocle and giving his eye a moment in which to rise to the surface before it was screwed down again.

And Mrs Norman Knight: 'Oh, Mr Warren, what happy socks?'

'I *am* so glad you like them,' said he, staring at his feet. 'They seem to have got so *much* whiter since the moon rose.' And he turned his lean sorrowful young face to Bertha. 'There *is* a moon, you know.'

She wanted to cry: 'I am sure there is—often—often!'

He really was a most attractive person. But so was Face, crouched before the fire in her banana skins, and so was Mug, smoking a cigarette and saying as he flicked the ash: 'Why doth the bridegroom tarry?'*

'There he is, now.'

Bang went the front door open and shut. Harry shouted: 'Hullo, you people. Down in five minutes.' And they heard him swarm up the stairs. Bertha couldn't help smiling; she knew how he loved doing things at high pressure. What, after all, did an extra five minutes matter? But he would pretend to himself that they mattered beyond measure. And then he would make a great point of coming into the drawing-room, extravagantly cool and collected.

Harry had such a zest for life. Oh, how she appreciated it in him. And his passion for fighting—for seeking in everything that came up against him another test of his power and of his courage—that, too, she understood. Even when it made him just occasionally, to other people, who didn't know him well, a little ridiculous perhaps. . . . For there were moments when he rushed into battle where no battle was. . . . She talked and laughed and positively forgot until he had come in (just as she had imagined) that Pearl Fulton had not turned up.

'I wonder if Miss Fulton has forgotten?'

'I expect so,' said Harry. 'Is she on the 'phone?'

'Ah! There's a taxi, now.' And Bertha smiled with that little air of proprietorship that she always assumed while her women finds were new and mysterious. 'She lives in taxis.'

'She'll run to fat if she does,' said Harry coolly, ringing the bell for dinner. 'Frightful danger for blond women.'

'Harry—don't,' warned Bertha, laughing up at him.

Came another tiny moment, while they waited, laughing and talking, just a trifle too much at their ease, a trifle too unaware. And then Miss Fulton, all in silver, with a silver fillet binding her pale blond hair, came in smiling, her head a little on one side.

'Am I late?'

'No, not at all,' said Bertha. 'Come along.' And she took her arm and they moved into the dining-room.

What was there in the touch of that cool arm that could fan—fan—start blazing—blazing—the fire of bliss that Bertha did not know what to do with?

Miss Fulton did not look at her; but then she seldom did look at people directly. Her heavy eyelids lay upon her eyes and the strange half smile came and went upon her lips as though she lived by listening rather than seeing. But Bertha knew, suddenly, as if the longest, most intimate look had passed between them—as if they had said to each other: 'You, too?'—that Pearl Fulton, stirring the beautiful red soup in the grey plate, was feeling just what she was feeling.

And the others? Face and Mug, Eddie and Harry, their spoons rising and falling—dabbing their lips with their napkins, crumbling bread, fiddling with the forks and glasses and talking.

'I met her at the Alpha show—the weirdest little person. She'd not only cut off her hair, but she seemed to have taken a dreadfully good snip off her legs and arms and her neck and her poor little nose as well.'

'Isn't she very *liée** with Michael Oat?'

'The man who wrote *Love in False Teeth*?'

'He wants to write a play for me. One act. One man. Decides to commit suicide. Gives all the reasons why he should and why he shouldn't. And just as he has made up his mind either to do it or not to do it—curtain. Not half a bad idea.'

'What's he going to call it—"Stomach Trouble"?'

'I *think* I've come across the *same* idea in a lit-tle French review, *quite* unknown in England.'

No, they didn't share it. They were dears—dears—and she loved having them there, at her table, and giving them delicious food and wine. In fact, she longed to tell them how delightful they were, and what a decorative group they made, how they seemed to set one another off and how they reminded her of a play by Tchekof!*

Harry was enjoying his dinner. It was part of his—well, not his nature, exactly, and certainly not his pose—his—something or other—to talk about food and to glory in his 'shameless passion for the white flesh of the lobster' and 'the green of pistachio ices—green and cold like the eyelids of Egyptian dancers'.

When he looked up at her and said: 'Bertha, this is a very admirable *soufflée*!' she almost could have wept with child-like pleasure.

Oh, why did she feel so tender towards the whole world to-night? Everything was good—was right. All that happened seemed to fill again her brimming cup of bliss.

And still, in the back of her mind, there was the pear tree. It would be silver now, in the light of poor dear Eddie's moon, silver as Miss Fulton, who sat there turning a tangerine in her slender fingers that were so pale a light seemed to come from them.

What she simply couldn't make out—what was miraculous—was how she should have guessed Miss Fulton's mood so exactly and so instantly. For she never doubted for a moment that she was right, and yet what had she to go on? Less than nothing.

'I believe this does happen very, very rarely between women. Never between men,' thought Bertha. 'But while I am making the coffee in the drawing-room perhaps she will "give a sign".'

What she meant by that she did not know, and what would happen after that she could not imagine.

While she thought like this she saw herself talking and laughing. She had to talk because of her desire to laugh.

'I must laugh or die.'

But when she noticed Face's funny little habit of tucking something down the front of her bodice—as if she kept a tiny, secret hoard of nuts there, too—Bertha had to dig her nails into her hands—so as not to laugh too much.

It was over at last. And: 'Come and see my new coffee machine,' said Bertha.

'We only have a new coffee machine once a fortnight,' said Harry. Face took her arm this time; Miss Fulton bent her head and followed after.

The fire had died down in the drawing-room to a red, flickering 'nest of baby phœnixes', said Face.

'Don't turn up the light for a moment. It is so lovely.' And down she crouched by the fire again. She was always cold . . . 'without her little red flannel jacket, of course,' thought Bertha.

At that moment Miss Fulton 'gave the sign'.

'Have you a garden?' said the cool, sleepy voice.

This was so exquisite on her part that all Bertha could do was to obey. She crossed the room, pulled the curtains apart, and opened those long windows.

'There!' she breathed.

And the two women stood side by side looking at the slender, flowering tree. Although it was so still it seemed, like the flame of a candle, to stretch up, to point, to quiver in the bright air, to grow taller and taller as they gazed—almost to touch the rim of the round, silver moon.

How long did they stand there? Both, as it were, caught in that circle of unearthly light, understanding each other perfectly, creatures of another world, and wondering what they were to do in this one with all this blissful treasure that burned in their bosoms and dropped, in silver flowers, from their hair and hands?

For ever—for a moment? And did Miss Fulton murmur: 'Yes. Just *that*.' Or did Bertha dream it?

Then the light was snapped on and Face made the coffee and Harry said: 'My dear Mrs Knight, don't ask me about my baby. I never see her. I shan't feel the slightest interest in her until she has a lover,' and Mug took his eye out of the conservatory for a moment and then put it under glass again and Eddie Warren drank his coffee and set down the cup with a face of anguish as though he had drunk and seen the spider.*

'What I want to do is to give the young men a show. I believe London is simply teeming with first-chop, unwritten plays. What I want to say to 'em is: "Here's the theatre. Fire ahead."'

'You know, my dear, I am going to decorate a room for the Jacob Nathans. Oh, I am so tempted to do a fried-fish scheme, with the backs of the chairs shaped like frying pans and lovely chip potatoes embroidered all over the curtains.'

'The trouble with our young writing men is that they are still too romantic. You can't put out to sea without being seasick and wanting a basin. Well, why won't they have the courage of those basins?'

'A *dreadful* poem about a *girl* who was *violated* by a beggar *without* a nose in a lit-tle wood. . . .'

Miss Fulton sank into the lowest, deepest chair and Harry handed round the cigarettes.

From the way he stood in front of her shaking the silver box and saying abruptly: 'Egyptian? Turkish? Virginian? They're all mixed up,' Bertha realized that she not only bored him; he really disliked her. And she decided from the way Miss Fulton said: 'No, thank you, I won't smoke,' that she felt it, too, and was hurt.

'Oh, Harry, don't dislike her. You are quite wrong about her. She's wonderful, wonderful. And, besides, how can you feel so differently about someone who means so much to me. I shall try to tell you when we are in bed to-night what has been happening. What she and I have shared.'

At those last words something strange and almost terrifying darted into Bertha's mind. And this something blind and smiling whispered to her: 'Soon these people will go. The house will be quiet—quiet. The lights will be out. And you and he will be alone together in the dark room—the warm bed. . . .'

She jumped up from her chair and ran over to the piano.

'What a pity someone does not play!' she cried. 'What a pity somebody does not play.'

For the first time in her life Bertha Young desired her husband.

Oh, she'd loved him—she'd been in love with him, of course, in every other way, but just not in that way. And, equally, of course, she'd understood that he was different. They'd discussed it so often. It had worried her dreadfully at first to find that she was so cold, but after a time it had not seemed to matter. They were so frank with each other—such good pals. That was the best of being modern.

But now—ardently! ardently! The word ached in her ardent body! Was this what that feeling of bliss had been leading up to? But then, then——

'My dear,' said Mrs Norman Knight, 'you know our shame. We are the victims of time and train. We live in Hampstead. It's been so nice.'

'I'll come with you into the hall,' said Bertha. 'I loved having you. But you must not miss the last train. That's so awful, isn't it?'

'Have a whisky, Knight, before you go?' called Harry.

'No, thanks, old chap.'

Bertha squeezed his hand for that as she shook it.

'Good night, good-bye,' she cried from the top step, feeling that this self of hers was taking leave of them for ever.

When she got back into the drawing-room the others were on the move.

'. . . Then you can come part of the way in my taxi.'

'I shall be *so* thankful *not* to have to face *another* drive *alone* after my *dreadful* experience.'

'You can get a taxi at the rank just at the end of the street. You won't have to walk more than a few yards.'

'That's a comfort. I'll go and put on my coat.'

Miss Fulton moved towards the hall and Bertha was following when Harry almost pushed past.

'Let me help you.'

Bertha knew that he was repenting his rudeness—she let him go. What a boy he was in some ways—so impulsive—so—simple.

And Eddie and she were left by the fire.

'I *wonder* if you have seen Bilks' *new* poem called *Table d'Hôte*,'* said Eddie softly. 'It's *so* wonderful. In the last Anthology. Have you got a copy? I'd *so* like to *show* it to you. It begins with an *incredibly* beautiful line: "Why Must it Always be Tomato Soup?"'

'Yes,' said Bertha. And she moved noiselessly to a table opposite the drawing-room door and Eddie glided noiselessly after her. She picked up the little book and gave it to him; they had not made a sound.

While he looked it up she turned her head towards the hall. And she saw ... Harry with Miss Fulton's coat in his arms and Miss Fulton with her back turned to him and her head bent. He tossed the coat away, put his hands on her shoulders and turned her violently to him. His lips said: 'I adore you,' and Miss Fulton laid her moonbeam fingers on his cheeks and smiled her sleepy smile. Harry's nostrils quivered; his lips curled back in a hideous grin while he whispered: 'To-morrow,' and with her eyelids Miss Fulton said: 'Yes.'

'Here it is,' said Eddie. ' "Why Must it Always be Tomato Soup?" It's so *deeply* true, don't you feel? Tomato soup is so *dreadfully* eternal.'

'If you prefer,' said Harry's voice, very loud, from the hall, 'I can phone you a cab to come to the door.'

'Oh, no. It's not necessary,' said Miss Fulton, and she came up to Bertha and gave her the slender fingers to hold.

'Good-bye. Thank you so much.'

'Good-bye,' said Bertha.

Miss Fulton held her hand a moment longer.

'Your lovely pear tree!' she murmured.

And then she was gone, with Eddie following, like the black cat following the grey cat.

'I'll shut up shop,' said Harry, extravagantly cool and collected.

'Your lovely pear tree—pear tree—pear tree!'

Bertha simply ran over to the long windows.

'Oh, what is going to happen now?' she cried.

But the pear tree was as lovely as ever and as full of flower and as still.

PSYCHOLOGY

When she opened the door and saw him standing there she was more pleased than ever before, and he, too, as he followed her into the studio, seemed very very happy to have come.

'Not busy?'

'No. Just going to have tea.'

'And you are not expecting anybody?'

'Nobody at all.'

'Ah! That's good.'

He laid aside his coat and hat gently, lingeringly, as though he had time and to spare for everything, or as though he were taking leave of them for ever, and came over to the fire and held out his hands to the quick, leaping flame.

Just for a moment both of them stood silent in that leaping light. Still, as it were, they tasted on their smiling lips the sweet shock of their greeting. Their secret selves whispered:

'Why should we speak? Isn't this enough?'

'More than enough. I never realized until this moment. . . .'

'How good it is just to be with you. . . .'

'Like this. . . .'

'It's more than enough.'

But suddenly he turned and looked at her and she moved quickly away.

'Have a cigarette? I'll put the kettle on. Are you longing for tea?'

'No. Not longing.'

'Well, I am.'

'Oh, you.' He thumped the Armenian cushion and flung on to the *sommier*.* 'You are a perfect little Chinee.'

'Yes, I am,' she laughed. 'I long for tea as strong men long for wine.'

She lighted the lamp under its broad orange shade, pulled the curtains and drew up the tea table. Two birds sang in the kettle; the fire fluttered. He sat up clasping his knees. It was delightful—this business of having tea—and she always had delicious things to eat— little sharp sandwiches, short sweet almond fingers, and a dark, rich cake tasting of rum—but it was an interruption. He wanted it over, the table pushed away, their two chairs drawn up to the light, and the moment came when he took out his pipe, filled it, and said, pressing the tobacco tight into the bowl: 'I have been thinking over what you said last time and it seems to me. . . .'

Yes, that was what he waited for and so did she. Yes, while she shook the teapot hot and dry over the spirit flame she saw those other two, him, leaning back, taking his ease among the cushions, and her, curled up *en escargot** in the blue shell arm-chair. The picture was so clear and so minute it might have been painted on the blue teapot lid. And yet she couldn't hurry. She could almost have cried: 'Give me time.' She must have time in which to grow calm. She wanted time in which to free herself from all these familiar things with which she lived so vividly. For all these gay things round her were part of her— her offspring—and they knew it and made the largest, most vehement claims. But now they must go. They must be swept away, shooed away—like children, sent up the shadowy stairs, packed into bed and commanded to go to sleep—at once—without a murmur!

For the special thrilling quality of their friendship was in their complete surrender. Like two open cities in the midst of some vast plain their two minds lay open to each other. And it wasn't as if he rode into hers like a conqueror, armed to the eyebrows and seeing nothing but a gay silken flutter—nor did she enter his like a queen walking soft on petals. No, they were eager, serious travellers, absorbed in understanding what was to be seen and discovering what was hidden—making the most of this extraordinary absolute chance which made it possible for him to be utterly truthful to her and for her to be utterly sincere with him.

And the best of it was they were both of them old enough to enjoy their adventure to the full without any stupid emotional complication. Passion would have ruined everything; they quite saw that. Besides, all that sort of thing was over and done with for both of them—he was thirty-one, she was thirty—they had had their experiences, and very rich and varied they had been, but now was the time for harvest—harvest. Weren't his novels to be very big novels indeed? And her plays. Who else had her exquisite sense of real English Comedy? . . .

Carefully she cut the cake into thick little wads and he reached across for a piece.

'Do realize how good it is,' she implored. 'Eat it imaginatively.

Roll your eyes if you can and taste it on the breath. It's not a sandwich from the hatter's bag*—it's the kind of cake that might have
been mentioned in the Book of Genesis. . . . And God said: "Let
there be cake. And there was cake. And God saw that it was good." *

'You needn't entreat me,' said he. 'Really you needn't. It's a queer
thing but I always do notice what I eat here and never anywhere else.
I suppose it comes of living alone so long and always reading while I
feed . . . my habit of looking upon food as just food . . . something
that's there, at certain times . . . to be devoured . . . to be . . . not
there.' He laughed. 'That shocks you. Doesn't it?'

'To the bone,' said she.

'But—look here—' He pushed away his cup and began to speak
very fast. 'I simply haven't got any external life at all. I don't know
the names of things a bit—trees and so on—and I never notice places
or furniture or what people look like. One room is just like another to
me—a place to sit and read or talk in—except,' and here he paused,
smiled in a strange naive way, and said, 'except this studio.' He
looked round him and then at her; he laughed in his astonishment
and pleasure. He was like a man who wakes up in a train to find that
he has arrived, already, at the journey's end.

'Here's another queer thing. If I shut my eyes I can see this place
down to every detail—every detail. . . . Now I come to think of it—
I've never realized this consciously before. Often when I am away
from here I revisit it in spirit—wander about among your red chairs,
stare at the bowl of fruit on the black table—and just touch, very
lightly, that marvel of a sleeping boy's head.'

He looked at it as he spoke. It stood on the corner of the mantelpiece; the head to one side down-drooping, the lips parted, as though
in his sleep the little boy listened to some sweet sound. . . .

'I love that little boy,' he murmured. And then they both were
silent.

A new silence came between them. Nothing in the least like the
satisfactory pause that had followed their greetings—the 'Well, here
we are together again, and there's no reason why we shouldn't go on
from just where we left off last time.' That silence could be contained in the circle of warm, delightful fire and lamplight. How
many times hadn't they flung something into it just for the fun of
watching the ripples break on the easy shores. But into this
unfamiliar pool the head of the little boy sleeping his timeless sleep

dropped—and the ripples flowed away, away—boundlessly far—into deep glittering darkness.

And then both of them broke it. She said: 'I must make up the fire,' and he said: 'I have been trying a new. . . .' Both of them escaped. She made up the fire and put the table back, the blue chair was wheeled forward, she curled up and he lay back among the cushions. Quickly! Quickly! They must stop it from happening again.

'Well, I read the book you left last time.'

'Oh, what do you think of it?'

They were off and all was as usual. But was it? Weren't they just a little too quick, too prompt with their replies, too ready to take each other up? Was this really anything more than a wonderfully good imitation of other occasions? His heart beat; her cheek burned and the stupid thing was she could not discover where exactly they were or what exactly was happening. She hadn't time to glance back. And just as she had got so far it happened again. They faltered, wavered, broke down, were silent. Again they were conscious of the boundless, questioning dark. Again, there they were—two hunters, bending over their fire, but hearing suddenly from the jungle beyond a shake of wind and a loud, questioning cry. . . .

She lifted her head. 'It's raining,' she murmured. And her voice was like his when he had said: 'I love that little boy.'

Well. Why didn't they just give way to it—yield—and see what will happen then? But no. Vague and troubled though they were, they knew enough to realize their precious friendship was in danger. She was the one who would be destroyed—not they—and they'd be no party to that.

He got up, knocked out his pipe, ran his hand through his hair and said: 'I have been wondering very much lately whether the novel of the future will be a psychological novel or not. How sure are you that psychology *qua* psychology has got anything to do with literature at all?'

'Do you mean you feel there's quite a chance that the mysterious non-existent creatures—the young writers of to-day—are trying simply to jump the psycho-analyst's claim?'*

'Yes, I do. And I think it's because this generation is just wise enough to know that it is sick and to realize that its only chance of recovery is by going into its symptoms—making an exhaustive study of them—tracking them down—trying to get at the root of the trouble.'

'But oh,' she wailed. 'What a dreadfully dismal outlook.'

'Not at all,' said he. 'Look here. . . . ' On the talk went. And now it seemed they really had succeeded. She turned in her chair to look at him while she answered. Her smile said: 'We have won.' And he smiled back, confident: 'Absolutely.'

But the smile undid them. It lasted too long; it became a grin. They saw themselves as two little grinning puppets jigging away in nothingness.

'What have we been talking about?' thought he. He was so utterly bored he almost groaned.

'What a spectacle we have made of ourselves,' thought she. And she saw him laboriously—oh, laboriously—laying out the grounds and herself running after, putting here a tree and there a flowery shrub and here a handful of glittering fish in a pool. They were silent this time from sheer dismay.

The clock struck six merry little pings and the fire made a soft flutter. What fools they were—heavy, stodgy, elderly—with positively upholstered minds.

And now the silence put a spell upon them like solemn music. It was anguish—anguish for her to bear it and he would die—he'd die if it were broken. . . . And yet he longed to break it. Not by speech. At any rate not by their ordinary maddening chatter. There was another way for them to speak to each other, and in the new way he wanted to murmur: 'Do you feel this too? Do you understand it at all?' . . .

Instead, to his horror, he heard himself say: 'I must be off; I'm meeting Brand at six.'

What devil made him say that instead of the other? She jumped— simply jumped out of her chair, and he heard her crying: 'You must rush, then. He's so punctual. Why didn't you say so before?'

'You've hurt me; you've hurt me! We've failed!' said her secret self while she handed him his hat and stick, smiling gaily. She wouldn't give him a moment for another word, but ran along the passage and opened the big outer door.

Could they leave each other like this? How could they? He stood on the step and she just inside holding the door. It was not raining now.

'You've hurt me—hurt me,' said her heart. 'Why don't you go? No, don't go. Stay. No—go!' And she looked out upon the night.

She saw the beautiful fall of the steps, the dark garden ringed with glittering ivy, on the other side of the road the huge bare willows and above them the sky big and bright with stars. But of course he would see nothing of all this. He was superior to it all. He—with his wonderful 'spiritual' vision!

She was right. He did see nothing at all. Misery! He'd missed it. It was too late to do anything now. Was it too late? Yes, it was. A cold snatch of hateful wind blew into the garden. Curse life! He heard her cry 'au revoir' and the door slammed.

Running back into the studio she behaved so strangely. She ran up and down lifting her arms and crying: 'Oh! Oh! How stupid! How imbecile! How stupid!' And then she flung herself down on the *sommier* thinking of nothing—just lying there in her rage. All was over. What was over? Oh—something was. And she'd never see him again—never. After a long long time (or perhaps ten minutes) had passed in that black gulf her bell rang a sharp quick jingle. It was he, of course. And equally, of course, she oughtn't to have paid the slightest attention to it but just let it go on ringing and ringing. She flew to answer.

On the doorstep there stood an elderly virgin, a pathetic creature who simply idolized her (heaven knows why) and had this habit of turning up and ringing the bell and then saying, when she opened the door: 'My dear, send me away!' She never did. As a rule she asked her in and let her admire everything and accepted the bunch of slightly soiled looking flowers—more than graciously. But to-day. . . .

'Oh, I am so sorry,' she cried. 'But I've got someone with me. We are working on some wood-cuts. I'm hopelessly busy all evening.'

'It doesn't matter. It doesn't matter at all, darling,' said the good friend. 'I was just passing and I thought I'd leave you some violets.' She fumbled down among the ribs of a large old umbrella. 'I put them down here. Such a good place to keep flowers out of the wind. Here they are,' she said, shaking out a little dead bunch.

For a moment she did not take the violets. But while she stood just inside, holding the door, a strange thing happened. . . . Again she saw the beautiful fall of the steps, the dark garden ringed with glittering ivy, the willows, the big bright sky. Again she felt the silence that

was like a question. But this time she did not hesitate. She moved
forward. Very softly and gently, as though fearful of making a ripple
in that boundless pool of quiet she put her arms round her friend.

'My dear,' murmured her happy friend, quite overcome by
this gratitude. 'They are really nothing. Just the simplest little
thrippenny bunch.'

But as she spoke she was enfolded—more tenderly, more beautifully embraced, held by such a sweet pressure and for so long that
the poor dear's mind positively reeled and she just had the strength
to quaver: 'Then you really don't mind me too much?'

'Good night, my friend,' whispered the other. 'Come again soon.'

'Oh, I will. I will.'

This time she walked back to the studio slowly, and standing in
the middle of the room with half-shut eyes she felt so light, so rested,
as if she had woken up out of a childish sleep. Even the act of
breathing was a joy. . . .

The *sommier* was very untidy. All the cushions 'like furious mountains' as she said; she put them in order before going over to the
writing-table.

'I have been thinking over our talk about the psychological novel,'
she dashed off, 'it really is intensely interesting.' . . . And so on and
so on.

At the end she wrote: 'Good night, my friend. Come again soon.'

PICTURES

Eight o'clock in the morning. Miss Ada Moss lay in a black iron bedstead, staring up at the ceiling. Her room, a Bloomsbury top-floor back, smelled of soot and face powder and the paper of fried potatoes she brought in for supper the night before.

'Oh, dear,' thought Miss Moss, 'I am cold. I wonder why it is that I always wake up so cold in the mornings now. My knees and feet and my back—especially my back; it's like a sheet of ice. And I always was such a one for being warm in the old days. It's not as if I was skinny—I'm just the same full figure that I used to be. No, it's because I don't have a good hot dinner in the evenings.'

A pageant of Good Hot Dinners passed across the ceiling, each of them accompanied by a bottle of Nourishing Stout. . . .

'Even if I were to get up now,' she thought, 'and have a sensible substantial breakfast. . . . ' A pageant of Sensible Substantial Breakfasts followed the dinners across the ceiling, shepherded by an enormous, white, uncut ham. Miss Moss shuddered and disappeared under the bedclothes. Suddenly, in bounced the landlady.

'There's a letter for you, Miss Moss.'

'Oh,' said Miss Moss, far too friendly, 'thank you very much, Mrs Pine. It's very good of you, I'm sure, to take the trouble.'

'No trouble at all,' said the landlady. 'I thought perhaps it was the letter you'd been expecting.'

'Why,' said Miss Moss brightly, 'yes, perhaps it is.' She put her head on one side and smiled vaguely at the letter. 'I shouldn't be surprised.'

The landlady's eyes popped. 'Well, I should, Miss Moss,' said she, 'and that's how it is. And I'll trouble you to open it, if you please. Many is the lady in my place as would have done it for you and have been within her rights. For things can't go on like this, Miss Moss, no indeed they can't. What with week in and week out and first you've got it and then you haven't, and then it's another letter lost in the post or another manager down at Brighton* but will be back on Tuesday for certain—I'm fair sick and tired and I won't stand it no more. Why should I, Miss Moss, I ask you, at a time like this, with prices flying up in the air and my poor dear lad in France?* My sister

Eliza was only saying to me yesterday—"Minnie," she says, "you're too soft-hearted. You could have let that room time and time again," says she, "and if people won't look after themselves in times like these, nobody else will," she says. "She may have had a College eddication and sung in West End concerts," says she, "but if your Lizzie says what's true," she says, "and she's washing her own wovens and drying them on the towel rail, it's easy to see where the finger's pointing.* And it's high time you had done with it," says she.'

Miss Moss gave no sign of having heard this. She sat up in bed, tore open her letter and read:

'Dear Madam,

Yours to hand. Am not producing at present, but have filed photo for future ref.

Yours truly,
BACKWASH FILM CO.'

This letter seemed to afford her peculiar satisfaction; she read it through twice before replying to the landlady.

'Well, Mrs Pine, I think you'll be sorry for what you said. This is from a manager, asking me to be there with evening dress at ten o'clock next Saturday morning.'

But the landlady was too quick for her. She pounced, secured the letter.

'Oh, is it! Is it indeed!' she cried.

'Give me back that letter. Give it back to me at once, you bad, wicked woman,' cried Miss Moss, who could not get out of bed because her nightdress was slit down the back. 'Give me back my private letter.' The landlady began slowly backing out of the room, holding the letter to her buttoned bodice.

'So it's come to this, has it?' said she. 'Well, Miss Moss, if I don't get my rent at eight o'clock to-night, we'll see who's a bad, wicked woman—that's all.' Here she nodded, mysteriously. 'And I'll keep this letter.' Here her voice rose. 'It will be a pretty little bit of evidence!' And here it fell, sepulchral, '*My lady.*'

The door banged and Miss Moss was alone. She flung off the bed clothes, and sitting by the side of the bed, furious and shivering, she stared at her fat white legs with their great knots of greeny-blue veins.

'Cockroach! That's what she is. She's a cockroach!' said Miss Moss. 'I could have her up for snatching my letter—I'm sure I could.' Still keeping on her nightdress she began to drag on her clothes.

'Oh, if I could only pay that woman, I'd give her a piece of my mind that she wouldn't forget. I'd tell her off proper.' She went over to her chest of drawers for a safety-pin, and seeing herself in the glass she gave a vague smile and shook her head. 'Well, old girl,' she murmured, 'you're up against it this time, and no mistake.' But the person in the glass made an ugly face at her.

'You silly thing,' scolded Miss Moss. 'Now what's the good of crying: you'll only make your nose red. No, you get dressed and go out and try your luck—that's what you've got to do.'

She unhooked her vanity bag* from the bedpost, rooted in it, shook it, turned it inside out.

'I'll have a nice cup of tea at an A B C* to settle me before I go anywhere,' she decided. 'I've got one and thrippence—yes, just one and three.'

Ten minutes later, a stout lady in blue serge, with a bunch of artificial 'parmas'* at her bosom, a black hat covered with purple pansies, white gloves, boots with white uppers, and a vanity bag containing one and three, sang in a low contralto voice:

> Sweet-heart, remember when days are forlorn
> It al-ways is dar-kest before the dawn.

But the person in the glass made a face at her, and Miss Moss went out. There were grey crabs all the way down the street slopping water over grey stone steps. With his strange, hawking cry and the jangle of the cans the milk boy went his rounds. Outside Brittweiler's Swiss House he made a splash, and an old brown cat without a tail appeared from nowhere, and began greedily and silently drinking up the spill. It gave Miss Moss a queer feeling to watch—a sinking—as you might say.

But when she came to the A B C she found the door propped open; a man went in and out carrying trays of rolls, and there was nobody inside except a waitress doing her hair and the cashier unlocking the cash-boxes. She stood in the middle of the floor but neither of them saw her.

'My boy came home last night,' sang the waitress.

'Oh, I say—how topping for you!' gurgled the cashier.

'Yes, wasn't it,' sang the waitress. 'He brought me a sweet little brooch. Look, it's got "Dieppe" written on it.'

The cashier ran across to look and put her arm round the waitress' neck.

'Oh, I say—how topping for you.'

'Yes, isn't it,' said the waitress. 'O-oh, he is brahn.* "Hullo," I said, "hullo, old mahogany."'

'Oh, I say,' gurgled the cashier, running back into her cage and nearly bumping into Miss Moss on the way. 'You are a *treat*!' Then the man with the rolls came in again, swerving past her.

'Can I have a cup of tea, Miss?' she asked.

But the waitress went on doing her hair. 'Oh,' she sang, 'we're not *open* yet.' She turned round and waved her comb at the cashier.

'*Are* we, dear?'

'Oh, no,' said the cashier. Miss Moss went out.

'I'll go to Charing Cross. Yes, that's what I'll do,' she decided. 'But I won't have a cup of tea. No, I'll have a coffee. There's more of a tonic in coffee. . . . Cheeky, those girls are! Her boy came home last night; he brought her a brooch with "Dieppe" written on it.' She began to cross the road. . . .

'Look out, Fattie; don't go to sleep!' yelled a taxi driver. She pretended not to hear.

'No, I won't go to Charing Cross,' she decided. 'I'll go straight to Kig and Kadgit. They're open at nine. If I get there early Mr Kadgit may have something by the morning's post. . . . I'm very glad you turned up so early, Miss Moss. I've just heard from a manager who wants a lady to play. . . . I think you'll just suit him. I'll give you a card to go and see him. It's three pounds a week and all found.* If I were you I'd hop round as fast as I could. Lucky you turned up so early. . . .'

But there was nobody at Kig and Kadgit's except the charwoman wiping over the 'lino'* in the passage.

'Nobody here yet, Miss,' said the char.

'Oh, isn't Mr Kadgit here?' said Miss Moss, trying to dodge the pail and brush. 'Well, I'll just wait a moment, if I may.'

'You can't wait in the waiting-room, Miss. I 'aven't done it yet. Mr Kadgit's never 'ere before 'leven-thirty Saturdays. Sometimes 'e don't come at all.' And the char began crawling towards her.

'Dear me—how silly of me,' said Miss Moss. 'I forgot it was Saturday.'

'Mind your feet, *please*, Miss,' said the char. And Miss Moss was outside again.

That was one thing about Beit and Bithems; it was lively. You walked into the waiting-room, into a great buzz of conversation, and there was everybody; you knew almost everybody. The early ones sat on chairs and the later ones sat on the early ones' laps, while the gentlemen leaned negligently against the walls or preened themselves in front of the admiring ladies.

'Hello,' said Miss Moss, very gay. 'Here we are again!'

And young Mr Clayton, playing the banjo on his walking-stick, sang: 'Waiting for the Robert E. Lee.'*

'Mr Bithem here yet?' asked Miss Moss, taking out an old dead powder puff and powdering her nose mauve.

'Oh, yes, dear,' cried the chorus. 'He's been here for ages. We've all been waiting here for more than an hour.'

'Dear me!' said Miss Moss. 'Anything doing, do you think?'

'Oh, a few jobs going for South Africa,' said young Mr Clayton. 'Hundred and fifty a week for two years, you know.'

'Oh!' cried the chorus. 'You *are* weird, Mr Clayton. Isn't he a *cure*?* Isn't he a *scream*,* dear? Oh, Mr Clayton, you do make me laugh. Isn't he a *comic*?'

A dark, mournful girl touched Miss Moss on the arm.

'I just missed a lovely job yesterday,' she said. 'Six weeks in the provinces and then the West End.* The manager said I would have got it for certain if only I'd been robust enough. He said if my figure had been fuller, the part was made for me.' She stared at Miss Moss, and the dirty dark red rose under the brim of her hat looked, somehow, as though it shared the blow with her, and was crushed, too.

'Oh, dear, that was hard lines,' said Miss Moss trying to appear indifferent. 'What was it—if I may ask?'

But the dark, mournful girl saw through her and a gleam of spite came into her heavy eyes.

'Oh, no good to you, my dear,' said she. 'He wanted someone young, you know—a dark Spanish type—my style, but more figure, that was all.'

The inner door opened and Mr Bithem appeared in his shirt

sleeves. He kept one hand on the door ready to whisk back again, and held up the other.

'Look here, ladies—' and then he paused, grinned his famous grin before he said—'*and bhoys.*' The waiting-room laughed so loudly at this that he had to hold both hands up. 'It's no good waiting this morning. Come back Monday; I'm expecting several calls on Monday.'

Miss Moss made a desperate rush forward. 'Mr Bithem, I wonder if you've heard from. . . .'

'Now let me see,' said Mr Bithem slowly, staring; he had only seen Miss Moss four times a week for the past—how many weeks? 'Now, who are you?'

'Miss Ada Moss.'

'Oh, yes, yes; of course, my dear. Not yet, my dear. Now I had a call for twenty-eight ladies to-day, but they had to be young and able to hop it* a bit—see? And I had another call for sixteen—but they had to know something about sand-dancing. Look here, my dear, I'm up to the eyebrows this morning. Come back on Monday week; it's no good coming before that.' He gave her a whole grin to herself and patted her fat back. 'Hearts of oak,* dear lady,' said Mr Bithem, 'hearts of oak!'

At the North-East Film Company the crowd was all the way up the stairs. Miss Moss found herself next to a fair little baby thing about thirty in a white lace hat with cherries round it.

'What a crowd!' said she. 'Anything special on?'

'*Didn't* you know, dear?' said the baby, opening her immense pale eyes. 'There was a call at nine-thirty for *attractive* girls. We've all been waiting for *hours.* Have you played for this company before?' Miss Moss put her head on one side. 'No, I don't think I have.'

'They're a lovely company to play for,' said the baby. 'A friend of mine has a friend who gets thirty pounds a day. . . . Have you *arcted* much for the *fil*-lums?'

'Well, I'm not an actress by profession,' confessed Miss Moss. 'I'm a contralto singer. But things have been so bad lately that I've been doing a little.'

'It's *like* that, isn't it, dear?' said the baby.

'I had a splendid education at the College of Music,' said Miss Moss, 'and I got my silver medal for singing. I've often sung at West End concerts. But I thought, for a change, I'd try my luck. . . .'

'Yes, it's *like* that, isn't it, dear?' said the baby.

At the moment a beautiful typist appeared at the top of the stairs.

'Are you all waiting for the North-East call?'

'Yes!' cried the chorus.

'Well, it's off. I've just had a phone through.'

'But look here! What about our expenses?' shouted a voice.

The typist looked down at them, and she couldn't help laughing.

'Oh, you weren't to have been *paid*. The North-East never *pay* their crowds.'*

There was only a little round window at the Bitter Orange Company. No waiting-room—nobody at all except a girl, who came to the window when Miss Moss knocked, and said: 'Well?'

'Can I see the producer, please?' said Miss Moss pleasantly. The girl leaned on the window-bar, half shut her eyes and seemed to go to sleep for a moment. Miss Moss smiled at her. The girl not only frowned; she seemed to smell something vaguely unpleasant; she sniffed. Suddenly she moved away, came back with a paper and thrust it at Miss Moss.

'Fill up the form!' said she. And banged the window down.

'Can you aviate*—high-dive—drive a car—buck-jump*—shoot?' read Miss Moss. She walked along the street asking herself those questions. There was a high, cold wind blowing; it tugged at her, slapped her face, jeered; it knew she could not answer them. In the Square Gardens she found a little wire basket to drop the form into. And then she sat down on one of the benches to powder her nose. But the person in the pocket mirror made a hideous face at her, and that was too much for Miss Moss; she had a good cry. It cheered her wonderfully.

'Well, that's over,' she sighed. 'It's one comfort to be off my feet. And my nose will soon get cool in the air. . . . It's very nice in here. Look at the sparrows. Cheep. Cheep. How close they come. I expect somebody feeds them. No, I've nothing for you, you cheeky little things. . . . ' She looked away from them. What was the big building opposite—the Café de Madrid? My goodness, what a smack that little child came down! Poor little mite! Never mind—up again. . . . By eight o'clock to-night . . . Café de Madrid. 'I could just go in and sit there and have a coffee, that's all,' thought Miss Moss. 'It's such a place for artists too. I might just have a stroke of luck. . . . A dark handsome gentleman in a fur coat comes in with a friend, and sits at

my table, perhaps. "No, old chap, I've searched London for a
contralto and I can't find a soul. You see, the music is difficult; have
a look at it." ' And Miss Moss heard herself saying: 'Excuse me, I
happen to be a contralto, and I have sung that part many times. . . .'
'Extraordinary! "Come back to my studio and I'll try your voice
now." . . . Ten pounds a week. . . . Why should I feel nervous? It's
not nervousness. Why shouldn't I go to the Café de Madrid? I'm a
respectable woman—I'm a contralto singer. And I'm only trembling
because I've had nothing to eat to-day. . . . "A nice little piece of
evidence, *my lady*." . . . Very well, Mrs Pine. Café de Madrid. They
have concerts there in the evenings. . . . "Why don't they begin?"
"The contralto has not arrived." . . . "Excuse me, I happen to be a
contralto; I have sung that music many times." '

It was almost dark in the café. Men, palms, red plush seats, white
marble tables, waiters in aprons, Miss Moss walked through them
all. Hardly had she sat down when a very stout gentleman wearing a
very small hat that floated on the top of his head like a little yacht
flopped into the chair opposite hers.

'Good evening!' said he.

Miss Moss said, in her cheerful way: 'Good evening!'

'Fine evening,' said the stout gentleman.

'Yes, very fine. Quite a treat, isn't it?' said she.

He crooked a sausage finger at the waiter—'Bring me a large
whisky'—and turned to Miss Moss. 'What's yours?'

'Well, I think I'll take a brandy if it's all the same.'

Five minutes later the stout gentleman leaned across the table and
blew a puff of cigar smoke full in her face.

'That's a tempting bit o' ribbon!' said he.

Miss Moss blushed until a pulse at the top of her head that she
never had felt before pounded away.

'I always was one for pink,' said she.

The stout gentleman considered her, drumming with her fingers
on the table.

'I like 'em firm and well covered,' said he.

Miss Moss, to her surprise, gave a loud snigger.

Five minutes later the stout gentleman heaved himself up. 'Well,
am I goin' your way, or are you comin' mine?' he asked.

'I'll come with you, if it's all the same,' said Miss Moss. And she
sailed after the little yacht out of the café.

THE MAN WITHOUT A TEMPERAMENT

He stood at the hall door turning the ring, turning the heavy signet ring upon his little finger while his glance travelled coolly, deliberately, over the round tables and basket-chairs scattered about the glassed-in verandah. He pursed his lips—he might have been going to whistle—but he did not whistle—only turned the ring—turned the ring on his pink, freshly washed hands.

Over in the corner sat The Two Topknots, drinking a decoction they always drank at this hour—something whitish, greyish, in glasses, with little husks floating on the top—and rooting in a tin full of paper shavings for pieces of speckled biscuit, which they broke, dropped into the glasses and fished for with spoons. Their two coils of knitting, like two snakes, slumbered beside the tray.

The American Woman sat where she always sat against the glass wall, in the shadow of a great creeping thing with wide open purple eyes that pressed—that flattened itself against the glass, hungrily watching her. And she knoo it was there—she knoo it was looking at her just that way. She played up to it; she gave herself little airs. Sometimes she even pointed at it, crying: 'Isn't that the most terrible thing you've ever seen! Isn't that ghoulish!' It was on the other side of the verandah, after all . . . and besides it couldn't touch her, could it, Klaymongso? She was an American Woman, wasn't she Klaymongso, and she'd just go right away to her Consul. Klaymongso, curled in her lap, with her torn antique brocade bag, a grubby handkerchief, and a pile of letters from home on top of him, sneezed for reply.

The other tables were empty. A glance passed between the American and the Topknots. She gave a foreign little shrug; they waved an understanding biscuit. But he saw nothing. Now he was still, now from his eyes you saw he listened. 'Hoo-e-zip-zoo-oo!' sounded the lift. The iron cage clanged open. Light dragging steps sounded across the hall, coming towards him. A hand, like a leaf, fell on his shoulder. A soft voice said: 'Let's go and sit over there—where we can see the drive. The trees are so lovely.' And he moved forward with the hand still on his shoulder, and the light, dragging steps beside his. He pulled out a chair and she sank into it, slowly, leaning her head against the back, her arms falling along the sides.

'Won't you bring the other up closer? It's such miles away.' But he did not move.

'Where's your shawl?' he asked.

'Oh!' She gave a little groan of dismay. 'How silly I am, I've left it upstairs on the bed. Never mind. Please don't go for it. I shan't want it, I know I shan't.'

'You'd better have it.' And he turned and swiftly crossed the verandah into the dim hall with its scarlet plush and gilt furniture— conjuror's furniture—its Notice of Services at the English Church, its green baize board with the unclaimed letters climbing the black lattice, huge 'Presentation' clock that struck the hours at the half-hours, bundles of sticks and umbrellas and sunshades in the clasp of a brown wooden bear,* past the two crippled palms, two ancient beggars at the foot of the staircase, up the marble stairs three at a time, past the life-size group on the landing of two stout peasant children with their marble pinnies* full of marble grapes, and along the corridor, with its piled-up wreckage of old tin boxes, leather trunks, canvas hold-alls, to their room.

The servant girl was in their room, singing loudly while she emptied soapy water into a pail. The windows were open wide, the shutters put back, and the light glared in. She had thrown the carpets and the big white pillows over the balcony rails; the nets* were looped up from the beds; on the writing table there stood a pan of fluff and match-ends. When she saw him her small impudent eyes snapped and her singing changed to humming. But he gave no sign. His eyes searched the glaring room. Where the devil was the shawl!

'*Vous desirez, Monsieur?*'* mocked the servant girl.

No answer. He had seen it. He strode across the room, grabbed the grey cobweb and went out, banging the door. The servant girl's voice at its loudest and shrillest followed him along the corridor.

'Oh, there you are. What happened? What kept you? The tea's here, you see. I've just sent Antonio off for the hot water. Isn't it extraordinary? I must have told him about it sixty times at least, and still he doesn't bring it. Thank you. That's very nice. One does just feel the air when one bends forward.'

'Thanks.' He took his tea and sat down in the other chair. 'No, nothing to eat.'

'Oh do! Just one, you had so little at lunch and it's hours before dinner.'

Her shawl dropped off as she bent forward to hand him the biscuits. He took one and put it in his saucer.

'Oh, those trees along the drive,' she cried, 'I could look at them for ever. They are like the most exquisite huge ferns. And you see that one with the grey-silver bark and the clusters of cream coloured flowers, I pulled down a head of them yesterday to smell and the scent'—she shut her eyes at the memory and her voice thinned away, faint, airy—'was like freshly ground nutmegs.' A little pause. She turned to him and smiled. 'You do know what nutmegs smell like— do you, Robert?'

And he smiled back at her. 'Now how am I going to prove to you that I do?'

Back came Antonio with not only the hot water—with letters on a salver and three rolls of paper.

'Oh, the post! Oh, how lovely! Oh, Robert, they mustn't be all for you! Have they just come, Antonio?' Her thin hands flew up and hovered over the letters that Antonio offered her, bending forward.

'Just this moment, Signora,' grinned Antonio. 'I took-a them from the postman myself. I made-a the postman give them for me.'

'Noble Antonio!' laughed she. 'There—those are mine, Robert; the rest are yours.'

Antonio wheeled sharply, stiffened, the grin went out of his face. His striped linen jacket and his flat gleaming fringe made him look like a wooden doll.

Mr Salesby put the letters into his pocket; the papers lay on the table. He turned the ring, turned the signet ring on his little finger and stared in front of him, blinking, vacant.

But she—with her teacup in one hand, the sheets of thin paper in the other, her head tilted back, her lips open, a brush of bright colour on her cheek-bones, sipped, sipped, drank . . . drank. . . .

'From Lottie,' came her soft murmur. 'Poor dear . . . such trouble . . . left foot. She thought . . . neuritis . . . Doctor Blyth . . . flat foot . . . massage. So many robins this year . . . maid most satisfactory . . . Indian Colonel . . . every grain of rice separate . . . very heavy fall of snow.' And her wide lighted eyes looked up from the letter. 'Snow, Robert! Think of it!' And she touched the little dark violets pinned on her thin bosom and went back to the letter.

*

. . . Snow. Snow in London. Millie with the early morning cup of tea. 'There's been a terrible fall of snow in the night, Sir.' 'Oh, has there, Millie?' The curtains ring apart, letting in the pale, reluctant light. He raises himself in the bed; he catches a glimpse of the solid houses opposite framed in white, of their window boxes full of great sprays of white coral. . . . In the bathroom—overlooking the back garden. Snow—heavy snow over everything. The lawn is covered with a wavy pattern of cat's paws; there is a thick, thick icing on the garden table; the withered pods of the laburnum tree are white tassels; only here and there in the ivy is a dark leaf showing. . . . Warming his back at the dining-room fire, the paper drying over a chair. Millie with the bacon. 'Oh, if you please, Sir, there's two little boys come as will do the steps and front for a shilling, shall I let them?' . . . And then flying lightly, lightly down the stairs—Jinnie. 'Oh, Robert, isn't it wonderful! Oh, what a pity it has to melt. Where's the pussy-wee?' 'I'll get him from Millie' . . . 'Millie, you might just hand me up the kitten if you've got him down there.' 'Very good, Sir.' He feels the little beating heart under his hand. 'Come on, old chap, your Missus wants you.' 'Oh, Robert, do show him the snow—his first snow. Shall I open the window and give him a little piece on his paw to hold? . . .'

'Well, that's very satisfactory on the whole—very. Poor Lottie! Darling Anne! How I only wish I could send them something of this,' she cried, waving her letters at the brilliant, dazzling garden. 'More tea, Robert? Robert dear, more tea?'

'No, thanks, no. It was very good,' he drawled.

'Well mine wasn't. Mine was just like chopped hay. Oh, here comes the Honeymoon Couple.'

Half striding, half running, carrying a basket between them and rods and lines, they came up the drive, up the shallow steps.

'My! have you been out fishing?' cried the American Woman.

They were out of breath, they panted: 'Yes, yes, we have been out in a little boat all day. We have caught seven. Four are good to eat. But three we shall give away. To the children.'

Mrs Salesby turned her chair to look; the Topknots laid the snakes down. They were a very dark young couple—black hair, olive skin, brilliant eyes and teeth. He was dressed 'English fashion' in a flannel jacket, white trousers and shoes. Round his neck he wore a silk scarf;

his head, with his hair brushed back, was bare. And he kept mopping his forehead, rubbing his hands with a brilliant handkerchief. Her white skirt had a patch of wet; her neck and throat were stained a deep pink. When she lifted her arms big half-hoops of perspiration showed under her arm-pits; her hair clung in wet curls to her cheeks. She looked as though her young husband had been dipping her in the sea, and fishing her out again to dry in the sun and then—in with her again—all day.

'Would Klaymongso like a fish?' they cried. Their laughing voices charged with excitement beat against the glassed-in verandah like birds, and a strange saltish smell came from the basket.

'You will sleep well to-night,' said a Topknot, picking her ear with a knitting needle while the other Topknot smiled and nodded.

The Honeymoon Couple looked at each other. A great wave seemed to go over them. They gasped, gulped, staggered a little and then came up laughing—laughing.

'We cannot go upstairs, we are too tired. We must have tea just as we are. Here—coffee. No—tea. No—coffee. Tea—coffee, Antonio!' Mrs Salesby turned.

'Robert! Robert!' Where was he? He wasn't there. Oh, there he was at the other end of the verandah, with his back turned, smoking a cigarette. 'Robert, shall we go for our little turn?'

'Right.' He stumped the cigarette into an ashtray and sauntered over, his eyes on the ground. 'Will you be warm enough?'

'Oh, quite.'

'Sure?'

'Well,' she put her hand on his arm, 'perhaps'—and gave his arm the faintest pressure—'it's not upstairs, it's only in the hall— perhaps you'd get me my cape. Hanging up.'

He came back with it and she bent her small head while he dropped it on her shoulders. Then, very stiff, he offered her his arm. She bowed sweetly to the people on the verandah while he just covered a yawn, and they went down the steps together.

'*Vous avez voo ça!*'* said the American Woman.

'He is not a man,' said the Two Topknots, 'he is an ox. I say to my sister in the morning and at night when we are in bed, I tell her—*No* man is he, but an ox!'

Wheeling, tumbling, swooping, the laughter of the Honeymoon Couple dashed against the glass of the verandah.

The sun was still high. Every leaf, every flower in the garden lay open, motionless, as if exhausted, and a sweet, rich, rank smell filled the quivering air. Out of the thick, fleshy leaves of a cactus there rose an aloe stem loaded with pale flowers that looked as though they had been cut out of butter; light flashed upon the lifted spears of the palms; over a bed of scarlet waxen flowers some big black insects 'zoomed-zoomed'; a great gaudy creeper, orange splashed with jet, sprawled against a wall.

'I don't need my cape after all,' said she. 'It's really too warm.' So he took it off and carried it over his arm. 'Let us go down this path here. I feel so well to-day—marvellously better. Good heavens—look at those children! And to think it's November!'

In a corner of the garden there were two brimming tubs of water. Three little girls, having thoughtfully taken off their drawers* and hung them on a bush, their skirts clasped to their waists, were standing in the tubs and tramping up and down. They screamed, their hair fell over their faces, they splashed one another. But suddenly, the smallest, who had a tub to herself, glanced up and saw who was looking. For a moment she seemed overcome with terror, then clumsily she struggled and strained out of her tub, and still holding her clothes above her waist. 'The Englishman! The Englishman!' she shrieked and fled away to hide. Shrieking and screaming, the other two followed her. In a moment they were gone; in a moment there was nothing but the two brimming tubs and their little drawers on the bush.

'How—very—extraordinary!' said she. 'What made them so frightened? Surely they were much too young to. . . . ' She looked up at him. She thought he looked pale—but wonderfully handsome with that great tropical tree behind him with its long, spiked thorns.

For a moment he did not answer. Then he met her glance, and smiling his slow smile, '*Très* rum!' said he.

Très rum! Oh, she felt quite faint. Oh, why should she love him so much just because he said a thing like that. *Très* rum! That was Robert all over. Nobody else but Robert could ever say such a thing. To be so wonderful, so brilliant, so learned, and then to say in that queer, boyish voice. . . . She could have wept.

'You know you're very absurd, sometimes,' said she.

'I am,' he answered. And they walked on.

But she was tired. She had had enough. She did not want to walk any more.

'Leave me here and go for a little constitutional, won't you? I'll be in one of these long chairs. What a good thing you've got my cape; you won't have to go upstairs for a rug. Thank you, Robert, I shall look at that delicious heliotrope. . . . You won't be gone long?'

'No—no. You don't mind being left?'

'Silly! I want you to go. I can't expect you to drag after your invalid wife every minute. . . . How long will you be?'

He took out his watch. 'It's just after half-past four. I'll be back at a quarter past five.'

'Back at a quarter past five,' she repeated, and she lay still in the long chair and folded her hands.

He turned away. Suddenly he was back again. 'Look here, would you like my watch?' And he dangled it before her.

'Oh!' She caught her breath. 'Very, very much.' And she clasped the watch, the watch, watch, the darling watch in her fingers. 'Now go quickly.'

The gates of the Pension Villa Excelsior were open wide, jammed open against some bold geraniums. Stooping a little, staring straight ahead, walking swiftly, he passed through them and began climbing the hill that wound behind the town like a great rope looping the villas together. The dust lay thick. A carriage came bowling along driving towards the Excelsior. In it sat the General and the Countess; they had been for his daily airing. Mr Salesby stepped to one side but the dust beat up, thick, white, stifling like wool. The Countess just had time to nudge the General.

'There he goes,' she said spitefully.

But the General gave a loud caw and refused to look.

'It is the Englishman,' said the driver, turning round and smiling. And the Countess threw up her hands and nodded so amiably that he spat with satisfaction and gave the stumbling horse a cut.

On—on—past the finest villas in the town, magnificent places, palaces, worth coming any distance to see, past the public gardens with the carved grottoes and statues and stone animals drinking at the fountain, into a poorer quarter. Here the road ran narrow and foul between high lean houses, the ground floors of which were scooped and hollowed into stables and carpenters' shops. At a fountain ahead of him two old hags were beating linen. As he passed them they squatted back on their haunches, stared, and then their

'A-hak-kak-kak!' with the slap, slap, of the stone on the linen sounded after him.

He reached the top of the hill; he turned a corner and the town was hidden. Down he looked into a deep valley with a dried up river bed at the bottom. This side and that was covered with small dilapidated houses that had broken stone verandahs where the fruit lay drying, tomato canes in the garden, and from the gates to the doors a trellis of vines. The late sunlight, deep, golden, lay in the cup of the valley; there was a smell of charcoal in the air. In the gardens the men were cutting grapes. He watched a man standing in the greenish shade, raising up, holding a black cluster in one hand, taking the knife from his belt, cutting, laying the bunch in a flat boat-shaped basket. The man worked leisurely, silently, taking hundreds of years over the job. On the hedges on the other side of the road there were grapes small as berries, growing wild, growing among the stones. He leaned against a wall, filled his pipe, put a match to it. . . .

Leaned across a gate, turned up the collar of his mackintosh. It was going to rain. It didn't matter, he was prepared for it. You didn't expect anything else in November. He looked over the bare field. From the corner by the gate there came the smell of swedes, a great stack of them, wet, rank coloured. Two men passed walking towards the straggling village. 'Good day!' 'Good day!' By Jove! he had to hurry if he was going to catch that train home. Over the gate, across a field, over the stile, into the lane, swinging along in the drifting rain and dusk. . . . Just home in time for a bath and then a change before supper. . . . In the drawing-room; Jinnie is sitting pretty nearly in the fire. 'Oh, Robert, I didn't hear you come in. Did you have a good time? How nice you smell! A present?' 'Some bits of blackberry I picked for you. Pretty colour.' 'Oh, lovely, Robert! Dennis and Beaty are coming to supper.' Supper—cold beef, potatoes in their jackets, claret, household bread. They are gay—everybody's laughing. 'Oh, we all know Robert,' says Dennis, breathing on his eyeglasses and polishing them. 'By the way, Dennis, I picked up a very jolly little edition of. . . .'

A clock struck. He wheeled sharply. What time was it. Five? A quarter past? Back, back the way he came. As he passed through the gates he saw her on the look-out. She got up, waved and slowly she came to meet him, dragging the heavy cape. In her hand she carried a spray of heliotrope.

'You're late,' she cried gaily. 'You're three minutes late. Here's your watch, it's been very good while you were away. Did you have a nice time? Was it lovely? Tell me. Where did you go?'

'I say—put this *on*,' he said taking the cape from her.

'Yes, I will. Yes, it's getting chilly. Shall we go up to our room?'

When they reached the lift she was coughing. He frowned.

'It's nothing. I haven't been out too late. Don't be cross.' She sat down on one of the red plush chairs while he rang and rang, and then, getting no answer, kept his finger on the bell.

'Oh, Robert, do you think you ought to?'

'Ought to what?'

The door of the *salon* opened. 'What is that? Who is making that noise?' sounded from within. Klaymongso began to yelp. 'Caw! Caw! Caw!' came from the General. A Topknot darted out with one hand to her ear, opened the staff door, 'Mr Queet! Mr Queet!' she bawled. That brought the manager up at a run.

'Is that you ringing the bell, Mr Salesby? Do you want the lift? Very good, Sir. I'll take you up myself. Antonio wouldn't have been a minute, he was just taking off his apron—' And having ushered them in, the oily manager went to the door of the *salon*. 'Very sorry you should have been troubled, ladies and gentlemen.' Salesby stood in the cage, sucking in his cheeks, staring at the ceiling and turning the ring, turning the signet ring on his little finger. . . .

Arrived in their room he went swiftly over to the washstand, shook the bottle, poured her out a dose and brought it across.

'Sit down. Drink it. And don't talk.' And he stood over her while she obeyed. Then he took the glass, rinsed it and put it back in its case. 'Would you like a cushion?'

'No, I'm quite all right. Come over here. Sit down by me just a minute, will you, Robert? Ah, that's very nice.' She turned and thrust the piece of heliotrope in the lapel of his coat. 'That,' she said, 'is most becoming.' And then she leaned her head against his shoulder, and he put his arm round her.

'Robert—' her voice like a sigh—like a breath.

'Yes—'

They sat there for a long while. The sky flamed, paled; the two white beds were like two ships. . . . At last he heard the servant girl running along the corridor with the hot water cans, and gently he released her and turned on the light.

'Oh, what time is it? Oh, what a heavenly evening. Oh, Robert, I was thinking while you were away this afternoon. . . .'

They were the last couple to enter the dining-room. The Countess was there with her lorgnette and her fan, the General was there with his special chair and the air cushion and the small rug over his knees. The American Woman was there showing Klaymongso a copy of the *Saturday Evening Post**. . . . 'We're having a feast of reason and a flow of soul.'* The Two Topknots were there feeling over the peaches and the pears in their dish of fruit, and putting aside all they considered unripe or overripe to show to the manager, and the Honeymoon Couple leaned across the table, whispering, trying not to burst out laughing.

Mr Queet, in everyday clothes and white canvas shoes, served the soup, and Antonio, in full evening dress, handed it round.

'No,' said the American Woman, 'take it away, Antonio. We can't eat soup. We can't eat anything mushy, can we, Klaymongso?'

'Take them back and fill them to the rim!' said the Topknots, and they turned and watched while Antonio delivered the message.

'What is it? Rice? Is it cooked?' The Countess peered through her lorgnette. 'Mr Queet, the General can have some of this soup if it is cooked.'

'Very good, Countess.'

The Honeymoon Couple had their fish instead.

'Give me that one. That's the one I caught. No it's not. Yes, it is. No it's not. Well, it's looking at me with its eye so it must be. Tee! Hee! Hee!' Their feet were locked together under the table.

'Robert, you're not eating again. Is anything the matter?'

'No. Off food, that's all.'

'Oh, what a bother. There are eggs and spinach coming. You don't like spinach, do you. I must tell them in future. . . .'

An egg and mashed potatoes for the General.

'Mr Queet! Mr Queet!'

'Yes, Countess.'

'The General's egg's too hard again.'

'Caw! Caw! Caw!'

'Very sorry, Countess. Shall I have you another cooked, General?'

. . . They are the first to leave the dining-room. She rises, gathering her shawl and he stands aside, waiting for her to pass, turning the ring, turning the signet ring on his little finger. In the hall Mr Queet hovers. 'I thought you might not want to wait for the lift. Antonio's just serving the finger bowls. And I'm sorry the bell won't ring, it's out of order. I can't think what's happened.'

'Oh, I do hope. . . .' from her.

'Get in,' says he.

Mr Queet steps after them and slams the door. . . .

. . . 'Robert, do you mind if I go to bed very soon? Won't you go down to the *salon* or out into the garden? Or perhaps you might smoke a cigar on the balcony. It's lovely out there. And I like cigar smoke. I always did. But if you'd rather. . . .'

'No, I'll sit here.'

He takes a chair and sits on the balcony. He hears her moving about in the room, lightly, lightly, moving and rustling. Then she comes over to him. 'Good night, Robert.'

'Good night.' He takes her hand and kisses the palm. 'Don't catch cold.'

The sky is the colour of jade. There are a great many stars; an enormous white moon hangs over the garden. Far away lightning flutters—flutters like a wing—flutters like a broken bird that tries to fly and sinks again and again struggles.

The lights from the *salon* shine across the garden path and there is the sound of a piano. And once the American Woman, opening the French window to let Klaymongso into the garden, cries: 'Have you seen this moon?' But nobody answers.

He gets very cold sitting there, staring at the balcony rail. Finally he comes inside. The moon—the room is painted white with moonlight. The light trembles in the mirrors; the two beds seem to float. She is asleep. He sees her through the nets, half sitting, banked up with pillows, her white hands crossed on the sheet. Her white cheeks, her fair hair pressed against the pillow, are silvered over. He undresses quickly, stealthily and gets into bed. Lying there, his hands clasped behind his head. . . .

. . . In his study. Late summer. The virginia creeper just on the turn. . . .

'Well, my dear chap, that's the whole story. That's the long and the short of it. If she can't cut away for the next two years and give a decent climate a chance she don't stand a dog's—h'm—show. Better be frank about these things.' 'Oh, certainly. . . . ' 'And hang it all, old man, what's to prevent you going with her? It isn't as though you've got a regular job like us wage earners. You can do what you do wherever you are—' 'Two years.' 'Yes, I should give it two years. You'll have no trouble about letting this house you know. As a matter of fact. . . .'

. . . He is with her. 'Robert, the awful thing is—I suppose it's my illness—I simply feel I could not go alone. You see—you're everything. You're bread and wine,* Robert, bread and wine. Oh, my darling—what am I saying? Of course I could, of course I won't take you away. . . .'

He hears her stirring. Does she want something?

'Boogles?'

Good Lord! She is talking in her sleep. They haven't used that name for years.

'Boogles. Are you awake?'

'Yes, do you want anything?'

'Oh, I'm going to be a bother. I'm so sorry. Do you mind? There's a wretched mosquito inside my net—I can hear him singing. Would you catch him? I don't want to move because of my heart.'

'No, don't move. Stay where you are.' He switches on the light, lifts the net. 'Where is the little beggar? Have you spotted him?'

'Yes, there, over by the corner. Oh, I do feel such a fiend to have dragged you out of bed. Do you mind dreadfully?'

'No, of course not.' For a moment he hovers in his blue and white pyjamas. Then, 'got him,' he said.

'Oh, good. Was he a juicy one?'

'Beastly.' He went over to the washstand and dipped his fingers in water. 'Are you all right now? Shall I switch off the light?'

'Yes, please. No. Boogles! Come back here a moment. Sit down by me. Give me your hand.' She turns his signet ring. 'Why weren't you asleep? Boogles, listen. Come closer. I sometimes wonder—do you mind awfully being out here with me?'

He bends down. He kisses her. He tucks her in, he smoothes the pillow.

'Rot!' he whispers.

THE STRANGER

It seemed to the little crowd on the wharf that she was never going to move again. There she lay, immense, motionless on the grey crinkled water, a loop of smoke above her, an immense flock of gulls screaming and diving after the galley droppings at the stern. You could just see little couples parading—little flies walking up and down the dish on the grey crinkled tablecloth. Other flies clustered and swarmed at the edge. Now there was a gleam of white on the lower deck—the cook's apron or the stewardess perhaps. Now a tiny black spider raced up the ladder on to the bridge.

In the front of the crowd a strong-looking, middle-aged man, dressed very well, very snugly in a grey overcoat, grey silk scarf, thick gloves and dark felt hat, marched up and down, twirling his folded umbrella. He seemed to be the leader of the little crowd on the wharf and at the same time to keep them together. He was something between the sheep-dog and the shepherd.

But what a fool—what a fool he had been not to bring any glasses! There wasn't a pair of glasses between the whole lot of them.

'Curious thing, Mr Scott, that none of us thought of glasses. We might have been able to stir 'em up a bit. We might have managed a little signalling. *Don't hesitate to land. Natives harmless.** Or: *A welcome awaits you. All is forgiven.** What? Eh?'

Mr Hammond's quick, eager glance, so nervous and yet so friendly and confiding, took in everybody on the wharf, roped in even those old chaps lounging against the gangways. They knew, every man-jack of them,* that Mrs Hammond was on that boat, and he was so tremendously excited it never entered his head not to believe that this marvellous fact meant something to them too. It warmed his heart towards them. They were, he decided, as decent a crowd of people—Those old chaps over by the gangways, too—fine, solid old chaps. What chests—by Jove! And he squared his own, plunged his thick-gloved hands into his pockets, rocked from heel to toe.

'Yes, my wife's been in Europe for the last ten months. On a visit to our eldest girl, who was married last year. I brought her up here, as far as Auckland, myself. So I thought I'd better come and fetch her back. Yes, yes, yes.' The shrewd grey eyes narrowed again and searched anxiously, quickly, the motionless liner. Again his overcoat was unbuttoned. Out came the thin, butter-yellow watch again, and for the twentieth—fiftieth—hundredth time he made the calculation.

'Let me see, now. It was two fifteen when the doctor's launch went off. Two fifteen. It is now exactly twenty-eight minutes past four. That is to say, the doctor's been gone two hours and thirteen minutes. Two hours and thirteen minutes! Whee-ooh!' He gave a queer little half-whistle and snapped his watch to again. 'But I think we should have been told if there was anything up—don't you, Mr Gaven?'

'Oh, yes, Mr Hammond! I don't think there's anything to— anything to worry about,' said Mr Gaven, knocking out his pipe against the heel of his shoe. 'At the same time—'

'Quite so! Quite so!' cried Mr Hammond. 'Dashed annoying!' He paced quickly up and down and came back again to his stand between Mr and Mrs Scott and Mr Gaven. 'It's getting quite dark, too,' and he waved his folded umbrella as though the dusk at least might have had the decency to keep off for a bit. But the dusk came slowly, spreading like a slow stain over the water. Little Jean Scott dragged at her mother's hand.

'I wan' my tea, mammy!' she wailed.

'I expect you do,' said Mr Hammond. 'I expect all these ladies want their tea.' And his kind, flushed, almost pitiful glance roped them all in again. He wondered whether Janey was having a final cup of tea in the saloon out there. He hoped so; he thought not. It would be just like her not to leave the deck. In that case perhaps the deck steward would bring her up a cup. If he'd been there he'd have got it for her—somehow. And for a moment he was on deck, standing over her, watching her little hand fold round the cup in the way she had, while she drank the only cup of tea to be got on board. . . . But now he was back here, and the Lord only knew when that cursed Captain would stop hanging about in the stream. He took another turn, up and down, up and down. He walked as far as the cab-stand to make sure his driver hadn't disappeared; back he swerved again to the little flock huddled in the shelter of the banana crates. Little Jean Scott was still wanting her tea. Poor little beggar! He wished he had a bit of chocolate on him.

'Here, Jean!' he said: 'Like a lift up?' And easily, gently, he swung the little girl on to a higher barrel. The movement of holding her, steadying her, relieved him wonderfully, lightened his heart.

'Hold on,' he said, keeping an arm round her.

'Oh, don't worry about *Jean*, Mr Hammond!' said Mrs Scott.

'That's all right, Mrs Scott. No trouble. It's a pleasure. Jean's a little pal of mine, aren't you, Jean?'

'Yes, Mr Hammond,' said Jean, and she ran her finger down the dent of his felt hat.

But suddenly she caught him by the ear and gave a loud scream. 'Lo-ok, Mr Hammond! She's moving! Look, she's coming in!'

By Jove! So she was. At last! She was slowly, slowly turning round. A bell sounded far over the water and a great spout of steam gushed into the air. The gulls rose; they fluttered away like bits of white paper. And whether that deep throbbing was her engines or his heart Mr Hammond couldn't say. He had to nerve himself to bear it, whatever it was. At that moment old Captain Johnson, the harbour-master, came striding down the wharf, a leather portfolio under his arm.

'Jean'll be all right,' said Mr Scott. 'I'll hold her.' He was just in time. Mr Hammond had forgotten about Jean. He sprang away to greet old Captain Johnson.

'Well, Captain,' the eager, nervous voice rang out again, 'you've taken pity on us at last.'

'It's no good blaming me, Mr Hammond,' wheezed old Captain Johnson, staring at the liner. 'You got Mrs Hammond on board, ain't yer?'

'Yes, yes!' said Hammond, and he kept by the harbour-master's side. 'Mrs Hammond's there. Hul-lo! We shan't be long now!'

With her telephone ring-ringing, the thrum of her screw filling the air, the big liner bore down on them, cutting sharp through the dark water so that big white shavings curled to either side. Hammond and the harbour-master kept in front of the rest. Hammond took off his hat; he raked the decks—they were crammed with passengers; he waved his hat and bawled a loud, strange 'Hul-lo!' across the water, and then turned round and burst out laughing and said something—nothing—to old Captain Johnson.

'Seen her?' asked the harbour-master.

'No, not yet. Steady—wait a bit!' And suddenly, between two

great clumsy idiots—'Get out of the way there!' he signed with his
umbrella—he saw a hand raised—a white glove shaking a handkerchief. Another moment, and—thank God, thank God!—there
she was. There was Janey. There was Mrs Hammond, yes, yes, yes—
standing by the rail and smiling and nodding and waving her
handkerchief.

'Well, that's first class—first class! Well, well, well!' He positively stamped. Like lightning he drew out his cigar-case and
offered it to old Captain Johnson. 'Have a cigar, Captain! They're
pretty good. Have a couple! Here'—and he pressed all the cigars in
the case on the harbour-master—'I've a couple of boxes up at the
hotel.'

'Thanks, Mr Hammond!' wheezed old Captain Johnson.

Hammond stuffed the cigar-case back. His hands were shaking,
but he'd got hold of himself again. He was able to face Janey. There
she was, leaning on the rail, talking to some woman and at the same
time watching him, ready for him. It struck him, as the gulf of water
closed, how small she looked on that huge ship. His heart was wrung
with such a spasm that he could have cried out. How little she looked
to have come all that long way and back by herself! Just like her,
though. Just like Janey. She had the courage of a——And now the
crew had come forward and parted the passengers; they had lowered
the rails for the gangways.

The voices on shore and the voices on board flew to greet each
other.

'All well?'

'All well.'

'How's mother?'

'Much better.'

'Hello, Jean!'

'Hillo, Aun' Emily!'

'Had a good voyage?'

'Splendid!'

'Shan't be long now!'

'Not long now.'

The engines stopped. Slowly she edged to the wharf-side.

'Make way there—make way—make way!' And the wharf hands
brought the heavy gangways along at a sweeping run. Hammond
signed to Janey to stay where she was. The old harbour-master

stepped forward; he followed. As to 'ladies first', or any rot like that, it never entered his head.

'After you, Captain!' he cried genially. And, treading on the old man's heels, he strode up the gangway on to the deck in a bee-line to Janey, and Janey was clasped in his arms.

'Well, well, well! Yes, yes! Here we are at last!' he stammered. It was all he could say. And Janey emerged, and her cool little voice— the only voice in the world for him—said,

'Well, darling! Have you been waiting long?'

No; not long. Or, at any rate, it didn't matter. It was over now. But the point was, he had a cab waiting at the end of the wharf. Was she ready to go off? Was her luggage ready? In that case they could cut off sharp with her cabin luggage and let the rest go hang until to-morrow. He bent over her and she looked up with her familiar half-smile. She was just the same. Not a day changed. Just as he'd always known her. She laid her small hand on his sleeve.

'How are the children, John?' she asked.

(Hang the children!) 'Perfectly well. Never better in their lives.'

'Haven't they sent me letters?'

'Yes, yes—of course! I've left them at the hotel for you to digest later on.'

'We can't go quite so fast,' said she. 'I've got people to say good-bye to—and then there's the Captain.' As his face fell she gave his arm a small understanding squeeze. 'If the Captain comes off the bridge I want you to thank him for having looked after your wife so beautifully.' Well, he'd got her. If she wanted another ten minutes— As he gave way she was surrounded. The whole first-class seemed to want to say good-bye to Janey.

'Good-bye, *dear* Mrs Hammond! And next time you're in Sydney I'll *expect* you.'

'Darling Mrs Hammond! You won't forget to write to me, will you?'

'Well, Mrs Hammond, what this boat would have been without you!'

It was as plain as a pikestaff that she was by far the most popular woman on board. And she took it all—just as usual. Absolutely composed. Just her little self—just Janey all over; standing there with her veil thrown back. Hammond never noticed what his wife had on. It was all the same to him whatever she wore. But to-day he

did notice that she wore a black 'costume'*—didn't they call it?—
with white frills, trimmings he supposed they were, at the neck and
sleeves. All this while Janey handed him round.

'John, dear!' And then: 'I want to introduce you to—'

Finally they did escape, and she led the way to her state-room.* To
follow Janey down the passage that she knew so well—that was so
strange to him; to part the green curtains after her and to step into
the cabin that had been hers gave him exquisite happiness. But—
confound it!—the stewardess was there on the floor, strapping up the
rugs.

'That's the last, Mrs Hammond,' said the stewardess, rising and
pulling down her cuffs.

He was introduced again, and then Janey and the stewardess disappeared into the passage. He heard whisperings. She was getting
the tipping business over, he supposed. He sat down on the striped
sofa and took his hat off. There were the rugs she had taken with her;
they looked good as new. All her luggage looked fresh, perfect. The
labels were written in her beautiful little clear hand—'Mrs. John
Hammond'.

'Mrs John Hammond!' He gave a long sigh of content and leaned
back, crossing his arms. The strain was over. He felt he could have
sat there for ever sighing his relief—the relief at being rid of that
horrible tug, pull, grip on his heart. The danger was over. That was
the feeling. They were on dry land again.

But at that moment Janey's head came round the corner.

'Darling—do you mind? I just want to go and say good-bye to the
doctor.'

Hammond started up. 'I'll come with you.'

'No, no!' she said. 'Don't bother. I'd rather not. I'll not be a
minute.'

And before he could answer she was gone. He had half a mind to
run after her; but instead he sat down again.

Would she really not be long? What was the time now? Out came
the watch; he stared at nothing. That was rather queer of Janey,
wasn't it? Why couldn't she have told the stewardess to say good-bye
for her? Why did she have to go chasing after the ship's doctor? She
could have sent a note from the hotel even if the affair had been
urgent. Urgent? Did it—could it mean that she had been ill on the
voyage—she was keeping something from him? That was it! He

seized his hat. He was going off to find that fellow and to wring the truth out of him at all costs. He thought he'd noticed just something. She was just a touch too calm—too steady. From the very first moment——

The curtains rang. Janey was back. He jumped to his feet.

'Janey, have you been ill on this voyage? You have!'

'Ill?' Her airy little voice mocked him. She stepped over the rugs, came up close, touched his breast, and looked up at him.

'Darling,' she said, 'don't frighten me. Of course I haven't! Whatever makes you think I have? Do I look ill?'

But Hammond didn't see her. He only felt that she was looking at him and that there was no need to worry about anything. She was here to look after things. It was all right. Everything was.

The gentle pressure of her hand was so calming that he put his over hers to hold it there. And she said:

'Stand still. I want to look at you. I haven't seen you yet. You've had your beard beautifully trimmed, and you look—younger, I think, and decidedly thinner! Bachelor life agrees with you.'

'Agrees with me!' He groaned for love and caught her close again. And again, as always, he had the feeling he was holding something that never was quite his—his. Something too delicate, too precious, that would fly away once he let go.

'For God's sake let's get off to the hotel so that we can be by ourselves!' And he rang the bell hard for some one to look sharp with the luggage.

*　　*　　*

Walking down the wharf together she took his arm. He had her on his arm again. And the difference it made to get into the cab after Janey—to throw the red-and-yellow striped blanket round them both—to tell the driver to hurry because neither of them had had any tea. No more going without his tea or pouring out his own. She was back. He turned to her, squeezed her hand, and said gently, teasingly, in the 'special' voice he had for her: 'Glad to be home again, dearie?' She smiled; she didn't even bother to answer, but gently she drew his hand away as they came to the lighted streets.

'We've got the best room in the hotel,' he said. 'I wouldn't be put off with another. And I asked the chambermaid to put in a bit of a fire in case you felt chilly. She's a nice, attentive girl. And I thought now we were here we wouldn't bother to go home to-morrow, but spend the day looking round and leave the morning after. Does that suit you? There's no hurry, is there? The children will have you soon enough. . . . I thought a day's sight-seeing might make a nice break in your journey—eh, Janey?'

'Have you taken the tickets for the day after?' she asked.

'I should think I have!' He unbuttoned his overcoat and took out his bulging pocket-book. 'Here we are! I reserved a first-class carriage to Napier. There it is—"Mr *and* Mrs John Hammond". I thought we might as well do ourselves comfortably, and we don't want other people butting in, do we? But if you'd like to stop here a bit longer—?'

'Oh, no!' said Janey quickly. 'Not for the world! The day after to-morrow, then. And the children—'

But they had reached the hotel. The manager was standing in the broad, brilliantly-lighted porch. He came down to greet them. A porter ran from the hall for their boxes.

'Well, Mr Arnold, here's Mrs Hammond at last!'

The manager led them through the hall himself and pressed the elevator-bell. Hammond knew there were business pals of his sitting at the little hall tables having a drink before dinner. But he wasn't going to risk interruption; he looked neither to the right nor the left. They could think what they pleased. If they didn't understand, the more fools they—and he stepped out of the lift, unlocked the door of their room, and shepherded Janey in. The door shut. Now, at last, they were alone together. He turned up the light. The curtains were drawn; the fire blazed. He flung his hat on to the huge bed and went towards her.

But—would you believe it!—again they were interrupted. This time it was the porter with the luggage. He made two journeys of it, leaving the door open in between, taking his time, whistling through his teeth in the corridor. Hammond paced up and down the room, tearing off his gloves, tearing off his scarf. Finally he flung his overcoat on to the bedside.

At last the fool was gone. The door clicked. Now they *were* alone. Said Hammond: 'I feel I'll never have you to myself again. These cursed people! Janey'—and he bent his flushed, eager gaze upon her—'let's have dinner up here. If we go down to the restaurant we'll be interrupted, and then there's the confounded music' (the music he'd praised so highly, applauded so loudly last night!). 'We shan't be able to hear each other speak. Let's have something up here in front of the fire. It's too late for tea. I'll order a little supper, shall I? How does the idea strike you?'

'Do, darling!' said Janey. 'And while you're away—the children's letters—'

'Oh, later on will do!' said Hammond.

'But then we'd get it over,' said Janey. 'And I'd first have time to—'

'Oh, I needn't go down!' explained Hammond. 'I'll just ring and give the order . . . you don't want to send me away, do you?'

Janey shook her head and smiled.

'But you're thinking of something else. You're worrying about something,' said Hammond. 'What is it? Come and sit here—come and sit on my knee before the fire.'

'I'll just unpin my hat,' said Janey, and she went over to the dressing-table. 'A-ah!' She gave a little cry.

'What is it?'

'Nothing, darling. I've just found the children's letters. That's all right! They will keep. No hurry now!' She turned to him, clasping them. She tucked them into her frilled blouse. She cried quickly, gaily: 'Oh, how typical this dressing-table is of you!'

'Why? What's the matter with it?' said Hammond.

'If it were floating in eternity I should say "John!"' laughed Janey, staring at the big bottle of hair tonic, the wicker bottle of eau-de-Cologne, the two hair-brushes, and a dozen new collars* tied with pink tape. 'Is this all your luggage?'

'Hang my luggage!' said Hammond; but all the same he liked being laughed at by Janey. 'Let's talk. Let's get down to things. Tell me'—and as Janey perched on his knees he leaned back and drew her into the deep, ugly chair—'tell me you're really glad to be back, Janey.'

'Yes, darling, I am glad,' she said.

But just as when he embraced her he felt she would fly away, so Hammond never knew—never knew for dead certain that she was as glad as he was. How could he know? Would he ever know? Would he always have this craving—this pang like hunger, somehow, to make Janey so much part of him that there wasn't any of her to escape? He wanted to blot out everybody, everything. He wished now he'd turned off the light. That might have brought her nearer. And now those letters from the children rustled in her blouse. He could have chucked them into the fire.

'Janey,' he whispered.

'Yes, dear?' She lay on his breast, but so lightly, so remotely. Their breathing rose and fell together.

'Janey!'

'What is it?'

'Turn to me,' he whispered. A slow, deep flush flowed into his forehead. 'Kiss me, Janey! You kiss me!'

It seemed to him there was a tiny pause—but long enough for him to suffer torture—before her lips touched his, firmly, lightly— kissing them as she always kissed him, as though the kiss—how could he describe it?—confirmed what they were saying, signed the contract. But that wasn't what he wanted; that wasn't at all what he thirsted for. He felt suddenly, horribly tired.

'If you knew,' he said, opening his eyes, 'what it's been like— waiting to-day. I thought the boat never would come in. There we were, hanging about. What kept you so long?'

She made no answer. She was looking away from him at the fire. The flames hurried—hurried over the coals, flickered, fell.

'Not asleep, are you?' said Hammond, and he jumped her up and down.

'No,' she said. And then: 'Don't do that, dear. No, I was thinking. As a matter of fact,' she said, 'one of the passengers died last night— a man. That's what held us up. We brought him in—I mean, he wasn't buried at sea. So, of course, the ship's doctor and the shore doctor—'

'What was it?' asked Hammond uneasily. He hated to hear of death. He hated this to have happened. It was, in some queer way, as though he and Janey had met a funeral on their way to the hotel.

'Oh, it wasn't anything in the least infectious!' said Janey. She was speaking scarcely above her breath. 'It was *heart*.' A pause. 'Poor fellow!' she said. 'Quite young.' And she watched the fire flicker and fall. 'He died in my arms,' said Janey.

The blow was so sudden that Hammond thought he would faint. He couldn't move; he couldn't breathe. He felt all his strength flowing—flowing into the big dark chair, and the big dark chair held him fast, gripped him, forced him to bear it.

'What?' he said dully. 'What's that you say?'

'The end was quite peaceful,' said the small voice. 'He just'—and Hammond saw her lift her gentle hand—'breathed his life away at the end.' And her hand fell.

'Who—else was there?' Hammond managed to ask.

'Nobody. I was alone with him.'

Ah, my God, what was she saying! What was she doing to him! This would kill him! And all the while she spoke:

'I saw the change coming and I sent the steward for the doctor, but the doctor was too late. He couldn't have done anything, anyway.'

'But—why *you*, why *you*?' moaned Hammond.

At that Janey turned quickly, quickly searched his face.

'You don't *mind*, John, do you?' she asked. 'You don't—It's nothing to do with you and me.'

Somehow or other he managed to shake some sort of smile at her. Somehow or other he stammered: 'No—go—on, go on! I want you to tell me.'

'But, John darling—'

'Tell me, Janey!'

'There's nothing to tell,' she said, wondering. 'He was one of the first-class passengers. I saw he was very ill when he came on board. . . . But he seemed to be so much better until yesterday. He had a severe attack in the afternoon—excitement—nervousness, I think, about arriving. And after that he never recovered.'

'But why didn't the stewardess—'

'Oh, my dear—the stewardess!' said Janey. 'What would he have felt? And besides . . . he might have wanted to leave a message . . . to—'

'Didn't he?' muttered Hammond. 'Didn't he say anything?'

'No, darling, not a word!' She shook her head softly. 'All the time I was with him he was too weak . . . he was too weak even to move a finger. . . .'

Janey was silent. But her words, so light, so soft, so chill, seemed to hover in the air, to rain into his breast like snow.

The fire had gone red. Now it fell in with a sharp sound and the room was colder. Cold crept up his arms. The room was huge, immense, glittering. It filled his whole world. There was the great blind bed, with his coat flung across it like some headless man saying his prayers. There was the luggage, ready to be carried away again, anywhere, tossed into trains, carted on to boats.

. . . 'He was too weak. He was too weak to move a finger.' And yet he died in Janey's arms. She—who'd never—never once in all these years—never on one single solitary occasion——

No; he mustn't think of it. Madness lay in thinking of it. No, he wouldn't face it. He couldn't stand it. It was too much to bear!

And now Janey touched his tie with her fingers. She pinched the edges of the tie together.

'You're not—sorry I told you, John darling? It hasn't made you sad? It hasn't spoilt our evening—our being alone together?'

But at that he had to hide his face. He put his face into her bosom and his arms enfolded her.

Spoilt their evening! Spoilt their being alone together! They would never be alone together again.

MISS BRILL

Although it was so brilliantly fine—the blue sky powdered with gold and great spots of light like white wine splashed over the Jardins Publiques*—Miss Brill was glad that she had decided on her fur. The air was motionless, but when you opened your mouth there was just a faint chill, like a chill from a glass of iced water before you sip, and now and again a leaf came drifting—from nowhere, from the sky. Miss Brill put up her hand and touched her fur. Dear little thing! It was nice to feel it again. She had taken it out of its box that afternoon, shaken out the moth-powder, given it a good brush, and rubbed the life back into the dim little eyes. 'What has been happening to me?' said the sad little eyes. Oh, how sweet it was to see them snap at her again from the red eiderdown! . . . But the nose, which was of some black composition, wasn't at all firm. It must have had a knock, somehow. Never mind—a little dab of black sealing-wax when the time came—when it was absolutely necessary. . . . Little rogue! Yes, she really felt like that about it. Little rogue biting its tail just by her left ear. She could have taken it off and laid it on her lap and stroked it. She felt a tingling* in her hands and arms, but that came from walking, she supposed. And when she breathed, something light and sad—no, not sad, exactly—something gentle seemed to move in her bosom.

There were a number of people out this afternoon, far more than last Sunday. And the band sounded louder and gayer. That was because the Season had begun. For although the band played all the year round on Sundays, out of season it was never the same. It was like some one playing with only the family to listen; it didn't care how it played if there weren't any strangers present. Wasn't the conductor wearing a new coat, too? She was sure it was new. He scraped with his foot and flapped his arms like a rooster about to crow, and the bandsmen sitting in the green rotunda* blew out their cheeks and glared at the music. Now there came a little 'flutey' bit—very pretty!—a little chain of bright drops. She was sure it would be repeated. It was; she lifted her head and smiled.

Only two people shared her 'special' seat: a fine old man in a velvet coat, his hands clasped over a huge carved walking-stick, and a big old woman, sitting upright, with a roll of knitting on her embroidered apron. They did not speak. This was disappointing, for Miss Brill always looked forward to the conversation. She had become really quite expert, she thought, at listening as though she didn't listen, at sitting in other people's lives just for a minute while they talked round her.

She glanced, sideways, at the old couple. Perhaps they would go soon. Last Sunday, too, hadn't been as interesting as usual. An Englishman and his wife, he wearing a dreadful Panama hat* and she button boots. And she'd gone on the whole time about how she ought to wear spectacles; she knew she needed them; but that it was no good getting any; they'd be sure to break and they'd never keep on. And he'd been so patient. He'd suggested everything—gold rims, the kind that curved round your ears, little pads inside the bridge. No, nothing would please her. 'They'll always be sliding down my nose!' Miss Brill had wanted to shake her.

The old people sat on the bench, still as statues. Never mind, there was always the crowd to watch. To and fro, in front of the flower-beds and the band rotunda, the couples and groups paraded, stopped to talk, to greet, to buy a handful of flowers from the old beggar who had his tray fixed to the railings. Little children ran among them, swooping and laughing; little boys with big white silk bows under their chins, little girls, little French dolls, dressed up in velvet and lace. And sometimes a tiny staggerer came suddenly rocking into the open from under the trees, stopped, stared, as suddenly sat down 'flop', until its small high-stepping mother, like a young hen, rushed scolding to its rescue. Other people sat on the benches and green chairs, but they were nearly always the same, Sunday after Sunday, and—Miss Brill had often noticed—there was something funny about nearly all of them. They were odd, silent, nearly all old, and from the way they stared they looked as though they'd just come from dark little rooms or even—even cupboards!

Behind the rotunda the slender trees with yellow leaves down drooping, and through them just a line of sea, and beyond the blue sky with gold-veined clouds.

Tum-tum-tum tiddle-um! tiddle-um! tum tiddley-um tum ta! blew the band.

Two young girls in red came by and two young soldiers in blue met them, and they laughed and paired and went off arm-in-arm.

Two peasant women with funny straw hats passed, gravely, leading beautiful smoke-coloured donkeys. A cold, pale nun hurried by. A beautiful woman came along and dropped her bunch of violets, and a little boy ran after to hand them to her, and she took them and threw them away as if they'd been poisoned. Dear me! Miss Brill didn't know whether to admire that or not! And now an ermine toque* and a gentleman in grey met just in front of her. He was tall, stiff, dignified, and she was wearing the ermine toque she'd bought when her hair was yellow. Now everything, her hair, her face, even her eyes, was the same colour as the shabby ermine, and her hand, in its cleaned glove, lifted to dab her lips, was a tiny yellowish paw. Oh, she was so pleased to see him—delighted! She rather thought they were going to meet that afternoon. She described where she'd been— everywhere, here, there, along by the sea. The day was so charming—didn't he agree? And wouldn't he, perhaps? . . . But he shook his head, lighted a cigarette, slowly breathed a great deep puff into her face, and, even while she was still talking and laughing, flicked the match away and walked on. The ermine toque was alone; she smiled more brightly than ever. But even the band seemed to know what she was feeling and played more softly, played tenderly, and the drum beat, 'The Brute! The Brute!' over and over. What would she do? What was going to happen now? But as Miss Brill wondered, the ermine toque turned, raised her hand as though she'd seen some one else, much nicer, just over there, and pattered away. And the band changed again and played more quickly, more gaily than ever, and the old couple on Miss Brill's seat got up and marched away, and such a funny old man with long whiskers hobbled along in time to the music and was nearly knocked over by four girls walking abreast.

Oh, how fascinating it was! How she enjoyed it! How she loved sitting here, watching it all! It was like a play. It was exactly like a play. Who could believe the sky at the back wasn't painted? But it wasn't till a little brown dog trotted on solemn and then slowly trotted off, like a little 'theatre' dog, a little dog that had been drugged, that Miss Brill discovered what it was that made it so exciting. They were all on the stage. They weren't only the audience, not only looking on; they were acting. Even she had a part and came every Sunday. No doubt somebody would have noticed if she hadn't been there; she was part of the performance after all. How strange

she'd never thought of it like that before! And yet it explained why
she made such a point of starting from home at just the same time
each week—so as not to be late for the performance—and it also
explained why she had quite a queer, shy feeling at telling her
English pupils how she spent her Sunday afternoons. No wonder!
Miss Brill nearly laughed out loud. She was on the stage. She
thought of the old invalid gentleman to whom she read the newspaper four afternoons a week* while he slept in the garden. She had
got quite used to the frail head on the cotton pillow, the hollowed
eyes, the open mouth and the high pinched nose. If he'd been dead
she mightn't have noticed for weeks; she wouldn't have minded. But
suddenly he knew he was having the paper read to him by an actress!
'An actress!' The old head lifted; two points of light quivered in the
old eyes. 'An actress—are ye?' And Miss Brill smoothed the newspaper as though it were the manuscript of her part and said gently:
'Yes, I have been an actress for a long time.'

The band had been having a rest. Now they started again. And
what they played was warm, sunny, yet there was just a faint chill—a
something, what was it?—not sadness—no, not sadness—a something that made you want to sing. The tune lifted, lifted, the light
shone; and it seemed to Miss Brill that in another moment all of
them, all the whole company, would begin singing. The young ones,
the laughing ones who were moving together, they would begin, and
the men's voices, very resolute and brave, would join them. And then
she too, she too, and the others on the benches—they would come in
with a kind of accompaniment—something low, that scarcely rose or
fell, something so beautiful—moving.... And Miss Brill's eyes
filled with tears and she looked smiling at all the other members of
the company. Yes, we understand, we understand, she thought—
though what they understood she didn't know.

Just at that moment a boy and a girl came and sat down where the
old couple had been. They were beautifully dressed; they were in
love. The hero and heroine, of course, just arrived from his father's
yacht. And still soundlessly singing, still with that trembling smile,
Miss Brill prepared to listen.

'No, not now,' said the girl. 'Not here, I can't.'

'But why? Because of that stupid old thing at the end there?' asked
the boy. 'Why does she come here at all—who wants her? Why
doesn't she keep her silly old mug at home?'

'It's her fu-fur which is so funny,' giggled the girl. 'It's exactly like a fried whiting.'

'Ah, be off with you!' said the boy in an angry whisper. Then: 'Tell me, ma petite chère—'

'No, not here,' said the girl. 'Not *yet*.'

*　　*　　*

On her way home she usually bought a slice of honey-cake at the baker's. It was her Sunday treat. Sometimes there was an almond in her slice, sometimes not. It made a great difference. If there was an almond it was like carrying home a tiny present—a surprise—something that might very well not have been there. She hurried on the almond Sundays and struck the match for the kettle in quite a dashing way.

But to-day she passed the baker's by, climbed the stairs, went into the little dark room—her room like a cupboard—and sat down on the red eiderdown. She sat there for a long time. The box that the fur came out of was on the bed. She unclasped the necklet quickly; quickly, without looking, laid it inside. But when she put the lid on she thought she heard something crying.

THE DAUGHTERS OF THE LATE COLONEL

I

The week after was one of the busiest weeks of their lives. Even when they went to bed it was only their bodies that lay down and rested; their minds went on, thinking things out, talking things over, wondering, deciding, trying to remember where. . . .

Constantia lay like a statue, her hands by her sides, her feet just overlapping each other, the sheet up to her chin. She stared at the ceiling.

'Do you think father would mind if we gave his top-hat* to the porter?'

'The porter?' snapped Josephine. 'Why ever the porter? What a very extraordinary idea!'

'Because,' said Constantia slowly, 'he must often have to go to funerals. And I noticed at—at the cemetery that he only had a bowler.'* She paused. 'I thought then how very much he'd appreciate a top-hat. We ought to give him a present, too. He was always very nice to father.'

'But,' cried Josephine, flouncing on her pillow and staring across the dark at Constantia, 'father's head!' And suddenly, for one awful moment, she nearly giggled. Not, of course, that she felt in the least like giggling. It must have been habit. Years ago, when they had stayed awake at night talking, their beds had simply heaved. And now the porter's head, disappearing, popped out, like a candle, under father's hat. . . . The giggle mounted, mounted; she clenched her hands; she fought it down; she frowned fiercely at the dark and said 'Remember'* terribly sternly.

'We can decide to-morrow,' she said.

Constantia had noticed nothing; she sighed.

'Do you think we ought to have our dressing-gowns dyed as well?'

'Black?' almost shrieked Josephine.

'Well, what else?' said Constantia. 'I was thinking—it doesn't seem quite sincere, in a way, to wear black* out of doors and when we're fully dressed, and then when we're at home—'

'But nobody sees us,' said Josephine. She gave the bedclothes such a twitch that both her feet came uncovered, and she had to creep up the pillows to get them well under again.

'Kate does,' said Constantia. 'And the postman very well might.'

Josephine thought of her dark-red slippers, which matched her dressing-gown, and of Constantia's favourite indefinite green ones which went with hers. Black! Two black dressing-gowns and two pairs of black woolly slippers, creeping off to the bath-room like black cats.

'I don't think it's absolutely necessary,' said she.

Silence. Then Constantia said, 'We shall have to post the papers with the notice in them to-morrow to catch the Ceylon* mail. . . . How many letters have we had up till now?'

'Twenty-three.'

Josephine had replied to them all, and twenty-three times when she came to 'We miss our dear father so much' she had broken down and had to use her handkerchief, and on some of them even to soak up a very light-blue tear with an edge of blotting-paper. Strange! She couldn't have put it on—but twenty-three times. Even now, though, when she said over to herself sadly 'We miss our dear father *so* much,' she could have cried if she'd wanted to.

'Have you got enough stamps?' came from Constantia.

'Oh, how can I tell?' said Josephine crossly. 'What's the good of asking me that now?'

'I was just wondering,' said Constantia mildly.

Silence again. There came a little rustle, a scurry, a hop.

'A mouse,' said Constantia.

'It can't be a mouse because there aren't any crumbs,' said Josephine.

'But it doesn't know there aren't,' said Constantia.

A spasm of pity squeezed her heart. Poor little thing! She wished she'd left a tiny piece of biscuit on the dressing-table. It was awful to think of it not finding anything. What would it do?

'I can't think how they manage to live at all,' she said slowly.

'Who?' demanded Josephine.

And Constantia said more loudly than she meant to, 'Mice.'

Josephine was furious. 'Oh, what nonsense, Con!' she said. 'What have mice got to do with it? You're asleep.'

'I don't think I am,' said Constantia. She shut her eyes to make sure. She was.

Josephine arched her spine, pulled up her knees, folded her arms so that her fists came under her ears, and pressed her cheek hard against the pillow.

II

Another thing which complicated matters was they had Nurse Andrews staying on with them that week. It was their own fault; they had asked her. It was Josephine's idea. On the morning—well, on the last morning, when the doctor had gone, Josephine had said to Constantia, 'Don't you think it would be rather nice if we asked Nurse Andrews to stay on for a week as our guest?'

'Very nice,' said Constantia.

'I thought,' went on Josephine quickly, 'I should just say this afternoon, after I've paid her, "My sister and I would be very pleased, after all you've done for us, Nurse Andrews, if you would stay on for a week as our guest." I'd have to put that in about being our guest in case—'

'Oh, but she could hardly expect to be paid!' cried Constantia.

'One never knows,' said Josephine sagely.

Nurse Andrews had, of course, jumped at the idea. But it was a bother. It meant they had to have regular sit-down meals at the proper times, whereas if they'd been alone they could just have asked Kate if she wouldn't have minded bringing them a tray wherever they were. And meal-times now that the strain was over were rather a trial.

Nurse Andrews was simply fearful about butter. Really they couldn't help feeling that about butter, at least, she took advantage of their kindness. And she had that maddening habit of asking for just an inch more bread to finish what she had on her plate, and then, at the last mouthful, absent-mindedly—of course it wasn't absent-mindedly—taking another helping. Josephine got very red when this happened, and she fastened her small, bead-like eyes on the table-cloth as if she saw a minute strange insect creeping through the web of it. But Constantia's long, pale face lengthened and set, and she gazed away—away—far over the desert, to where that line of camels unwound like a thread of wool. . . .

'When I was with Lady Tukes,' said Nurse Andrews, 'she had such a dainty little contra-vance for the buttah. It was a silvah Cupid balanced on the—on the bordah of a glass dish, holding a tayny fork. And when you wanted some buttah you simply pressed his foot and he bent down and speared you a piece. It was quite a gayme.'

Josephine could hardly bear that. But 'I think those things are very extravagant' was all she said.

'But whey?' asked Nurse Andrews, beaming through her eye-glasses. 'No one, surely, would take more buttah than one wanted— would one?'

'Ring, Con,' cried Josephine. She couldn't trust herself to reply.

And proud young Kate, the enchanted princess, came in to see what the old tabbies wanted now. She snatched away their plates of mock something or other and slapped down a white, terrified blancmange.*

'Jam, please, Kate,' said Josephine kindly.

Kate knelt and burst open the sideboard, lifted the lid of the jam-pot, saw it was empty, put it on the table, and stalked off.

'I'm afraid,' said Nurse Andrews a moment later, 'there isn't any.'

'Oh, what a bother!' said Josephine. She bit her lip. 'What had we better do?'

Constantia looked dubious. 'We can't disturb Kate again,' she said softly.

Nurse Andrews waited, smiling at them both. Her eyes wandered, spying at everything behind her eye-glasses. Constantia in despair went back to her camels. Josephine frowned heavily—concentrated. If it hadn't been for this idiotic woman she and Con would, of course, have eaten their blancmange without. Suddenly the idea came.

'I know,' she said. 'Marmalade. There's some marmalade in the sideboard. Get it, Con.'

'I hope,' laughed Nurse Andrews, and her laugh was like a spoon tinkling against a medicine-glass—'I hope it's not very bittah marmalayde.'

III

But, after all, it was not long now, and then she'd be gone for good. And there was no getting over the fact that she had been very kind to father. She had nursed him day and night at the end. Indeed, both

Constantia and Josephine felt privately she had rather overdone the not leaving him at the very last. For when they had gone in to say good-bye Nurse Andrews had sat beside his bed the whole time, holding his wrist* and pretending to look at her watch. It couldn't have been necessary. It was so tactless, too. Supposing father had wanted to say something—something private to them. Not that he had. Oh, far from it! He lay there, purple, a dark, angry purple in the face, and never even looked at them when they came in. Then, as they were standing there, wondering what to do, he had suddenly opened one eye. Oh, what a difference it would have made, what a difference to their memory of him, how much easier to tell people about it, if he had only opened both! But no—one eye only. It glared at them a moment and then . . . went out.

IV

It had made it very awkward for them when Mr Farolles, of St John's, called the same afternoon.

'The end was quite peaceful, I trust?' were the first words he said as he glided towards them through the dark drawing-room.

'Quite,' said Josephine faintly. They both hung their heads. Both of them felt certain that eye wasn't at all a peaceful eye.

'Won't you sit down?' said Josephine.

'Thank you, Miss Pinner,'* said Mr Farolles gratefully. He folded his coat-tails and began to lower himself into father's arm-chair, but just as he touched it he almost sprang up and slid into the next chair instead.

He coughed. Josephine clasped her hands; Constantia looked vague.

'I want you to feel, Miss Pinner,' said Mr Farolles, 'and you, Miss Constantia, that I'm trying to be helpful. I want to be helpful to you both, if you will let me. These are the times,' said Mr Farolles, very simply and earnestly, 'when God means us to be helpful to one another.'

'Thank you very much, Mr Farolles,' said Josephine and Constantia.

'Not at all,' said Mr Farolles gently. He drew his kid gloves through his fingers and leaned forward. 'And if either of you would like a little Communion, either or both of you, here *and* now, you have only to tell me. A little Communion is often very help—a great comfort,' he added tenderly.

But the idea of a little Communion terrified them. What! In the drawing-room by themselves—with no—no altar or anything! The piano would be much too high, thought Constantia, and Mr Farolles could not possibly lean over it with the chalice. And Kate would be sure to come bursting in and interrupt them, thought Josephine. And supposing the bell rang in the middle? It might be somebody important—about their mourning. Would they get up reverently and go out, or would they have to wait . . . in torture?

'Perhaps you will send round a note by your good Kate if you would care for it later,' said Mr Farolles.

'Oh yes, thank you very much!' they both said.

Mr Farolles got up and took his black straw hat from the round table.

'And about the funeral,' he said softly. 'I may arrange that—as your dear father's old friend and yours, Miss Pinner—and Miss Constantia?

Josephine and Constantia got up too.

'I should like it to be quite simple,' said Josephine firmly, 'and not too expensive. At the same time, I should like—'

'A good one that will last,' thought dreamy Constantia, as if Josephine were buying a nightgown. But of course Josephine didn't say that. 'One suitable to our father's position.' She was very nervous.

'I'll run round to our good friend Mr Knight,' said Mr Farolles soothingly. 'I will ask him to come and see you. I am sure you will find him very helpful indeed.'

V

Well, at any rate, all that part of it was over, though neither of them could possibly believe that father was never coming back. Josephine had had a moment of absolute terror at the cemetery, while the coffin was lowered, to think that she and Constantia had done this thing without asking his permission. What would father say when he found out? For he was bound to find out sooner or later. He always did. 'Buried. You two girls had me *buried*!' She heard his stick thumping. Oh, what would they say? What possible excuse could they make? It sounded such an appallingly heartless thing to do. Such a wicked advantage to take of a person because he happened to be helpless at the moment. The other people seemed to treat it all as a matter of course. They were strangers; they couldn't be expected to understand that father was the very last person for such a thing to happen to. No, the entire blame for it all would fall on her and Constantia. And the expense, she thought, stepping into the tight-buttoned* cab. When she had to show him the bills. What would he say then?

She heard him absolutely roaring, 'And do you expect me to pay for this gimcrack excursion of yours?'

'Oh,' groaned poor Josephine aloud, 'we shouldn't have done it, Con!'

And Constantia, pale as a lemon in all that blackness, said in a frightened whisper, 'Done what, Jug?'

'Let them bu-bury father like that,' said Josephine, breaking down and crying into her new, queer-smelling mourning handkerchief.

'But what else could we have done?' asked Constantia wonderingly. 'We couldn't have kept him, Jug—we couldn't have kept him unburied. At any rate, not in a flat that size.'

Josephine blew her nose; the cab was dreadfully stuffy.

'I don't know,' she said forlornly. 'It is all so dreadful. I feel we ought to have tried to, just for a time at least. To make perfectly sure. One thing's certain'—and her tears sprang out again—'father will never forgive us for this—never!'

VI

Father would never forgive them. That was what they felt more than ever when, two mornings later, they went into his room to go through his things. They had discussed it quite calmly. It was even down on Josephine's list of things to be done. *Go through father's things and settle about them.* But that was a very different matter from saying after breakfast:

'Well, are you ready, Con?'

'Yes, Jug—when you are.'

'Then I think we'd better get it over.'

It was dark in the hall. It had been a rule for years never to disturb father in the morning, whatever happened. And now they were going to open the door without knocking even. . . . Constantia's eyes were enormous at the idea; Josephine felt weak in the knees.

'You—you go first,' she gasped, pushing Constantia.

But Constantia said, as she always had said on those occasions, 'No, Jug, that's not fair. You're eldest.'

Josephine was just going to say—what at other times she wouldn't have owned to for the world—what she kept for her very last weapon, 'But you're tallest,' when they noticed that the kitchen door was open, and there stood Kate. . . .

'Very stiff,' said Josephine, grasping the door-handle and doing her best to turn it. As if anything ever deceived Kate!

It couldn't be helped. That girl was. . . . Then the door was shut behind them, but—but they weren't in father's room at all. They might have suddenly walked through the wall by mistake into a different flat altogether. Was the door just behind them? They were too frightened to look. Josephine knew that if it was it was holding itself tight shut; Constantia felt that, like the doors in dreams, it hadn't any handle at all. It was the coldness which made it so awful. Or the whiteness—which? Everything was covered. The blinds were down, a cloth hung over the mirror, a sheet hid the bed; a huge fan of white paper filled the fire-place. Constantia timidly put out her hand; she almost expected a snowflake to fall. Josephine felt a queer tingling in her nose, as if her nose was freezing. Then a cab klop-klopped over the cobbles below, and the quiet seemed to shake into little pieces.

'I had better pull up a blind,' said Josephine bravely.

'Yes, it might be a good idea,' whispered Constantia.

They only gave the blind a touch, but it flew up and the cord flew after, rolling round the blind-stick, and the little tassel tapped as if trying to get free. That was too much for Constantia.

'Don't you think—don't you think we might put it off for another day?' she whispered.

'Why?' snapped Josephine, feeling, as usual, much better now that she knew for certain that Constantia was terrified. 'It's got to be done. But I do wish you wouldn't whisper, Con.'

'I didn't know I was whispering,' whispered Constantia.

'And why do you keep on staring at the bed?' said Josephine, raising her voice almost defiantly. 'There's nothing *on* the bed.'

'Oh, Jug, don't say so!' said poor Connie. 'At any rate, not so loudly.'

Josephine felt herself that she had gone too far. She took a wide swerve over to the chest of drawers, put out her hand, but quickly drew it back again.

'Connie!' she gasped, and she wheeled round and leaned with her back against the chest of drawers.

'Oh, Jug—what?'

Josephine could only glare. She had the most extraordinary feeling that she had just escaped something simply awful. But how could she explain to Constantia that father was in the chest of drawers? He was in the top drawer with his handkerchiefs and neck-ties, or in the next with his shirts and pyjamas, or in the lowest of all with his suits. He was watching there, hidden away—just behind the door-handle—ready to spring.

She pulled a funny old-fashioned face at Constantia, just as she used to in the old days when she was going to cry.

'I can't open,' she nearly wailed.

'No, don't, Jug,' whispered Constantia earnestly. 'It's much better not to. Don't let's open anything. At any rate, not for a long time.'

'But—but it seems so weak,' said Josephine, breaking down.

'But why not be weak for once, Jug?' argued Constantia, whispering quite fiercely. 'If it is weak.' And her pale stare flew from the locked writing-table—so safe—to the huge glittering wardrobe, and she began to breathe in a queer, panting way. 'Why shouldn't we be weak for once in our lives, Jug? It's quite excusable. Let's be weak—be weak, Jug. It's much nicer to be weak than to be strong.'

And then she did one of those amazingly bold things that she'd done about twice before in their lives; she marched over to the wardrobe, turned the key, and took it out of the lock. Took it out of the lock and held it up to Josephine, showing Josephine by her extraordinary smile that she knew what she'd done, she'd risked deliberately father being in there among his overcoats.

If the huge wardrobe had lurched forward, had crashed down on Constantia, Josephine wouldn't have been surprised. On the contrary, she would have thought it the only suitable thing to happen. But nothing happened. Only the room seemed quieter than ever, and bigger flakes of cold air fell on Josephine's shoulders and knees. She began to shiver.

'Come, Jug,' said Constantia, still with that awful callous smile, and Josephine followed just as she had that last time, when Constantia had pushed Benny into the Round Pond.*

VII

But the strain told on them when they were back in the dining-room. They sat down, very shaky, and looked at each other.

'I don't feel I can settle to anything,' said Josephine, 'until I've had something. Do you think we could ask Kate for two cups of hot water?'

'I really don't see why we shouldn't,' said Constantia carefully. She was quite normal again. 'I won't ring. I'll go to the kitchen door and ask her.'

'Yes, do,' said Josephine, sinking down into a chair. 'Tell her, just two cups, Con, nothing else—on a tray.'

'She needn't even put the jug on, need she?' said Constantia, as though Kate might very well complain if the jug had been there.

'Oh no, certainly not! The jug's not at all necessary. She can pour it direct out of the kettle,' cried Josephine, feeling that would be a labour-saving indeed.

Their cold lips quivered at the greenish brims. Josephine curved her small red hands round the cup; Constantia sat up and blew on the wavy steam, making it flutter from one side to the other.

'Speaking of Benny,' said Josephine.

And though Benny hadn't been mentioned Constantia immediately looked as though he had.

'He'll expect us to send him something of father's, of course. But it's so difficult to know what to send to Ceylon.'

'You mean things get unstuck so on the voyage,' murmured Constantia.

'No, lost,' said Josephine sharply. 'You know there's no post. Only runners.'

Both paused to watch a black man in white linen drawers* running through the pale fields for dear life, with a large brown-paper parcel in his hands. Josephine's black man was tiny; he scurried along glistening like an ant. But there was something blind and tireless about Constantia's tall, thin fellow, which made him, she decided, a very unpleasant person indeed. . . . On the verandah, dressed all in white and wearing a cork helmet,* stood Benny. His right hand shook up and down, as father's did when he was impatient. And behind him, not in the least interested, sat Hilda, the unknown sister-in-law. She swung in a cane rocker and flicked over the leaves of the *Tatler*.*

'I think his watch would be the most suitable present,' said Josephine.

Constantia looked up; she seemed surprised.

'Oh, would you trust a gold watch to a native?'

'But of course I'd disguise it,' said Josephine. 'No one would know it was a watch.' She liked the idea of having to make a parcel such a curious shape that no one could possibly guess what it was. She even thought for a moment of hiding the watch in a narrow cardboard corset-box that she'd kept by her for a long time, waiting for it to come in for something. It was such beautiful firm cardboard. But, no, it wouldn't be appropriate for this occasion. It had lettering on it: *Medium Women's* 28. *Extra Firm Busks*.* It would be almost too much of a surprise for Benny to open that and find father's watch inside.

'And of course it isn't as though it would be going—ticking, I mean,' said Constantia, who was still thinking of the native love of jewellery. 'At least,' she added, 'it would be very strange if after all that time it was.'

VIII

Josephine made no reply. She had flown off on one of her tangents. She had suddenly thought of Cyril. Wasn't it more usual for the only grandson to have the watch? And then dear Cyril was so appreciative, and a gold watch meant so much to a young man. Benny, in all probability, had quite got out of the habit of watches; men so seldom wore waistcoats* in those hot climates. Whereas Cyril in London wore them from year's end to year's end. And it would be so nice for her and Constantia, when he came to tea, to know it was there. 'I see you've got on grandfather's watch, Cyril.' It would be somehow so satisfactory.

Dear boy! What a blow his sweet, sympathetic little note had been! Of course they quite understood; but it was most unfortunate.

'It would have been such a point, having him,' said Josephine.

'And he would have enjoyed it so,' said Constantia, not thinking what she was saying.

However, as soon as he got back he was coming to tea with his aunties. Cyril to tea was one of their rare treats.

'Now, Cyril, you mustn't be frightened of our cakes. Your Auntie Con and I bought them at Buszard's this morning. We know what a man's appetite is. So don't be ashamed of making a good tea.'

Josephine cut recklessly into the rich dark cake that stood for her winter gloves or the soling and heeling of Constantia's only respectable shoes. But Cyril was most unmanlike in appetite.

'I say, Aunt Josephine, I simply can't. I've only just had lunch, you know.'

'Oh, Cyril, that can't be true! It's after four,' cried Josephine. Constantia sat with her knife poised over the chocolate-roll.

'It is, all the same,' said Cyril. 'I had to meet a man at Victoria, and he kept me hanging about till . . . there was only time to get lunch and to come on here. And he gave me—phew'—Cyril put his hand to his forehead—'a terrific blow-out,' he said.

It was disappointing—today of all days. But still he couldn't be expected to know.

'But you'll have a meringue, won't you, Cyril?' said Aunt Josephine. 'These meringues were bought specially for you. Your dear father was so fond of them. We were sure you are, too.'

'I *am*, Aunt Josephine,' cried Cyril ardently. 'Do you mind if I take half to begin with?'

'Not at all, dear boy; but we mustn't let you off with that.'

'Is your dear father still so fond of meringues?' asked Auntie Con gently. She winced faintly as she broke through the shell of hers.

'Well, I don't quite know, Auntie Con,' said Cyril breezily.

At that they both looked up.

'Don't know?' almost snapped Josephine. 'Don't know a thing like that about your own father, Cyril?'

'Surely,' said Auntie Con softly.

Cyril tried to laugh it off. 'Oh, well,' he said, 'it's such a long time since—' He faltered. He stopped. Their faces were too much for him.

'Even *so*,' said Josephine.

And Auntie Con looked.

Cyril put down his teacup. 'Wait a bit,' he cried. 'Wait a bit, Aunt Josephine. What am I thinking of?'

He looked up. They were beginning to brighten. Cyril slapped his knee.

'Of course,' he said, 'it was meringues. How could I have forgotten? Yes, Aunt Josephine, you're perfectly right. Father's most frightfully keen on meringues.'

They didn't only beam. Aunt Josephine went scarlet with pleasure; Auntie Con gave a deep, deep sigh.

'And now, Cyril, you must come and see father,' said Josephine. 'He knows you were coming to-day.'

'Right,' said Cyril, very firmly and heartily. He got up from his chair; suddenly he glanced at the clock.

'I say, Auntie Con, isn't your clock a bit slow? I've got to meet a man at—at Paddington just after five. I'm afraid I shan't be able to stay very long with grandfather.'

'Oh, he won't expect you to stay *very* long!' said Aunt Josephine.

Constantia was still gazing at the clock. She couldn't make up her mind if it was fast or slow. It was one or the other, she felt almost certain of that. At any rate, it had been.

Cyril still lingered. 'Aren't you coming along, Auntie Con?'

'Of course,' said Josephine, 'we shall all go. Come on, Con.'

IX

They knocked at the door, and Cyril followed his aunts into grandfather's hot, sweetish room.

'Come on,' said Grandfather Pinner. 'Don't hang about. What is it? What've you been up to?'

He was sitting in front of a roaring fire, clasping his stick. He had a thick rug over his knees. On his lap there lay a beautiful pale yellow silk handkerchief.

'It's Cyril, father,' said Josephine shyly. And she took Cyril's hand and led him forward.

'Good afternoon, grandfather,' said Cyril, trying to take his hand out of Aunt Josephine's. Grandfather Pinner shot his eyes at Cyril in the way he was famous for. Where was Auntie Con? She stood on the other side of Aunt Josephine; her long arms hung down in front of her; her hands were clasped. She never took her eyes off grandfather.

'Well,' said Grandfather Pinner, beginning to thump, 'What have you got to tell me?'

What had he, what had he got to tell him? Cyril felt himself smiling like a perfect imbecile. The room was stifling, too.

But Aunt Josephine came to his rescue. She cried brightly, 'Cyril says his father is still very fond of meringues, father dear.'

'Eh?' said Grandfather Pinner, curving his hand like a purple meringue-shell over one ear.

Josephine repeated, 'Cyril says his father is still very fond of meringues.'

'Can't hear,' said old Colonel Pinner. And he waved Josephine away with his stick, then pointed with his stick to Cyril. 'Tell me what she's trying to say,' he said.

(My God!) 'Must I?' said Cyril, blushing and staring at Aunt Josephine.

'Do, dear,' she smiled. 'It will please him so much.'

'Come on, out with it!' cried Colonel Pinner testily, beginning to thump again.

And Cyril leaned forward and yelled, 'Father's still very fond of meringues.'

At that Grandfather Pinner jumped as though he had been shot.

'Don't shout!' he cried. 'What's the matter with the boy? *Meringues!* What about 'em?'

'Oh, Aunt Josephine, must we go on?' groaned Cyril desperately.

'It's quite all right, dear boy,' said Aunt Josephine, as though he and she were at the dentist's together. 'He'll understand in a minute.' And she whispered to Cyril, 'He's getting a bit deaf, you know.' Then she leaned forward and really bawled at Grandfather Pinner, 'Cyril only wanted to tell you, father dear, that *his* father is still very fond of meringues.'

Colonel Pinner heard that time, heard and brooded, looking Cyril up and down.

'What an esstrordinary thing!' said old Grandfather Pinner. 'What an esstrordinary thing to come all this way here to tell me!'

And Cyril felt it *was*.

*

'Yes, I shall send Cyril the watch,' said Josephine.

'That would be very nice,' said Constantia. 'I seem to remember last time he came there was some little trouble about the time.'

X

They were interrupted by Kate bursting through the door in her usual fashion, as though she had discovered some secret panel in the wall.

'Fried or boiled?' asked the bold voice.

Fried or boiled? Josephine and Constantia were quite bewildered for the moment. They could hardly take it in.

'Fried or boiled what, Kate?' asked Josephine, trying to begin to concentrate.

Kate gave a loud sniff. 'Fish.'

'Well, why didn't you say so immediately?' Josephine reproached her gently. 'How could you expect us to understand, Kate? There are a great many things in this world, you know, which are fried or boiled.' And after such a display of courage she said quite brightly to Constantia, 'Which do you prefer, Con?'

'I think it might be nice to have it fried,' said Constantia. 'On the other hand, of course boiled fish is very nice. I think I prefer both equally well. . . . Unless you. . . . In that case—'

'I shall fry it,' said Kate, and she bounced back, leaving their door open and slamming the door of her kitchen.

Josephine gazed at Constantia; she raised her pale eyebrows until they rippled away into her pale hair. She got up. She said in a very lofty, imposing way, 'Do you mind following me into the drawing-room, Constantia? I've something of great importance to discuss with you.'

For it was always to the drawing-room they retired when they wanted to talk over Kate.

Josephine closed the door meaningly. 'Sit down, Constantia,' she said, still very grand. She might have been receiving Constantia for the first time. And Con looked round vaguely for a chair, as though she felt indeed quite a stranger.

'Now the question is,' said Josephine, bending forward, 'whether we shall keep her or not.'

'That is the question,' agreed Constantia.

'And this time,' said Josephine firmly, 'we must come to a definite decision.'

Constantia looked for a moment as though she might begin going over all the other times, but she pulled herself together and said, 'Yes, Jug.'

'You see, Con,' explained Josephine, 'everything is so changed now.' Constantia looked up quickly. 'I mean,' went on Josephine, 'we're not dependent on Kate as we were.' And she blushed faintly. 'There's not father to cook for.'

'That is perfectly true,' agreed Constantia. 'Father certainly doesn't want any cooking now whatever else—'

Josephine broke in sharply, 'You're not sleepy, are you, Con?'

'Sleepy, Jug?' Constantia was wide-eyed.

'Well, concentrate more,' said Josephine sharply, and she returned to the subject. 'What it comes to is, if we did'—and this she barely breathed, glancing at the door—'give Kate notice'—she raised her voice again—'we could manage our own food.'

'Why not?' cried Constantia. She couldn't help smiling. The idea was so exciting. She clasped her hands. 'What should we live on, Jug?'

'Oh, eggs in various forms!' said Jug, lofty again. 'And, besides, there are all the cooked foods.'

'But I've always heard,' said Constantia, 'they are considered so very expensive.'

'Not if one buys them in moderation,' said Josephine. But she tore herself away from this fascinating bypath and dragged Constantia after her.

'What we've got to decide now, however, is whether we really do trust Kate or not.'

Constantia leaned back. Her flat little laugh flew from her lips.

'Isn't it curious, Jug,' said she, 'that just on this one subject I've never been able to quite make up my mind?'

XI

She never had. The whole difficulty was to prove anything. How did one prove things, how could one? Suppose Kate had stood in front of her and deliberately made a face. Mightn't she very well have been in pain? Wasn't it impossible, at any rate, to ask Kate if she was making a face at her? If Kate answered 'No'—and of course she would say 'No'—what a position! How undignified! Then again Constantia suspected, she was almost certain that Kate went to her chest of drawers when she and Josephine were out, not to take things but to spy. Many times she had come back to find her amethyst cross in the most unlikely places, under her lace ties or on top of her evening Bertha.* More than once she had laid a trap for Kate. She had arranged things in a special order and then called Josephine to witness.

'You see, Jug?'

'Quite, Con.'

'Now we shall be able to tell.'

But, oh dear, when she did go to look, she was as far off from a proof as ever! If anything was displaced, it might so very well have happened as she closed the drawer; a jolt might have done it so easily.

'You come, Jug, and decide. I really can't. It's too difficult.'

But after a pause and a long glare Josephine would sigh, 'Now you've put the doubt into my mind, Con, I'm sure I can't tell myself.'

'Well, we can't postpone it again,' said Josephine. 'If we postpone it this time—'

XII

But at that moment in the street below a barrel-organ* struck up. Josephine and Constantia sprang to their feet together.

'Run, Con,' said Josephine. 'Run quickly. There's sixpence on the—'

Then they remembered. It didn't matter. They would never have to stop the organ-grinder again. Never again would she and Constantia be told to make that monkey take his noise somewhere else. Never would sound that loud, strange bellow when father thought they were not hurrying enough. The organ-grinder might play there all day and the stick would not thump.

> *It never will thump again,*
> *It never will thump again,*

played the barrel-organ.

What was Constantia thinking? She had such a strange smile; she looked different. She couldn't be going to cry.

'Jug, Jug,' said Constantia softly, pressing her hands together. 'Do you know what day it is? It's Saturday. It's a week to-day, a whole week.'

> *A week since father died,*
> *A week since father died,*

cried the barrel-organ. And Josephine, too, forgot to be practical and sensible; she smiled faintly, strangely. On the Indian carpet there fell a square of sunlight, pale red; it came and went and came—and stayed, deepened—until it shone almost golden.

'The sun's out,' said Josephine, as though it really mattered.

A perfect fountain of bubbling notes shook from the barrel-organ, round, bright notes, carelessly scattered.

Constantia lifted her big, cold hands as if to catch them, and then her hands fell again. She walked over to the mantelpiece to her favourite Buddha. And the stone and gilt image, whose smile always gave her such a queer feeling, almost a pain and yet a pleasant pain, seemed to-day to be more than smiling. He knew something; he had a secret. 'I know something that you don't know,' said her Buddha. Oh, what was it, what could it be? And yet she had always felt there was . . . something.

The sunlight pressed through the windows, thieved its way in, flashed its light over the furniture and the photographs. Josephine watched it. When it came to mother's photograph, the enlargement over the piano, it lingered as though puzzled to find so little remained of mother, except the ear-rings shaped like tiny pagodas* and a black feather boa.* Why did the photographs of dead people always fade so? wondered Josephine. As soon as a person was dead their photograph died too. But, of course, this one of mother was very old. It was thirty-five years old. Josephine remembered standing on a chair and pointing out that feather boa to Constantia and telling her that it was a snake that had killed their mother in Ceylon. . . . Would everything have been different if mother hadn't died? She didn't see why. Aunt Florence had lived with them until they had left school, and they had moved three times and had their yearly holiday and . . . and there'd been changes of servants, of course.

Some little sparrows, young sparrows they sounded, chirped on the window-ledge. *Yeep—eyeep—yeep*. But Josephine felt they were not sparrows, not on the window-ledge. It was inside her, that queer little crying noise. *Yeep—eyeep—yeep*. Ah, what was it crying, so weak and forlorn?

If mother had lived, might they have married? But there had been nobody for them to marry. There had been father's Anglo-Indian* friends before he quarrelled with them. But after that she and Constantia never met a single man except clergymen. How did one meet men? Or even if they'd met them, how could they have got to know men well enough to be more than strangers? One read of people having adventures, being followed, and so on. But nobody had ever followed Constantia and her. Oh yes, there had been one year at Eastbourne* a mysterious man at their boarding-house who had put a note on the jug of hot water outside their bedroom door! But by the time Connie had found it the steam had made the writing too faint to read; they couldn't even make out to which of them it was addressed. And he had left next day. And that was all. The rest had been looking after father, and at the same time keeping out of father's way. But now? But now? The thieving sun touched Josephine gently. She lifted her face. She was drawn over to the window by gentle beams. . . .

Until the barrel-organ stopped playing Constantia stayed before the Buddha, wondering, but not as usual, not vaguely. This time her wonder was like longing. She remembered the times she had come in here, crept out of bed in her nightgown when the moon was full, and lain on the floor with her arms outstretched, as though she was crucified. Why? The big, pale moon had made her do it. The horrible dancing figures on the carved screen* had leered at her and she hadn't minded. She remembered too how, whenever they were at the seaside, she had gone off by herself and got as close to the sea as she could, and sung something, something she had made up, while she gazed all over that restless water. There had been this other life, running out, bringing things home in bags, getting things on approval,* discussing them with Jug, and taking them back to get more things on approval, and arranging father's trays and trying not to annoy father. But it all seemed to have happened in a kind of tunnel. It wasn't real. It was only when she came out of the tunnel into the moonlight or by the sea or into a thunderstorm that she really felt herself. What did it mean? What was it she was always wanting? What did it all lead to? Now? Now?

She turned away from the Buddha with one of her vague gestures. She went over to where Josephine was standing. She wanted to say something to Josephine, something frightfully important, about—about the future and what. . . .

'Don't you think perhaps—' she began.

But Josephine interrupted her. 'I was wondering if now—' she murmured. They stopped; they waited for each other.

'Go on, Con,' said Josephine.

'No, no, Jug; after you,' said Constantia.

'No, say what you were going to say. You began,' said Josephine.

'I . . . I'd rather hear what you were going to say first,' said Constantia.

'Don't be absurd, Con.'

'Really, Jug.'

'Connie!'

'Oh, *Jug!*'

A pause. Then Constantia said faintly, 'I can't say what I was going to say, Jug, because I've forgotten what it was . . . that I was going to say.'

Josephine was silent for a moment. She stared at a big cloud where the sun had been. Then she replied shortly, 'I've forgotten too.'

LIFE OF MA PARKER

When the literary gentleman, whose flat old Ma Parker cleaned every Tuesday, opened the door to her that morning, he asked after her grandson. Ma Parker stood on the doormat inside the dark little hall, and she stretched out her hand to help her gentleman shut the door before she replied. 'We buried 'im yesterday, sir,' she said quietly.

'Oh, dear me! I'm sorry to hear that,' said the literary gentleman in a shocked tone. He was in the middle of his breakfast. He wore a very shabby dressing-gown and carried a crumpled newspaper in one hand. But he felt awkward. He could hardly go back to the warm sitting-room without saying something—something more. Then because these people set such store by funerals he said kindly, 'I hope the funeral went off all right.'

'Beg parding, sir?' said old Ma Parker huskily.

Poor old bird! She did look dashed. 'I hope the funeral was a—a—success,' said he. Ma Parker gave no answer. She bent her head and hobbled off to the kitchen, clasping the old fish bag that held her cleaning things and an apron and a pair of felt shoes. The literary gentleman raised his eyebrows and went back to his breakfast.

'Overcome, I suppose,' he said aloud, helping himself to the marmalade.

Ma Parker drew the two jetty spears* out of her toque* and hung it behind the door. She unhooked her worn jacket and hung that up too. Then she tied her apron and sat down to take off her boots. To take off her boots or to put them on was an agony to her, but it had been an agony for years. In fact, she was so accustomed to the pain that her face was drawn and screwed up ready for the twinge before she'd so much as untied the laces. That over, she sat back with a sigh and softly rubbed her knees. . . .

'Gran! Gran!' Her little grandson stood on her lap in his button boots. He'd just come in from playing in the street.

'Look what a state you've made your gran's skirt into—you wicked boy!'

But he put his arms round her neck and rubbed his cheek against hers.

'Gran, gi' us a penny!' he coaxed.

'Be off with you; Gran ain't got no pennies.'

'Yes, you 'ave.'

'No, I ain't.'

'Yes, you 'ave. Gi' us one!'

Already she was feeling for the old, squashed, black leather purse.

'Well, what'll you give your gran?'

He gave a shy little laugh and pressed closer. She felt his eyelid quivering against her check. 'I ain't got nothing,' he murmured. . . .

The old woman sprang up, seized the iron kettle off the gas stove and took it over to the sink. The noise of the water drumming in the kettle deadened her pain, it seemed. She filled the pail, too, and the washing-up bowl.

It would take a whole book to describe the state of that kitchen. During the week the literary gentleman 'did' for himself. That is to say, he emptied the tea leaves now and again into a jam jar set aside for that purpose, and if he ran out of clean forks he wiped over one or two on the roller towel. Otherwise, as he explained to his friends, his 'system' was quite simple, and he couldn't understand why people made all this fuss about housekeeping.

'You simply dirty everything you've got, get a hag in once a week to clean up, and the thing's done.'

The result looked like a gigantic dustbin. Even the floor was littered with toast crusts, envelopes, cigarette ends. But Ma Parker bore him no grudge. She pitied the poor young gentleman for having no one to look after him. Out of the smudgy little window you could see an immense expanse of sad-looking sky, and whenever there were clouds they looked very worn, old clouds, frayed at the edges, with holes in them, or dark stains like tea.

While the water was heating, Ma Parker began sweeping the floor. 'Yes,' she thought, as the broom knocked, 'what with one thing and another I've had my share. I've had a hard life.'

Even the neighbours said that of her. Many a time, hobbling home with her fish bag she heard them, waiting at the corner, or leaning over the area railings, say among themselves, 'She's had a hard life, has Ma Parker.' And it was so true she wasn't in the least proud of it. It was just as if you were to say she lived in the basement-back at Number 27. A hard life! . . .

*

At sixteen she'd left Stratford and come up to London as kitching-maid. Yes, she was born in Stratford-on-Avon. Shakespeare,* sir? No, people were always arsking her about him. But she'd never heard his name until she saw it on the theatres.

Nothing remained of Stratford except that 'sitting in the fire-place of a evening you could see the stars through the chimley,' and 'Mother always 'ad 'er side of bacon 'anging from the ceiling.' And there was something—a bush, there was—at the front door, that smelt ever so nice. But the bush was very vague. She'd only remembered it once or twice in the hospital, when she'd been taken bad.

That was a dreadful place—her first place. She was never allowed out. She never went upstairs except for prayers morning and even-ing. It was a fair cellar. And the cook was a cruel woman. She used to snatch away her letters from home before she'd read them, and throw them in the range because they made her dreamy. . . . And the beedles! Would you believe it?—until she came to London she'd never seen a black beedle. Here Ma always gave a little laugh, as though—not to have seen a black beedle! Well! It was as if to say you'd never seen your own feet.

When that family was sold up she went as 'help' to a doctor's house, and after two years there, on the run from morning till night, she married her husband. He was a baker.

'A baker, Mrs Parker!' the literary gentleman would say. For occasionally he laid aside his tomes and lent an ear, at least, to this product called Life. 'It must be rather nice to be married to a baker!'

Mrs Parker didn't look so sure.

'Such a clean trade,' said the gentleman.

Mrs Parker didn't look convinced.

'And didn't you like handing the new loaves to the customers?'

'Well, sir,' said Mrs Parker, 'I wasn't in the shop above a great deal. We had thirteen little ones and buried seven of them. If it wasn't the 'ospital it was the infirmary, you might say!'

'You might, *indeed*, Mrs Parker!' said the gentleman, shuddering, and taking up his pen again.

Yes, seven had gone, and while the six were still small her husband was taken ill with consumption.* It was flour on the lungs, the doctor told her at the time. . . . Her husband sat up in bed with his shirt pulled over his head, and the doctor's finger drew a circle on his back.

'Now, if we were to cut him open *here*, Mrs Parker,' said the doctor, 'you'd find his lungs chock-a-block with white powder. Breathe, my good fellow!' And Mrs Parker never knew for certain whether she saw or whether she fancied she saw a great fan of white dust come out of her poor dear husband's lips. . . .

But the struggle she'd had to bring up those six little children and keep herself to herself. Terrible it had been! Then, just when they were old enough to go to school her husband's sister came to stop with them to help things along, and she hadn't been there more than two months when she fell down a flight of steps and hurt her spine. And for five years Ma Parker had another baby—and such a one for crying!—to look after. Then young Maudie went wrong and took her sister Alice with her; the two boys emigrimated, and young Jim went to India with the army, and Ethel, the youngest, married a good-for-nothing little waiter who died of ulcers the year little Lennie was born. And now little Lennie—my grandson. . . .

The piles of dirty cups, dirty dishes, were washed and dried. The ink-black knives were cleaned with a piece of potato and finished off with a piece of cork. The table was scrubbed, and the dresser and the sink that had sardine tails swimming in it. . . .

He'd never been a strong child—never from the first. He'd been one of those fair babies that everybody took for a girl. Silvery fair curls he had, blue eyes, and a little freckle like a diamond on one side of his nose. The trouble she and Ethel had had to rear that child! The things out of the newspapers they tried him with! Every Sunday morning Ethel would read aloud while Ma Parker did her washing.

'Dear Sir,—Just a line to let you know my little Myrtil was laid out for dead. . . . After four bottils . . . gained 8 lbs. in 9 weeks, *and is still putting it on*.'

And then the egg-cup of ink would come off the dresser and the letter would be written, and Ma would buy a postal order on her way to work next morning. But it was no use. Nothing made little Lennie put it on. Taking him to the cemetery, even, never gave him a colour; a nice shake-up in the bus never improved his appetite.

But he was gran's boy from the first. . . .

'Whose boy are you?' said old Ma Parker, straightening up from the stove and going over to the smudgy window. And a little voice, so warm, so close, it half stifled her—it seemed to be in her breast under her heart—laughed out, and said, 'I'm gran's boy!'

At that moment there was a sound of steps, and the literary gentleman appeared, dressed for walking.

'Oh, Mrs Parker, I'm going out.'

'Very good, sir.'

'And you'll find your half-crown in the tray of the inkstand.'

'Thank you, sir.'

'Oh, by the way, Mrs Parker,' said the literary gentleman quickly, 'you didn't throw away any cocoa last time you were here—did you?'

'No, sir.'

'*Very* strange. I could have sworn I left a teaspoonful of cocoa in the tin.' He broke off. He said softly and firmly, 'You'll always tell me when you throw things away—won't you, Mrs Parker?' And he walked off very well pleased with himself, convinced, in fact, he'd shown Mrs Parker that under his apparent carelessness he was as vigilant as a woman.

The door banged. She took her brushes and cloths into the bed-room. But when she began to make the bed, smoothing, tucking, patting, the thought of little Lennie was unbearable. Why did he have to suffer so? That's what she couldn't understand. Why should a little angel child have to arsk for his breath and fight for it? There was no sense in making a child suffer like that.

. . . From Lennie's little box of a chest there came a sound as though something was boiling. There was a great lump of something bubbling in his chest that he couldn't get rid of. When he coughed the sweat sprang out on his head; his eyes bulged, his hands waved, and the great lump bubbled as a potato knocks in a saucepan. But what was more awful than all was when he didn't cough he sat against the pillow and never spoke or answered, or even made as if he heard. Only he looked offended.

'It's not your poor old gran's doing it, my lovey,' said old Ma Parker, patting back the damp hair from his little scarlet ears. But Lennie moved his head and edged away. Dreadfully offended with her he looked—and solemn. He bent his head and looked at her sideways as though he couldn't have believed it of his gran.

But at the last . . . Ma Parker threw the counterpane over the bed. No, she simply couldn't think about it. It was too much—she'd had too much in her life to bear. She'd borne it up till now, she'd kept herself to herself, and never once had she been seen to cry. Never by a living soul. Not even her own children had seen Ma break down. She'd kept a proud face always. But now! Lennie gone—what had she? She had nothing. He was all she'd got from life, and now he was took too. Why must it all have happened to me? she wondered. 'What have I done?' said old Ma Parker. 'What have I done?'

As she said those words she suddenly let fall her brush. She found herself in the kitchen. Her misery was so terrible that she pinned on her hat, put on her jacket and walked out of the flat like a person in a dream. She did not know what she was doing. She was like a person so dazed by the horror of what has happened that he walks away—anywhere, as though by walking away he could escape. . . .

It was cold in the street. There was a wind like ice. People went flitting by, very fast; the men walked like scissors; the women trod like cats. And nobody knew—nobody cared. Even if she broke down, if at last, after all these years, she were to cry, she'd find herself in the lock-up* as like as not.

But at the thought of crying it was as though little Lennie leapt in his gran's arms. Ah, that's what she wants to do, my dove. Gran wants to cry. If she could only cry now, cry for a long time, over everything, beginning with her first place and the cruel cook, going on to the doctor's, and then the seven little ones, death of her husband, the children's leaving her, and all the years of misery that led up to Lennie. But to have a proper cry over all these things would take a long time. All the same, the time for it had come. She must do it. She couldn't put it off any longer; she couldn't wait any more. . . . Where could she go?

'She's had a hard life, has Ma Parker.' Yes, a hard life, indeed! Her chin began to tremble; there was no time to lose. But where? Where?

She couldn't go home; Ethel was there. It would frighten Ethel out of her life. She couldn't sit on a bench anywhere; people would come arsking her questions. She couldn't possibly go back to the gentleman's flat; she had no right to cry in strangers' houses. If she sat on some steps a policeman would speak to her.

Oh, wasn't there anywhere where she could hide and keep herself to herself and stay as long as she liked, not disturbing anybody, and nobody worrying her? Wasn't there anywhere in the world where she could have her cry out—at last?

Ma Parker stood, looking up and down. The icy wind blew out her apron into a balloon. And now it began to rain. There was nowhere.

MR AND MRS DOVE

Of course he knew—no man better—that he hadn't a ghost of a chance, he hadn't an earthly. The very idea of such a thing was preposterous. So preposterous that he'd perfectly understand it if her father—well, whatever her father chose to do he'd perfectly understand. In fact, nothing short of desperation, nothing short of the fact that this was positively his last day in England for God knows how long, would have screwed him up to it. And even now. . . . He chose a tie out of the chest of drawers, a blue and cream check tie, and sat on the side of his bed. Supposing she replied, 'What impertinence!' would he be surprised? Not in the least, he decided, turning up his soft collar and turning it down over the tie. He expected her to say something like that. He didn't see, if he looked at the affair dead soberly, what else she could say.

Here he was! And nervously he tied a bow in front of the mirror, jammed his hair down with both hands, pulled out the flaps of his jacket pockets. Making between £500 and £600 a year on a fruit farm in—of all places—Rhodesia.* No capital. Not a penny coming to him. No chance of his income increasing for at least four years. As for looks and all that sort of thing, he was completely out of the running. He couldn't even boast of top-hole health, for the East Africa business had knocked him out so thoroughly that he'd had to take six months' leave. He was still fearfully pale—worse even than usual this afternoon, he thought, bending forward and peering into the mirror. Good heavens! What had happened? His hair looked almost bright green. Dash it all, he hadn't green hair at all events. That was a bit too steep. And then the green light trembled in the glass; it was the shadow from the tree outside. Reggie turned away, took out his cigarette case, but remembering how the mater* hated him to smoke in his bedroom, put it back again and drifted over to the chest of drawers. No, he was dashed if he could think of one blessed thing in his favour, while she. . . . Ah! . . . He stopped dead, folded his arms, and leaned hard against the chest of drawers.

And in spite of her position, her father's wealth, the fact that she was an only child and far and away the most popular girl in the neighbourhood; in spite of her beauty and her cleverness—

cleverness!—it was a great deal more than that, there was really nothing she couldn't do; he fully believed, had it been necessary, she would have been a genius at anything—in spite of the fact that her parents adored her, and she them, and they'd as soon let her go all that way as . . . . In spite of every single thing you could think of, so terrific was his love that he couldn't help hoping. Well, was it hope? Or was this queer, timid longing to have the chance of looking after her, of making it his job to see that she had everything she wanted, and that nothing came near her that wasn't perfect—just love? How he loved her! He squeezed hard against the chest of drawers and murmured to it, 'I love her, I love her!' And just for the moment he was with her on the way to Umtali.* It was night. She sat in a corner asleep. Her soft chin was tucked into her soft collar, her gold-brown lashes lay on her cheeks. He doted on her delicate little nose, her perfect lips, her ear like a baby's, and the gold-brown curl that half covered it. They were passing through the jungle. It was warm and dark and far away. Then she woke up and said, 'Have I been asleep?' and he answered, 'Yes. Are you all right? Here, let me—' And he leaned forward to . . . . He bent over her. This was such bliss that he could dream no further. But it gave him the courage to bound downstairs, to snatch his straw hat from the hall, and to say as he closed the front door, 'Well, I can only try my luck, that's all.'

But his luck gave him a nasty jar, to say the least, almost immediately. Promenading up and down the garden path with Chinny and Biddy, the ancient Pekes,* was the mater. Of course Reginald was fond of the mater and all that. She—she meant well, she had no end of grit, and so on. But there was no denying it, she was rather a grim parent. And there had been moments, many of them, in Reggie's life, before Uncle Alick died and left him the fruit farm, when he was convinced that to be a widow's only son was about the worst punishment a chap could have. And what made it rougher than ever was that she was positively all that he had. She wasn't only a combined parent, as it were, but she had quarrelled with all her own and the governor's* relations before Reggie had won his first trouser pockets.* So that whenever Reggie was homesick out there, sitting on his dark verandah by starlight, while the gramophone cried, 'Dear, what is Life but Love?' his only vision was of the mater, tall and stout, rustling down the garden path, with Chinny and Biddy at her heels. . . .

The mater, with her scissors outspread to snap the head of a dead something or other, stopped at the sight of Reggie.

'You are not going out, Reginald?' she asked, seeing that he was.

'I'll be back for tea, mater,' said Reggie weakly, plunging his hands into his jacket pockets.

Snip. Off came a head. Reggie almost jumped.

'I should have thought you could have spared your mother your last afternoon,' said she.

Silence. The Pekes stared. They understood every word of the mater's. Biddy lay down with her tongue poked out; she was so fat and glossy she looked like a lump of half-melted toffee. But Chinny's porcelain eyes gloomed at Reginald, and he sniffed faintly, as though the whole world were one unpleasant smell. Snip, went the scissors again. Poor little beggars; they were getting it!

'And where are you going, if your mother may ask?' asked the mater.

It was over at last, but Reggie did not slow down until he was out of sight of the house and half-way to Colonel Proctor's. Then only he noticed what a top-hole afternoon it was. It had been raining all the morning, late summer rain, warm, heavy, quick, and now the sky was clear, except for a long tail of little clouds, like ducklings, sailing over the forest. There was just enough wind to shake the last drops off the trees; one warm star splashed on his hand. Ping!—another drummed on his hat. The empty road gleamed, the hedges smelled of briar, and how big and bright the hollyhocks glowed in the cottage gardens. And here was Colonel Proctor's—here it was already. His hand was on the gate, his elbow jogged the syringa bushes, and petals and pollen scattered over his coat sleeve. But wait a bit. This was too quick altogether. He'd meant to think the whole thing out again. Here, steady. But he was walking up the path, with the huge rose bushes on either side. It can't be done like this. But his hand had grasped the bell, given it a pull, and started it pealing wildly, as if he'd come to say the house was on fire. The housemaid must have been in the hall, too, for the front door flashed open, and Reggie was shut in the empty drawing-room before that confounded bell had stopped ringing. Strangely enough, when it did, the big room, shadowy, with some one's parasol lying on top of the grand piano, bucked him up—or rather, excited him. It was so quiet, and yet in one moment the door would open, and his fate be decided. The feeling was not unlike that of being at the dentist's; he was almost reckless. But at the same time, to his immense surprise, Reggie heard himself saying, 'Lord, Thou knowest, Thou hast not done *much* for me. . . . ' That pulled him up; that made him realise again how dead serious it was. Too late. The door handle turned. Anne came in, crossed the shadowy space between them, gave him her hand, and said, in her small, soft voice, 'I'm so sorry, father is out. And mother is having a day in town, hat-hunting. There's only me to entertain you, Reggie.'

Reggie gasped, pressed his own hat to his jacket buttons, and stammered out, 'As a matter of fact, I've only come . . . to say good-bye.'

'Oh!' cried Anne softly—she stepped back from him and her grey eyes danced—'what a *very* short visit!'

Then, watching him, her chin tilted, she laughed outright, a long, soft peal, and walked away from him over to the piano, and leaned against it, playing with the tassel of the parasol.

'I'm so sorry,' she said, 'to be laughing like this. I don't know why I do. It's just a bad ha-habit.' And suddenly she stamped her grey shoe, and took a pocket-handkerchief out of her white woolly jacket. 'I really must conquer it, it's too absurd,' said she.

'Good heavens, Anne,' cried Reggie, 'I love to hear you laughing! I can't imagine anything more—'

But the truth was, and they both knew it, she wasn't always laughing; it wasn't really a habit. Only ever since the day they'd met, ever since that very first moment, for some strange reason that Reggie wished to God he understood, Anne had laughed at him. Why? It didn't matter where they were or what they were talking about. They might begin by being as serious as possible, dead serious—at any rate, as far as he was concerned—but then suddenly, in the middle of a sentence, Anne would glance at him, and a little quick quiver passed over her face. Her lips parted, her eyes danced, and she began laughing.

Another queer thing about it was, Reggie had an idea she didn't herself know why she laughed. He had seen her turn away, frown, suck in her cheeks, press her hands together. But it was no use. The long, soft peal sounded, even while she cried, 'I don't know why I'm laughing.' It was a mystery. . . .

Now she tucked the handkerchief away. 'Do sit down,' said she.

'And smoke, won't you? There are cigarettes in that little box beside you. I'll have one too.' He lighted a match for her, and as she bent forward he saw the tiny flame glow in the pearl ring she wore. 'It is to-morrow that you're going, isn't it?' said Anne.

'Yes, to-morrow as ever is,' said Reggie, and he blew a little fan of smoke. Why on earth was he so nervous? Nervous wasn't the word for it.

'It's—it's frightfully hard to believe,' he added.

'Yes—isn't it?' said Anne softly, and she leaned forward and rolled the point of her cigarette round the green ash-tray. How beautiful she looked like that!—simply beautiful—and she was so small in that immense chair. Reginald's heart swelled with tenderness, but it was her voice, her soft voice, that made him tremble. 'I feel you've been here for years,' she said.

Reginald took a deep breath of his cigarette. 'It's ghastly, this idea of going back,' he said.

'*Coo-roo-coo-coo-coo*,' sounded from the quiet.

'But you're fond of being out there, aren't you?' said Anne. She hooked her finger through her pearl necklace. 'Father was saying only the other night how lucky he thought you were to have a life of your own.' And she looked up at him. Reginald's smile was rather wan. 'I don't feel fearfully lucky,' he said lightly.

'*Roo-coo-coo-coo*,' came again. And Anne murmured, 'You mean it's lonely.'

'Oh, it isn't the loneliness I care about,' said Reginald, and he stumped his cigarette savagely on the green ash-tray. 'I could stand any amount of it, used to like it even. It's the idea of—' Suddenly, to his horror, he felt himself blushing.

'*Roo-coo-coo-coo! Roo-coo-coo-coo!*'

Anne jumped up. 'Come and say good-bye to my doves,' she said. 'They've been moved to the side veranda. You do like doves, don't you, Reggie?'

'Awfully,' said Reggie, so fervently that as he opened the french window for her and stood to one side, Anne ran forward and laughed at the doves instead.

To and fro, to and fro over the fine red sand on the floor of the dove house, walked the two doves. One was always in front of the other. One ran forward, uttering a little cry, and the other followed, solemnly bowing and bowing. 'You see,' explained Anne, 'the one in front, she's Mrs Dove. She looks at Mr Dove and gives that little laugh and runs forward, and he follows her, bowing and bowing. And that makes her laugh again. Away she runs, and after her,' cried Anne, and she sat back on her heels, 'comes poor Mr Dove, bowing and bowing . . . and that's their whole life. They never do anything else, you know.' She got up and took some yellow grains out of a bag on the roof of the dove house. 'When you think of them, out in Rhodesia, Reggie, you can be sure that is what they will be doing. . . .'

Reggie gave no sign of having seen the doves or of having heard a word. For the moment he was conscious only of the immense effort it took to tear his secret out of himself and offer it to Anne. 'Anne, do you think you could ever care for me?' It was done. It was over. And in the little pause that followed Reginald saw the garden open to the light, the blue quivering sky, the flutter of leaves on the veranda poles, and Anne turning over the grains of maize on her palm with one finger. Then slowly she shut her hand, and the new world faded as she murmured slowly, 'No, never in that way.' But he had scarcely time to feel anything before she walked quickly away, and he followed her down the steps, along the garden path, under the pink rose arches, across the lawn. There, with the gay herbaceous border behind her, Anne faced Reginald. 'It isn't that I'm not awfully fond of you,' she said. 'I am. But'—her eyes widened—'not in the way'— a quiver passed over her face—'one ought to be fond of—' Her lips parted, and she couldn't stop herself. She began laughing. 'There, you see, you see,' she cried, 'it's your check t-tie. Even at this moment, when one would think one really would be solemn, your tie reminds me fearfully of the bow-tie that cats wear in pictures! Oh, please forgive me for being so horrid, please!'

Reggie caught hold of her little warm hand. 'There's no question of forgiving you,' he said quickly. 'How could there be? And I do believe I know why I make you laugh. It's because you're so far above me in every way that I am somehow ridiculous. I see that, Anne. But if I were to—'

'No, no.' Anne squeezed his hand hard. 'It's not that. That's all wrong. I'm not far above you at all. You're much better than I am. You're marvellously unselfish and . . . and kind and simple. I'm none of those things. You don't know me. I'm the most awful character,' said Anne. 'Please don't interrupt. And besides, that's not the point. The point is'—she shook her head—'I couldn't possibly marry a man I laughed at. Surely you see that. The man I marry—' breathed Anne softly. She broke off. She drew her hand away, and looking at Reggie she smiled strangely, dreamily. 'The man I marry—'

And it seemed to Reggie that a tall, handsome, brilliant stranger stepped in front of him and took his place—the kind of man that Anne and he had seen often at the theatre, walking on to the stage from nowhere, without a word catching the heroine in his arms, and after one long, tremendous look, carrying her off to anywhere. . . .

Reggie bowed to his vision. 'Yes, I see,' he said huskily.

'Do you?' said Anne. 'Oh, I do hope you do. Because I feel so horrid about it. It's so hard to explain. You know I've never—' She stopped. Reggie looked at her. She was smiling. 'Isn't it funny?' she said. 'I can say anything to you. I always have been able to from the very beginning.'

He tried to smile, to say 'I'm glad.' She went on. 'I've never known anyone I like as much as I like you. I've never felt so happy with anyone. But I'm sure it's not what people and what books mean when they talk about love. Do you understand? Oh, if you only knew how horrid I feel. But we'd be like . . . like Mr and Mrs Dove.'

That did it. That seemed to Reginald final, and so terribly true that he could hardly bear it. 'Don't drive it home,' he said, and he turned away from Anne and looked across the lawn. There was the gardener's cottage, with the dark ilex-tree* beside it. A wet, blue thumb of transparent smoke hung above the chimney. It didn't look real. How his throat ached! Could he speak? He had a shot. 'I must be getting along home,' he croaked, and he began walking across the lawn. But Anne ran after him. 'No, don't. You can't go yet,' she said imploringly. 'You can't possibly go away feeling like that.' And she stared up at him frowning, biting her lip.

'Oh, that's all right,' said Reggie, giving himself a shake. 'I'll . . . I'll—' And he waved his hand as much as to say 'get over it'.

'But this is awful,' said Anne. She clasped her hands and stood in front of him. 'Surely you do see how fatal it would be for us to marry, don't you?'

'Oh, quite, quite,' said Reggie, looking at her with haggard eyes.

'How wrong, how wicked, feeling as I do. I mean, it's all very well for Mr and Mrs Dove. But imagine that in real life—imagine it!'

'Oh, absolutely,' said Reggie, and he started to walk on. But again Anne stopped him. She tugged at his sleeve, and to his astonishment, this time, instead of laughing, she looked like a little girl who was going to cry.

'Then why, if you understand, are you so un-unhappy?' she wailed. 'Why do you mind so fearfully? Why do you look so aw-awful?'

Reggie gulped, and again he waved something away. 'I can't help it,' he said, 'I've had a blow. If I cut off now, I'll be able to—'

'How can you talk of cutting off now?' said Anne scornfully. She stamped her foot at Reggie; she was crimson. 'How can you be so cruel? I can't let you go until I know for certain that you are just as happy as you were before you asked me to marry you. Surely you must see that, it's so simple.'

But it did not seem at all simple to Reginald. It seemed impossibly difficult.

'Even if I can't marry you, how can I know that you're all that way away, with only that awful mother to write to, and that you're miserable, and that it's all my fault?'

'It's not your fault. Don't think that. It's just fate.' Reggie took her hand off his sleeve and kissed it. 'Don't pity me, dear little Anne,' he said gently. And this time he nearly ran, under the pink arches, along the garden path.

'*Roo-coo-coo-coo! Roo-coo-coo-coo!*' sounded from the verandah. 'Reggie, Reggie,' from the garden.

He stopped, he turned. But when she saw his timid, puzzled look, she gave a little laugh.

'Come back, Mr Dove,' said Anne. And Reginald came slowly across the lawn.

HER FIRST BALL

Exactly when the ball began Leila would have found it hard to say. Perhaps her first real partner was the cab. It did not matter that she shared the cab with the Sheridan girls* and their brother. She sat back in her own little corner of it, and the bolster on which her hand rested felt like the sleeve of an unknown young man's dress suit; and away they bowled, past waltzing lamp-posts and houses and fences and trees.

'Have you really never been to a ball before, Leila? But, my child, how too weird'—cried the Sheridan girls.

'Our nearest neighbour was fifteen miles,' said Leila softly, gently opening and shutting her fan.

Oh, dear, how hard it was to be indifferent like the others! She tried not to smile too much; she tried not to care. But every single thing was so new and exciting. . . . Meg's tuberoses,* Jose's long loop of amber, Laura's little dark head, pushing above her white fur like a flower through snow. She would remember for ever. It even gave her a pang to see her cousin Laurie throw away the wisps of tissue paper he pulled from the fastenings of his new gloves. She would like to have kept those wisps as a keepsake, as a remembrance. Laurie leaned forward and put his hand on Laura's knee.

'Look here, darling,' he said. 'The third and the ninth as usual. Twig?'*

Oh, how marvellous to have a brother! In her excitement Leila felt that if there had been time, if it hadn't been impossible, she couldn't have helped crying because she was an only child, and no brother had ever said 'Twig?' to her; no sister would ever say, as Meg said to Jose that moment, 'I've never known your hair go up more success-fully than it has to-night!'

But, of course, there was no time. They were at the drill hall already; there were cabs in front of them and cabs behind. The road was bright on either side with moving fan-like lights, and on the pavement gay couples seemed to float through the air; little satin shoes chased each other like birds.

'Hold on to me, Leila; you'll get lost,' said Laura.

'Come on, girls, let's make a dash for it,' said Laurie.

Leila put two fingers on Laura's pink velvet cloak, and they were somehow lifted past the big golden lantern, carried along the passage, and pushed into the little room marked 'Ladies'. Here the crowd was so great there was hardly space to take off their things; the noise was deafening. Two benches on either side were stacked high with wraps. Two old women in white aprons ran up and down tossing fresh armfuls. And everybody was pressing forward trying to get at the little dressing-table and mirror at the far end.

A great quivering jet of gas lighted the ladies' room. It couldn't wait; it was dancing already. When the door opened again and there came a burst of tuning from the drill hall, it leaped almost to the ceiling.

Dark girls, fair girls were patting their hair, tying ribbons again, tucking handkerchiefs down the fronts of their bodices, smoothing marble-white gloves. And because they were all laughing it seemed to Leila that they were all lovely.

'Aren't there any invisible hair-pins?' cried a voice. 'How most extraordinary! I can't see a single invisible hair-pin.'

'Powder my back, there's a darling,' cried some one else.

'But I must have a needle and cotton. I've torn simply miles and miles of the frill,' wailed a third.

Then, 'Pass them along, pass them along!' The straw basket of programmes* was tossed from arm to arm. Darling little pink-and-silver programmes, with pink pencils and fluffy tassels. Leila's fingers shook as she took one out of the basket. She wanted to ask some one, 'Am I meant to have one too?' but she had just time to read: 'Waltz 3. *Two, Two in a Canoe*. Polka 4. *Making the Feathers Fly*,' when Meg cried, 'Ready, Leila?' and they pressed their way through the crush in the passage towards the big double doors of the drill hall.

Dancing had not begun yet, but the band had stopped tuning, and the noise was so great it seemed that when it did begin to play it would never be heard. Leila, pressing close to Meg, looking over Meg's shoulder, felt that even the little quivering coloured flags strung across the ceiling were talking. She quite forgot to be shy; she forgot how in the middle of dressing she had sat down on the bed with one shoe off and one shoe on and begged her mother to ring up her cousins and say she couldn't go after all. And the rush of longing she had had to be sitting on the verandah of their forsaken up-country home, listening to the baby owls crying 'More pork'* in the moonlight, was changed to a rush of joy so sweet that it was hard to bear alone. She clutched her fan, and, gazing at the gleaming, golden floor, the azaleas, the lanterns, the stage at one end with its red carpet and gilt chairs and the band in a corner, she thought breathlessly, 'How heavenly; how simply heavenly!'

All the girls stood grouped together at one side of the doors, the men at the other, and the chaperones* in dark dresses, smiling rather foolishly, walked with little careful steps over the polished floor towards the stage.

'This is my little country cousin Leila. Be nice to her. Find her partners; she's under my wing,' said Meg, going up to one girl after another.

Strange faces smiled at Leila—sweetly, vaguely. Strange voices answered, 'Of course, my dear.' But Leila felt the girls didn't really see her. They were looking towards the men. Why didn't the men begin? What were they waiting for? There they stood, smoothing their gloves, patting their glossy hair and smiling among themselves. Then, quite suddenly, as if they had only just made up their minds that that was what they had to do, the men came gliding over the parquet.* There was a joyful flutter among the girls. A tall, fair man flew up to Meg, seized her programme, scribbled something; Meg passed him on to Leila. 'May I have the pleasure?' He ducked and smiled. There came a dark man wearing an eyeglass, then cousin Laurie with a friend, and Laura with a little freckled fellow whose tie was crooked. Then quite an old man—fat, with a big bald patch on his head—took her programme and murmured, 'Let me see, let me see!' And he was a long time comparing his programme, which looked black with names, with hers. It seemed to give him so much trouble that Leila was ashamed. 'Oh, please don't bother,' she said eagerly. But instead of replying the fat man wrote something, glanced at her again. 'Do I remember this bright little face?' he said softly. 'Is it known to me of yore?' At that moment the band began playing; the fat man disappeared. He was tossed away on a great wave of music that came flying over the gleaming floor, breaking the groups up into couples, scattering them, sending them spinning. . . .

Leila had learned to dance at boarding school. Every Saturday afternoon the boarders were hurried off to a little corrugated iron mission hall where Miss Eccles (of London) held her 'select' classes.

But the difference between that dusty-smelling hall—with calico texts on the walls, the poor terrified little woman in a brown velvet toque with rabbit's ears thumping the cold piano, Miss Eccles poking the girls' feet with her long white wand—and this was so tremendous that Leila was sure if her partner didn't come and she had to listen to that marvellous music and to watch the others sliding, gliding over the golden floor, she would die at least, or faint, or lift her arms and fly out of one of those dark windows that showed the stars.

'Ours, I think—' Some one bowed, smiled, and offered her his arm; she hadn't to die after all. Some one's hand pressed her waist, and she floated away like a flower that is tossed into a pool.

'Quite a good floor, isn't it?' drawled a faint voice close to her ear.

'I think it's most beautifully slippery,' said Leila.

'Pardon!' The faint voice sounded surprised. Leila said it again. And there was a tiny pause before the voice echoed, 'Oh, quite!' and she was swung round again.

He steered so beautifully. That was the great difference between dancing with girls and men, Leila decided. Girls banged into each other, and stamped on each other's feet; the girl who was gentleman always clutched you so.

The azaleas were separate flowers no longer; they were pink and white flags streaming by.

'Were you at the Bells' last week?' the voice came again. It sounded tired. Leila wondered whether she ought to ask him if he would like to stop.

'No, this is my first dance,' said she.

Her partner gave a little gasping laugh. 'Oh, I say,' he protested.

'Yes, it is really the first dance I've ever been to.' Leila was most fervent. It was such a relief to be able to tell somebody. 'You see, I've lived in the country all my life up till now. . . .'

At that moment the music stopped, and they went to sit on two chairs against the wall. Leila tucked her pink satin feet under and fanned herself, while she blissfully watched the other couples passing and disappearing through the swing doors.

'Enjoying yourself, Leila?' asked Jose, nodding her golden head.

Laura passed and gave her the faintest little wink; it made Leila wonder for a moment whether she was quite grown up after all. Certainly her partner did not say very much. He coughed, tucked his handkerchief away, pulled down his waistcoat, took a minute thread off his sleeve. But it didn't matter. Almost immediately the band started, and her second partner seemed to spring from the ceiling.

'Floor's not bad,' said the new voice. Did one always begin with the floor? And then, 'Were you at the Neaves' on Tuesday?' And again Leila explained. Perhaps it was a little strange that her partners were not more interested. For it was thrilling. Her first ball! She was only at the beginning of everything. It seemed to her that she had never known what the night was like before. Up till now it had been dark, silent, beautiful very often—oh, yes—but mournful somehow. Solemn. And now it would never be like that again—it had opened dazzling bright.

'Care for an ice?' said her partner. And they went through the swing doors, down the passage, to the supper room. Her cheeks burned, she was fearfully thirsty. How sweet the ices looked on little glass plates, and how cold the frosted spoon was, iced too! And when they came back to the hall there was the fat man waiting for her by the door. It gave her quite a shock again to see how old he was; he ought to have been on the stage with the fathers and mothers. And when Leila compared him with her other partners he looked shabby. His waistcoat was creased, there was a button off his glove, his coat looked as if it was dusty with French chalk.

'Come along, little lady,' said the fat man. He scarcely troubled to clasp her, and they moved away so gently, it was more like walking than dancing. But he said not a word about the floor. 'Your first dance, isn't it?' he murmured.

'How *did* you know?'

'Ah,' said the fat man, 'that's what it is to be old!' He wheezed faintly as he steered her past an awkward couple. 'You see, I've been doing this kind of thing for the last thirty years.'

'Thirty years?' cried Leila. Twelve years before she was born!

'It hardly bears thinking about, does it?' said the fat man gloomily. Leila looked at his bald head, and she felt quite sorry for him.

'I think it's marvellous to be still going on,' she said kindly.

'Kind little lady,' said the fat man, and he pressed her a little closer, and hummed a bar of the waltz. 'Of course,' he said, 'you can't hope to last anything like as long as that. No-o,' said the fat man, 'long before that you'll be sitting up there on the stage, looking on, in your nice black velvet. And these pretty arms will have turned into little short fat ones, and you'll beat time with such a different kind of fan—a black bony one.' The fat man seemed to shudder. 'And you'll smile away like the poor old dears up there, and point to your daughter, and tell the elderly lady next to you how some dreadful man tried to kiss her at the club ball. And your heart will ache, ache'—the fat man squeezed her closer still, as if he really was sorry for that poor heart—'because no one wants to kiss you now. And you'll say how unpleasant these polished floors are to walk on, how dangerous they are. Eh, Mademoiselle Twinkletoes?' said the fat man softly.

Leila gave a light little laugh, but she did not feel like laughing. Was it—could it all be true? It sounded terribly true. Was this first ball only the beginning of her last ball after all? At that the music seemed to change; it sounded sad, sad; it rose upon a great sigh. Oh, how quickly things changed! Why didn't happiness last for ever? For ever wasn't a bit too long.

'I want to stop,' she said in a breathless voice. The fat man led her to the door.

'No,' she said, 'I won't go outside. I won't sit down. I'll just stand here, thank you.' She leaned against the wall, tapping with her foot, pulling up her gloves and trying to smile. But deep inside her a little girl threw her pinafore over her head and sobbed. Why had he spoiled it all?

'I say, you know,' said the fat man, 'you mustn't take me seriously, little lady.'

'As if I should!' said Leila, tossing her small dark head and sucking her underlip. . . .

Again the couples paraded. The swing doors opened and shut. Now new music was given out by the bandmaster. But Leila didn't want to dance any more. She wanted to be home, or sitting on the verandah listening to those baby owls. When she looked through the dark windows at the stars, they had long beams like wings. . . .

But presently a soft, melting, ravishing tune began, and a young man with curly hair bowed before her. She would have to dance, out of politeness, until she could find Meg. Very stiffly she walked into the middle; very haughtily she put her hand on his sleeve. But in one minute, in one turn, her feet glided, glided. The lights, the azaleas, the dresses, the pink faces, the velvet chairs, all became one beautiful flying wheel. And when her next partner bumped her into the fat man and he said, 'Par*don*,' she smiled at him more radiantly than ever. She didn't even recognize him again.

MARRIAGE À LA MODE

On his way to the station William remembered with a fresh pang of disappointment that he was taking nothing down to the kiddies. Poor little chaps! It was hard lines on them. Their first words always were as they ran to greet him, 'What have you got for me, daddy?' and he had nothing. He would have to buy them some sweets at the station. But that was what he had done for the past four Saturdays; their faces had fallen last time when they saw the same old boxes produced again.

And Paddy had said, 'I had red ribbing on mine *bee*-fore!'

And Johnny had said, 'It's always pink on mine. I hate pink.'

But what was William to do? The affair wasn't so easily settled. In the old days, of course, he would have taken a taxi off to a decent toyshop and chosen them something in five minutes. But nowadays they had Russian toys, French toys, Serbian toys—toys from God knows where. It was over a year since Isabel had scrapped the old donkeys and engines and so on because they were so 'dreadfully sentimental' and 'so appallingly bad for the babies' sense of form.'

'It's so important,' the new Isabel had explained, 'that they should like the right things from the very beginning. It saves so much time later on. Really, if the poor pets have to spend their infant years staring at these horrors, one can imagine them growing up and asking to be taken to the Royal Academy.'*

And she spoke as though a visit to the Royal Academy was certain immediate death to anyone. . . .

'Well, I don't know,' said William slowly. 'When I was their age I used to go to bed hugging an old towel with a knot in it.'

The new Isabel looked at him, her eyes narrowed, her lips apart.

'*Dear* William! I'm sure you did!' She laughed in the new way.

Sweets it would have to be, however, thought William gloomily, fishing in his pocket for change for the taxi-man. And he saw the kiddies handing the boxes round—they were awfully generous little chaps—while Isabel's precious friends didn't hesitate to help themselves. . . .

What about fruit? William hovered before a stall just inside the station. What about a melon each? Would they have to share that, too? Or a pineapple for Pad, and a melon for Johnny? Isabel's friends could hardly go sneaking up to the nursery at the children's meal-times. All the same, as he bought the melon William had a horrible vision of one of Isabel's young poets lapping up a slice, for some reason, behind the nursery door.

With his two very awkward parcels he strode off to his train. The platform was crowded, the train was in. Doors banged open and shut. There came such a loud hissing from the engine that people looked dazed as they scurried to and fro. William made straight for a first-class smoker, stowed away his suit-case and parcels, and taking a huge wad of papers out of his inner pocket, he flung down in the corner and began to read.

'Our client moreover is positive. . . . We are inclined to reconsider . . . in the event of—' Ah, that was better. William pressed back his flattened hair and stretched his legs across the carriage floor. The familiar dull gnawing in his breast quietened down. 'With regard to our decision—' He took out a blue pencil and scored a paragraph slowly.

Two men came in, stepped across him, and made for the farther corner. A young fellow swung his golf clubs into the rack and sat down opposite. The train gave a gentle lurch, they were off. William glanced up and saw the hot, bright station slipping away. A red-faced girl raced along by the carriages, there was something strained and almost desperate in the way she waved and called. 'Hysterical!' thought William dully. Then a greasy, black-faced workman at the end of the platform grinned at the passing train. And William thought, 'A filthy life!' and went back to his papers.

When he looked up again there were fields, and beasts standing for shelter under the dark trees. A wide river, with naked children splashing in the shallows, glided into sight and was gone again. The sky shone pale, and one bird drifted high like a dark fleck in a jewel.

'We have examined our client's correspondence files. . . .' The last sentence he had read echoed in his mind. 'We have examined. . . .' William hung on to that sentence, but it was no good; it snapped in the middle, and the fields, the sky, the sailing bird, the water, all said, 'Isabel'. The same thing happened every Saturday afternoon. When he was on his way to meet Isabel there began those countless imaginary meetings. She was at the station, standing just a little apart from everybody else; she was sitting in the open taxi outside; she was at the garden gate; walking across the parched grass; at the door, or just inside the hall.

And her clear, light voice said, 'It's William,' or 'Hillo, William!' or 'So William has come!' He touched her cool hand, her cool cheek.

The exquisite freshness of Isabel! When he had been a little boy, it was his delight to run into the garden after a shower of rain and shake the rose-bush over him. Isabel was that rose-bush, petal-soft, sparkling and cool. And he was still that little boy. But there was no running into the garden now, no laughing and shaking. The dull, persistent gnawing in his breast started again. He drew up his legs, tossed the papers aside, and shut his eyes.

'What is it, Isabel? What is it?' he said tenderly. They were in their bedroom in the new house. Isabel sat on a painted stool before the dressing-table that was strewn with little black and green boxes.

'What is what, William?' And she bent forward, and her fine light hair fell over her cheeks.

'Ah, you know!' He stood in the middle of the strange room and he felt a stranger. At that Isabel wheeled round quickly and faced him.

'Oh, William!' she cried imploringly, and she held up the hair-brush. 'Please! Please don't be so dreadfully stuffy and—tragic. You're always saying or looking or hinting that I've changed. Just because I've got to know really congenial people, and go about more, and am frightfully keen on—on everything, you behave as though I'd—' Isabel tossed back her hair and laughed—'killed our love or something. It's so awfully absurd'—she bit her lip—'and it's so maddening, William. Even this new house and the servants you grudge me.'

'Isabel!'

'Yes, yes, it's true in a way,' said Isabel quickly. 'You think they are another bad sign. Oh, I know you do. I feel it,' she said softly, 'every time you come up the stairs. But we couldn't have gone on living in that other poky little hole, William. Be practical, at least! Why, there wasn't enough room for the babies even.'

No, it was true. Every evening when he came back from chambers it was to find the babies with Isabel in the back drawing-room. They were having rides on the leopard skin thrown over the sofa back, or they were playing shops with Isabel's desk for a counter, or Pad was sitting on the hearthrug rowing away for dear life with a little brass fire-shovel, while Johnny shot at pirates with the tongs.* Every

evening they each had a pick-a-back up the narrow stairs to their fat
old Nanny.

Yes, he supposed it was a poky little house. A little white house
with blue curtains and a window-box full of petunias. William met
their friends at the door with 'Seen our petunias? Pretty terrific for
London, don't you think?'

But the imbecile thing, the absolutely extraordinary thing was that
he hadn't the slightest idea that Isabel wasn't as happy as he. God,
what blindness! He hadn't the remotest notion in those days that she
really hated that inconvenient little house, that she thought the fat
Nanny was ruining the babies, that she was desperately lonely, pin-
ing for new people and new music and pictures and so on. If they
hadn't gone to that studio party at Moira Morrison's—if Moira
Morrison hadn't said as they were leaving, 'I'm going to rescue your
wife, selfish man. She's like an exquisite little Titania'*—if Isabel
hadn't gone with Moira to Paris—if—if. . . .

The train stopped at another station. Bettingford. Good heavens!
They'd be there in ten minutes. William stuffed the papers back into
his pockets; the young man opposite had long since disappeared.
Now the other two got out. The late afternoon sun shone on women
in cotton frocks and little sunburnt, barefoot children. It blazed on a
silky yellow flower with coarse leaves which sprawled over a bank of
rock. The air ruffling through the window smelled of the sea. Had
Isabel the same crowd with her this week-end, wondered William?

And he remembered the holidays they used to have, the four of
them, with a little farm girl, Rose, to look after the babies. Isabel
wore a jersey and her hair in a plait; she looked about fourteen. Lord!
how his nose used to peel! And the amount they ate, and the amount
they slept in that immense feather bed with their feet locked
together. . . . William couldn't help a grim smile as he thought of
Isabel's horror if she knew the full extent of his sentimentality.

*   *   *

'Hillo, William!' She was at the station after all, standing just as he
had imagined, apart from the others, and—William's heart leapt—
she was alone.

'Hullo, Isabel!' William stared. He thought she looked so beautiful
that he had to say something, 'You look very cool.'

'Do I?' said Isabel. 'I don't feel very cool. Come along, your horrid old train is late. The taxi's outside.' She put her hand lightly on his arm as they passed the ticket collector. 'We've all come to meet you,' she said. 'But we've left Bobby Kane at the sweet shop, to be called for.'

'Oh!' said William. It was all he could say for the moment.

There in the glare waited the taxi, with Bill Hunt and Dennis Green sprawling on one side, their hats tilted over their faces, while on the other, Moira Morrison, in a bonnet like a huge strawberry, jumped up and down.

'No ice! No ice! No ice!' she shouted gaily.

And Dennis chimed in from under his hat. '*Only* to be had from the fishmonger's.'

And Bill Hunt, emerging, added, 'With *whole* fish in it.'

'Oh, what a bore!' wailed Isabel. And she explained to William how they had been chasing round the town for ice while she waited for him. 'Simply everything is running down the steep cliffs into the sea, beginning with the butter.'

'We shall have to anoint ourselves with the butter,' said Dennis. 'May thy head, William, lack not ointment.'

'Look here,' said William, 'how are we going to sit? I'd better get up by the driver.'

'No, Bobby Kane's by the driver,' said Isabel. 'You're to sit between Moira and me.' The taxi started. 'What have you got in those mysterious parcels?'

'De-cap-it-ated heads!' said Bill Hunt, shuddering beneath his hat.

'Oh, fruit!' Isabel sounded very pleased. 'Wise William! A melon and a pineapple. How too nice!'

'No, wait a bit,' said William, smiling. But he really was anxious. 'I brought them down for the kiddies.'

'Oh, my dear!' Isabel laughed, and slipped her hand through his arm. 'They'd be rolling in agonies if they were to eat them. No'— she patted his hand—'you must bring them something next time. I refuse to part with my pineapple.'

'Cruel Isabel! Do let me smell it!' said Moira. She flung her arms across William appealingly. 'Oh!' The strawberry bonnet fell forward: she sounded quite faint.

'A Lady in Love with a Pineapple,' said Dennis, as the taxi drew up before a little shop with a striped blind. Out came Bobby Kane, his arms full of little packets.

'I do hope they'll be good. I've chosen them because of the colours. There are some round things which really look too divine. And
just look at this nougat,' he cried ecstatically, 'just look at it! It's a
perfect little ballet!'

But at that moment the shopman appeared. 'Oh, I forgot. They're
none of them paid for,' said Bobby, looking frightened. Isabel gave
the shopman a note, and Bobby was radiant again. 'Hullo, William!
I'm sitting by the driver.' And bare-headed, all in white, with his
sleeves rolled up to the shoulders, he leapt into his place. 'Avanti!'* he
cried. . . .

After tea the others went off to bathe, while William stayed and
made his peace with the kiddies. But Johnny and Paddy were asleep,
the rose-red glow had paled, bats were flying, and still the bathers
had not returned. As William wandered downstairs, the maid
crossed the hall carrying a lamp. He followed her into the sitting-
room. It was a long room, coloured yellow. On the wall opposite
William some one had painted a young man, over life-size, with very
wobbly legs, offering a wide-eyed daisy to a young woman who had
one very short arm and one very long, thin one. Over the chairs and
sofa there hung strips of black material, covered with big splashes
like broken eggs, and everywhere one looked there seemed to be an
ash-tray full of cigarette ends. William sat down in one of the armchairs. Nowadays, when one felt with one hand down the sides, it
wasn't to come upon a sheep with three legs or a cow that had lost
one horn, or a very fat dove out of the Noah's Ark. One fished up yet
another little paper-covered book of smudged-looking poems. . . .
He thought of the wad of papers in his pocket, but he was too
hungry and tired to read. The door was open; sounds came from the
kitchen. The servants were talking as if they were alone in the house.
Suddenly there came a loud screech of laughter and an equally loud
'Sh!' They had remembered him. William got up and went through
the french windows into the garden, and as he stood there in the
shadow he heard the bathers coming up the sandy road; their voices
rang through the quiet.

'I think it's up to Moira to use her little arts and wiles.'

A tragic moan from Moira.

'We ought to have a gramophone for the week-ends that played
"The Maid of the Mountains".'

'Oh no! Oh no!' cried Isabel's voice. 'That's not fair to William.

Be nice to him, my children! He's only staying until tomorrow evening.'

'Leave him to me,' cried Bobby Kane. 'I'm awfully good at looking after people.'

The gate swung open and shut. William moved on the terrace; they had seen him. 'Hallo, William!' And Bobby Kane, flapping his towel, began to leap and pirouette on the parched lawn. 'Pity you didn't come, William. The water was divine. And we all went to a little pub afterwards and had sloe gin.'*

The others had reached the house. 'I say, Isabel,' called Bobby, 'would you like me to wear my Nijinsky dress* to-night?'

'No,' said Isabel, 'nobody's going to dress. We're all starving. William's starving, too. Come along, *mes amis*,* let's begin with sardines.'

'I've found the sardines,' said Moira, and she ran into the hall, holding a box high in the air.

'A Lady with a Box of Sardines,' said Dennis gravely.

'Well, William, and how's London?' asked Bill Hunt, drawing the cork out of a bottle of whisky.

'Oh, London's not much changed,' answered William.

'Good old London,' said Bobby, very hearty, spearing a sardine.

But a moment later William was forgotten. Moira Morrison began wondering what colour one's legs really were under water.

'Mine are the palest, palest mushroom colour.'

Bill and Dennis ate enormously. And Isabel filled glasses, and changed plates, and found matches, smiling blissfully. At one moment she said, 'I do wish, Bill, you'd paint it.'

'Paint what?' said Billy loudly, stuffing his mouth with bread.

'Us,' said Isabel, 'round the table. It would be so fascinating in twenty years' time.'

Bill screwed up his eyes and chewed. 'Light's wrong,' he said rudely, 'far too much yellow'; and went on eating. And that seemed to charm Isabel, too.

But after supper they were all so tired they could do nothing but yawn until it was late enough to go to bed. . . .

*   *   *

It was not until William was waiting for his taxi the next afternoon that he found himself alone with Isabel. When he brought his

suit-case down into the hall, Isabel left the others and went over to
him. She stooped down and picked up the suit-case. 'What a weight!'
she said, and she gave a little awkward laugh. 'Let me carry it! To the
gate.'

'No, why should you?' said William. 'Of course not. Give it to me.'

'Oh, please do let me,' said Isabel. 'I want to, really.' They walked
together silently. William felt there was nothing to say now.

'There,' said Isabel triumphantly, setting the suit-case down, and
she looked anxiously along the sandy road. 'I hardly seem to have
seen you this time,' she said breathlessly. 'It's so short, isn't it? I feel
you've only just come. Next time—' The taxi came into sight. 'I
hope they look after you properly in London. I'm so sorry the babies
have been out all day, but Miss Neil had arranged it. They'll hate
missing you. Poor William, going back to London.' The taxi turned.
'Good-bye!' She gave him a little hurried kiss; she was gone.

Fields, trees, hedges streamed by. They shook through the empty,
blind-looking little town, ground up the steep pull to the station.
The train was in. William made straight for a first-class smoker,
flung back into the corner, but this time he let the papers alone. He
folded his arms against the dull, persistent gnawing, and began in his
mind to write a letter to Isabel.

*   *   *

The post was late as usual. They sat outside the house in long chairs
under coloured parasols. Only Bobby Kane lay on the turf at Isabel's
feet. It was dull, stifling; the day drooped like a flag.

'Do you think there will be Mondays in Heaven?' asked Bobby
childishly.

And Dennis murmured, 'Heaven will be one long Monday.'

But Isabel couldn't help wondering what had happened to the
salmon they had for supper last night. She had meant to have fish
mayonnaise for lunch and now. . . .

Moira was asleep. Sleeping was her latest discovery. 'It's *so* wonderful. One simply shuts one's eyes, that's all. It's *so* delicious.'

When the old ruddy postman came beating along the sandy road
on his tricycle one felt the handle-bars ought to have been oars.

Bill Hunt put down his book. 'Letters,' he said complacently, and
they all waited. But, heartless postman—O malignant world! There
was only one, a fat one for Isabel. Not even a paper.

'And mine's only from William,' said Isabel mournfully.

'From William—already?'

'He's sending you back your marriage lines* as a gentle reminder.'

'Does everybody have marriage lines? I thought they were only for servants.'

'Pages and pages! Look at her! A Lady reading a Letter,'* said Dennis.

My darling, precious Isabel. Pages and pages there were. As Isabel read on her feeling of astonishment changed to a stifled feeling. What on earth had induced William . . . ? How extraordinary it was. . . . What could have made him . . . ? She felt confused, more and more excited, even frightened. It was just like William. Was it? It was absurd, of course, it must be absurd, ridiculous. 'Ha, ha, ha! Oh dear!' What was she to do? Isabel flung back in her chair and laughed till she couldn't stop laughing.

'Do, do tell us,' said the others. 'You must tell us.'

'I'm longing to,' gurgled Isabel. She sat up, gathered the letter, and waved it at them. 'Gather round,' she said. 'Listen, it's too marvellous. A love-letter!'

'A love-letter! But how divine!' *Darling, precious Isabel.* But she had hardly begun before their laughter interrupted her.

'Go on, Isabel, it's perfect.'

'It's the most marvellous find.'

'Oh, do go on, Isabel!'

God forbid, my darling, that I should be a drag on your happiness.

'Oh! oh! oh!'

'Sh! sh! sh!'

And Isabel went on. When she reached the end they were hysterical: Bobby rolled on the turf and almost sobbed.

'You must let me have it just as it is, entire, for my new book,' said Dennis firmly. 'I shall give it a whole chapter.'

'Oh, Isabel,' moaned Moira, 'that wonderful bit about holding you in his arms!'

'I always thought those letters in divorce cases were made up. But they pale before this.'

'Let me hold it. Let me read it, mine own self,' said Bobby Kane.

But, to their surprise, Isabel crushed the letter in her hand. She was laughing no longer. She glanced quickly at them all; she looked exhausted. 'No, not just now. Not just now,' she stammered.

And before they could recover she had run into the house, through the hall, up the stairs into her bedroom. Down she sat on the side of the bed. 'How vile, odious, abominable, vulgar,' muttered Isabel. She pressed her eyes with her knuckles and rocked to and fro. And again she saw them, but not four, more like forty, laughing, sneering, jeering, stretching out their hands while she read them William's letter. Oh, what a loathsome thing to have done. How could she have done it! *God forbid, my darling, that I should be a drag on your happiness.* William! Isabel pressed her face into the pillow. But she felt that even the grave bedroom knew her for what she was, shallow, tinkling, vain. . . .

Presently from the garden below there came voices.

'Isabel, we're all going for a bathe. Do come!'

'Come, thou wife of William!'

'Call her once before you go, call once yet!'

Isabel sat up. Now was the moment, now she must decide. Would she go with them, or stay here and write to William. Which, which should it be? 'I must make up my mind.' Oh, but how could there be any question? Of course she would stay here and write.

'Titania!' piped Moira.

'Isa-bel?'

No, it was too difficult. 'I'll—I'll go with them, and write to William later. Some other time. Later. Not now. But I shall *certainly* write,' thought Isabel hurriedly.

And, laughing in the new way, she ran down the stairs.

AT THE BAY

I

Very early morning. The sun was not yet risen, and the whole of Crescent Bay was hidden under a white sea-mist. The big bush-covered hills* at the back were smothered. You could not see where they ended and the paddocks* and bungalows* began. The sandy road was gone and the paddocks and bungalows the other side of it; there were no white dunes covered with reddish grass beyond them; there was nothing to mark which was beach and where was the sea. A heavy dew had fallen. The grass was blue. Big drops hung on the bushes and just did not fall; the silvery, fluffy toi-toi* was limp on its long stalks, and all the marigolds and the pinks in the bungalow gardens were bowed to the earth with wetness. Drenched were the cold fuchsias, round pearls of dew lay on the flat nasturtium leaves. It looked as though the sea had beaten up softly in the darkness, as though one immense wave had come rippling, rippling—how far? Perhaps if you had waked up in the middle of the night you might have seen a big fish flicking in at the window and gone again. . . .

Ah-Aah! sounded the sleepy sea. And from the bush there came the sound of little streams flowing, quickly, lightly, slipping between the smooth stones, gushing into ferny basins and out again; and there was the splashing of big drops on large leaves, and something else—what was it?—a faint stirring and shaking, the snapping of a twig and then such silence that it seemed some one was listening.

Round the corner of Crescent Bay, between the piled-up masses of broken rock, a flock of sheep came pattering. They were huddled together, a small, tossing, woolly mass, and their thin, stick-like legs trotted along quickly as if the cold and the quiet had frightened them. Behind them an old sheep-dog, his soaking paws covered with sand, ran along with his nose to the ground, but carelessly, as if thinking of something else. And then in the rocky gateway the shepherd himself appeared. He was a lean, upright old man, in a frieze* coat that was covered with a web of tiny drops, velvet trousers tied under the knee, and a wideawake* with a folded blue handkerchief round the brim. One hand was crammed into his belt, the other grasped a beautifully smooth yellow stick. And as he walked, taking his time, he kept up a very soft light whistling, an airy, far-away fluting that sounded mournful and tender. The old dog cut an ancient caper or two and then drew up sharp, ashamed of his levity, and walked a few dignified paces by his master's side. The sheep ran forward in little pattering rushes; they began to bleat, and ghostly flocks and herds answered them from under the sea. 'Baa! Baaa!' For a time they seemed to be always on the same piece of ground. There ahead was stretched the sandy road with shallow puddles, the same soaking bushes showed on either side and the same shadowy palings. Then something immense came into view; an enormous shock-haired giant with his arms stretched out. It was the big gum-tree outside Mrs Stubbs's shop, and as they passed by there was a strong whiff of eucalyptus. And now big spots of light gleamed in the mist. The shepherd stopped whistling; he rubbed his red nose and wet beard on his wet sleeve and, screwing up his eyes, glanced in the direction of the sea. The sun was rising. It was marvellous how quickly the mist thinned, sped away, dissolved from the shallow plain, rolled up from the bush and was gone as if in a hurry to escape; big twists and curls jostled and shouldered each other as the silvery beams broadened. The far-away sky—a bright, pure blue—was reflected in the puddles, and the drops, swimming along the telegraph wires, flashed into points of light. Now the leaping, glittering sea was so bright it made one's eyes ache to look at it. The shepherd drew a pipe, the bowl as small as an acorn, out of his breast pocket, fumbled for a chunk of speckled tobacco, pared off a few shavings and stuffed the bowl. He was a grave, fine-looking old man. As he lit up and the blue smoke wreathed his head, the dog, watching, looked proud of him.

'Baa! Baaa!' The sheep spread out into a fan. They were just clear of the summer colony before the first sleeper turned over and lifted a drowsy head; their cry sounded in the dreams of little children . . . who lifted their arms to drag down, to cuddle the darling little woolly lambs of sleep. Then the first inhabitant appeared; it was the Burnells' cat Florrie, sitting on the gatepost, far too early as usual, looking for their milk-girl. When she saw the old sheep-dog she sprang up quickly, arched her back, drew in her tabby head, and seemed to give a little fastidious shiver. 'Ugh! What a coarse, revolting creature!' said Florrie. But the old sheepdog, not looking up, waggled past, flinging out his legs from side to side. Only one of his ears twitched to prove that he saw, and thought her a silly young female.

The breeze of morning lifted in the bush and the smell of leaves and wet black earth mingled with the sharp smell of the sea. Myriads of birds were singing. A goldfinch flew over the shepherd's head and, perching on the tiptop of a spray, it turned to the sun, ruffling its small breast feathers. And now they had passed the fisherman's hut, passed the charred-looking little *whare** where Leila the milk-girl lived with her old Gran. The sheep strayed over a yellow swamp and Wag, the sheep-dog, padded after, rounded them up and headed them for the steeper, narrower rocky pass that led out of Crescent Bay and towards Daylight Cove. 'Baa! Baaa!' Faint the cry came as they rocked along the fast-drying road. The shepherd put away his pipe, dropping it into his breast-pocket so that the little bowl hung over. And straightway the soft airy whistling began again. Wag ran out along a ledge of rock after something that smelled, and ran back again disgusted. Then pushing, nudging, hurrying, the sheep rounded the bend and the shepherd followed after out of sight.

II

A few moments later the back door of one of the bungalows opened, and a figure in a broad-striped bathing suit flung down the paddock, cleared the stile, rushed through the tussock grass into the hollow, staggered up the sandy hillock, and raced for dear life over the big porous stones, over the cold, wet pebbles, on to the hard sand that gleamed like oil. Splish-Splosh! Splish-Splosh! The water bubbled round his legs as Stanley Burnell waded out exulting. First man in as usual! He'd beaten them all again. And he swooped down to souse his head and neck.

'Hail, brother! All hail, Thou Mighty One!' A velvety bass voice came booming over the water.

Great Scott! Damnation take it! Stanley lifted up to see a dark head bobbing far out and an arm lifted. It was Jonathan Trout— there before him! 'Glorious morning!' sang the voice.

'Yes, very fine!' said Stanley briefly. Why the dickens didn't the fellow stick to his part of the sea? Why should he come barging

over to this exact spot? Stanley gave a kick, a lunge and struck out,
swimming overarm. But Jonathan was a match for him. Up he came,
his black hair sleek on his forehead, his short beard sleek.

'I had an extraordinary dream last night!' he shouted.

What was the matter with the man? This mania for conversation
irritated Stanley beyond words. And it was always the same—always
some piffle about a dream he'd had, or some cranky idea he'd got
hold of, or some rot he'd been reading. Stanley turned over on his
back and kicked with his legs till he was a living waterspout. But
even then. . . . 'I dreamed I was hanging over a terrifically high cliff,
shouting to some one below.' You would be! thought Stanley. He
could stick no more of it. He stopped splashing. 'Look here, Trout,'
he said, 'I'm in rather a hurry this morning.'

'You're WHAT?' Jonathan was so surprised—or pretended to be—
that he sank under the water, then reappeared again blowing.

'All I mean is,' said Stanley, 'I've no time to—to—to fool about. I
want to get this over. I'm in a hurry. I've work to do this morning—
see?'

Jonathan was gone before Stanley had finished. 'Pass, friend!' said
the bass voice gently, and he slid away through the water with
scarcely a ripple. . . . But curse the fellow! He'd ruined Stanley's
bathe. What an unpractical idiot the man was! Stanley struck out to
sea again, and then as quickly swam in again, and away he rushed up
the beach. He felt cheated.

Jonathan stayed a little longer in the water. He floated, gently
moving his hands like fins, and letting the sea rock his long, skinny
body. It was curious, but in spite of everything he was fond of
Stanley Burnell. True, he had a fiendish desire to tease him sometimes, to poke fun at him, but at bottom he was sorry for the fellow.
There was something pathetic in his determination to make a job of
everything. You couldn't help feeling he'd be caught out one day, and
then what an almighty cropper he'd come! At that moment an
immense wave lifted Jonathan, rode past him, and broke along the
beach with a joyful sound. What a beauty! And now there came
another. That was the way to live—carelessly, recklessly, spending
oneself. He got on to his feet and began to wade towards the shore,
pressing his toes into the firm, wrinkled sand. To take things easy,
not to fight against the ebb and flow of life, but to give way to it—
that was what was needed. It was this tension that was all wrong. To

live—to live! And the perfect morning, so fresh and fair, basking in the light, as though laughing at its own beauty, seemed to whisper, 'Why not?'

But now he was out of the water Jonathan turned blue with cold. He ached all over; it was as though some one was wringing the blood out of him. And stalking up the beach, shivering, all his muscles tight, he too felt his bathe was spoilt. He'd stayed in too long.

III

Beryl was alone in the living-room when Stanley appeared, wearing a blue serge suit, a stiff collar and a spotted tie. He looked almost uncannily clean and brushed; he was going to town for the day. Dropping into his chair, he pulled out his watch and put it beside his plate.

'I've just got twenty-five minutes,' he said. 'You might go and see if the porridge is ready, Beryl?'

'Mother's just gone for it,' said Beryl. She sat down at the table and poured out his tea.

'Thanks!' Stanley took a sip. 'Hallo!' he said in an astonished voice, 'you've forgotten the sugar.'

'Oh, sorry!' But even then Beryl didn't help him; she pushed the basin across. What did this mean? As Stanley helped himself his blue eyes widened; they seemed to quiver. He shot a quick glance at his sister-in-law and leaned back.

'Nothing wrong, is there?' he asked carelessly, fingering his collar.

Beryl's head was bent; she turned her plate in her fingers.

'Nothing,' said her light voice. Then she too looked up, and smiled at Stanley. 'Why should there be?'

'O-oh! No reason at all as far as I know. I thought you seemed rather—'

At that moment the door opened and the three little girls appeared, each carrying a porridge plate. They were dressed alike in blue jerseys and knickers; their brown legs were bare, and each had her hair plaited and pinned up in what was called a horse's tail. Behind them came Mrs Fairfield with the tray.

'Carefully, children,' she warned. But they were taking the very greatest care. They loved being allowed to carry things. 'Have you said good morning to your father?'

'Yes, grandma.' They settled themselves on the bench opposite Stanley and Beryl.

'Good morning, Stanley!' Old Mrs Fairfield gave him his plate.

'Morning, mother! How's the boy?'

'Splendid! He only woke up once last night. What a perfect morning!' The old woman paused, her hand on the loaf of bread, to gaze out of the open door into the garden. The sea sounded. Through the wide-open window streamed the sun on to the yellow varnished walls and bare floor. Everything on the table flashed and glittered. In the middle there was an old salad bowl filled with yellow and red nasturtiums. She smiled, and a look of deep content shone in her eyes.

'You might *cut* me a slice of that bread, mother,' said Stanley. 'I've only twelve and a half minutes before the coach passes. Has anyone given my shoes to the servant girl?'

'Yes, they're ready for you.' Mrs Fairfield was quite unruffled.

'Oh, Kezia! Why are you such a messy child!' cried Beryl despairingly.

'Me, Aunt Beryl?' Kezia stared at her. What had she done now? She had only dug a river down the middle of her porridge, filled it, and was eating the banks away. But she did that every single morning, and no one had said a word up till now.

'Why can't you eat your food properly like Isabel and Lottie?' How unfair grownups are!

'But Lottie always makes a floating island, don't you, Lottie?'

'I don't,' said Isabel smartly. 'I just sprinkle mine with sugar and put on the milk and finish it. Only babies play with their food.'

Stanley pushed back his chair and got up.

'Would you get me those shoes, mother? And, Beryl, if you've finished, I wish you'd cut down to the gate and stop the coach. Run in to your mother, Isabel, and ask her where my bowler hat's been put. Wait a minute—have you children been playing with my stick?'

'No, father!'

'But I put it here,' Stanley began to bluster. 'I remember distinctly putting it in this corner. Now, who's had it? There's no time to lose. Look sharp! The stick's got to be found.'

Even Alice, the servant-girl, was drawn into the chase. 'You haven't been using it to poke the kitchen fire with by any chance?'

Stanley dashed into the bedroom where Linda was lying. 'Most extraordinary thing. I can't keep a single possession to myself. They've made away with my stick, now!'

'Stick, dear? What stick?' Linda's vagueness on these occasions could not be real, Stanley decided. Would nobody sympathize with him?

'Coach! Coach, Stanley!' Beryl's voice cried from the gate.

Stanley waved his arm to Linda. 'No time to say good-bye!' he cried. And he meant that as a punishment to her.

He snatched his bowler hat, dashed out of the house, and swung down the garden path. Yes, the coach was there waiting, and Beryl, leaning over the open gate, was laughing up at somebody or other just as if nothing had happened. The heartlessness of women! The way they took it for granted it was your job to slave away for them while they didn't even take the trouble to see that your walking-stick wasn't lost. Kelly trailed his whip across the horses.

'Good-bye, Stanley,' called Beryl, sweetly and gaily. It was easy enough to say good-bye! And there she stood, idle, shading her eyes with her hand. The worst of it was Stanley had to shout good-bye too, for the sake of appearances. Then he saw her turn, give a little skip and run back to the house. She was glad to be rid of him!

Yes, she was thankful. Into the living-room she ran and called 'He's gone!' Linda cried from her room: 'Beryl! Has Stanley gone?' Old Mrs Fairfield appeared, carrying the boy in his little flannel coatee.

'Gone?'

'Gone!'

Oh, the relief, the difference it made to have the man out of the house. Their very voices were changed as they called to one another; they sounded warm and loving and as if they shared a secret. Beryl went over to the table. 'Have another cup of tea, mother. It's still hot.' She wanted, somehow, to celebrate the fact that they could do what they liked now. There was no man to disturb them; the whole perfect day was theirs.

'No, thank you, child,' said old Mrs Fairfield, but the way at that moment she tossed the boy up and said 'a-goos-a-goos-a-ga!' to him meant that she felt the same. The little girls ran into the paddock like chickens let out of a coop.

Even Alice, the servant-girl, washing up the dishes in the kitchen, caught the infection and used the precious tank water in a perfectly reckless fashion.

'Oh, these men!' said she, and she plunged the teapot into the bowl and held it under the water even after it had stopped bubbling, as if it too was a man and drowning was too good for them.

IV

'Wait for me, Isa-bel! Kezia, wait for me!'

There was poor little Lottie, left behind again, because she found it so fearfully hard to get over the stile by herself. When she stood on the first step her knees began to wobble; she grasped the post. Then you had to put one leg over. But which leg? She never could decide. And when she did finally put one leg over with a sort of stamp of despair—then the feeling was awful. She was half in the paddock still and half in the tussock grass. She clutched the post desperately and lifted up her voice. 'Wait for me!'

'No, don't you wait for her, Kezia!' said Isabel. 'She's such a little silly. She's always making a fuss. Come on!' And she tugged Kezia's jersey. 'You can use my bucket if you come with me,' she said kindly. 'It's bigger than yours.' But Kezia couldn't leave Lottie all by herself. She ran back to her. By this time Lottie was very red in the face and breathing heavily.

'Here, put your other foot over,' said Kezia.

'Where?'

Lottie looked down at Kezia as if from a mountain height.

'Here where my hand is.' Kezia patted the place.

'Oh, *there* do you mean?' Lottie gave a deep sigh and put the second foot over.

'Now—sort of turn round and sit down and slide,' said Kezia.

'But there's nothing to sit down *on*, Kezia,' said Lottie.

She managed it at last, and once it was over she shook herself and began to beam.

'I'm getting better at climbing over stiles, aren't I, Kezia?'

Lottie's was a very hopeful nature.

The pink and the blue sunbonnet followed Isabel's bright red sunbonnet up that sliding, slipping hill. At the top they paused to decide where to go and to have a good stare at who was there already. Seen from behind, standing against the skyline, gesticulating largely with their spades, they looked like minute puzzled explorers.

The whole family of Samuel Josephs was there already with their lady-help, who sat on a camp-stool and kept order with a whistle that she wore tied round her neck, and a small cane with which she directed operations. The Samuel Josephs never played by themselves or managed their own game. If they did, it ended in the boys pouring water down the girls' necks or the girls trying to put little black crabs into the boys' pockets. So Mrs S. J. and the poor lady-help drew up what she called a 'brogramme' every morning to keep them 'abused and out of bischief'. It was all competitions or races or round games. Everything began with a piercing blast of the lady-help's whistle and ended with another. There were even prizes—large, rather dirty paper parcels which the lady-help with a sour little smile drew out of a bulging string kit. The Samuel Josephs fought fearfully for the prizes and cheated and pinched one another's arms—they were all expert pinchers. The only time the Burnell children ever played with them Kezia had got a prize, and when she undid three bits of paper she found a very small rusty button-hook. She couldn't understand why they made such a fuss. . . .

But they never played with the Samuel Josephs now or even went to their parties. The Samuel Josephs were always giving children's parties at the Bay and there was always the same food. A big wash-hand basin of very brown fruit-salad, buns cut into four and a wash-hand jug full of something the lady-help called 'Limmonadear'.* And you went away in the evening with half the frill torn off your frock or something spilled all down the front of your open-work pinafore, leaving the Samuel Josephs leaping like savages on their lawn. No. They were too awful.

On the other side of the beach, close down to the water, two little boys, their knickers rolled up, twinkled like spiders. One was digging, the other pattered in and out of the water, filling a small bucket. They were the Trout boys, Pip and Rags. But Pip was so busy digging and Rags was so busy helping that they didn't see their little cousins until they were quite close.

'Look!' said Pip. 'Look what I've discovered.' And he showed them an old, wet, squashed-looking boot. The three little girls stared.

'Whatever are you going to do with it?' asked Kezia.

'Keep it, of course!' Pip was very scornful. 'It's a find—see?'

Yes, Kezia saw that. All the same. . . .

'There's lots of things buried in the sand,' explained Pip. 'They get chucked up from wrecks. Treasure. Why—you might find—'

'But why does Rags have to keep on pouring water in?' asked Lottie.

'Oh, that's to moisten it,' said Pip, 'to make the work a bit easier. Keep it up, Rags.'

And good little Rags ran up and down, pouring in the water that turned brown like cocoa.

'Here, shall I show you what I found yesterday?' said Pip mysteriously, and he stuck his spade into the sand. 'Promise not to tell.'

They promised.

'Say, cross my heart straight dinkum.'*

The little girls said it.

Pip took something out of his pocket, rubbed it a long time on the front of his jersey, then breathed on it and rubbed it again.

'Now turn round!' he ordered.

They turned round.

'All look the same way! Keep still! Now!'

And his hand opened; he held up to the light something that flashed, that winked, that was a most lovely green.

'It's a nemeral,' said Pip solemnly.

'Is it really, Pip?' Even Isabel was impressed.

The lovely green thing seemed to dance in Pip's fingers. Aunt Beryl had a nemeral in a ring, but it was a very small one. This one was as big as a star and far more beautiful.

V

As the morning lengthened whole parties appeared over the sand-hills and came down on the beach to bathe. It was understood that at eleven o'clock the women and children of the summer colony had the sea to themselves. First the women undressed, pulled on their bathing dresses and covered their heads in hideous caps like sponge bags; then the children were unbuttoned. The beach was strewn with little heaps of clothes and shoes; the big summer hats, with stones on them to keep them from blowing away, looked like immense shells. It was strange that even the sea seemed to sound differently when all those leaping, laughing figures ran into the waves. Old Mrs Fairfield, in a lilac cotton dress and a black hat tied under the chin, gathered her little brood and got them ready. The little Trout boys whipped their shirts over their heads, and away the five sped, while their grandma sat with one hand in her knitting-bag ready to draw out the ball of wool when she was satisfied they were safely in.

The firm compact little girls were not half so brave as the tender, delicate-looking little boys. Pip and Rags, shivering, crouching down, slapping the water, never hesitated. But Isabel, who could swim twelve strokes, and Kezia, who could nearly swim eight, only followed on the strict understanding they were not to be splashed. As for Lottie, she didn't follow at all. She liked to be left to go in her own way, please. And that way was to sit down at the edge of the water, her legs straight, her knees pressed together, and to make vague motions with her arms as if she expected to be wafted out to sea. But when a bigger wave than usual, an old whiskery one, came lolloping along in her direction, she scrambled to her feet with a face of horror and flew up the beach again.

'Here, mother, keep those for me, will you?'

Two rings and a thin gold chain were dropped into Mrs Fairfield's lap.

'Yes, dear. But aren't you going to bathe here?'

'No-o,' Beryl drawled. She sounded vague. 'I'm undressing farther along. I'm going to bathe with Mrs Harry Kember.'

'Very well.' But Mrs Fairfield's lips set. She disapproved of Mrs Harry Kember. Beryl knew it.

Poor old mother, she smiled as she skimmed over the stones. Poor old mother! Old! Oh, what joy, what bliss it was to be young. . . .

'You look very pleased,' said Mrs Harry Kember. She sat hunched up on the stones, her arms round her knees, smoking.

'It's such a lovely day,' said Beryl, smiling down at her.

'Oh, my *dear*!' Mrs Harry Kember's voice sounded as though she knew better than that. But then her voice always sounded as though she knew something more about you than you did yourself. She was a long, strange-looking woman with narrow hands and feet. Her face, too, was long and narrow and exhausted-looking;

even her fair curled fringe looked burnt out and withered. She was the only woman at the Bay who smoked, and she smoked incessantly, keeping the cigarette between her lips while she talked, and only taking it out when the ash was so long you could not understand why it did not fall. When she was not playing bridge— she played bridge every day of her life—she spent her time lying in the full glare of the sun. She could stand any amount of it; she never had enough. All the same, it did not seem to warm her. Parched, withered, cold, she lay stretched on the stones like a piece of tossed-up driftwood. The women at the Bay thought she was very, very fast. Her lack of vanity, her slang, the way she treated men as though she was one of them, and the fact that she didn't care twopence about her house and called the servant Gladys 'Glad-eyes', was disgraceful. Standing on the veranda steps Mrs Kember would call in her indifferent, tired voice, 'I say, Glad-eyes, you might heave me a handkerchief if I've got one, will you?' And Glad-eyes, a red bow in her hair instead of a cap, and white shoes, came running with an impudent smile. It was an absolute scandal! True, she had no children, and her husband. . . . Here the voices were always raised; they became fervent. How can he have married her? How can he, how can he? It must have been money, of course, but even then!

Mrs Kember's husband was at least ten years younger than she was, and so incredibly handsome that he looked like a mask or a most perfect illustration in an American novel rather than a man. Black hair, dark blue eyes, red lips, a slow sleepy smile, a fine tennis player, a perfect dancer, and with it all a mystery. Harry Kember was like a man walking in his sleep. Men couldn't stand him, they couldn't get a word out of the chap; he ignored his wife just as she ignored him. How did he live? Of course there were stories, but such stories! They simply couldn't be told. The women he'd been seen with, the places he'd been seen in . . . but nothing was ever certain, nothing definite. Some of the women at the Bay privately thought he'd commit a murder one day. Yes, even while they talked to Mrs Kember and took in the awful concoction she was wearing, they saw her, stretched as she lay on the beach; but cold, bloody, and still with a cigarette stuck in the corner of her mouth.

Mrs Kember rose, yawned, unsnapped her belt buckle, and tugged at the tape of her blouse. And Beryl stepped out of her skirt and shed her jersey, and stood up in her short white petticoat, and her camisole with ribbon bows on the shoulders.

'Mercy on us,' said Mrs Harry Kember, 'what a little beauty you are!'

'Don't!' said Beryl softly; but, drawing off one stocking and then the other, she felt a little beauty.

'My dear—why not?' said Mrs Harry Kember, stamping on her own petticoat. Really—her underclothes! A pair of blue cotton knickers and a linen bodice that reminded one somehow of a pillow-case. . . . 'And you don't wear stays,* do you?' She touched Beryl's waist, and Beryl sprang away with a small affected cry. Then 'Never!' she said firmly.

'Lucky little creature,' sighed Mrs Kember, unfastening her own.

Beryl turned her back and began the complicated movements of some one who is trying to take off her clothes and to pull on her bathing-dress all at one and the same time.

'Oh, my dear—don't mind me,' said Mrs Harry Kember. 'Why be shy? I shan't eat you. I shan't be shocked like those other ninnies.' And she gave her strange neighing laugh and grimaced at the other women.

But Beryl was shy. She never undressed in front of anybody. Was that silly? Mrs Harry Kember made her feel it was silly, even something to be ashamed of. Why be shy indeed! She glanced quickly at her friend standing so boldly in her torn chemise and lighting a fresh cigarette; and a quick, bold, evil feeling started up in her breast. Laughing recklessly, she drew on the limp, sandy-feeling bathing-dress that was not quite dry and fastened the twisted buttons.

'That's better,' said Mrs Harry Kember. They began to go down the beach together. 'Really, it's a sin for you to wear clothes, my dear. Somebody's got to tell you some day.'

The water was quite warm. It was that marvellous transparent blue, flecked with silver, but the sand at the bottom looked gold; when you kicked with your toes there rose a little puff of gold-dust. Now the waves just reached her breast. Beryl stood, her arms out-stretched, gazing out, and as each wave came she gave the slightest little jump, so that it seemed it was the wave which lifted her so gently.

'I believe in pretty girls having a good time,' said Mrs Harry Kember. 'Why not? Don't you make a mistake, my dear. Enjoy

yourself.' And suddenly she turned turtle,* disappeared, and swam
away quickly, quickly, like a rat. Then she flicked round and began
swimming back. She was going to say something else. Beryl felt that
she was being poisoned by this cold woman, but she longed to hear.
But oh, how strange, how horrible! As Mrs Harry Kember came up
close she looked, in her black waterproof bathing-cap, with her
sleepy face lifted above the water, just her chin touching, like a
horrible caricature of her husband.

VI

In a steamer chair,* under a manuka tree* that grew in the middle of
the front grass patch, Linda Burnell dreamed the morning away. She
did nothing. She looked up at the dark, close, dry leaves of the
manuka, at the chinks of blue between, and now and again a tiny
yellowish flower dropped on her. Pretty—yes, if you held one of
those flowers on the palm of your hand and looked at it closely, it was
an exquisite small thing. Each pale yellow petal shone as if each was
the careful work of a loving hand. The tiny tongue in the centre gave
it the shape of a bell. And when you turned it over the outside was a
deep bronze colour. But as soon as they flowered, they fell and were
scattered. You brushed them off your frock as you talked; the horrid
little things got caught in one's hair. Why, then, flower at all? Who
takes the trouble—or the joy—to make all these things that are
wasted, wasted. . . . It was uncanny.

On the grass beside her, lying between two pillows, was the boy.
Sound asleep he lay, his head turned away from his mother. His fine
dark hair looked more like a shadow than like real hair, but his ear
was a bright, deep coral. Linda clasped her hands above her head and
crossed her feet. It was very pleasant to know that all these bungalows were empty, that everybody was down on the beach, out of
sight, out of hearing. She had the garden to herself; she was alone.

Dazzling white the picotees* shone; the golden-eyed marigolds
glittered; the nasturtiums wreathed the veranda poles in green and
gold flame. If only one had time to look at these flowers long enough,
time to get over the sense of novelty and strangeness, time to know
them! But as soon as one paused to part the petals, to discover the
under-side of the leaf, along came Life and one was swept away. And

lying in her cane chair, Linda felt so light; she felt like a leaf. Along came Life like a wind and she was seized and shaken; she had to go. Oh dear, would it always be so? Was there no escape?

... Now she sat on the veranda of their Tasmanian* home, leaning against her father's knee. And he promised, 'As soon as you and I are old enough, Linny, we'll cut off somewhere, we'll escape. Two boys together. I have a fancy I'd like to sail up a river in China.' Linda saw that river, very wide, covered with little rafts and boats. She saw the yellow hats of the boatmen and she heard their high, thin voices as they called. ...

'Yes, papa.'

But just then a very broad young man with bright ginger hair walked slowly past their house, and slowly, solemnly even, uncovered.* Linda's father pulled her ear teasingly, in the way he had.

'Linny's beau,' he whispered.

'Oh, papa, fancy being married to Stanley Burnell!'

Well, she was married to him. And what was more she loved him. Not the Stanley whom every one saw, not the everyday one; but a timid, sensitive, innocent Stanley who knelt down every night to say his prayers, and who longed to be good. Stanley was simple. If he believed in people—as he believed in her, for instance—it was with his whole heart. He could not be disloyal; he could not tell a lie. And how terribly he suffered if he thought anyone—she—was not being dead straight, dead sincere with him! 'This is too subtle for me!' He flung out the words, but his open quivering, distraught look was like the look of a trapped beast.

But the trouble was—here Linda felt almost inclined to laugh, though Heaven knows it was no laughing matter—she saw *her* Stanley so seldom. There were glimpses, moments, breathing spaces of calm, but all the rest of the time it was like living in a house that couldn't be cured of the habit of catching on fire, on a ship that got wrecked every day. And it was always Stanley who was in the thick of the danger. Her whole time was spent in rescuing him, and restoring him, and calming him down, and listening to his story. And what was left of her time was spent in the dread of having children.

Linda frowned; she sat up quickly in her steamer chair and clasped her ankles. Yes, that was her real grudge against life; that was what she could not understand. That was the question she asked and asked, and listened in vain for the answer. It was all very well to say it was the common lot of women to bear children. It wasn't true. She, for one, could prove that wrong. She was broken, made weak, her courage was gone, through child-bearing. And what made it doubly hard to bear was, she did not love her children. It was useless pretending. Even if she had had the strength she never would have nursed and played with the little girls. No, it was as though a cold breath had chilled her through and through on each of those awful journeys; she had no warmth left to give them. As to the boy—well, thank Heaven, mother had taken him; he was mother's, or Beryl's, or anybody's who wanted him. She had hardly held him in her arms. She was so indifferent about him that as he lay there. . . . Linda glanced down.

The boy had turned over. He lay facing her, and he was no longer asleep. His dark-blue, baby eyes were open; he looked as though he was peeping at his mother. And suddenly his face dimpled; it broke into a wide, toothless smile, a perfect beam, no less.

'I'm here!' that happy smile seemed to say. 'Why don't you like me?'

There was something so quaint, so unexpected about that smile that Linda smiled herself. But she checked herself and said to the boy coldly, 'I don't like babies.'

'Don't like babies?' The boy couldn't believe her. 'Don't like *me*?' He waved his arms foolishly at his mother.

Linda dropped off her chair on to the grass.

'Why do you keep on smiling?' she said severely. 'If you knew what I was thinking about, you wouldn't.'

But he only squeezed up his eyes, slyly, and rolled his head on the pillow. He didn't believe a word she said.

'We know all about that!' smiled the boy.

Linda was so astonished at the confidence of this little creature. . . . Ah no, be sincere. That was not what she felt; it was something far different, it was something so new, so. . . . The tears danced in her eyes; she breathed in a small whisper to the boy, 'Hallo, my funny!'

But by now the boy had forgotten his mother. He was serious again. Something pink,* something soft waved in front of him. He made a grab at it and it immediately disappeared. But when he lay back, another, like the first, appeared. This time he determined to catch it. He made a tremendous effort and rolled right over.

VII

The tide was out; the beach was deserted; lazily flopped the warm sea. The sun beat down, beat down hot and fiery on the fine sand, baking the grey and blue and black and white-veined pebbles. It sucked up the little drop of water that lay in the hollow of the curved shells; it bleached the pink convolvulus that threaded through and through the sand-hills. Nothing seemed to move but the small sand-hoppers.* Pit-pit-pit! They were never still.

Over there on the weed-hung rocks that looked at low tide like shaggy beasts come down to the water to drink, the sunlight seemed to spin like a silver coin dropped into each of the small rock pools. They danced, they quivered, and minute ripples laved the porous shores. Looking down, bending over, each pool was like a lake with pink and blue houses clustered on the shores; and oh! the vast mountainous country behind those houses—the ravines, the passes, the dangerous creeks and fearful tracks that led to the water's edge. Underneath waved the sea-forest—pink thread-like trees, velvet anemones, and orange berry-spotted weeds. Now a stone on the bottom moved, rocked, and there was a glimpse of a black feeler; now a thread-like creature wavered by and was lost. Something was happening to the pink waving trees; they were changing to a cold moonlight blue. And now there sounded the faintest 'plop'. Who made that sound? What was going on down there? And how strong, how damp the seaweed smelt in the hot sun. . . .

The green blinds were drawn in the bungalows of the summer colony. Over the verandas, prone on the paddock, flung over the fences, there were exhausted-looking bathing-dresses and rough striped towels. Each back window seemed to have a pair of sand-shoes on the sill and some lumps of rock or a bucket or a collection of pawa shells.* The bush quivered in a haze of heat; the sandy road was empty except for the Trouts' dog Snooker, who lay stretched in the very middle of it. His blue eye was turned up, his legs stuck out stiffly, and he gave an occasional desperate-sounding puff, as much as to say he had decided to make an end of it and was only waiting for some kind cart to come along.

'What are you looking at, my grandma? Why do you keep stopping and sort of staring at the wall?'

Kezia and her grandmother were taking their siesta together. The little girl, wearing only her short drawers and her under-bodice, her arms and legs bare, lay on one of the puffed-up pillows of her grandma's bed, and the old woman, in a white ruffled dressing-gown, sat in a rocker at the window, with a long piece of pink knitting in her lap. This room that they shared, like the other rooms of the bungalow, was of light varnished wood and the floor was bare. The furniture was of the shabbiest, the simplest. The dressing-table for instance, was a packing-case in a sprigged muslin petticoat, and the mirror above was very strange; it was as though a little piece of forked lightning was imprisoned in it. On the table there stood a jar of sea-pinks, pressed so tightly together they looked more like a velvet pincushion, and a special shell which Kezia had given her grandma for a pin-tray, and another even more special which she had thought would make a very nice place for a watch to curl up in.

'Tell me, grandma,' said Kezia.

The old woman sighed, whipped the wool twice round her thumb, and drew the bone needle through. She was casting on.*

'I was thinking of your Uncle William, darling,' she said quietly.

'My Australian Uncle William?' said Kezia. She had another.

'Yes, of course.'

'The one I never saw?'

'That was the one.'

'Well, what happened to him?' Kezia knew perfectly well, but she wanted to be told again.

'He went to the mines,* and he got a sunstroke there and died,' said old Mrs Fairfield.

Kezia blinked and considered the picture again. . . . A little man fallen over like a tin soldier by the side of a big black hole.

'Does it make you sad to think about him, grandma?' She hated her grandma to be sad.

It was the old woman's turn to consider. Did it make her sad? To look back, back. To stare down the years, as Kezia had seen her doing. To look after *them* as a woman does, long after *they* were out of sight. Did it make her sad? No, life was like that.

'No, Kezia.'

'But why?' asked Kezia. She lifted one bare arm and began to draw things in the air. 'Why did Uncle William have to die? He wasn't old.'

Mrs Fairfield began counting the stitches in threes. 'It just happened,' she said in an absorbed voice.

'Does everybody have to die?' asked Kezia.

'Everybody!'

'*Me?*' Kezia sounded fearfully incredulous.

'Some day, my darling.'

'But, grandma.' Kezia waved her left leg and waggled the toes. They felt sandy. 'What if I just won't?'

The old woman sighed again and drew a long thread from the ball.

'We're not asked, Kezia,' she said sadly. 'It happens to all of us sooner or later.'

Kezia lay still thinking this over. She didn't want to die. It meant she would have to leave here, leave everywhere, for ever, leave—leave her grandma. She rolled over quickly.

'Grandma,' she said in a startled voice.

'What, my pet!'

'*You're* not to die.' Kezia was very decided.

'Ah, Kezia'—her grandma looked up and smiled and shook her head—'don't let's talk about it.'

'But you're not to. You couldn't leave me. You couldn't not be there.' This was awful. 'Promise me you won't ever do it, grandma,' pleaded Kezia.

The old woman went on knitting.

'Promise me! Say never!'

But still her grandma was silent.

Kezia rolled off the bed; she couldn't bear it any longer, and lightly she leapt on to her grandma's knees, clasped her hands round the old woman's throat and began kissing her, under the chin, behind the ear, and blowing down her neck.

'Say never . . . say never . . . say never—' She gasped between the kisses. And then she began, very softly and lightly, to tickle her grandma.

'Kezia!' The old woman dropped her knitting. She swung back in the rocker. She began to tickle Kezia. 'Say never, say never, say never,' gurgled Kezia, while they lay there laughing in each other's arms. 'Come, that's enough, my squirrel! That's enough, my wild pony!' said old Mrs Fairfield, setting her cap straight. 'Pick up my knitting.'

Both of them had forgotten what the 'never' was about.

VIII

The sun was still full on the garden when the back door of the Burnells' shut with a bang, and a very gay figure walked down the path to the gate. It was Alice, the servant-girl, dressed for her afternoon out. She wore a white cotton dress with such large red spots on it, and so many that they made you shudder, white shoes and a leghorn* turned up under the brim with poppies. Of course she wore gloves, white ones, stained at the fastenings with iron-mould, and in one hand she carried a very dashed-looking sunshade which she referred to as her *perishall*.*

Beryl, sitting in the window, fanning her freshly-washed hair, thought she had never seen such a guy. If Alice had only blacked her face with a piece of cork before she started out, the picture would have been complete. And where did a girl like that go to in a place like this? The heart-shaped Fijian fan beat scornfully at that lovely bright mane. She supposed Alice had picked up some horrible common larrikin* and they'd go off into the bush together. Pity to make herself so conspicuous; they'd have hard work to hide with Alice in that rig-out.

But no, Beryl was unfair. Alice was going to tea with Mrs Stubbs, who'd sent her an 'invite' by the little boy who called for orders. She had taken ever such a liking to Mrs Stubbs ever since the first time she went to the shop to get something for her mosquitoes.*

'Dear heart!' Mrs Stubbs had clapped her hand to her side. 'I never seen anyone so eaten. You might have been attacked by canningbals.'*

Alice did wish there'd been a bit of life on the road though. Made her feel so queer, having nobody behind her. Made her feel all weak in the spine. She couldn't believe that some one wasn't watching her. And yet it was silly to turn round; it gave you away. She pulled up her gloves, hummed to herself and said to the distant gum-tree, 'Shan't be long now.' But that was hardly company.

Mrs Stubbs's shop was perched on a little hillock just off the road.

It had two big windows for eyes, a broad veranda for a hat, and the sign on the roof, scrawled MRS. STUBBS's, was like a little card stuck rakishly in the hat crown.

On the veranda there hung a long string of bathing-dresses, clinging together as though they'd just been rescued from the sea rather than waiting to go in, and beside them there hung a cluster of sand-shoes so extraordinarily mixed that to get at one pair you had to tear apart and forcibly separate at least fifty. Even then it was the rarest thing to find the left that belonged to the right. So many people had lost patience and gone off with one shoe that fitted and one that was a little too big. . . . Mrs Stubbs prided herself on keeping something of everything. The two windows, arranged in the form of precarious pyramids, were crammed so tight, piled so high, that it seemed only a conjuror could prevent them from toppling over. In the left-hand corner of one window, glued to the pane by four gelatine lozenges, there was—and there had been from time immemorial—a notice.

LOST! HANSOME GOLE BROOCH
SOLID GOLD
ON OR NEAR BEACH
REWARD OFFERED

Alice pressed open the door. The bell jangled, the red serge curtains parted, and Mrs Stubbs appeared. With her broad smile and the long bacon knife in her hand, she looked like a friendly brigand. Alice was welcomed so warmly that she found it quite difficult to keep up her 'manners'. They consisted of persistent little coughs and hems, pulls at her gloves, tweaks at her skirt, and a curious difficulty in seeing what was set before her or understanding what was said.

Tea was laid on the parlour table—ham, sardines, a whole pound of butter, and such a large johnny cake* that it looked like an advertisement for somebody's baking-powder. But the Primus stove* roared so loudly that it was useless to try to talk above it. Alice sat down on the edge of a basket-chair while Mrs Stubbs pumped the stove still higher. Suddenly Mrs Stubbs whipped the cushion off a chair and disclosed a large brown-paper parcel.

'I've just had some new photers taken, my dear,' she shouted cheerfully to Alice. 'Tell me what you think of them.'

In a very dainty, refined way Alice wet her finger and put the tissue back from the first one. Life! How many there were! There were three dozzing* at least. And she held hers up to the light.

Mrs Stubbs sat in an arm-chair, leaning very much to one side. There was a look of mild astonishment on her large face, and well there might be. For though the arm-chair stood on a carpet, to the left of it, miraculously skirting the carpet-border, there was a dashing water-fall. On her right stood a Grecian pillar with a giant fern-tree on either side of it, and in the background towered a gaunt mountain, pale with snow.*

'It is a nice style, isn't it?' shouted Mrs Stubbs; and Alice had just screamed 'Sweetly' when the roaring of the Primus stove died down, fizzled out, ceased, and she said 'Pretty' in a silence that was frightening.

'Draw up your chair, my dear,' said Mrs Stubbs, beginning to pour out. 'Yes,' she said thoughtfully, as she handed the tea, 'but I don't care about the size. I'm having an enlargemint. All very well for Christmas cards, but I never was the one for small photers myself. You get no comfort out of them. To say the truth, I find them dis'eartening.'

Alice quite saw what she meant.

'Size,' said Mrs Stubbs. 'Give me size. That was what my poor dear husband was always saying. He couldn't stand anything small. Gave him the creeps. And, strange as it may seem, my dear'—here Mrs Stubbs creaked and seemed to expand herself at the memory— 'it was dropsy* that carried him off at the larst. Many's the time they drawn one and a half pints from 'im at the 'ospital. . . . It seemed like a judgmint.'

Alice burned to know exactly what it was that was drawn from him. She ventured, 'I suppose it was water.'

But Mrs Stubbs fixed Alice with her eyes and replied meaningly, 'It was *liquid*, my dear.'

Liquid! Alice jumped away from the word like a cat and came back to it, nosing and wary.

'That's 'im!' said Mrs Stubbs, and she pointed dramatically to the life-size head and shoulders of a burly man with a dead white rose in the button-hole of his coat that made you think of a curl of cold mutting* fat. Just below, in silver letters on a red cardboard ground, were the words, 'Be not afraid, it is I.'*

'It's ever such a fine face,' said Alice faintly.

The pale-blue bow on the top of Mrs Stubbs's fair frizzy hair quivered. She arched her plump neck. What a neck she had! It was bright pink where it began and then it changed to warm apricot, and that faded to the colour of a brown egg and then to a deep creamy.

'All the same, my dear,' she said surprisingly, 'freedom's best!' Her soft, fat chuckle sounded like a purr. 'Freedom's best,' said Mrs Stubbs again.

Freedom! Alice gave a loud, silly little titter. She felt awkward. Her mind flew back to her own kitching. Ever so queer! She wanted to be back in it again.

IX

A strange company assembled in the Burnells' washhouse after tea. Round the table there sat a bull, a rooster, a donkey that kept forgetting it was a donkey, a sheep and a bee. The washhouse was the perfect place for such a meeting because they could make as much noise as they liked, and nobody ever interrupted. It was a small tin shed standing apart from the bungalow. Against the wall there was a deep trough and in the corner a copper* with a basket of clothes-pegs on top of it. The little window, spun over with cobwebs, had a piece of candle and a mouse-trap on the dusty sill. There were clothes-lines criss-crossed overhead and, hanging from a peg on the wall, a very big, a huge, rusty horseshoe. The table was in the middle with a form at either side.

'You can't be a bee, Kezia. A bee's not an animal. It's a ninseck.'*

'Oh, but I do want to be a bee frightfully,' wailed Kezia. . . . A tiny bee, all yellow-furry, with striped legs. She drew her legs up under her and leaned over the table. She felt she was a bee.

'A ninseck must be an animal,' she said stoutly. 'It makes a noise. It's not like a fish.'

'I'm a bull, I'm a bull!' cried Pip. And he gave such a tremendous bellow—how did he make that noise?—that Lottie looked quite alarmed.

'I'll be a sheep,' said little Rags. 'A whole lot of sheep went past this morning.'

'How do you know?'

'Dad heard them. Baa!' He sounded like the little lamb that trots behind and seems to wait to be carried.

'Cock-a-doodle-do!' shrilled Isabel. With her red cheeks and bright eyes she looked like a rooster.

'What'll I be?' Lottie asked everybody, and she sat there smiling, waiting for them to decide for her. It had to be an easy one.

'Be a donkey, Lottie.' It was Kezia's suggestion. 'Hee-haw! You can't forget that.'

'Hee-haw!' said Lottie solemnly. 'When do I have to say it?'

'I'll explain, I'll explain,' said the bull. It was he who had the cards. He waved them round his head. 'All be quiet! All listen!' And he waited for them. 'Look here, Lottie.' He turned up a card. 'It's got two spots on it—see? Now, if you put that card in the middle and somebody else has one with two spots as well, you say "Hee-haw," and the card's yours.'

'Mine?' Lottie was round-eyed. 'To keep?'

'No, silly. Just for the game, see? Just while we're playing.' The bull was very cross with her.

'Oh, Lottie, you *are* a little silly,' said the proud rooster.

Lottie looked at both of them. Then she hung her head; her lip quivered. 'I don't not want to play,' she whispered. The others glanced at one another like conspirators. All of them knew what that meant. She would go away and be discovered somewhere standing with her pinny* thrown over her head, in a corner, or against a wall, or even behind a chair.

'Yes, you *do*, Lottie. It's quite easy,' said Kezia.

And Isabel, repentant, said exactly like a grown-up, 'Watch *me*, Lottie, and you'll soon learn.'

'Cheer up, Lot,' said Pip. 'There, I know what I'll do. I'll give you the first one. It's mine, really, but I'll give it to you. Here you are.' And he slammed the card down in front of Lottie.

Lottie revived at that. But now she was in another difficulty. 'I haven't got a hanky,' she said; 'I want one badly, too.'

'Here, Lottie, you can use mine.' Rags dipped into his sailor blouse and brought up a very wet-looking one, knotted together. 'Be very careful,' he warned her. 'Only use that corner. Don't undo it. I've got a little starfish inside I'm going to try and tame.'

'Oh, come on, you girls,' said the bull. 'And mind—you're not to look at your cards. You've got to keep your hands under the table till I say "Go." '

Smack went the cards round the table. They tried with all their might to see, but Pip was too quick for them. It was very exciting, sitting there in the washhouse; it was all they could do not to burst into a little chorus of animals before Pip had finished dealing.

'Now, Lottie, you begin.'

Timidly Lottie stretched out a hand, took the top card off her pack, had a good look at it—it was plain she was counting the spots—and put it down.

'No, Lottie, you can't do that. You mustn't look first. You must turn it the other way over.'

'But then everybody will see it the same time as me,' said Lottie.

The game proceeded. Mooe-ooo-er! The bull was terrible. He charged over the table and seemed to eat the cards up.

Bss-ss! said the bee.

Cock-a-doodle-do! Isabel stood up in her excitement and moved her elbows like wings.

Baa! Little Rags put down the King of Diamonds and Lottie put down the one they called the King of Spain. She had hardly any cards left.

'Why don't you call out, Lottie?'

'I've forgotten what I am,' said the donkey woefully.

'Well, change! Be a dog instead! Bow-wow!'

'Oh yes. That's *much* easier.' Lottie smiled again. But when she and Kezia both had a one Kezia waited on purpose. The others made signs to Lottie and pointed. Lottie turned very red; she looked bewildered, and at last she said, 'Hee-haw! Ke-zia.'

'Ss! Wait a minute!' They were in the very thick of it when the bull stopped them, holding up his hand. 'What's that? What's that noise?'

'What noise? What do you mean?' asked the rooster.

'Ss! Shut up! Listen!' They were mouse-still. 'I thought I heard a—a sort of knocking,' said the bull.

'What was it like?' asked the sheep faintly.

No answer.

The bee gave a shudder. 'Whatever did we shut the door for?' she said softly. Oh, why, why had they shut the door?

While they were playing, the day had faded; the gorgeous sunset had blazed and died. And now the quick dark came racing over the sea, over the sand-hills, up the paddock. You were frightened to look in the corners of the washhouse, and yet you had to look with all your might. And somewhere, far away, grandma was lighting a lamp. The blinds were being pulled down; the kitchen fire leapt in the tins on the mantelpiece.

'It would be awful now,' said the bull, 'if a spider was to fall from the ceiling on to the table, wouldn't it?'

'Spiders don't fall from ceilings.'

'Yes, they do. Our Min told us she'd seen a spider as big as a saucer, with long hairs on it like a gooseberry.'

Quickly all the little heads were jerked up; all the little bodies drew together, pressed together.

'Why doesn't somebody come and call us?' cried the rooster.

Oh, those grown-ups, laughing and snug, sitting in the lamp-light, drinking out of cups! They'd forgotten about them. No, not really forgotten. That was what their smile meant. They had decided to leave them there all by themselves.

Suddenly Lottie gave such a piercing scream that all of them jumped off the forms, all of them screamed too. 'A face—a face looking!' shrieked Lottie.

It was true, it was real. Pressed against the window was a pale face, black eyes, a black beard.

'Grandma! Mother! Somebody!'

But they had not got to the door, tumbling over one another, before it opened for Uncle Jonathan. He had come to take the little boys home.

X

He had meant to be there before, but in the front garden he had come upon Linda walking up and down the grass, stopping to pick off a dead pink or give a top-heavy carnation something to lean against, or to take a deep breath of something, and then walking on again, with her little air of remoteness. Over her white frock she wore a yellow, pink-fringed shawl from the Chinaman's shop.

'Hallo, Jonathan!' called Linda. And Jonathan whipped off his shabby panama, pressed it against his breast, dropped on one knee, and kissed Linda's hand.

'Greeting, my Fair One! Greeting, my Celestial Peach Blossom!' boomed the bass voice gently. 'Where are the other noble dames?'

'Beryl's out playing bridge and mother's giving the boy his bath. . . . Have you come to borrow something?'

The Trouts were for ever running out of things and sending across to the Burnells' at the last moment.

But Jonathan only answered, 'A little love, a little kindness'; and he walked by his sister-in-law's side.

Linda dropped into Beryl's hammock under the manuka tree, and Jonathan stretched himself on the grass beside her, pulled a long stalk and began chewing it. They knew each other well. The voices of children cried from the other gardens. A fisherman's light cart shook along the sandy road, and from far away they heard a dog barking; it was muffled as though the dog had its head in a sack. If you listened you could just hear the soft swish of the sea at full tide sweeping the pebbles. The sun was sinking.

'And so you go back to the office on Monday, do you, Jonathan?' asked Linda.

'On Monday the cage door opens and clangs to upon the victim for another eleven months and a week,' answered Jonathan.

Linda swung a little. 'It must be awful,' she said slowly.

'Would ye have me laugh, my fair sister? Would ye have me weep?'

Linda was so accustomed to Jonathan's way of talking that she paid no attention to it.

'I suppose,' she said vaguely, 'one gets used to it. One gets used to anything.'

'Does one? Hum!' The 'Hum' was so deep it seemed to boom from underneath the ground. 'I wonder how it's done,' brooded Jonathan; 'I've never managed it.'

Looking at him as he lay there, Linda thought again how attractive he was. It was strange to think that he was only an ordinary clerk, that Stanley earned twice as much money as he. What was the matter with Jonathan? He had no ambition; she supposed that was it. And yet one felt he was gifted, exceptional. He was passionately fond of music; every spare penny he had went on books. He was always full of new ideas, schemes, plans. But nothing came of it all. The new fire blazed in Jonathan; you almost heard it roaring softly as he explained, described and dilated on the new thing; but a moment later it had fallen in and there was nothing but ashes, and Jonathan went about with a look like hunger in his black eyes. At these times he exaggerated his absurd manner of speaking, and he sang in church—he was the leader of the choir—with such fearful dramatic intensity that the meanest hymn put on an unholy splendour.

'It seems to me just as imbecile, just as infernal, to have to go to the office on Monday,' said Jonathan, 'as it always has done and always will do. To spend all the best years of one's life sitting on a stool from nine to five, scratching in somebody's ledger!* It's a queer use to make of one's . . . one and only life, isn't it? Or do I fondly dream?'* He rolled over on the grass and looked up at Linda. 'Tell me, what is the difference between my life and that of an ordinary prisoner. The only difference I can see is that I put myself in jail and nobody's ever going to let me out. That's a more intolerable situation than the other. For if I'd been—pushed in, against my will—kicking, even—once the door was locked, or at any rate in five years or so, I might have accepted the fact and begun to take an interest in the flight of flies or counting the warder's steps along the passage with particular attention to variations of tread and so on. But as it is, I'm like an insect that's flown into a room of its own accord. I dash against the walls, dash against the windows, flop against the ceiling, do everything on God's earth, in fact, except fly out again. And all the while I'm thinking, like that moth, or that butterfly, or whatever it is, "The shortness of life! The shortness of life!" I've only one night or one day, and there's this vast dangerous garden, waiting out there, undiscovered, unexplored.'

'But, if you feel like that, why—' began Linda quickly.

'*Ah!*' cried Jonathan. And that 'Ah!' was somehow almost exultant. 'There you have me. Why? Why indeed? There's the maddening, mysterious question. Why don't I fly out again? There's the window or the door or whatever it was I came in by. It's not hopelessly shut—is it? Why don't I find it and be off? Answer me that, little sister.' But he gave her no time to answer.

'I'm exactly like that insect again. For some reason'—Jonathan paused between the words—'it's not allowed, it's forbidden, it's against the insect law, to stop banging and flopping and crawling up the pane even for an instant. Why don't I leave the office? Why don't I seriously consider, this moment, for instance, what it is that prevents me leaving? It's not as though I'm tremendously tied. I've two boys to provide for, but, after all, they're boys. I could cut off to sea, or get a job up-country, or—' Suddenly he smiled at Linda and said in a changed voice, as if he were confiding a secret, 'Weak . . . weak. No stamina. No anchor. No guiding principle, let us call it.' But then the dark velvety voice rolled out:

> Would ye hear the story
> How it unfolds itself . . .

and they were silent.

The sun had set. In the western sky there were great masses of crushed-up rose-coloured clouds. Broad beams of light shone through the clouds and beyond them as if they would cover the whole sky. Overhead the blue faded; it turned a pale gold, and the bush outlined against it gleamed dark and brilliant like metal. Sometimes when those beams of light show in the sky they are very awful. They remind you that up there sits Jehovah,* the jealous God, the Almighty, Whose eye is upon you, ever watchful, never weary. You remember that at His coming the whole earth will shake into one ruined graveyard; the cold, bright angels will drive you this way and that, and there will be no time to explain what could be explained so simply.* . . . But to-night it seemed to Linda there was something infinitely joyful and loving in those silver beams. And now no sound came from the sea. It breathed softly as if it would draw that tender, joyful beauty into its own bosom.

'It's all wrong, it's all wrong,' came the shadowy voice of Jonathan. 'It's not the scene, it's not the setting for . . . three stools, three desks, three inkpots and a wire blind.'

Linda knew that he would never change, but she said, 'Is it too late, even now?'

'I'm old—I'm old,' intoned Jonathan. He bent towards her, he passed his hand over his head. 'Look!' His black hair was speckled all over with silver, like the breast plumage of a black fowl.

Linda was surprised. She had no idea that he was grey. And yet, as he stood up beside her and sighed and stretched, she saw him, for the first time, not resolute, not gallant, not careless, but touched already with age. He looked very tall on the darkening grass, and the thought crossed her mind, 'He is like a weed.'

Jonathan stooped again and kissed her fingers.

'Heaven reward thy sweet patience, lady mine,' he murmured. 'I must go seek those heirs to my fame and fortune. . . .' He was gone.

XI

Light shone in the windows of the bungalow. Two square patches of gold fell upon the pinks and the peaked marigolds. Florrie, the cat, came out on to the veranda, and sat on the top step, her white paws close together, her tail curled round. She looked content, as though she had been waiting for this moment all day.

'Thank goodness, it's getting late,' said Florrie. 'Thank goodness, the long day is over.' Her greengage* eyes opened.

Presently there sounded the rumble of the coach, the crack of Kelly's whip. It came near enough for one to hear the voices of the men from town, talking loudly together. It stopped at the Burnells' gate.

Stanley was half-way up the path before he saw Linda. 'Is that you, darling?'

'Yes, Stanley.'

He leapt across the flower-bed and seized her in his arms. She was enfolded in that familiar, eager, strong embrace.

'Forgive me, darling, forgive me,' stammered Stanley, and he put his hand under her chin and lifted her face to him.

'Forgive you?' smiled Linda. 'But whatever for?'

'Good God! You can't have forgotten,' cried Stanley Burnell. 'I've thought of nothing else all day. I've had the hell of a day. I made up my mind to dash out and telegraph, and then I thought the wire* mightn't reach you before I did. I've been in tortures, Linda.'

'But, Stanley,' said Linda, 'what must I forgive you for?'

'Linda!'—Stanley was very hurt—'didn't you realize—you must have realized—I went away without saying good-bye to you this morning? I can't imagine how I can have done such a thing. My confounded temper, of course. But—well'—and he sighed and took her in his arms again—'I've suffered for it enough to-day.'

'What's that you've got in your hand?' asked Linda. 'New gloves? Let me see.'

'Oh, just a cheap pair of wash-leather* ones,' said Stanley humbly. 'I noticed Bell was wearing some in the coach this morning, so, as I was passing the shop, I dashed in and got myself a pair. What are you smiling at? You don't think it was wrong of me, do you?'

'On the *con*-trary, darling,' said Linda, 'I think it was most sensible.'

She pulled one of the large, pale gloves on her own fingers and looked at her hand, turning it this way and that. She was still smiling.

Stanley wanted to say, 'I was thinking of you the whole time I bought them.' It was true, but for some reason he couldn't say it. 'Let's go in,' said he.

XII

Why does one feel so different at night? Why is it so exciting to be awake when everybody else is asleep? Late—it is very late! And yet every moment you feel more and more wakeful, as though you were slowly, almost with every breath, waking up into a new, wonderful, far more thrilling and exciting world than the daylight one. And what is this queer sensation that you're a conspirator? Lightly, stealthily you move about your room. You take something off the dressing-table and put it down again without a sound. And everything, even the bed-post, knows you, responds, shares your secret. . . .

You're not very fond of your room by day. You never think about it. You're in and out, the door opens and slams, the cupboard creaks. You sit down on the side of your bed, change your shoes and dash out again. A dive down to the glass, two pins in your hair, powder your nose and off again. But now—it's suddenly dear to you. It's a darling little funny room. It's yours. Oh, what a joy it is to own things! Mine—my own!

'My very own for ever?'

'Yes.' Their lips met.

No, of course, that had nothing to do with it. That was all nonsense and rubbish. But, in spite of herself, Beryl saw so plainly two people standing in the middle of her room. Her arms were round his neck; he held her. And now he whispered, 'My beauty, my little beauty!' She jumped off her bed, ran over to the window and kneeled on the window-seat, with her elbows on the sill. But the beautiful night, the garden, every bush, every leaf, even the white palings, even the stars, were conspirators too. So bright was the moon that the flowers were bright as by day; the shadow of the nasturtiums, exquisite lily-like leaves and wide-open flowers, lay across the silvery veranda. The manuka tree, bent by the southerly winds, was like a bird on one leg stretching out a wing.

But when Beryl looked at the bush, it seemed to her the bush was sad.

'We are dumb trees, reaching up in the night, imploring we know not what,' said the sorrowful bush.

It is true when you are by yourself and you think about life, it is always sad. All that excitement and so on has a way of suddenly leaving you, and it's as though, in the silence, somebody called your name, and you heard your name for the first time. 'Beryl!'

'Yes, I'm here. I'm Beryl. Who wants me?'

'Beryl!'

'Let me come.'

It is lonely living by oneself. Of course, there are relations, friends, heaps of them; but that's not what she means. She wants some one who will find the Beryl they none of them know, who will expect her to be that Beryl always. She wants a lover.

'Take me away from all these other people, my love. Let us go far away. Let us live our life, all new, all ours, from the very beginning. Let us make our fire. Let us sit down to eat together. Let us have long talks at night.'

And the thought was almost, 'Save me, my love. Save me!'

. . . 'Oh, go on! Don't be a prude, my dear. You enjoy yourself while you're young. That's my advice.' And a high rush of silly laughter joined Mrs Harry Kember's loud, indifferent neigh.

You see, it's so frightfully difficult when you've nobody. You're so at the mercy of things. You can't just be rude. And you've always this horror of seeming inexperienced and stuffy like the other ninnies at the Bay. And—and it's fascinating to know you've power over people. Yes, that is fascinating. . . .

Oh why, oh why doesn't 'he' come soon?

If I go on living here, thought Beryl, anything may happen to me.

'But how do you know he is coming at all?' mocked a small voice within her.

But Beryl dismissed it. She couldn't be left. Other people, perhaps, but not she. It wasn't possible to think that Beryl Fairfield never married, that lovely fascinating girl.

'Do you remember Beryl Fairfield?'

'Remember her! As if I could forget her! It was one summer at the Bay that I saw her. She was standing on the beach in a blue'—no, pink—'muslin frock, holding on a big cream'—no, black—'straw hat. But it's years ago now.'

'She's as lovely as ever, more so if anything.'

Beryl smiled, bit her lip, and gazed over the garden. As she gazed, she saw somebody, a man, leave the road, step along the paddock beside their palings as if he was coming straight towards her. Her heart beat. Who was it? Who could it be? It couldn't be a burglar, certainly not a burglar, for he was smoking and he strolled lightly. Beryl's heart leapt; it seemed to turn right over, and then to stop. She recognized him.

'Good evening, Miss Beryl,' said the voice softly.

'Good evening.'

'Won't you come for a little walk?' it drawled.

Come for a walk—at that time of night! 'I couldn't. Everybody's in bed. Everybody's asleep.'

'Oh,' said the voice lightly, and a whiff of sweet smoke reached her. 'What does everybody matter? Do come! It's such a fine night. There's not a soul about.'

Beryl shook her head. But already something stirred in her, something reared its head.

The voice said, 'Frightened?' It mocked, 'Poor little girl!'

'Not in the least,' said she. As she spoke that weak thing within her seemed to uncoil, to grow suddenly tremendously strong; she longed to go!

And just as if this was quite understood by the other, the voice said, gently and softly, but finally, 'Come along!'

Beryl stepped over her low window, crossed the veranda, ran down the grass to the gate. He was there before her.

'That's right,' breathed the voice, and it teased, 'You're not frightened, are you? You're not frightened?'

She was; now she was here she was terrified, and it seemed to her everything was different. The moonlight stared and glittered; the shadows were like bars of iron. Her hand was taken.

'Not in the least,' she said lightly. 'Why should I be?'

Her hand was pulled gently, tugged. She held back.

'No, I'm not coming any farther,' said Beryl.

'Oh, rot!' Harry Kember didn't believe her. 'Come along! We'll just go as far as that fuchsia bush. Come along!'

The fuchsia bush was tall. It fell over the fence in a shower. There was a little pit of darkness beneath.

'No, really, I don't want to,' said Beryl.

For a moment Harry Kember didn't answer. Then he came close to her, turned to her, smiled and said quickly, 'Don't be silly! Don't be silly!'

His smile was something she'd never seen before. Was he drunk? That bright, blind, terrifying smile froze her with horror. What was she doing? How had she got here? The stern garden asked her as the gate pushed open, and quick as a cat Harry Kember came through and snatched her to him.

'Cold little devil! Cold little devil!' said the hateful voice.

But Beryl was strong. She slipped, ducked, wrenched free.

'You are vile, vile,' said she.

'Then why in God's name did you come?' stammered Harry Kember.

Nobody answered him.

XIII

A cloud, small, serene, floated across the moon. In that moment of darkness the sea sounded deep, troubled. Then the cloud sailed away, and the sound of the sea was a vague murmur, as though it waked out of a dark dream. All was still.*

THE VOYAGE

The Picton boat* was due to leave at half-past eleven. It was a beautiful night, mild, starry, only when they got out of the cab and started to walk down the Old Wharf that jutted out into the harbour, a faint wind blowing off the water ruffled under Fenella's hat, and she put up her hand to keep it on. It was dark on the Old Wharf, very dark; the wool sheds, the cattle trucks, the cranes standing up so high, the little squat railway engine, all seemed carved out of solid darkness. Here and there on a rounded wood-pile, that was like the stalk of a huge black mushroom, there hung a lantern, but it seemed afraid to unfurl its timid, quivering light in all that blackness; it burned softly, as if for itself.

Fenella's father pushed on with quick, nervous strides. Beside him her grandma bustled along in her crackling black ulster;* they went so fast that she had now and again to give an undignified little skip to keep up with them. As well as her luggage strapped into a neat sausage, Fenella carried clasped to her her grandma's umbrella, and the handle, which was a swan's head, kept giving her shoulder a sharp little peck as if it too wanted her to hurry. . . . Men, their caps pulled down, their collars turned up, swung by; a few women all muffled scurried along; and one tiny boy, only his little black arms and legs showing out of a white woolly shawl, was jerked along angrily between his father and mother; he looked like a baby fly that had fallen into the cream.

Then suddenly, so suddenly that Fenella and her grandma both leapt, there sounded from behind the largest wool shed, that had a trail of smoke hanging over it, *Mia-oo-oo-O-O!*

'First whistle,' said her father briefly, and at that moment they came in sight of the Picton boat. Lying beside the dark wharf, all strung, all beaded with round golden lights, the Picton boat looked as if she was more ready to sail among stars than out into the cold sea. People pressed along the gangway. First went her grandma, then her father, then Fenella. There was a high step down on to the deck, and an old sailor in a jersey standing by gave her his dry, hard hand. They were there; they stepped out of the way of the hurrying people, and standing under a little iron stairway that led to the upper deck they began to say good-bye.

'There, mother, there's your luggage!' said Fenella's father, giving grandma another strapped-up sausage.

'Thank you, Frank.'

'And you've got your cabin tickets safe?'

'Yes, dear.'

'And your other tickets?'

Grandma felt for them inside her glove and showed him the tips. 'That's right.'

He sounded stern, but Fenella, eagerly watching him, saw that he looked tired and sad. *Mia-oo-oo-O-O!* The second whistle blared just above their heads, and a voice like a cry shouted, 'Any more for the gangway?'

'You'll give my love to father,' Fenella saw her father's lips say. And her grandma, very agitated, answered. 'Of course I will, dear. Go now. You'll be left. Go now, Frank. Go now.'

'It's all right, mother. I've got another three minutes.' To her surprise Fenella saw her father take off his hat. He clasped grandma in his arms and pressed her to him. 'God bless you, mother!' she heard him say.

And grandma put her hand, with the black thread glove that was worn through on her ring finger, against his cheek, and she sobbed, 'God bless you, my own brave son!'

This was so awful that Fenella quickly turned her back on them, swallowed once, twice, and frowned terribly at a little green star on a mast head. But she had to turn round again; her father was going.

'Good-bye, Fenella. Be a good girl.' His cold, wet moustache brushed her cheek. But Fenella caught hold of the lapels of his coat.

'How long am I going to stay?' she whispered anxiously. He wouldn't look at her. He shook her off gently, and gently said, 'We'll see about that. Here! Where's your hand?' He pressed something into her palm. 'Here's a shilling in case you should need it.'

A shilling! She must be going away for ever! 'Father!' cried Fenella. But he was gone. He was the last off the ship. The sailors put their shoulders to the gangway. A huge coil of dark rope went flying through the air and fell 'thump' on the wharf. A bell rang; a whistle shrilled. Silently the dark wharf began to slip, to slide, to edge away from them. Now there was a rush of water between.

Fenella strained to see with all her might. 'Was that father turning round?'—or waving?—or standing alone?—or walking off by him-self? The strip of water grew broader, darker. Now the Picton boat began to swing round steady, pointing out to sea. It was no good looking any longer. There was nothing to be seen but a few lights, the face of the town clock hanging in the air, and more lights, little patches of them, on the dark hills.

The freshening wind tugged at Fenella's skirts; she went back to her grandma. To her relief grandma seemed no longer sad. She had put the two sausages of luggage one on top of the other, and she was sitting on them, her hands folded, her head a little on one side. There was an intent, bright look on her face. Then Fenella saw that her lips were moving and guessed that she was praying. But the old woman gave her a bright nod as if to say the prayer was nearly over. She unclasped her hands, sighed, clasped them again, bent forward, and at last gave herself a soft shake.

'And now, child,' she said fingering the bow of her bonnet-strings, 'I think we ought to see about our cabins. Keep close to me, and mind you don't slip.'

'Yes, grandma!'

'And be careful the umbrellas aren't caught in the stair rail. I saw a beautiful umbrella broken in half like that on my way over.'

'Yes, grandma.'

Dark figures of men lounged against the rails. In the glow of their pipes a nose shone out, or the peak of a cap, or a pair of surprised-looking eyebrows. Fenella glanced up. High in the air, a little figure, his hands thrust in his short jacket pockets, stood staring out to sea. The ship rocked ever so little, and she thought the stars rocked too. And now a pale steward in a linen coat, holding a tray high in the palm of his hand, stepped out of a lighted doorway and skimmed past them. They went through that doorway. Carefully over the high brass-bound step on to the rubber mat and then down such a terribly steep flight of stairs that grandma had to put both feet on each step, and Fenella clutched the clammy brass rail and forgot all about the swan-necked umbrella.

At the bottom grandma stopped; Fenella was rather afraid she was going to pray again. But no, it was only to get out the cabin tickets. They were in the saloon. It was glaring bright and stifling; the air smelled of paint and burnt chop-bones and indiarubber. Fenella

wished her grandma would go on, but the old woman was not to be
hurried. An immense basket of ham sandwiches caught her eye. She
went up to them and touched the top one delicately with her finger.

'How much are the sandwiches?' she asked.

'Tuppence!' bawled a rude steward, slamming down a knife and
fork.

Grandma could hardly believe it.

'Twopence *each*?' she asked.

'That's right,' said the steward, and he winked at his companion.

Grandma made a small, astonished face. Then she whispered
primly to Fenella. 'What wickedness!' And they sailed out at the
further door and along a passage that had cabins on either side. Such
a very nice stewardess came to meet them. She was dressed all in
blue, and her collar and cuffs were fastened with large brass buttons.
She seemed to know grandma well.

'Well, Mrs Crane,' said she, unlocking their washstand. 'We've got
you back again. It's not often you give yourself a cabin.'

'No,' said grandma. 'But this time my dear son's
thoughtfulness—'

'I hope—' began the stewardess. Then she turned round and took
a long mournful look at grandma's blackness and at Fenella's black
coat and skirt, black blouse, and hat with a crêpe* rose.

Grandma nodded. 'It was God's will,' said she.

The stewardess shut her lips and, taking a deep breath, she
seemed to expand.

'What I always say is,' she said, as though it was her own discovery, 'sooner or later each of us has to go, and that's a certingty.'
She paused. 'Now, can I bring you anything, Mrs Crane? A cup of
tea? I know it's no good offering you a little something* to keep the
cold out.'

Grandma shook her head. 'Nothing, thank you. We've got a few
wine biscuits, and Fenella has a very nice banana.'

'Then I'll give you a look later on,' said the stewardess, and she
went out, shutting the door.

What a very small cabin it was! It was like being shut up in a box
with grandma. The dark round eye above the washstand gleamed at
them dully. Fenella felt shy. She stood against the door, still clasping
her luggage and the umbrella. Were they going to get undressed in
here? Already her grandma had taken off her bonnet, and, rolling up

the strings, she fixed each with a pin to the lining before she hung the bonnet up. Her white hair shone like silk; the little bun at the back was covered with a black net. Fenella hardly ever saw her grandma with her head uncovered; she looked strange.

'I shall put on the woollen fascinator* your dear mother crocheted for me,' said grandma, and, unstrapping the sausage, she took it out and wound it round her head; the fringe of grey bobbles danced at her eyebrows as she smiled tenderly and mournfully at Fenella. Then she undid her bodice, and something under that, and something else underneath that. Then there seemed a short, sharp tussle, and grandma flushed faintly. Snip! Snap! She had undone her stays. She breathed a sigh of relief, and sitting on the plush* couch, she slowly and carefully pulled off her elastic-sided boots and stood them side by side.

By the time Fenella had taken off her coat and skirt and put on her flannel dressing-gown grandma was quite ready.

'Must I take off my boots, grandma? They're lace.'*

Grandma gave them a moment's deep consideration. 'You'd feel a great deal more comfortable if you did, child,' said she. She kissed Fenella. 'Don't forget to say your prayers. Our dear Lord is with us when we are at sea even more than when we are on dry land. And because I am an experienced traveller,' said grandma briskly, 'I shall take the upper berth.'

'But, grandma, however will you get up there?'

Three little spider-like steps were all Fenella saw. The old woman gave a small silent laugh before she mounted them nimbly, and she peered over the high bunk at the astonished Fenella.

'You didn't think your grandma could do that, did you?' said she. And as she sank back Fenella heard her light laugh again.

The hard square of brown soap would not lather, and the water in the bottle was like a kind of blue jelly. How hard it was, too, to turn down those stiff sheets; you simply had to tear your way in. If everything had been different, Fenella might have got the giggles. . . . At last she was inside, and while she lay there panting, there sounded from above a long, soft whispering, as though some one was gently, gently rustling among tissue paper to find something. It was grandma saying her prayers. . . .

A long time passed. Then the stewardess came in; she trod softly and leaned her hand on grandma's bunk.

'We're just entering the Straits,'* she said.

'Oh!'

'It's a fine night, but we're rather empty. We may pitch a little.'

And indeed at that moment the Picton boat rose and rose and hung in the air just long enough to give a shiver before she swung down again, and there was the sound of heavy water slapping against her sides. Fenella remembered she had left that swan-necked umbrella standing up on the little couch. If it fell over, would it break? But grandma remembered too, at the same time.

'I wonder if you'd mind, stewardess, laying down my umbrella,' she whispered.

'Not at all, Mrs Crane.' And the stewardess, coming back to grandma breathed, 'Your little granddaughter's in such a beautiful sleep.'

'God be praised for that!' said grandma.

'Poor little motherless mite!' said the stewardess. And grandma was still telling the stewardess all about what happened when Fenella fell asleep.

But she hadn't been asleep long enough to dream before she woke up again to see something waving in the air above her head. What was it? What could it be? It was a small grey foot. Now another joined it. They seemed to be feeling about for something; there came a sigh.

'I'm awake, grandma,' said Fenella.

'Oh, dear, am I near the ladder?' asked grandma. 'I thought it was this end.'

'No, grandma, it's the other. I'll put your foot on it. Are we there?' asked Fenella.

'In the harbour,' said grandma. 'We must get up, child. You'd better have a biscuit to steady yourself before you move.'

But Fenella had hopped out of her bunk. The lamp was still burning, but night was over, and it was cold. Peering through that round eye, she could see far off some rocks. Now they were scattered over with foam; now a gull flipped by; and now there came a long piece of real land.

'It's land, grandma,' said Fenella, wonderingly, as though they had been at sea for weeks together. She hugged herself; she stood on one leg and rubbed it with the toes of the other foot; she was trembling. Oh, it had all been so sad lately. Was it going to change? But all her grandma said was, 'Make haste, child. I should leave your nice banana for the stewardess as you haven't eaten it.' And Fenella put on her black clothes again, and a button sprang off one of her gloves and rolled to where she couldn't reach it. They went up on deck.

But if it had been cold in the cabin, on deck it was like ice. The sun was not up yet, but the stars were dim, and the cold pale sky was the same colour as the cold pale sea. On the land a white mist rose and fell. Now they could see quite plainly dark bush. Even the shapes of the umbrella ferns showed, and those strange silvery withered trees* that are like skeletons. . . . Now they could see the landing-stage and some little houses, pale too, clustered together, like shells on the lid of a box.* The other passengers tramped up and down, but more slowly than they had the night before, and they looked gloomy.

And now the landing-stage came out to meet them. Slowly it swam towards the Picton boat, and a man holding a coil of rope, and a cart with a small drooping horse and another man sitting on the step, came too.

'It's Mr Penreddy, Fenella, come for us,' said grandma. She sounded pleased. Her white waxen cheeks were blue with cold, her chin trembled, and she had to keep wiping her eyes and her little pink nose.

'You've got my—'

'Yes, grandma.' Fenella showed it to her.

The rope came flying through the air, and 'smack' it fell on to the deck. The gangway was lowered. Again Fenella followed her grandma on to the wharf over to the little cart, and a moment later they were bowling away. The hooves of the little horse drummed over the wooden piles, then sank softly into the sandy road. Not a soul was to be seen; there was not even a feather of smoke. The mist rose and fell, and the sea still sounded asleep as slowly it turned on the beach.

'I seen Mr Crane yestiddy,' said Mr Penreddy. 'He looked himself then. Missus knocked him up a batch of scones last week.'

And now the little horse pulled up before one of the shell-like houses. They got down. Fenella put her hand on the gate, and the big, trembling dew-drops soaked through her glove-tips. Up a little path of round white pebbles they went, with drenched sleeping flowers on either side. Grandma's delicate white picotees were so heavy with dew that they were fallen, but their sweet smell was part of the cold morning. The blinds were down in the little house; they mounted the steps on to the verandah. A pair of old bluchers* was on one side of the door, and a large red watering-can on the other.

'Tut! tut! Your grandpa,' said grandma. She turned the handle. Not a sound. She called, 'Walter!' And immediately a deep voice that sounded half stifled called back, 'Is that you, Mary?'

'Wait, dear,' said grandma. 'Go in there.' She pushed Fenella gently into a small dusky sitting-room.

On the table a white cat, that had been folded up like a camel, rose, stretched itself, yawned, and then sprang on to the tips of its toes. Fenella buried one cold little hand in the white, warm fur, and smiled timidly while she stroked and listened to grandma's gentle voice and the rolling tones of grandpa.

A door creaked. 'Come in, dear.' The old woman beckoned, Fenella followed. There, lying to one side of an immense bed, lay grandpa. Just his head with a white tuft, and his rosy face and long silver beard showed over the quilt. He was like a very old wide-awake bird.

'Well, my girl!' said grandpa. 'Give us a kiss!' Fenella kissed him. 'Ugh!' said grandpa. 'Her little nose is as cold as a button. What's that she's holding? Her grandma's umbrella?'

Fenella smiled again, and crooked the swan neck over the bed-rail. Above the bed there was a big text in a deep-black frame:——

> *Lost! One Golden Hour*
> *Set with Sixty Diamond Minutes.*
> No *Reward Is Offered*
> *For It is* GONE FOR EVER!

'Yer grandma painted that,' said grandpa. And he ruffled his white tuft and looked at Fenella so merrily she almost thought he winked at her.

A MARRIED MAN'S STORY

It is evening. Supper is over. We have left the small, cold dining room; we have come back to the sitting room where there is a fire. All is as usual. I am sitting at my writing table which is placed across a corner so that I am behind it, as it were, and facing the room. The lamp with the green shade is alight; I have before me two large books of reference, both open, a pile of papers. . . . All the paraphernalia, in fact, of an extremely occupied man. My wife, with our little boy on her lap, is in a low chair before the fire. She is about to put him to bed before she clears away the dishes and piles them up in the kitchen for the servant girl to-morrow morning. But the warmth, the quiet, and the sleepy baby, have made her dreamy. One of his red woollen boots is off; one is on. She sits, bent forward, clasping the little bare foot, staring into the glow, and as the fire quickens, falls, flares again, her shadow—an immense *Mother and Child**—is here and gone again upon the wall. . . .

Outside it is raining. I like to think of that cold drenched window behind the blind, and beyond, the dark bushes in the garden, their broad leaves bright with rain, and beyond the fence, the gleaming road with the two hoarse little gutters singing against each other, and the wavering reflections of the lamps, like fishes' tails. . . . While I am here, I am there, lifting my face to the dim sky, and it seems to me it must be raining all over the world—that the whole earth is drenched, is sounding with a soft quick patter or hard steady drumming, or gurgling and something that is like sobbing and laughing mingled together, and that light playful splashing that is of water falling into still lakes and flowing rivers. And all at one and the same moment I am arriving in a strange city, slipping under the hood of the cab while the driver whips the cover* off the breathing horse, running from shelter to shelter, dodging someone, swerving by someone else. I am conscious of tall houses, their doors and shutters sealed against the night, of dripping balconies and sodden flower pots, I am brushing through deserted gardens and peering into moist smelling summer-houses (you know how soft and almost crumbling the wood of a summer-house is in the rain), I am standing on the dark quayside, giving my ticket into the wet red hand of the old sailor in an oilskin—How strong the sea smells! How loudly those tied-up boats knock against one another! I am crossing the wet stackyard, hooded in an old sack, carrying a lantern, while the house-dog, like a soaking doormat, springs, shakes himself over me. And now I am walking along a deserted road—it is impossible to miss the puddles and the trees are stirring—stirring. . . .

But one could go on with such a catalogue for ever—on and on—until one lifted the single arum lily leaf* and discovered the tiny snails clinging, until one counted . . . and what then? Aren't those just the signs, the traces of my feeling? The bright green streaks made by someone who walks over the dewy grass? Not the feeling itself. And as I think that, a mournful glorious voice begins to sing in my bosom. Yes, perhaps that is nearer what I mean. What a voice! What power! What velvety softness! Marvellous!

Suddenly my wife turns round quickly. She knows—how long has she known?—that I am not 'working'! It is strange that with her full, open gaze, she should smile so timidly—and that she should say in such a hesitating voice: 'What are you thinking?'

I smile and draw two fingers across my forehead in the way I have. 'Nothing,' I answer softly.

At that she stirs, and still trying not to make it sound important, she says: 'Oh, but you must have been thinking of something!'

Then I really meet her gaze, meet it fully, and I fancy her face quivers. Will she never grow accustomed to these simple—one might say—everyday little lies? Will she never learn not to expose herself—or to build up defences?

'Truly, I was thinking of nothing!'

There! I seem to see it dart at her. She turns away, pulls the other red sock off the baby—sits him up, and begins to unbutton him behind. I wonder if that little soft rolling bundle sees anything, feels anything? Now she turns him over on her knee, and in this light, his soft arms and legs waving, he is extraordinarily like a young crab. A queer thing is I can't connect him with my wife and myself; I've never accepted him as ours. Each time when I come into the hall and see the perambulator, I catch myself thinking: 'H'm, someone has brought a baby.' Or, when his crying wakes me at night, I feel inclined to blame my wife for having brought the baby in from outside. The truth is, that though one might suspect her of strong maternal feelings, my wife doesn't seem to me the type of woman who bears children in her own body. There's an immense difference! Where is that . . . animal ease and playfulness, that quick kissing and cuddling one has been taught to expect of young mothers? She hasn't a sign of it. I believe that when she ties its bonnet she feels like an aunt and not a mother. But of course I may be wrong; she may be passionately devoted. . . . I don't think so. At any rate, isn't it a trifle indecent to feel like this about one's own wife? Indecent or not, one has these feelings. And one other thing. How can I reasonably expect my wife, *a broken-hearted woman*, to spend her time tossing the baby? But that is beside the mark. She never even began to toss when her heart was whole.

And now she has carried the baby to bed. I hear her soft deliberate steps moving between the dining room and the kitchen, there and back again, to the tune of the clattering dishes. And now all is quiet. What is happening now? Oh, I know just as surely as if I'd gone to see—she is standing in the middle of the kitchen, facing the rainy window. Her head is bent, with one finger she is tracing something— nothing—on the table. It is cold in the kitchen; the gas jumps; the tap drips; it's a forlorn picture. And nobody is going to come behind her, to take her in his arms, to kiss her soft hair, to lead her to the fire and to rub [her] hands warm again. Nobody is going to call her or to wonder what she is doing out there. And she knows it. And yet, being a woman, deep down, deep down, she really does expect the miracle to happen; she really could embrace that dark, dark deceit, rather than live—like this.

To live like this. . . . I write those words, very carefully, very beauti- fully. For some reason I feel inclined to sign them, or to write underneath—Trying a New Pen. But seriously, isn't it staggering to think what may be contained in one innocent-looking little phrase? It tempts me—it tempts me terribly. Scene. The supper-table. My wife has just handed me my tea. I stir it, lift the spoon, idly chase and then carefully capture a speck of tea-leaf, and having brought it ashore, I murmur, quite gently, 'How long shall we continue to live—like— this?' And immediately there is that famous 'blinding flash and deaf- ening roar. Huge pieces of débris (I must say I like débris) are flung into the air . . . and when the dark clouds of smoke have drifted away. . . . ' But this will never happen; I shall never know it. It will be found upon me 'intact' as they say. 'Open my heart and you will see. . . . '

Why? Ah, there you have me! There is the most difficult question
of all to answer. Why do people stay together? Putting aside 'for the
sake of the children', and 'the habit of years' and 'economic reasons'
as lawyers' nonsense—it's not much more—if one really does try to
find out why it is that people don't leave each other, one discovers a
mystery. It is because they can't; they are bound. And nobody on
earth knows what are the bands that bind them except those two. Am
I being obscure? Well, the thing itself isn't so frightfully crystal clear,
is it? Let me put it like this. Supposing you are taken, absolutely, first
into his confidence and then into hers. Supposing you know all there
is to know about the situation. And having given it not only your
deepest sympathy but your most honest impartial criticism, you
declare, very calmly (but not without the slightest suggestion of
relish—for there is—I swear there is—in the very best of us—
something that leaps up and cries 'A-ahh!' for joy at the thought of
destroying), 'Well, my opinion is that you two people ought to part.
You'll do no earthly good together. Indeed, it seems to me, it's the
duty of either to set the other free.' What happens then? He—and
she—agree. It is their conviction too. You are only saying what they
have been thinking all last night. And away they go to act on your
advice, immediately. . . . And the next time you hear of them they are
still together. You see—you've reckoned without the unknown
quantity—which is their secret relation to each other—and that they
can't disclose even if they want to. Thus far you may tell and no
further. Oh, don't misunderstand me! It need not necessarily have
anything to do with their sleeping together. . . . But this brings me to
a thought I've often half entertained. Which is, that human beings,
as we know them, don't choose each other at all. It is the owner, the
second self inhabiting them, who makes the choice for his own particular purposes, and—this may sound absurdly far-fetched—it's
the second self in the other which responds. Dimly—dimly—or so it
has seemed to me—we realise this, at any rate to the extent that we
realise the hopelessness of trying to escape. So that, what it all
amounts to is—if the impermanent selves of my wife and me are
happy—*tant mieux pour nous**—if miserable—*tant pis.** . . . But I
don't know, I don't know. And it may be that it's something entirely
individual in me—this sensation (yes, it is even a sensation) of how
extraordinarily *shell-like* we are as we are—little creatures, peering
out of the sentry-box at the gate, ogling through our glass case at the

entry, wan little servants, who never can say for certain, even, if the master is out or in. . . .

The door opens. . . . My wife. She says: 'I am going to bed.'

And I look up vaguely, and vaguely say: 'You are going to bed.'

'Yes.' A tiny pause. 'Don't forget—will you?—to turn out the gas in the hall.'

And again I repeat: 'The gas in the hall.'

There was a time—the time before—when this habit of mine (it really has become a habit now—it wasn't one then) was one of our sweetest jokes together. It began, of course, when, on several occasions, I really was deeply engaged and I didn't hear. I emerged only to see her shaking her head and laughing at me, 'You haven't heard a word!'

'No. What did you say?'

Why should she think that so funny and charming? She did; it delighted her. 'Oh, my darling, it's so like you! It's so—so—.' And I knew she loved me for it—knew she positively looked forward to coming in and disturbing me, and so—as one does—I played up. I was guaranteed to be wrapped away every evening at 10.30 p.m. But now? For some reason I feel it would be crude to stop my performance. It's simplest to play on. But what is she waiting for to-night? Why doesn't she go? Why prolong this? She is going. No, her hand on the door-knob, she turns round again, and she says in the most curious, small, breathless voice, 'You're not cold?'

Oh, it's not fair to be as pathetic as that! That was simply damnable. I shudder all over before I manage to bring out a slow 'No-o,' while my left hand ruffles the reference pages.

She is gone; she will not come back again to-night. It is not only I who recognise that; the room changes, too. It relaxes, like an old actor. Slowly the mask is rubbed off; the look of strained attention changes to an air of heavy, sullen brooding. Every line, every fold breathes fatigue. The mirror is quenched; the ash whitens; only my shy lamp burns on. . . . But what a cynical indifference to me it all shows! Or should I perhaps be flattered? No, we understand each other. You know those stories of little children* who are suckled by wolves and accepted by the tribe, and how for ever after they move freely among their fleet grey brothers? Something like that has happened to me. But wait—that about the wolves won't do. Curious!

Before I wrote it down, while it was still in my head, I was delighted
with it. It seemed to express, and more, to suggest, just what I
wanted to say. But written, I can smell the falseness immediately and
the . . . source of the smell is in that word fleet. Don't you agree?
Fleet, grey brothers! 'Fleet.' A word I never use. When I wrote
'wolves' it skimmed across my mind like a shadow and I couldn't
resist it. Tell me! Tell me! Why it is so difficult to write simply—and
not only simply but *sotto voce*,* if you know what I mean? That is how
I long to write. No fine effects—no bravuras.* But just the plain
truth, as only a liar can tell it.

I light a cigarette, lean back, inhale deeply—and find myself wondering if my wife is asleep. Or is she lying in her cold bed, staring into
the dark with those trustful, bewildered eyes? Her eyes are like the
eyes of a cow that is being driven along a road. 'Why am I being
driven—what harm have I done?' But I really am not responsible for
that look; it's her natural expression. One day, when she was turning
out a cupboard, she found a little old photograph of herself, taken
when she was a girl at school. In her confirmation dress,* she
explained. And there were the eyes, even then. I remember saying to
her: 'Did you always look so sad?' Leaning over my shoulder, she
laughed lightly. 'Do I look sad? I think it's just . . . me.' And she
waited for me to say something about it. But I was marvelling at her
courage at having shown it to me at all. It was a hideous photograph!
And I wondered again if she realised how plain she was, and comforted herself with the idea that people who loved each other didn't
criticise but accepted everything, or if she really rather liked her
appearance and expected me to say something complimentary. Oh,
that was base of me! How could I have forgotten all the countless
times when I have known her turn away, avoid the light, press her
face into my shoulders. And above all, how could I have forgotten the
afternoon of our wedding day, when we sat on the green bench in the
Botanical Gardens* and listened to the band, how, in an interval
between two pieces, she suddenly turned to me and said in the voice
in which one says: 'Do you think the grass is damp?' or 'Do you
think it's time for tea?' . . . 'Tell me—do you think physical beauty is
so very important?' I don't like to think how often she had rehearsed
that question. And do you know what I answered? At that moment,
as if at my command, there came a great gush of hard bright sound

from the band. And I managed to shout above it—cheerfully—'I didn't hear what you said.' Devilish! Wasn't it? Perhaps not wholly. She looked like the poor patient who hears the surgeon say, 'It will certainly be necessary to perform the operation—but not now!'

But all this conveys the impression that my wife and I were never really happy together. Not true! Not true! We were marvellously, radiantly happy. We were a model couple. If you had seen us together, any time, any place, if you had followed us, tracked us down, spied, taken us off our guard, you still would have been forced to confess, 'I have never seen a more ideally suited pair.' Until last autumn.

But really to explain what happened then I should have to go back and back, I should have to dwindle until my tiny hands clutched the bannisters, the stair-rail was higher than my head, and I peered through to watch my father padding softly up and down. There were coloured windows on the landings. As he came up, first his bald head was scarlet; then it was yellow. How frightened I was! And when they put me to bed, it was to dream that we were living inside one of my father's big coloured bottles. For he was a chemist. I was born nine years after my parents were married; I was an only child, and the effort to produce even me—small, withered bud I must have been— sapped all my mother's strength. She never left her room again. Bed, sofa, window, she moved between the three. Well I can see her, on the window days, sitting, her cheek in her hand, staring out. Her room looked over the street. Opposite there was a wall plastered with advertisement for travelling shows and circuses and so on. I stand beside her, and we gaze at the slim lady in a red dress hitting a dark gentleman over the head with her parasol, or at the tiger peering through the jungle while the clown, close by, balances a bottle on his nose, or at a little golden-haired girl sitting on the knee of an old black man in a broad cotton hat. . . . She says nothing. On sofa days there is a flannel dressing-gown that I loathe, and a cushion that keeps on slipping off the hard sofa. I pick it up. It has flowers and writing sewn on. I ask what the writing says, and she whispers, 'Sweet Repose!' In bed her fingers plait, in tight little plaits, the fringe of the quilt, and her lips are thin. And that is all there is of my mother, except the last queer 'episode' that comes later. . . .

My father—curled up in the corner on the lid of a round box that held sponges, I stared at my father so long it's as though his image, cut off at the waist by the counter, has remained solid in my memory. Perfectly bald, polished head, shaped like a thin egg, creased creamy cheeks, little bags under the eyes, large pale ears like handles. His manner was discreet, sly, faintly amused and tinged with impudence. Long before I could appreciate it I knew the mixture. . . . I even used to copy him in my corner, bending forward, with a small reproduction of his faint sneer. In the evening his customers were, chiefly, young women; some of them came in every day for his famous five-penny pick-me-up. Their gaudy looks, their voices, their free ways, fascinated me. I longed to be my father, handing them across the counter the little glass of bluish stuff they tossed off so greedily. God knows what it was made of. Years after I drank some, just to see what it tasted like, and I felt as though someone had given me a terrific blow on the head; I felt stunned. One of those evenings I remember vividly. It was cold; it must have been autumn, for the flaring gas was lighted after my tea. I sat in my corner and my father was mixing something; the shop was empty. Suddenly the bell jangled and a young woman rushed in, crying so loud, sobbing so hard, that it didn't sound real. She wore a green cape trimmed with fur and a hat with cherries dangling. My father came from behind the screen. But she couldn't stop herself at first. She stood in the middle of the shop and wrung her hands, and moaned. I've never heard such crying since. Presently she managed to gasp out, 'Give me a pick-me-up.' Then she drew a long breath, trembled away from him and qua-vered: 'I've had *bad news*!' And in the flaring gaslight I saw the whole side of her face was puffed up and purple; her lip was cut, and her eyelid looked as though it was gummed fast over the wet eye. My father pushed the glass across the counter, and she took her purse out of her stocking and paid him. But she couldn't drink; clutching the glass, she stared in front of her as if she could not believe what she saw. Each time she put her head back the tears spurted out again. Finally she put the glass down. It was no use. Holding the cape with one hand, she ran in the same way out of the shop again. My father gave no sign. But long after she had gone I crouched in my corner, and when I think back it's as though I felt my whole body vibrating—'So that's what it is outside,' I thought. 'That's what it's like out there.'

*

Do you remember your childhood? I am always coming across these marvellous accounts by writers who declare that they remember 'everything, everything'. I certainly don't. The dark stretches, the blanks, are much bigger than the bright glimpses. I seem to have spent most of my time like a plant in a cupboard. Now and again, when the sun shone, a careless hand thrust me out on to the window-sill, and a careless hand whipped me in again—and that was all. But what happened in the darkness—I wonder? Did one grow? Pale stem . . . timid leaves . . . white, reluctant bud. No wonder I was hated at school. Even the masters shrank from me. I somehow knew that my soft hesitating voice disgusted them. I knew, too, how they turned away from my shocked, staring eyes. I was small and thin, and I smelled of the shop; my nickname was Gregory Powder.* School was a tin building stuck on the raw hillside. There were dark red streaks like blood in the oozing clay banks of the playground. I hide in the dark passage, where the coats hang, and am discovered there by one of the masters. 'What are you doing there in the dark?' His terrible voice kills me; I die before his eyes. I am standing in a ring of thrust-out heads; some are grinning, some look greedy, some are spitting. And it is always cold. Big crushed up clouds press across the sky; the rusty water in the school tank is frozen; the bell sounds numb. One day they put a dead bird in my overcoat pocket. I found it just when I reached home. Oh, what a strange flutter there was at my heart, when I drew out that terribly soft, cold little body, with the legs thin as pins and the claws wrung. I sat on the back door step in the yard and put the bird in my cap. The feathers round the neck looked wet and there was a tiny tuft just above the closed eyes that stood up too. How tightly the beak was shut; I could not see the mark where it was divided. I stretched out one wing and touched the soft, secret down underneath; I tried to make the claws curl round my little finger. But I didn't feel sorry for it—no! I wondered. The smoke from our kitchen chimney poured downwards, and flakes of soot floated—soft, light in the air. Through a big crack in the cement yard a poor-looking plant with dull reddish flowers had pushed its way. I looked at the dead bird again. . . . And that is the first time that I remember singing, rather . . . listening to a silent voice inside a little cage that was me.

*

But what has all this to do with my married happiness? How can all this affect my wife and me? Why—to tell what happened last autumn—do I run all this way back into the Past? The Past—what is the Past? I might say the star-shaped flake of soot on a leaf of the poor-looking plant, and the bird lying on the quilted lining of my cap, and my father's pestle* and my mother's cushion, belong to it. But that is not to say they are any less mine than they were when I looked upon them with my very eyes, and touched them with these fingers. No, they are more; they are a living part of me. Who am I, in fact, as I sit here at this table, but my own past? If I deny that, I am nothing. And if I were to try and divide my life into childhood, youth, early manhood and so on, it would be a kind of affectation; I should know I was doing it just because of the pleasantly important sensation it gives one to rule lines, and to use green ink for child-hood, red for the next stage, and purple for the period of ado-lescence. For, one thing I have learnt, one thing I do believe is, Nothing Happens Suddenly. Yes, that is my religion, I suppose. . . .

My mother's death, for instance. Is it more distant from me to-day than it was then? It is just as close, as strange, as puzzling, and in spite of all the countless times I have recalled the circumstances, I know no more now than I did then whether I dreamed them or whether they really occurred. It happened when I was thirteen and I slept in a little strip of a room on what was called the Half Landing. One night I woke up with a start to see my mother, in her nightgown, without even the hated flannel dressing-gown, sitting on my bed. But the strange thing which frightened me was, she wasn't looking at me. Her head was bent; the short thin tail of hair lay between her shoulders; her hands were pressed between her knees, and my bed shook; she was shivering. It was the first time I had ever seen her out of her own room. I said, or I think I said, 'Is that you, mother?' And as she turned round I saw in the moonlight how queer she looked. Her face looked small—quite different. She looked like one of the boys at the school baths, who sits on a step, shivering just like that, and wants to go in and yet is frightened.

'Are you awake?' she said. Her eyes opened; I think she smiled. She leaned towards me. 'I've been poisoned,' she whispered. 'Your father's poisoned me.' And she nodded. Then, before I could say a word, she was gone, and I thought I heard the door shut. I sat quite still; I couldn't move. I think I expected something else to happen.

For a long time I listened for something; there wasn't a sound. The candle was by my bed, but I was too frightened to stretch out my hand for the matches. But even while I wondered what I ought to do, even while my heart thumped—everything became confused. I lay down and pulled the blankets round me. I fell asleep, and the next morning my mother was found dead of failure of the heart.

Did that visit happen? Was it a dream? Why did she come to tell me? Or why, if she came, did she go away so quickly? And her expression—so joyous under the frightened look—was that real? I believed it fully the afternoon of the funeral, when I saw my father dressed up for his part, hat and all. That tall hat so gleaming black and round was like a cork covered with black sealing-wax, and the rest of my father was awfully like a bottle, with his face for the label—*Deadly Poison*. It flashed into my mind as I stood opposite him in the hall. And Deadly Poison, or old D.P., was my private name for him from that day.

Late, it grows late. I love the night. I love to feel the tide of darkness rising slowly and slowly washing, turning over and over, lifting, floating, all that lies strewn upon the dark beach, all that lies hid in rocky hollows. I love, I love this strange feeling of drifting—whither? After my mother's death I hated to go to bed. I used to sit on the window-sill, folded up, and watch the sky. It seemed to me the moon moved much faster than the sun. And one big, bright green star I chose for my own. My star! But I never thought of it beckoning to me or twinkling merrily for my sake. Cruel, indifferent, splendid—it burned in the airy night. No matter—it was mine! But growing close up against the window there was a creeper with small, bunched up pink and purple flowers. These did know me. These, when I touched them at night, welcomed my fingers; the little tendrils, so weak, so delicate, knew I would not hurt them. When the wind moved the leaves I felt I understood their shaking. When I came to the window, it seemed to me the flowers said among themselves, 'The boy is here.'

As the months passed, there was often a light in my father's room below. And I heard voices and laughter. 'He's got some woman with him,' I thought. But it meant nothing to me. Then the gay voice, the sound of the laughter, gave me the idea it was one of the girls who used to come to the shop in the evenings—and gradually I began to

imagine which girl it was. It was the dark one in the red coat and
skirt, who once had given me a penny. A merry face stooped over
me—warm breath tickled my neck—there were little beads of black*
on her long lashes, and when she opened her arms to kiss me, there
came a marvellous wave of scent! Yes, that was the one. Time passed,
and I forgot the moon and my green star and my shy creeper—I
came to the window to wait for the light in my father's window, to
listen for the laughing voice, until one night I dozed and I dreamed
she came again—again she drew me to her, something soft, scented,
warm and merry hung over me like a cloud. But when I tried to
see, her eyes only mocked me, her red lips opened and she hissed,
'Little sneak! Little sneak!' But not as if she were angry, as if she
understood, and her smile somehow was like a rat . . . hateful!

The night after, I lighted the candle and sat down at the table
instead. By and by, as the flame steadied, there was a small lake of
liquid wax, surrounded by a white, smooth wall. I took a pin and
made little holes in this wall and then sealed them up faster than the
wax could escape. After a time I fancied the candle flame joined in
the game; it leapt up, quivered, wagged; it even seemed to laugh. But
while I played with the candle and smiled and broke off the tiny
white peaks of wax that rose above the wall and floated them on my
lake, a feeling of awful dreariness fastened on me—yes, that is the
word. It crept up from my knees to my thighs, into my arms; I ached
all over with misery. And I felt so strangely that I couldn't move.
Something bound me there by the table—I couldn't even let the pin
drop that I held between my finger and thumb. For a moment I came
to a stop, as it were.

Then the shrivelled case of the bud split and fell, the plant in the
cupboard came into flower. 'Who am I?' I thought. 'What is all this?'
And I looked at my room, at the broken bust of the man called
Hahnemann* on top of the cupboard, at my little bed with the pillow
like an envelope. I saw it all, but not as I had seen before. . . . Everything lived, but everything. But that was not all. I was equally alive
and—it's the only way I can express it—the barriers were down
between us—I had come into my own world!

The barriers were down. I had been all my life a little outcast; but
until that moment no one had 'accepted' me; I had lain in the
cupboard—or the cave forlorn. But now—I was taken, I was

accepted, claimed. I did not consciously turn away from the world of human beings; I had never known it; but I from that night did beyond words consciously turn towards my silent brothers. . . .

THE GARDEN PARTY

And after all the weather was ideal. They could not have had a more perfect day for a garden party if they had ordered it. Windless, warm, the sky without a cloud. Only the blue was veiled with a haze of light gold, as it is sometimes in early summer. The gardener had been up since dawn, mowing the lawns and sweeping them, until the grass and the dark flat rosettes where the daisy plants had been seemed to shine. As for the roses, you could not help feeling they understood that roses are the only flowers that impress people at garden parties; the only flowers that everybody is certain of knowing. Hundreds, yes, literally hundreds, had come out in a single night; the green bushes bowed down as though they had been visited by archangels.

Breakfast was not yet over before the men came to put up the marquee.

'Where do you want the marquee put, mother?'

'My dear child, it's no use asking me. I'm determined to leave everything to you children this year. Forget I am your mother. Treat me as an honoured guest.'

But Meg could not possibly go and supervise the men. She had washed her hair before breakfast, and she sat drinking her coffee in a green turban, with a dark wet curl stamped on each cheek. Jose,* the butterfly, always came down in a silk petticoat and a kimono jacket.

'You'll have to go, Laura, you're the artistic one.'

Away Laura flew, still holding her piece of bread-and-butter. It's so delicious to have an excuse for eating out of doors, and besides, she loved having to arrange things; she always felt she could do it so much better than anybody else.

Four men in their shirt-sleeves stood grouped together on the garden path. They carried staves covered with rolls of canvas, and they had big tool-bags slung on their backs. They looked impressive. Laura wished now that she was not holding that piece of bread-and-butter, but there was nowhere to put it, and she couldn't possibly throw it away. She blushed and tried to look severe and even a little bit short-sighted as she came up to them.

'Good morning,' she said, copying her mother's voice. But that sounded so fearfully affected that she was ashamed, and stammered like a little girl, 'Oh—er—have you come—is it about the marquee?'

'That's right, miss,' said the tallest of the men, a lanky, freckled fellow, and he shifted his tool-bag, knocked back his straw hat and smiled down at her. 'That's about it.'

His smile was so easy, so friendly, that Laura recovered. What nice eyes he had, small, but such a dark blue! And now she looked at the others, they were smiling too. 'Cheer up, we won't bite,' their smile seemed to say. How very nice workmen were! And what a beautiful morning! She mustn't mention the morning; she must be business-like. The marquee.

'Well, what about the lily-lawn? Would that do?'

And she pointed to the lily-lawn with the hand that didn't hold the bread-and-butter. They turned, they stared in the direction. A little fat chap thrust out his under-lip, and the tall fellow frowned.

'I don't fancy it,' said he. 'Not conspicuous enough. You see, with a thing like a marquee,' and he turned to Laura in his easy way, 'you want to put it somewhere where it'll give you a bang slap in the eye, if you follow me.'

Laura's upbringing made her wonder for a moment whether it was quite respectful of a workman to talk to her of bangs slap in the eye. But she did quite follow him.

'A corner of the tennis-court,' she suggested. 'But the band's going to be in one corner.'

'H'm, going to have a band, are you?' said another of the workmen. He was pale. He had a haggard look as his dark eyes scanned the tennis-court. What was he thinking?

'Only a very small band,' said Laura gently. Perhaps he wouldn't mind so much if the band was quite small. But the tall fellow interrupted.

'Look here, miss, that's the place. Against those trees. Over there. That'll do fine.'

Against the karakas.* Then the karaka-trees would be hidden. And they were so lovely, with their broad, gleaming leaves, and their clusters of yellow fruit. They were like trees you imagined growing on a desert island, proud, solitary, lifting their leaves and fruits to the sun in a kind of silent splendour. Must they be hidden by a marquee?

They must. Already the men had shouldered their staves and were making for the place. Only the tall fellow was left. He bent down, pinched a sprig of lavender, put his thumb and forefinger to his nose and snuffed up the smell. When Laura saw the gesture she forgot all about the karakas in her wonder at him caring for things like that— caring for the smell of lavender. How many men that she knew would have done such a thing. Oh, how extraordinarily nice workmen were, she thought. Why couldn't she have workmen for friends rather than the silly boys she danced with and who came to Sunday night supper? She would get on much better with men like these.

It's all the fault, she decided, as the tall fellow drew something on the back of an envelope, something that was to be looped up or left to hang, of these absurd class distinctions. Well, for her part, she didn't feel them. Not a bit, not an atom. . . . And now there came the chock-chock of wooden hammers. Some one whistled, some one sang out, 'Are you right there, matey?' 'Matey!' The friendliness of it, the—the—Just to prove how happy she was, just to show the tall fellow how at home she felt, and how she despised stupid conven- tions, Laura took a big bite of her bread-and-butter as she stared at the little drawing. She felt just like a work-girl.

'Laura, Laura, where are you? Telephone, Laura!' a voice cried from the house.

'Coming!' Away she skimmed, over the lawn, up the path, up the steps, across the veranda, and into the porch. In the hall her father and Laurie were brushing their hats ready to go to the office.

'I say, Laura,' said Laurie very fast, 'you might just give a squiz* at my coat before this afternoon. See if it wants pressing.'

'I will,' said she. Suddenly she couldn't stop herself. She ran at Laurie and gave him a small, quick squeeze. 'Oh, I do love parties, don't you?' gasped Laura.

'Ra-ther,' said Laurie's warm, boyish voice, and he squeezed his sister too, and gave her a gentle push. 'Dash off to the telephone, old girl.'

The telephone. 'Yes, yes; oh yes. Kitty? Good morning, dear. Come to lunch? Do, dear. Delighted of course. It will only be a very scratch meal—just the sandwich crusts and broken meringue-shells and what's left over. Yes, isn't a perfect morning? Your white? Oh, I certainly should. One moment—hold the line. Mother's calling.' And Laura sat back. 'What, mother? Can't hear.'

Mrs Sheridan's voice floated down the stairs. 'Tell her to wear that sweet hat she had on last Sunday.'

'Mother says you're to wear that *sweet* hat you had on last Sunday. Good. One o'clock. Bye-bye.'

Laura put back the receiver, flung her arms over her head, took a deep breath, stretched and let them fall. 'Huh,' she sighed, and the moment after the sigh she sat up quickly. She was still, listening. All the doors in the house seemed to be open. The house was alive with soft, quick steps and running voices. The green baize* door that led to the kitchen regions swung open and shut with a muffled thud. And now there came a long, chuckling absurd sound. It was the heavy piano being moved on its stiff castors. But the air! If you stopped to notice, was the air always like this? Little faint winds were playing chase in at the tops of the windows, out at the doors. And there were two tiny spots of sun, one on the inkpot, one on a silver photograph frame, playing too. Darling little spots. Especially the one on the inkpot lid. It was quite warm. A warm little silver star. She could have kissed it.

The front door bell pealed, and there sounded the rustle of Sadie's print skirt on the stairs. A man's voice murmured; Sadie answered, careless, 'I'm sure I don't know. Wait. I'll ask Mrs Sheridan.'

'What is it, Sadie?' Laura came into the hall.

'It's the florist, Miss Laura.'

It was, indeed. There, just inside the door, stood a wide, shallow tray full of pots of pink lilies. No other kind. Nothing but lilies— canna lilies,* big pink flowers, wide open, radiant, almost frighten- ingly alive on bright crimson stems.

'O-oh, Sadie!' said Laura, and the sound was like a little moan. She crouched down as if to warm herself at that blaze of lilies; she felt they were in her fingers, on her lips, growing in her breast.

'It's some mistake,' she said faintly. 'Nobody ever ordered so many. Sadie, go and find mother.'

But at that moment Mrs Sheridan joined them.

'It's quite right,' she said calmly. 'Yes, I ordered them. Aren't they lovely?' She pressed Laura's arm. 'I was passing the shop yesterday, and I saw them in the window. And I suddenly thought for once in my life I shall have enough canna lilies. The garden party will be a good excuse.'

'But I thought you said you didn't mean to interfere,' said Laura. Sadie had gone. The florist's man was still outside at his van. She put her arm round her mother's neck and gently, very gently, she bit her mother's ear.

'My darling child, you wouldn't like a logical mother, would you? Don't do that. Here's the man.'

He carried more lilies still, another whole tray.

'Bank them up, just inside the door, on both sides of the porch, please,' said Mrs Sheridan. 'Don't you agree, Laura?'

'Oh, I *do*, mother.'

In the drawing-room Meg, Jose and good little Hans had at last succeeded in moving the piano.

'Now, if we put this chesterfield* against the wall and move everything out of the room except the chairs, don't you think?'

'Quite.'

'Hans, move these tables into the smoking-room, and bring a sweeper to take these marks off the carpet and—one moment, Hans—' Jose loved giving orders to the servants, and they loved obeying her. She always made them feel they were taking part in some drama. 'Tell mother and Miss Laura to come here at once.'

'Very good, Miss Jose.'

She turned to Meg. 'I want to hear what the piano sounds like, just in case I'm asked to sing this afternoon. Let's try over "This Life is Weary".'

Pom! Ta-ta-ta *Tee*-ta! The piano burst out so passionately that Jose's face changed. She clasped her hands. She looked mournfully and enigmatically at her mother and Laura as they came in.

> This Life is *Wee*-ary,
> A Tear—a Sigh.
> A Love that *Chan*-ges,
> This Life is *Wee*-ary,
> A Tear—a Sigh.
> A Love that *Chan*-ges,
> And then . . . Good-bye!

But at the word 'Good-bye', and although the piano sounded more desperate than ever, her face broke into a brilliant, dreadfully unsympathetic smile.

'Aren't I in good voice, mummy?' she beamed.

> This Life is *Wee*-ary,
> Hope comes to Die.
> A Dream—a *Wa*-kening.

But now Sadie interrupted them. 'What is it, Sadie?'

'If you please, m'm, cook says have you got the flags* for the sandwiches?'

'The flags for the sandwiches, Sadie?' echoed Mrs Sheridan dreamily. And the children knew by her face that she hadn't got them. 'Let me see.' And she said to Sadie firmly, 'Tell cook I'll let her have them in ten minutes.'

Sadie went.

'Now, Laura,' said her mother quickly, 'come with me into the smoking-room. I've got the names somewhere on the back of an envelope. You'll have to write them out for me. Meg, go upstairs this minute and take that wet thing off your head. Jose, run and finish dressing this instant. Do you hear me, children, or shall I have to tell your father when he comes home to-night? And—and, Jose, pacify cook if you do go into the kitchen, will you? I'm terrified of her this morning.'

The envelope was found at last behind the dining-room clock, though how it had got there Mrs Sheridan could not imagine.

'One of you children must have stolen it out of my bag, because I remember vividly—cream-cheese and lemon-curd. Have you done that?'

'Yes.'

'Egg and—' Mrs Sheridan held the envelope away from her. 'It looks like mice. It can't be mice, can it?'

'Olive, pet,' said Laura, looking over her shoulder.

'Yes, of course, olive. What a horrible combination it sounds. Egg and olive.'

They were finished at last, and Laura took them off to the kitchen. She found Jose there pacifying the cook, who did not look at all terrifying.

'I have never seen such exquisite sandwiches,' said Jose's rapturous voice. 'How many kinds did you say there were, cook? Fifteen?'

'Fifteen, Miss Jose.'

'Well, cook, I congratulate you.'

Cook swept up crusts with the long sandwich knife, and smiled broadly.

'Godber's has come,' announced Sadie, issuing out of the pantry. She had seen the man pass the window.

That meant the cream puffs had come. Godber's were famous

for their cream puffs. Nobody ever thought of making them at home.

'Bring them in and put them on the table, my girl,' ordered cook.

Sadie brought them in and went back to the door. Of course Laura and Jose were far too grown-up to really care about such things. All the same, they couldn't help agreeing that the puffs looked very attractive. Very. Cook began arranging them, shaking off the extra icing sugar.

'Don't they carry one back to all one's parties?' said Laura.

'I suppose they do,' said practical Jose, who never liked to be carried back. 'They look beautifully light and feathery, I must say.'

'Have one each, my dears,' said cook in her comfortable voice. 'Yer ma won't know.'

Oh, impossible. Fancy cream puffs so soon after breakfast. The very idea made one shudder. All the same, two minutes later Jose and Laura were licking their fingers with that absorbed inward look that only comes from whipped cream.

'Let's go into the garden, out by the back way,' suggested Laura. 'I want to see how the men are getting on with the marquee. They're such awfully nice men.'

But the back door was blocked by cook, Sadie, Godber's man and Hans.

Something had happened.

'Tuk-tuk-tuk,' clucked cook like an agitated hen. Sadie had her hand clapped to her cheek as though she had toothache. Hans's face was screwed up in the effort to understand. Only Godber's man seemed to be enjoying himself; it was his story.

'What's the matter? What's happened?'

'There's been a horrible accident,' said cook. 'A man killed.'

'A man killed! Where? How? When?'

But Godber's man wasn't going to have his story snatched from under his very nose.

'Know those little cottages just below here, miss?' Know them? Of course, she knew them. 'Well, there's a young chap living there, name of Scott, a carter. His horse shied at a traction-engine,* corner of Hawke Street this morning, and he was thrown out on the back of his head. Killed.'

'Dead!' Laura stared at Godber's man.

'Dead when they picked him up,' said Godber's man with relish. 'They were taking the body home as I come up here.' And he said to the cook, 'He's left a wife and five little ones.'

'Jose, come here.' Laura caught hold of her sister's sleeve and dragged her through the kitchen to the other side of the green baize door. There she paused and leaned against it. 'Jose!' she said, horrified, 'however are we going to stop everything?'

'Stop everything, Laura!' cried Jose in astonishment. 'What do you mean?'

'Stop the garden party, of course.' Why did Jose pretend?

But Jose was still more amazed. 'Stop the garden party? My dear Laura, don't be so absurd. Of course we can't do anything of the kind. Nobody expects us to. Don't be so extravagant.'

'But we can't possibly have a garden party with a man dead just outside the front gate.'

That really was extravagant, for the little cottages were in a lane to themselves at the very bottom of a steep rise that led up to the house. A broad road ran between. True, they were far too near. They were the greatest possible eyesore, and they had no right to be in that neighbourhood at all. They were little mean dwellings painted a chocolate brown. In the garden patches there was nothing but cabbage stalks, sick hens and tomato cans. The very smoke coming out of their chimneys was poverty-stricken. Little rags and shreds of smoke, so unlike the great silvery plumes that uncurled from the Sheridans' chimneys. Washerwomen lived in the lane and sweeps and a cobbler, and a man whose house-front was studded all over with minute bird-cages. Children swarmed. When the Sheridans were little they were forbidden to set foot there because of the revolting language and of what they might catch. But since they were grown up, Laura and Laurie on their prowls sometimes walked through. It was disgusting and sordid. They came out with a shudder. But still one must go everywhere; one must see everything. So through they went.

'And just think of what the band would sound like to that poor woman,' said Laura.

'Oh, Laura!' Jose began to be seriously annoyed. 'If you're going to stop a band playing every time some one has an accident, you'll lead a very strenuous life. I'm every bit as sorry about it as you. I feel just as sympathetic.' Her eyes hardened. She looked at her sister just as she used to when they were little and fighting together. 'You won't bring a drunken workman back to life by being sentimental,' she said softly.

'Drunk! Who said he was drunk?' Laura turned furiously on Jose. She said just as they had used to say on those occasions, 'I'm going straight up to tell mother.'

'Do, dear,' cooed Jose.

'Mother, can I come into your room?' Laura turned the big glass door-knob.

'Of course, child. Why, what's the matter? What's given you such a colour?' And Mrs Sheridan turned round from her dressing-table. She was trying on a new hat.

'Mother, a man's been killed,' began Laura.

'*Not* in the garden?' interrupted her mother.

'No, no!'

'Oh, what a fright you gave me!' Mrs Sheridan sighed with relief, and took off the big hat and held it on her knees.

'But listen, mother,' said Laura. Breathless, half-choking, she told the dreadful story. 'Of course, we can't have our party, can we?' she pleaded. 'The band and everybody arriving. They'd hear us, mother; they're nearly neighbours!'

To Laura's astonishment her mother behaved just like Jose; it was harder to bear because she seemed amused. She refused to take Laura seriously.

'But, my dear child, use your common sense. It's only by accident we've heard of it. If some one had died there normally—and I can't understand how they keep alive in those poky little holes—we should still be having our party, shouldn't we?'

Laura had to say 'yes' to that, but she felt it was all wrong. She sat down on her mother's sofa and pinched the cushion frill.

'Mother, isn't it really terribly heartless of us?' she asked.

'Darling!' Mrs Sheridan got up and came over to her, carrying the hat. Before Laura could stop her she had popped it on. 'My child!' said her mother, 'the hat is yours. It's made for you. It's much too young for me. I have never seen you look such a picture. Look at yourself!' And she held up her hand-mirror.

'But, mother,' Laura began again. She couldn't look at herself; she turned aside.

This time Mrs Sheridan lost patience just as Jose had done.

'You are being very absurd, Laura,' she said coldly. 'People like that don't expect sacrifices from us. And it's not very sympathetic to spoil everybody's enjoyment as you're doing now.'

'I don't understand,' said Laura, and she walked quickly out of the room into her own bedroom. There, quite by chance, the first thing she saw was this charming girl in the mirror, in her black hat trimmed with gold daisies, and a long black velvet ribbon. Never had she imagined she could look like that. Is mother right? she thought. And now she hoped her mother was right. Am I being extravagant? Perhaps it was extravagant. Just for a moment she had another glimpse of that poor woman and those little children, and the body being carried into the house. But it all seemed blurred, unreal, like a picture in the newspaper. I'll remember it again after the party's over, she decided. And somehow that seemed quite the best plan. . . .

Lunch was over by half-past one. By half-past two they were all ready for the fray. The green-coated band had arrived and was established in a corner of the tennis-court.

'My dear!' trilled Kitty Maitland, 'aren't they too like frogs for words? You ought to have arranged them round the pond with the conductor in the middle on a leaf.'

Laurie arrived and hailed them on his way to dress. At the sight of him Laura remembered the accident again. She wanted to tell him. If Laurie agreed with the others, then it was bound to be all right. And she followed him into the hall.

'Laurie!'

'Hallo!' He was half-way upstairs, but when he turned round and saw Laura he suddenly puffed out his cheeks and goggled his eyes at her. 'My word, Laura! You do look stunning,' said Laurie. 'What an absolutely topping hat!'

Laura said faintly 'Is it?' and smiled up at Laurie, and didn't tell him after all.

Soon after that people began coming in streams. The band struck up; the hired waiters ran from the house to the marquee. Wherever you looked there were couples strolling, bending to the flowers, greeting, moving on over the lawn. They were like bright birds that had alighted in the Sheridans' garden for this one afternoon, on their way to—where? Ah, what happiness it is to be with people who all are happy, to press hands, press cheeks, smile into eyes.

'Darling Laura, how well you look!'

'What a becoming hat, child!'

'Laura, you look quite Spanish. I've never seen you look so striking.'

And Laura, glowing, answered softly, 'Have you had tea? Won't you have an ice? The passion-fruit ices really are rather special.' She ran to her father and begged him. 'Daddy darling, can't the band have something to drink?'

And the perfect afternoon slowly ripened, slowly faded, slowly its petals closed.

'Never a more delightful garden party. . . .' 'The greatest success. . . . ' 'Quite the most. . . .'

Laura helped her mother with the good-byes. They stood side by side in the porch till it was all over.

'All over, all over, thank heaven,' said Mrs Sheridan. 'Round up the others, Laura. Let's go and have some fresh coffee. I'm exhausted. Yes, it's been very successful. But oh, these parties, these parties! Why will you children insist on giving parties!' And they all of them sat down in the deserted marquee.

'Have a sandwich, daddy dear. I wrote the flag.'

'Thanks.' Mr Sheridan took a bite and the sandwich was gone. He took another. 'I suppose you didn't hear of a beastly accident that happened to-day?' he said.

'My dear,' said Mrs Sheridan, holding up her hand, 'we did. It nearly ruined the party. Laura insisted we should put it off.'

'Oh, mother!' Laura didn't want to be teased about it.

'It was a horrible affair all the same,' said Mr Sheridan. 'The chap was married too. Lived just below in the lane, and leaves a wife and half a dozen kiddies, so they say.'

An awkward little silence fell. Mrs Sheridan fidgeted with her cup. Really, it was very tactless of father. . . .

Suddenly she looked up. There on the table were all those sandwiches, cakes, puffs, all un-eaten, all going to be wasted. She had one of her brilliant ideas.

'I know,' she said. 'Let's make up a basket. Let's send that poor creature some of this perfectly good food. At any rate, it will be the greatest treat for the children. Don't you agree? And she's sure to have neighbours calling in and so on. What a point to have it all ready prepared. Laura!' She jumped up. 'Get me the big basket out of the stairs cupboard.'

'But, mother, do you really think it's a good idea?' said Laura.

Again, how curious, she seemed to be different from them all. To take scraps from their party. Would the poor woman really like that?

'Of course! What's the matter with you to-day? An hour or two ago you were insisting on us being sympathetic, and now—'

Oh well! Laura ran for the basket. It was filled, it was heaped by her mother.

'Take it yourself, darling,' said she. 'Run down just as you are. No, wait, take the arum lilies too. People of that class are so impressed by arum lilies.'

'The stems will ruin her lace frock,' said practical Jose.

So they would. Just in time. 'Only the basket, then. And, Laura!'—her mother followed her out of the marquee—'don't on any account—'

'What mother?'

No, better not put such ideas into the child's head! 'Nothing! Run along.'

It was just growing dusky as Laura shut their garden gates. A big dog ran by like a shadow. The road gleamed white, and down below in the hollow the little cottages were in deep shade. How quiet it seemed after the afternoon. Here she was going down the hill to somewhere where a man lay dead, and she couldn't realize it. Why couldn't she? She stopped a minute. And it seemed to her that kisses, voices, tinkling spoons, laughter, the smell of crushed grass were somehow inside her. She had no room for anything else. How strange! She looked up at the pale sky, and all she thought was, 'Yes, it was the most successful party.'

Now the broad road was crossed. The lane began, smoky and dark. Women in shawls and men's tweed caps hurried by. Men hung over the palings; the children played in the doorways. A low hum came from the mean little cottages. In some of them there was a flicker of light, and a shadow, crab-like, moved across the window. Laura bent her head and hurried on. She wished now she had put on a coat. How her frock shone! And the big hat with the velvet streamer—if only it was another hat! Were the people looking at her? They must be. It was a mistake to have come; she knew all along it was a mistake. Should she go back even now?

No, too late. This was the house. It must be. A dark knot of people stood outside. Beside the gate an old, old woman with a crutch sat in a chair, watching. She had her feet on a newspaper. The voices stopped as Laura drew near. The group parted. It was as though she was expected, as though they had known she was coming here.

Laura was terribly nervous. Tossing the velvet ribbon over her shoulder, she said to a woman standing by, 'Is this Mrs Scott's house?' and the woman, smiling queerly, said, 'It is, my lass.'

Oh, to be away from this! She actually said, 'Help me, God,' as she walked up the tiny path and knocked. To be away from those staring eyes, or to be covered up in anything, one of those women's shawls even. I'll just leave the basket and go, she decided. I shan't even wait for it to be emptied.

Then the door opened. A little woman in black showed in the gloom.

Laura said, 'Are you Mrs Scott?' But to her horror the woman answered, 'Walk in, please, miss,' and she was shut in the passage.

'No,' said Laura, 'I don't want to come in. I only want to leave this basket. Mother sent—'

The little woman in the gloomy passage seemed not to have heard her. 'Step this way, please, miss,' she said in an oily voice, and Laura followed her.

She found herself in a wretched little low kitchen, lighted by a smoky lamp. There was a woman sitting before the fire.

'Em,' said the little creature who had let her in. 'Em! It's a young lady.' She turned to Laura. She said meaningly, 'I'm 'er sister, miss. You'll excuse 'er, won't you?'

'Oh, but of course!' said Laura. 'Please, please don't disturb her. I—I only want to leave—'

But at that moment the woman at the fire turned round. Her face, puffed up, red, with swollen eyes and swollen lips, looked terrible. She seemed as though she couldn't understand why Laura was there. What did it mean? Why was this stranger standing in the kitchen with a basket? What was it all about? And the poor face puckered up again.

'All right, my dear,' said the other. 'I'll thenk the young lady.'

And again she began, 'You'll excuse her, miss, I'm sure,' and her face, swollen too, tried an oily smile.

Laura only wanted to get out, to get away. She was back in the passage. The door opened. She walked straight through into the bedroom where the dead man was lying.

'You'd like a look at 'im, wouldn't you?' said Em's sister, and she brushed past Laura over to the bed. 'Don't be afraid, my lass,'—and now her voice sounded fond and sly, and fondly she drew down the sheet—''e looks a picture. There's nothing to show. Come along, my dear.'

Laura came.

There lay a young man, fast asleep—sleeping so soundly, so deeply, that he was far, far away from them both. Oh, so remote, so peaceful. He was dreaming. Never wake him up again. His head was sunk in the pillow, his eyes were closed; they were blind under the closed eyelids. He was given up to his dream. What did garden parties and baskets and lace frocks matter to him? He was far from all those things. He was wonderful, beautiful. While they were laughing and while the band was playing, this marvel had come to the lane. Happy . . . happy. . . . All is well, said that sleeping face. This is just as it should be. I am content.

But all the same you had to cry, and she couldn't go out of the room without saying something to him. Laura gave a loud childish sob.

'Forgive my hat,' she said.

And this time she didn't wait for Em's sister. She found her way out of the door, down the path, past all those dark people. At the corner of the lane she met Laurie.

He stepped out of the shadow. 'Is that you, Laura?'

'Yes.'

'Mother was getting anxious. Was it all right?'

'Yes, quite. Oh, Laurie!' She took his arm, she pressed up against him.

'I say, you're not crying, are you?' asked her brother.

Laura shook her head. She was.

Laurie put his arm round her shoulder. 'Don't cry,' he said in his warm, loving voice. 'Was it awful?'

'No,' sobbed Laura. 'It was simply marvellous. But, Laurie—' She stopped, she looked at her brother. 'Isn't life,' she stammered, 'isn't life—' But what life was she couldn't explain. No matter. He quite understood.

'*Isn't* it, darling?' said Laurie.

THE DOLL'S HOUSE

When dear old Mrs Hay went back to town after staying with the Burnells she sent the children a doll's house. It was so big that the carter and Pat* carried it into the courtyard, and there it stayed, propped up on two wooden boxes beside the feed-room door. No harm could come to it; it was summer. And perhaps the smell of paint would have gone off by the time it had to be taken in. For, really, the smell of paint coming from that doll's house ('Sweet of old Mrs Hay, of course; most sweet and generous!')—but the smell of paint was quite enough to make anyone seriously ill, in Aunt Beryl's opinion. Even before the sacking was taken off. And when it was. . . .

There stood the doll's house, a dark, oily, spinach green, picked out with bright yellow. Its two solid little chimneys, glued on to the roof, were painted red and white, and the door, gleaming with yellow varnish, was like a little slab of toffee. Four windows, real windows, were divided into panes by a broad streak of green. There was actually a tiny porch, too, painted yellow, with big lumps of congealed paint hanging along the edge.

But perfect, perfect little house! Who could possibly mind the smell? It was part of the joy, part of the newness.

'Open it quickly, someone!'

The hook at the side was stuck fast. Pat prised it open with his penknife, and the whole house-front swung back, and—there you were, gazing at one and the same moment into the drawing-room and dining-room, the kitchen and two bedrooms. That is the way for a house to open! Why don't all houses open like that? How much more exciting than peering through the slit of a door into a mean little hall with a hatstand and two umbrellas! That is—isn't it?—what you long to know about a house when you put your hand on the knocker. Perhaps it is the way God opens houses at dead of night when He is taking a quiet turn* with an angel. . . .

'O-oh!' The Burnell children sounded as though they were in despair. It was too marvellous; it was too much for them. They had never seen anything like it in their lives. All the rooms were papered. There were pictures on the walls, painted on the paper, with gold frames complete. Red carpet covered all the floors except the kitchen; red plush chairs in the drawing-room, green in the dining-room; tables, beds with real bedclothes, a cradle, a stove, a dresser with tiny plates and one big jug. But what Kezia liked more than anything, what she liked frightfully, was the lamp. It stood in the middle of the dining-room table, an exquisite little amber lamp with a white globe. It was even filled all ready for lighting, though of course you couldn't light it. But there was something inside that looked like oil* and that moved when you shook it.

The father and mother dolls, who sprawled very stiff as though they had fainted in the drawing-room, and their two little children asleep upstairs, were really too big for the doll's house. They didn't look as though they belonged. But the lamp was perfect. It seemed to smile at Kezia, to say, 'I live here.' The lamp was real.

The Burnell children could hardly walk to school fast enough the next morning. They burned to tell everybody, to describe, too—well—to boast about their doll's house before the school-bell rang.

'I'm to tell,' said Isabel, 'because I'm the eldest. And you two can join in after. But I'm to tell first.'

There was nothing to answer. Isabel was bossy, but she was always right, and Lottie and Kezia knew too well the powers that went with being eldest. They brushed through the thick buttercups at the road edge and said nothing.

'And I'm to choose who's to come and see it first. Mother said I might.'

For it had been arranged that while the doll's house stood in the courtyard they might ask the girls at school, two at a time, to come and look. Not to stay to tea, of course, or to come traipsing through the house. But just to stand quietly in the courtyard while Isabel pointed out the beauties, and Lottie and Kezia looked pleased. . . .

But hurry as they might, by the time they had reached the tarred palings of the boys' playground the bell had begun to jangle. They only just had time to whip off their hats and fall into line before the roll was called. Never mind. Isabel tried to make up for it by looking very important and mysterious and by whispering behind her hand to the girls near her, 'Got something to tell you at playtime.'

Playtime came and Isabel was surrounded. The girls of her class nearly fought to put their arms round her, to walk away with her, to beam flatteringly, to be her special friend. She held quite a court under the huge pine trees at the side of the playground. Nudging, giggling together, the little girls pressed up close. And the only two who stayed outside the ring were the two who were always outside, the little Kelveys. They knew better than to come anywhere near the Burnells.

For the fact was, the school the Burnell children went to was not at all the kind of place their parents would have chosen if there had been any choice. But there was none. It was the only school for miles. And the consequence was all the children of the neighbourhood, the Judge's little girls, the doctor's daughters, the store-keeper's children, the milkman's, were forced to mix together. Not to speak of there being an equal number of rude, rough little boys as well. But the line had to be drawn somewhere. It was drawn at the Kelveys. Many of the children, including the Burnells, were not allowed even to speak to them. They walked past the Kelveys with their heads in the air, and as they set the fashion in all matters of behaviour, the Kelveys were shunned by everybody. Even the teacher had a special voice for them, and a special smile for the other children when Lil Kelvey came up to her desk with a bunch of dreadfully common-looking flowers.

They were the daughters of a spry, hard-working little washer-woman, who went about from house to house by the day. This was awful enough. But where was Mr Kelvey? Nobody knew for certain. But everybody said he was in prison. So they were the daughters of a washerwoman and a jailbird. Very nice company for other people's children! And they looked it. Why Mrs Kelvey made them so con-spicuous was hard to understand. The truth was they were dressed in 'bits' given to her by the people for whom she worked. Lil, for instance, who was a stout, plain child, with big freckles, came to school in a dress made from a green art-serge* table-cloth of the Burnells', with red plush sleeves from the Logans' curtains. Her hat, perched on top of her high forehead, was a grown-up woman's hat, once the property of Miss Lecky, the postmistress. It was turned up at the back and trimmed with a large scarlet quill. What a little guy she looked! It was impossible not to laugh. And her little sister, our Else, wore a long white dress, rather like a nightgown, and a pair of little boy's boots. But whatever our Else wore she would have looked strange. She was a tiny wishbone* of a child, with cropped hair and enormous solemn eyes—a little white owl. Nobody had ever seen her smile; she scarcely ever spoke. She went through life holding on to

Lil, with a piece of Lil's skirt screwed up in her hand. Where Lil went, our Else followed. In the playground, on the road going to and from school, there was Lil marching in front and our Else holding on behind. Only when she wanted anything, or when she was out of breath, our Else gave Lil a tug, a twitch, and Lil stopped and turned round. The Kelveys never failed to understand each other.

Now they hovered at the edge; you couldn't stop them listening. When the little girls turned round and sneered, Lil, as usual, gave her silly shamefaced smile, but our Else only looked.

And Isabel's voice, so very proud, went on telling. The carpet made a great sensation, but so did the beds with real bedclothes, and the stove with an oven door.

When she finished Kezia broke in. 'You've forgotten the lamp, Isabel.'

'Oh, yes,' said Isabel, 'and there's a teeny little lamp, all made of yellow glass, with a white globe that stands on the dining-room table. You couldn't tell it from a real one.'

'The lamp's best of all,' cried Kezia. She thought Isabel wasn't making half enough of the little lamp. But nobody paid any attention. Isabel was choosing the two who were to come back with them that afternoon and see it. She chose Emmie Cole and Lena Logan. But when the others knew they were all to have a chance, they couldn't be nice enough to Isabel. One by one they put their arms round Isabel's waist and walked her off. They had something to whisper to her, a secret. 'Isabel's *my* friend.'

Only the little Kelveys moved away forgotten; there was nothing more for them to hear.

Days passed, and as more children saw the doll's house, the fame of it spread. It became the one subject, the rage. The one question was, 'Have you seen Burnells' doll's house? Oh, ain't it lovely!' 'Haven't you seen it? Oh, I say!'

Even the dinner hour was given up to talking about it. The little girls sat under the pines eating their thick mutton sandwiches and big slabs of johnny cake* spread with butter. While always, as near as they could get, sat the Kelveys, our Else holding on to Lil, listening too, while they chewed their jam sandwiches out of a newspaper soaked with large red blobs. . . .

'Mother,' said Kezia, 'can't I ask the Kelveys just once?'

'Certainly not, Kezia.'

'But why not?'

'Run away, Kezia; you know quite well why not.'

At last everybody had seen it except them. On that day the subject rather flagged. It was the dinner hour. The children stood together under the pine trees, and suddenly, as they looked at the Kelveys eating out of their paper, always by themselves, always listening, they wanted to be horrid to them. Emmie Cole started the whisper.

'Lil Kelvey's going to be a servant when she grows up.'

'O-oh, how awful!' said Isabel Burnell, and she made eyes at Emmie.

Emmie swallowed in a very meaning way and nodded to Isabel as she'd seen her mother do on those occasions.

'It's true—it's true—it's true,' she said.

Then Lena Logan's little eyes snapped. 'Shall I ask her?' she whispered.

'Bet you don't,' said Jessie May.

'Pooh, I'm not frightened,' said Lena. Suddenly she gave a little squeal and danced in front of the other girls. 'Watch! Watch me! Watch me now!' said Lena. And sliding, gliding, dragging one foot, giggling behind her hand, Lena went over to the Kelveys.

Lil looked up from her dinner. She wrapped the rest quickly away. Our Else stopped chewing. What was coming now?

'Is it true you're going to be a servant when you grow up, Lil Kelvey?' shrilled Lena.

Dead silence. But instead of answering, Lil only gave her silly shamefaced smile. She didn't seem to mind the question at all. What a sell for Lena! The girls began to titter.

Lena couldn't stand that. She put her hands on her hips; she shot forward. 'Yah, yer father's in prison!' she hissed, spitefully.

This was such a marvellous thing to have said that the little girls rushed away in a body, deeply, deeply excited, wild with joy. Someone found a long rope, and they began skipping. And never did they skip so high, run in and out so fast, or do such daring things as on that morning.

In the afternoon Pat called for the Burnell children with the buggy and they drove home. There were visitors. Isabel and Lottie, who liked visitors, went upstairs to change their pinafores. But Kezia thieved out at the back. Nobody was about; she began to swing on the big white gates of the courtyard. Presently, looking along the road, she saw two little dots. They grew bigger, they were coming towards her. Now she could see that one was in front and one close behind. Now she could see that they were the Kelveys. Kezia stopped swinging. She slipped off the gate as if she was going to run away. Then she hesitated. The Kelveys came nearer, and beside them walked their shadows, very long, stretching right across the road with their heads in the buttercups. Kezia clambered back on the gate; she had made up her mind; she swung out.

'Hullo,' she said to the passing Kelveys.

They were so astounded that they stopped. Lil gave her silly smile. Our Else stared.

'You can come and see our doll's house if you want to,' said Kezia, and she dragged one toe on the ground. But at that Lil turned red and shook her head quickly.

'Why not?' asked Kezia.

Lil gasped, then she said, 'Your ma told our ma you wasn't to speak to us.'

'Oh, well,' said Kezia. She didn't know what to reply. 'It doesn't matter. You can come and see our doll's house all the same. Come on. Nobody's looking.'

But Lil shook her head still harder.

'Don't you want to?' asked Kezia.

Suddenly there was a twitch, a tug at Lil's skirt. She turned round. Our Else was looking at her with big imploring eyes; she was frowning; she wanted to go. For a moment Lil looked at our Else very doubtfully. But then our Else twitched her skirt again. She started forward. Kezia led the way. Like two little stray cats they followed across the courtyard to where the doll's house stood.

'There it is,' said Kezia.

There was a pause. Lil breathed loudly, almost snorted; our Else was still as a stone.

'I'll open it for you,' said Kezia kindly. She undid the hook and they looked inside.

'There's the drawing-room and the dining-room, and that's the—'

'Kezia!'

Oh, what a start they gave!

'Kezia!'

It was Aunt Beryl's voice. They turned round. At the back door stood Aunt Beryl, staring as if she couldn't believe what she saw.

'How dare you ask the little Kelveys into the courtyard?' said her cold, furious voice. 'You know as well as I do you're not allowed to talk to them. Run away, children, run away at once. And don't come back again,' said Aunt Beryl. And she stepped into the yard and shooed them out as if they were chickens.

'Off you go immediately' she called, cold and proud.

They did not need telling twice. Burning with shame, shrinking together, Lil huddling along like her mother, our Else dazed, somehow they crossed the big courtyard and squeezed through the white gate.

'Wicked, disobedient little girl!' said Aunt Beryl bitterly to Kezia, and she slammed the doll's house to.

The afternoon had been awful. A letter had come from Willie Brent, a terrifying, threatening letter, saying if she did not meet him that evening in Pulman's Bush, he'd come to the front door and ask the reason why! But now that she had frightened those little rats of Kelveys and given Kezia a good scolding, her heart felt lighter. That ghastly pressure was gone. She went back to the house humming.

When the Kelveys were well out of sight of Burnells', they sat down to rest on a big red drainpipe by the side of the road. Lil's cheeks were still burning; she took off the hat with the quill and held it on her knee. Dreamily they looked over the hay paddocks, past the creek,* to the group of wattles* where Logan's cows stood waiting to be milked. What were their thoughts?

Presently our Else nudged up close to her sister. By now she had forgotten the cross lady. She put out a finger and stroked her sister's quill; she smiled her rare smile.

'I seen the little lamp,' she said, softly.

Then both were silent once more.

THE FLY

'Y'are very snug in here,' piped old Mr Woodifield, and he peered out of the great, green leather armchair by his friend the boss's desk as a baby peers out of its pram. His talk was over; it was time for him to be off. But he did not want to go. Since he had retired, since his . . . stroke, the wife and the girls kept him boxed up in the house every day of the week except Tuesday. On Tuesday he was dressed and brushed and allowed to cut back to the City for the day. Though what he did there the wife and girls couldn't imagine. Made a nuisance of himself to his friends, they supposed. . . . Well, perhaps so. All the same, we cling to our last pleasures as the tree clings to its last leaves. So there sat old Woodifield, smoking a cigar and staring almost greedily at the boss, who rolled in his office chair, stout, rosy, five years older than he, and still going strong, still at the helm. It did one good to see him.

Wistfully, admiringly, the old voice added, 'It's snug in here—upon my word!'

'Yes, it's comfortable enough,' agreed the boss, and he flipped the *Financial Times* with a paper-knife. As a matter of fact he was proud of his room; he liked to have it admired, especially by old Woodifield. It gave him a feeling of deep, solid satisfaction to be planted there in the midst of it in full view of that frail old figure in the muffler.

'I've had it done up lately,' he explained, as he had explained for the past—how many?—weeks. 'New carpet,' and he pointed to the bright red carpet with a pattern of large white rings. 'New furniture,' and he nodded towards the massive bookcase and the table with legs like twisted treacle. 'Electric heating!' He waved almost exultantly towards the five transparent, pearly sausages glowing so softly in the tilted copper pan.

But he did not draw old Woodifield's attention to the photograph over the table of a grave-looking boy in uniform standing in one of those spectral photographers' parks with photographers' storm-clouds behind him. It was not new. It had been there for over six years.

'There was something I wanted to tell you,' said old Woodifield, and his eyes grew dim remembering. 'Now what was it? I had it in

my mind when I started out this morning.' His hands began to
tremble, and patches of red showed above his beard.

Poor old chap, he's on his last pins, thought the boss. And, feeling
kindly, he winked at the old man, and said jokingly, 'I tell you what.
I've got a little drop of something here that'll do you good before you
go out into the cold again. It's beautiful stuff. It wouldn't hurt a
child.' He took a key off his watch-chain, unlocked a cupboard below
his desk, and drew forth a dark, squat bottle. 'That's the medicine,'
said he. 'And the man from whom I got it told me on the strict Q.T.*
it came from the cellars at Windsor Cassel.'*

Old Woodifield's mouth fell open at the sight. He couldn't have
looked more surprised if the boss had produced a rabbit.

'It's whisky, ain't it?' he piped, feebly.

The boss turned the bottle and lovingly showed him the label.
Whisky it was.

'D'you know,' said he, peering up at the boss wonderingly, 'they
won't let me touch it at home.' And he looked as though he was
going to cry.

'Ah, that's where we know a bit more than the ladies,' cried the
boss, swooping across for two tumblers that stood on the table with
the water-bottle, and pouring a generous finger* into each. 'Drink it
down. It'll do you good. And don't put any water with it. It's sacri-
lege to tamper with stuff like this. Ah!' He tossed off his, pulled out
his handkerchief, hastily wiped his moustaches, and cocked an eye at
old Woodifield, who was rolling his in his chaps.

The old man swallowed, was silent a moment, and then said
faintly, 'It's nutty!'

But it warmed him; it crept into his chill old brain—he
remembered.

'That was it,' he said, heaving himself out of his chair. 'I thought
you'd like to know. The girls were in Belgium* last week having a look
at poor Reggie's grave, and they happened to come across your boy's.
They're quite near each other, it seems.'

Old Woodifield paused, but the boss made no reply. Only a quiver
in his eyelids showed that he heard.

'The girls were delighted with the way the place is kept,' piped the
old voice. 'Beautifully looked after. Couldn't be better if they were at
home. You've not been across, have yer?'

'No, no!' For various reasons the boss had not been across.

'There's miles of it,' quavered old Woodifield, 'and it's all as neat as a garden. Flowers growing on all the graves. Nice broad paths.' It was plain from his voice how much he liked a nice broad path.

The pause came again. Then the old man brightened wonderfully.

'D'you know what the hotel made the girls pay for a pot of jam?' he piped. 'Ten francs! Robbery, I call it. It was a little pot, so Gertrude says, no bigger than a half-crown. And she hadn't taken more than a spoonful when they charged her ten francs. Gertrude brought the pot away with her to teach 'em a lesson. Quite right, too; it's trading on our feelings. They think because we're over there having a look round we're ready to pay anything. That's what it is.' And he turned towards the door.

'Quite right, quite right!' cried the boss, though what was quite right he hadn't the least idea. He came round by his desk, followed the shuffling footsteps to the door, and saw the old fellow out. Woodifield was gone.

For a long moment the boss stayed, staring at nothing, while the grey-haired office messenger, watching him, dodged in and out of his cubby hole like a dog that expects to be taken for a run. Then: 'I'll see nobody for half an hour, Macey,' said the boss. 'Understand? Nobody at all.'

'Very good, sir.'

The door shut, the firm heavy steps recrossed the bright carpet, the fat body plumped down in the spring chair, and leaning forward, the boss covered his face with his hands. He wanted, he intended, he had arranged to weep. . . .

It had been a terrible shock to him when old Woodifield sprang that remark upon him about the boy's grave. It was exactly as though the earth had opened and he had seen the boy lying there with Woodifield's girls staring down at him. For it was strange. Although over six years had passed away, the boss never thought of the boy except as lying unchanged, unblemished in his uniform, asleep for ever. 'My son!' groaned the boss. But no tears came yet. In the past, in the first months and even years after the boy's death, he had only to say those words to be overcome by such grief that nothing short of a violent fit of weeping could relieve him. Time, he had declared then, he had told everybody, could make no difference. Other men perhaps might recover, might live their loss down, but not he. How was it possible? His boy was an only son. Ever since his birth the boss had worked at building up this business for him; it had no other meaning if it was not for the boy. Life itself had come to have no other meaning. How on earth could he have slaved, denied himself, kept going all those years without the promise for ever before him of the boy's stepping into his shoes and carrying on where he left off?

And that promise had been so near being fulfilled. The boy had been in the office learning the ropes for a year before the war. Every morning they had started off together; they had come back by the same train. And what congratulations he had received as the boy's father! No wonder; he had taken to it marvellously. As to his popularity with the staff, every man jack of them down to old Macey couldn't make enough of the boy. And he wasn't in the least spoilt. No, he was just his bright, natural self, with the right word for everybody, with that boyish look and his habit of saying, 'Simply splendid.'

But all that was over and done with as though it never had been. The day had come when Macey had handed him the telegram* that brought the whole place crashing about his head. 'Deeply regret to inform you. . . .' And he had left the office a broken man, with his life in ruins.

Six years ago, six years. . . . How quickly time passed! It might have happened yesterday. The boss took his hands from his face; he was puzzled. Something seemed to be wrong with him. He wasn't feeling as he wanted to feel. He decided to get up and have a look at the boy's photograph. But it wasn't a favourite photograph of his; the expression was unnatural. It was cold, even stern-looking. The boy had never looked like that.

At that moment the boss noticed that a fly had fallen into his broad inkpot, and was trying feebly but desperately to clamber out again. Help! help! said those struggling legs. But the sides of the inkpot were wet and slippery; it fell back again and began to swim. The boss took up a pen, picked the fly out of the ink, and shook it on to a piece of blotting-paper. For a fraction of a second it lay still on the dark patch that oozed round it. Then the front legs waved, took hold, and, pulling its small, sodden body up it began the immense task of cleaning the ink from its wings. Over and under, over and under, went a leg along a wing, as the stone goes over and under the scythe. Then there was a pause, while the fly, seeming to stand on the tips of its toes, tried to expand first one wing and then the other. It succeeded at last, and, sitting down, it began, like a minute cat, to clean its face. Now one could imagine that the little front legs rubbed against each other lightly, joyfully. The horrible danger was over; it had escaped; it was ready for life again.

But just then the boss had an idea. He plunged his pen back into the ink, leaned his thick wrist on the blotting paper, and as the fly tried its wings down came a great heavy blot. What would it make of that? What indeed! The little beggar seemed absolutely cowed, stunned, and afraid to move because of what would happen next. But then, as if painfully, it dragged itself forward. The front legs waved, caught hold, and, more slowly this time, the task began from the beginning.

He's a plucky little devil, thought the boss, and he felt a real admiration for the fly's courage. That was the way to tackle things; that was the right spirit. Never say die; it was only a question of. . . . But the fly had again finished its laborious task, and the boss had just time to refill his pen, to shake fair and square on the new-cleaned body yet another dark drop. What about it this time? A painful moment of suspense followed. But behold, the front legs were again waving; the boss felt a rush of relief. He leaned over the fly and said to it tenderly, 'You artful little b . . . .' And he actually had the brilliant notion of breathing on it to help the drying process. All the same, there was something timid and weak about its efforts now, and the boss decided that this time should be the last, as he dipped the pen deep into the inkpot.

It was. The last blot fell on the soaked blotting-paper, and the draggled fly lay in it and did not stir. The back legs were stuck to the body; the front legs were not to be seen.

'Come on,' said the boss. 'Look sharp!' And he stirred it with his pen—in vain. Nothing happened or was likely to happen. The fly was dead.

The boss lifted the corpse on the end of the paper-knife and flung it into the waste-paper basket. But such a grinding feeling of wretchedness seized him that he felt positively frightened. He started forward and pressed the bell for Macey.

'Bring me some fresh blotting-paper,' he said, sternly, 'and look sharp about it.' And while the old dog padded away he fell to wondering what it was he had been thinking about before. What was it? It was. . . . He took out his handkerchief and passed it inside his collar. For the life of him he could not remember.

A CUP OF TEA

Rosemary Fell was not exactly beautiful. No, you couldn't have called her beautiful. Pretty? Well, if you took her to pieces. . . . But why be so cruel as to take anyone to pieces? She was young, brilliant, extremely modern, exquisitely well dressed, amazingly well read in the newest of the new books, and her parties were the most delicious mixture of the really important people and . . . artists—quaint creatures, discoveries of hers, some of them too terrifying for words, but others quite presentable and amusing.

Rosemary had been married two years. She had a duck of a boy. No, not Peter—Michael. And her husband absolutely adored her. They were rich, really rich, not just comfortably well off, which is odious and stuffy and sounds like one's grandparents. But if Rosemary wanted to shop she would go to Paris as you and I would go to Bond Street. If she wanted to buy flowers, the car pulled up at that perfect shop in Regent Street, and Rosemary inside the shop just gazed in her dazzled, rather exotic way, and said: 'I want those and those and those. Give me four bunches of those. And that jar of roses. Yes, I'll have all the roses in the jar. No, no lilac. I hate lilac. It's got no shape.' The attendant bowed and put the lilac out of sight, as though this was only too true; lilac was dreadfully shapeless. 'Give me those stumpy little tulips. Those red and white ones.' And she was followed to the car by a thin shop-girl staggering under an immense white paper armful that looked like a baby in long clothes. . . .*

One winter afternoon she had been buying something in a little antique shop in Curzon Street.* It was a shop she liked. For one thing, one usually had it to oneself. And then the man who kept it was ridiculously fond of serving her. He beamed whenever she came in. He clasped his hands; he was so gratified he could scarcely speak. Flattery, of course. All the same, there was something . . .

'You see, madam,' he would explain in his low respectful tones, 'I love my things. I would rather not part with them than sell them to someone who does not appreciate them, who has not that fine feeling which is so rare. . . .' And, breathing deeply, he unrolled a tiny square of blue velvet and pressed it on the glass counter with his pale finger-tips.

Today it was a little box. He had been keeping it for her. He had shown it to nobody as yet. An exquisite little enamel box with a glaze so fine it looked as though it had been baked in cream. On the lid a minute creature stood under a flowery tree, and a more minute creature still had her arms round his neck. Her hat, really no bigger than a geranium petal, hung from a branch; it had green ribbons. And there was a pink cloud like a watchful cherub floating above their heads. Rosemary took her hands out of her long gloves. She always took off her gloves to examine such things. Yes, she liked it very much. She loved it; it was a great duck. She must have it. And, turning the creamy box, opening and shutting it, she couldn't help noticing how charming her hands were against the blue velvet. The shopman, in some dim cavern of his mind, may have dared to think so too. For he took a pencil, leant over the counter, and his pale bloodless fingers crept timidly towards those rosy, flashing ones, as he murmured gently: 'If I may venture to point out to madam, the flowers on the little lady's bodice.'

'Charming!' Rosemary admired the flowers. But what was the price? For a moment the shopman did not seem to hear. Then a murmur reached her. 'Twenty-eight guineas, madam.'

'Twenty-eight guineas.' Rosemary gave no sign. She laid the little box down; she buttoned her gloves again. Twenty-eight guineas. Even if one is rich . . . She looked vague. She stared at a plump tea-kettle like a plump hen above the shopman's head, and her voice was dreamy as she answered: 'Well, keep it for me—will you? I'll . . .'

But the shopman had already bowed as though keeping it for her was all any human being could ask. He would be willing, of course, to keep it for her for ever.

The discreet door shut with a click. She was outside on the step, gazing at the winter afternoon. Rain was falling, and with the rain it seemed the dark came too, spinning down like ashes. There was a cold bitter taste in the air, and the new-lighted lamps looked sad. Sad were the lights in the houses opposite. Dimly they burned as if regretting something. And people hurried by, hidden under their hateful umbrellas. Rosemary felt a strange pang. She pressed her muff against her breast; she wished she had the little box, too, to cling to. Of course, the car was there. She'd only to cross the pavement. But still she waited. There are moments, horrible moments in life, when one emerges from shelter and looks out, and it's awful. One oughtn't to give way to them. One ought to go home and have an extra-special tea. But at the very instant of thinking that, a young girl, thin, dark, shadowy—where had she come from?—was standing at Rosemary's elbow and a voice like a sigh, almost like a sob, breathed: 'Madam, may I speak to you a moment?'

'Speak to me?' Rosemary turned. She saw a little battered creature with enormous eyes, someone quite young, no older than herself, who clutched at her coat-collar with reddened hands, and shivered as though she had just come out of the water.

'M-madam,' stammered the voice. 'Would you let me have the price of a cup of tea?'

'A cup of tea?' There was something simple, sincere in that voice; it wasn't in the least the voice of a beggar. 'Then have you no money at all?' asked Rosemary.

'None, madam,' came the answer.

'How extraordinary!' Rosemary peered through the dusk, and the girl gazed back at her. How more than extraordinary! And suddenly it seemed to Rosemary such an adventure. It was like something out of a novel by Dostoevsky,* this meeting in the dusk. Supposing she took the girl home? Supposing she did do one of those things she was always reading about or seeing on the stage, what would happen? It would be thrilling. And she heard herself saying afterwards to the amazement of her friends: 'I simply took her home with me,' as she stepped forward and said to that dim person beside her: 'Come home to tea with me.'

The girl drew back startled. She even stopped shivering for a moment. Rosemary put out a hand and touched her arm. 'I mean it,' she said, smiling. And she felt how simple and kind her smile was. 'Why won't you? Do. Come home with me now in my car and have tea.'

'You—you don't mean it, madam,' said the girl, and there was pain in her voice.

'But I do,' cried Rosemary. 'I want you to. To please me. Come along.'

The girl put her fingers to her lips and her eyes devoured Rosemary. 'You're—you're not taking me to the police station?' she stammered.

'The police station!' Rosemary laughed out. 'Why should I be so cruel? No, I only want to make you warm and to hear—anything you care to tell me.'

Hungry people are easily led. The footman held the door of the car open, and a moment later they were skimming through the dusk.

'There!' said Rosemary. She had a feeling of triumph as she slipped her hand through the velvet strap.* She could have said, 'Now I've got you,' as she gazed at the little captive she had netted. But of course she meant it kindly. Oh, more than kindly. She was going to prove to this girl that—wonderful things did happen in life, that— fairy godmothers were real, that—rich people had hearts, and that women *were* sisters.* She turned impulsively, saying: 'Don't be frightened. After all, why shouldn't you come back with me? We're both women. If I'm the more fortunate, you ought to expect. . . .'

But happily at that moment, for she didn't know how the sentence was going to end, the car stopped. The bell was rung, the door opened, and with a charming, protecting, almost embracing movement, Rosemary drew the other into the hall. Warmth, softness, light, a sweet scent, all those things so familiar to her she never even thought about them, she watched that other receive. It was fascinating. She was like the rich little girl in her nursery with all the cupboards to open, all the boxes to unpack.

'Come, come upstairs,' said Rosemary, longing to begin to be generous. 'Come up to my room.' And, besides, she wanted to spare this poor little thing from being stared at by the servants; she decided as they mounted the stairs she would not even ring for Jeanne, but take off her things by herself. The great thing was to be natural!

And 'There!' cried Rosemary again, as they reached her beautiful big bedroom with the curtains drawn, the fire leaping on her wonderful lacquer furniture,* her gold cushions and the primrose and blue rugs.

The girl stood just inside the door; she seemed dazed. But Rosemary didn't mind that.

'Come and sit down,' she cried, dragging her big chair up to the fire, 'in this comfy chair. Come and get warm. You look so dreadfully cold.'

'I daren't, madam,' said the girl, and she edged backwards.

'Oh, please,'—Rosemary ran forward—'you mustn't be frightened, you mustn't, really. Sit down, and when I've taken off my things we shall go into the next room and have tea and be cosy. Why are you afraid?' And gently she half pushed the thin figure into its deep cradle.

But there was no answer. The girl stayed just as she had been put, with her hands by her sides and her mouth slightly open. To be quite sincere, she looked rather stupid. But Rosemary wouldn't acknowledge it. She leant over her, saying: 'Won't you take off your hat? Your pretty hair is all wet. And one is so much more comfortable without a hat, isn't one?'

There was a whisper that sounded like 'Very good, madam,' and the crushed hat was taken off.

'And let me help you off with your coat, too,' said Rosemary.

The girl stood up. But she held on to the chair with one hand and let Rosemary pull. It was quite an effort. The other scarcely helped her at all. She seemed to stagger like a child, and the thought came and went through Rosemary's mind, that if people wanted helping they must respond a little, just a little, otherwise it became very difficult indeed. And what was she to do with the coat now? She left it on the floor, and the hat too. She was just going to take a cigarette off the mantelpiece when the girl said quickly, but so lightly and strangely: 'I'm very sorry, madam, but I'm going to faint. I shall go off, madam, if I don't have something.'

'Good heavens, how thoughtless I am!' Rosemary rushed to the bell.

'Tea! Tea at once! And some brandy immediately!'

The maid was gone again, but the girl almost cried out: 'No, I don't want no brandy. I never drink brandy. It's a cup of tea I want, madam.' And she burst into tears.

It was a terrible and fascinating moment. Rosemary knelt beside her chair.

'Don't cry, poor little thing,' she said. 'Don't cry.' And she gave the other her lace handkerchief. She really was touched beyond words. She put her arm round those thin, bird-like shoulders.

Now at last the other forgot to be shy, forgot everything except that they were both women, and gasped out: 'I can't go on no longer like this. I can't bear it. I can't bear it. I shall do away with myself. I can't bear no more.'

'You shan't have to. I'll look after you. Don't cry any more. Don't you see what a good thing it was that you met me? We'll have tea and you'll tell me everything. And I shall arrange something. I promise. *Do* stop crying. It's so exhausting. Please!'

The other girl did stop just in time for Rosemary to get up before the tea came. She had the table placed between them. She plied the poor little creature with everything, all the sandwiches, all the bread and butter, and every time her cup was empty she filled it with tea, cream and sugar. People always said sugar was so nourishing. As for herself she didn't eat; she smoked and looked away tactfully so that the other should not be shy.

And really the effect of that slight meal was marvellous. When the tea-table was carried away a new being, a light, frail creature with tangled hair, dark lips, deep, lighted eyes, lay back in the big chair in a kind of sweet languor, looking at the blaze. Rosemary lit a fresh cigarette; it was time to begin.

'And when did you have your last meal?' she asked softly.

But at that moment the door-handle turned.

'Rosemary, may I come in?' It was Philip.

'Of course.'

He came in. 'Oh, I'm so sorry,' he said, and stopped and stared.

'It's quite all right,' said Rosemary, smiling. 'This is my friend, Miss——'

'Smith, madam,' said the languid figure, who was strangely still and unafraid.

'Smith,' said Rosemary. 'We are going to have a little talk.'

'Oh yes,' said Philip. 'Quite,' and his eye caught sight of the coat and hat on the floor. He came over to the fire and turned his back to it. 'It's a beastly afternoon,' he said curiously, still looking at that listless figure, looking at its hands and boots, and then at Rosemary again.

'Yes, isn't it?' said Rosemary enthusiastically. 'Vile.'

Philip smiled his charming smile. 'As a matter of fact,' said he, 'I wanted you to come into the library for a moment. Would you? Will Miss Smith excuse us?'

The big eyes were raised to him, but Rosemary answered for her: 'Of course she will.' And they went out of the room together.

'I say,' said Philip, when they were alone. 'Explain. Who is she? What does it all mean?'

Rosemary, laughing, leaned against the door and said: 'I picked her up in Curzon Street. Really. She's a real pick-up. She asked me for the price of a cup of tea, and I brought her home with me.'

'But what on earth are you going to do with her?' cried Philip.

'Be nice to her,' said Rosemary quickly. 'Be frightfully nice to her. Look after her. I don't know how. We haven't talked yet. But show her—treat her—make her feel——'

'My darling girl,' said Philip, 'you're quite mad, you know. It simply can't be done.'

'I knew you'd say that,' retorted Rosemary. 'Why not? I want to. Isn't that a reason? And besides, one's always reading about these things. I decided——'

'But,' said Philip slowly, and he cut the end of a cigar, 'she's so astonishingly pretty.'

'Pretty?' Rosemary was so surprised that she blushed. 'Do you think so? I—I hadn't thought about it.'

'Good Lord!' Philip struck a match. 'She's absolutely lovely. Look again, my child. I was bowled over when I came into your room just now. However . . . I think you're making a ghastly mistake. Sorry, darling, if I'm crude and all that. But let me know if Miss Smith is going to dine with us in time for me to look up *The Milliner's Gazette*.'*

'You absurd creature!' said Rosemary, and she went out of the library, but not back to her bedroom. She went to her writing-room and sat down at her desk. Pretty! Absolutely lovely! Bowled over! Her heart beat like a heavy bell. Pretty! Lovely! She drew her cheque-book towards her. But no, cheques would be no use, of course. She opened a drawer and took out five pound notes, looked at them, put two back, and holding the three squeezed in her hand, she went back to her bedroom.

Half an hour later Philip was still in the library, when Rosemary came in.

'I only wanted to tell you,' said she, and she leaned against the door again and looked at him with her dazzled exotic gaze, 'Miss Smith won't dine with us tonight.'

Philip put down the paper. 'Oh, what's happened? Previous engagement?'

Rosemary came over and sat down on his knee. 'She insisted on going,' said she, 'so I gave the poor little thing a present of money. I couldn't keep her against her will, could I?' she added softly.

Rosemary had just done her hair, darkened her eyes a little, and put on her pearls. She put up her hands and touched Philip's cheeks.

'Do you like me?' said she, and her tone, sweet, husky, troubled him.

'I like you awfully,' he said, and he held her tighter. 'Kiss me.'

There was a pause.

Then Rosemary said dreamily: 'I saw a fascinating little box today. It cost twenty-eight guineas. May I have it?'

Philip jumped her on his knee. 'You may, little wasteful one,' said he.

But that was not really what Rosemary wanted to say.

'Philip,' she whispered, and she pressed his head against her bosom, 'am I *pretty*?'

THE CANARY

. . . You see that big nail to the right of the front door? I can scarcely look at it even now and yet I could not bear to take it out. I should like to think it was there always even after my time. I sometimes hear the next people saying, 'There must have been a cage hanging from there.' And it comforts me. I feel he is not quite forgotten.

. . . You cannot imagine how wonderfully he sang. It was not like the singing of other canaries. And that isn't just my fancy. Often, from the window I used to see people stop at the gate to listen, or they would lean over the fence by the mock-orange* for quite a long time—carried away. I suppose it sounds absurd to you—it wouldn't if you had heard him—but it really seemed to me he sang whole songs, with a beginning and an end to them.

For instance, when I'd finished the house in the afternoon, and changed my blouse and brought my sewing on to the verandah here, he used to hop, hop, hop from one perch to the other, tap against the bars as if to attract my attention, sip a little water, just as a professional singer might, and then break into a song so exquisite that I had to put my needle down to listen to him. I can't describe it; I wish I could. But it was always the same, every afternoon, and I felt that I understood every note of it.

. . . I loved him. How I loved him! Perhaps it does not matter so very much what it is one loves in this world. But love something one must! Of course there was always my little house and the garden, but for some reason they were never enough. Flowers respond wonderfully, but they don't sympathise. Then I loved the evening star. Does that sound ridiculous? I used to go into the backyard, after sunset, and wait for it until it shone above the dark gum tree. I used to whisper, 'There you are, my darling.' And just in that first moment it seemed to be shining for me alone. It seemed to understand this . . . something which is like longing, and yet it is not longing. Or regret—it is more like regret. And yet regret for what? I have much to be thankful for!

. . . But after he came into my life I forgot the evening star; I did not need it any more. But it was strange. When the Chinaman who came to the door with birds to sell held him up in his tiny cage, and instead of fluttering, fluttering, like the poor little goldfinches, he gave a faint, small chirp, I found myself saying, just as I had said to the star over the gum tree, 'There you are, my darling.' From that moment he was mine!

. . . It surprises even me now to remember how he and I shared each other's lives. The moment I came down in the morning and took the cloth off his cage he greeted me with a drowsy little note. I knew it meant 'Missus! Missus!' Then I hung him on the nail outside while I got my three young men their breakfasts, and I never brought him in, to do his cage, until we had the house to ourselves again. Then, when the washing-up was done, it was quite a little entertainment. I spread a newspaper over a corner of the table and when I put the cage on it he used to beat with his wings, despairingly, as if he didn't know what was coming. 'You're a regular little actor,' I used to scold him. I scraped the tray, dusted it with fresh sand, filled his seed and water tins, tucked a piece of chickweed and half a chili between the bars. And I am perfectly certain he understood and appreciated every item of this little performance. You see by nature he was exquisitely neat. There was never a speck on his perch. And you'd only to see him enjoy his bath to realise he had a real small passion for cleanliness. His bath was put in last. And the moment it was in he positively leapt into it. First he fluttered one wing, then the other, then he ducked his head and dabbled his breast feathers. Drops of water were scattered all over the kitchen, but still he would not get out. I used to say to him, 'Now that's quite enough. You're only showing off.' And at last out he hopped and standing on one leg he began to peck himself dry. Finally he gave a shake, a flick, a twitter and he lifted his throat—Oh, I can hardly bear to recall it. I was always cleaning the knives by then. And it almost seemed to me the knives sang too, as I rubbed them bright on the board.

. . . Company, you see, that was what he was. Perfect company. If you have lived alone you will realise how precious that is. Of course there were my three young men who came in to supper every evening, and sometimes they stayed in the dining-room afterwards reading the paper. But I could not expect them to be interested in the little things that made my day. Why should they be? I was nothing to them. In fact, I overheard them one evening talking about me on the stairs as 'the Scarecrow'. No matter. It doesn't matter. Not in the least. I quite understand. They are young. Why should I mind? But I remember feeling so especially thankful that I was not quite alone that evening. I told him, after they had gone. I said 'Do you know what they call Missus?' And he put his head on one side and looked at me with his little bright eye until I could not help laughing. It seemed to amuse him.

. . . Have you kept birds? If you haven't, all this must sound, perhaps, exaggerated. People have the idea that birds are heartless, cold little creatures, not like dogs or cats. My washerwoman used to say every Monday when she wondered why I didn't keep 'a nice fox terrier', 'There's no comfort, Miss, in a canary.' Untrue! Dreadfully untrue! I remember one night. I had had a very awful dream— dreams can be terribly cruel—even after I had woken up I could not get over it. So I put on my dressing-gown and came down to the kitchen for a glass of water. It was a winter night and raining hard. I suppose I was half asleep still, but through the kitchen window, that hadn't a blind, it seemed to me the dark was staring in, spying. And suddenly I felt it was unbearable that I had no one to whom I could say 'I've had such a dreadful dream,' or—'Hide me from the dark.' I even covered my face for a minute. And then there came a little 'Sweet! Sweet!' His cage was on the table, and the cloth had slipped so that a chink of light shone through. 'Sweet! Sweet!' said the darling little fellow again, softly, as much as to say, 'I'm here, Missus. I'm here!' That was so beautifully comforting that I nearly cried.

. . . And now he's gone. I shall never have another bird, another pet of any kind. How could I? When I found him, lying on his back, with his eye dim and his claws wrung, when I realised that never again should I hear my darling sing, something seemed to die in me. My breast felt hollow, as if it was his cage. I shall get over it. Of course. I must. One can get over anything in time. And people always say I have a cheerful disposition. They are quite right. I thank God I have.

. . . All the same, without being morbid, or giving way to—to memories and so on, I must confess that there does seem to me something sad in life. It is hard to say what it is. I don't mean the sorrow that we all know, like illness and poverty and death. No, it is something different. It is there, deep down, deep down, part of one, like one's breathing. However hard I work and tire myself I have only to stop to know it is there, waiting. I often wonder if everybody feels the same. One can never know. But isn't it extraordinary that under his sweet, joyful little singing it was just this—sadness?—Ah, what is it?—that I heard.

EXPLANATORY NOTES

Frau Brechenmacher Attends a Wedding

First published in the *New Age*, vol. 7, no. 12 (21 July 1910), 273–5; revised and reprinted in *In a German Pension*, 1911.

3   '*Bub*': lad.

    '*Nu*': well, now.

4   *Gasthaus*: inn.

5   *Festsaal*: hall.

    '*Na*': well.

    three mourning rings: this implies that Frau Rupp has been widowed three times.

    free-born: child born outside marriage.

8   *worsted*: woollen.

The Woman at the Store

First published in *Rhythm*, vol. 1, no. 4 (Spring 1912), 7–21, illustrated by a header by Marguerite Thompson. Mansfield, wanting to publish somewhere other than the *New Age*, sent John Middleton Murry, the editor of the new magazine *Rhythm*, a story which he rejected because it did not conform with the magazine's maxim, 'Before art can be human again it must learn to be brutal'. She then sent him 'The Woman at the Store', which he accepted. The setting draws on a camping trip Mansfield made in 1907: see Ian Gordon (ed.), *The Urewera Notebook*. Mansfield would not allow the story to be reprinted during her lifetime: 'I couldn't have The Woman at the Store reprinted par exemple' (*Collected Letters*, iii. 210). When Murry reprinted the story in *Something Childish and Other Stories* he corrected two confusing sentences in the *Rhythm* version, but also altered the punctuation and changed 'Hin' to 'Jim' throughout. 'Hin' suggests the Maori name 'Hinemoa', usually used of a woman. The original name and fluid punctuation are restored here.

10   *pack horse*: horse carrying bundles or luggage.

    manuka: *leptospernum scoparium*, a flowering bush or tree, common in New Zealand, which has yellow flowers. Linda sits under a manuka tree in the sixth part of 'At the Bay'.

    galatea: cotton material, striped in blue on a white ground.

    wideawake: soft felt hat with a broad brim and low crown.

    Jaeger: woollen.

10 *duck*: strong cotton used for sails and men's trousers.

fly biscuits: Garibaldi biscuits: currants sandwiched between two layers of biscuit dough.

11 *whare*: Maori word for house, and used by pakeha (white New Zealanders) to mean 'shack'.

12 *Bluchers*: strong leather half-boots, named after Field Marshal von Blücher.

pawa: paua shell, a type of abalone.

Queen Victoria's Jubilee: probably the sixtieth (diamond) jubilee celebration, on 20 June 1897, of Queen Victoria's accession to the throne.

Richard Seddon: popular Liberal premier of New Zealand until his death in 1906.

13 *treacle papers*: to attract and trap flies.

14 *Els*: an abbreviation of Elsie.

tittivating: Mansfield's spelling.

Napier: a town in the North Island on Hawke Bay.

15 *sundowners*: swagmen, or tramps, often arriving at a house or store as the sun went down, looking for food and/or somewhere to sleep.

billy: billy can, a tin with a handle for holding liquid.

'with no . . . me from': Murry altered this, to clarify that the narrator is a woman; the *Rhythm* version contained a misprint and read: ' "I'll draw all of you when you're gone, and your horses and the tent, and that one"— she pointed at me—"with no clothes on in the creek." I looked at her where she wouldn't see me frown.'

16 *calico*: plain white unprinted cotton.

sateen: cotton with a glossy surface like satin.

spuds: potatoes.

18 *Camp Coffee*: the advertisements for this coffee substitute, made of chicory and coffee essence mixed with sugar, would feature an image of empire; Camp coffee's trademark was a picture of a turbaned sepoy serving coffee to an officer in the military uniform of a Highland regiment, with a pennant on the tent behind him inscribed with the words 'READY AYE READY'.

How Pearl Button Was Kidnapped

First published in *Rhythm*, no. 8 (September 1912), 136–9 under the pseudonym Lili Heron, with a woodcut of a heron by Gaudier-Brzeska and a header by Marguerite Thompson. Reprinted in *Something Childish*, where Murry dates it as 1910, and divides into shorter paragraphs than are contained in the *Rhythm* version; the version here is the *Rhythm* one. The 'dark women' are not identified as Maori as they are seen mostly from the child's perspective and she cannot categorize in that way, but their clothes, domestic equipment, and way of life indicate who they are. Mansfield draws on the experience recorded in *The Urewera Notebook* in the story. Another tale about Pearl, 'The Story of Pearl Button', written about 1908, appears in *The Katherine Mansfield Notebooks* (i. 112–13) but was not published in Mansfield's lifetime.

20 *flax basket of ferns*: kits, baskets of plaited flax which Maori use for carrying, and for storing food.

21 *feather mats*: the tail-feathers of the huia were once worn by Maori as a badge of rank.

22 *green ornament*: a greenstone (jade) pendant or (hei)tiki, often a carved representation of an ancestor, also referred to in *The Urewera Notebook* (p. 84) as part of a Maori girl's dress.

two pieces of black hair: plaits like the Maori girl 'with her hair in two long braids' in *The Urewera Notebook* (p. 43).

Millie

First published in the *Blue Review* vol. 1, no. 2 (June 1913), 82–7. Reprinted with alterations in the paragraphing in *Something Childish*. The *Blue Review* was an attempt at prolonging the life of *Rhythm* in an altered form, though J. D. Fergusson was no longer the art editor. Three monthly issues appeared from May to July, but the magazine lacked the dynamism of *Rhythm*, partly because of the editorial intervention of its backers, and folded.

24 *johnny*: an inexperienced new hand, used in New Zealand of a new immigrant.

strung up: hanged.

25 *Mount Cook*: in the South Island and permanently snow-covered, the highest peak in Australasia, named after Captain Cook; the Maori name is Aoraki.

28 *skunk*: unpleasant, contemptible person.

Something Childish but very Natural

Published posthumously by Murry, in the *Adelphi*, vol. 1, nos. 9–10 (February–March), 777–90, 913–22, and then in the volume of the same name; Murry dates it 1914. The title comes from a poem of the same name by Samuel Taylor Coleridge which imitates a German folk-song and is quoted in the story. It was sent by Coleridge in a letter to his wife in 1799 and first published in the *Annual Anthology*, 1800.

29 *Charing Cross Road*: a street in Soho renowned for its second-hand bookshops.

Had I . . .: a misquotation, which should read 'If I had but two . . .'.

30 *Bolton Abbey*: a priory founded in 1150, ruined since the sixteenth century, painted by Turner and described by Ruskin; train compartments were decorated with photographs of famous beauty spots, presumably as an incentive to train travel.

31 *have her hair up*: wearing her hair in a bun or chignon would indicate that she was old enough for paid employment.

35 *pollies*: perhaps parrots, copying each other.

36 *eat anything . . . fountain*: for fear of food-poisoning.

39 *Polytechnic*: the Polytechnic of Central London, in Regent Street, founded in 1882 for the mental, moral, and physical development of youth.

44 *two T's*: two ticks, that is, very soon.

   white pinks: pinks, like carnations, belong to the genus *dianthus*; they are fragrant and are characteristic of cottage gardens.

45 *to-morrow and to-morrow and to-morrow*: a quotation from *Macbeth* v.v, though when Macbeth says it he is oppressed by the strain and tedium of human life.

   telegram: before the universal availability of telephones, a message sent telegraphically to a decoding office; the written message was then delivered, usually by a boy on a bicycle.

The Little Governess

First published in *Signature*, Part I: no. 2 (18 October 1915) 11–18; Part II: no. 3 (1 November 1915), 11–18, under the pseudonym Matilda Berry. Reprinted without revision in *Bliss and Other Stories*.

47 *Governess Bureau*: agency for the employment of governesses, female teachers in private households.

   Ladies' Cabin: compartment for women only on the cross-Channel ferry.

   dress-basket: equivalent of a suitcase.

48 *Dames Seules*: Women Only.

49 *Trrrès bien*: Verrry well.

   motor veil: a veil used by women travelling in early motor-cars, to protect them from dust.

   alpaca: fabric made from llama wool.

   En voiture: All aboard.

50 *Un, deux, trois*: One, two, three.

51 *Ja, ein wenig, mehr als Franzosisch*: Yes, a little, more than French.

   Ja, es ist eine Tragœdie: Yes, it's a tragedy.

53 *Standard roses*: roses growing as a small tree, with the flowers in a bunch at the top of a straight stem.

Nein, danke: No, thank you.

Wie viel?: How much?

54 *Danke . . . sehr schön*: Thank you very much. They are so very lovely.

Englischer Garten: the proper name of a public park in Munich.

Nicht wahr?: Don't you agree?

55 *Regierungsrat*: senior civil servant.

Hauptbahnhof: main or central station.

Gewiss: certainly.

Gehen Sie: Go!

Gehen Sie sofort: Go immediately!

58 *hochwohlgebildete Dame*: highly cultured/extremely well-bred lady.

Na, sagen Sie 'mal: Well, really! (literally: well, tell me then).

An Indiscreet Journey

First published in *Something Childish*, and dated by Murry as 1915, based on an episode in Mansfield's life. Bored by her relationship with Murry, and intrigued by a developing attraction to the writer Francis Carco, who was serving with the French army near Gray, in the *Zone des Armées*, Mansfield travelled in February 1915 to the war zone and spent four nights with Carco. The adventure is described in *The Katherine Mansfield Notebooks*, ii. 9–12, and in her letters from Paris and Gray in *Collected Letters*, 1. 148–50.

60 *St Anne*: mother of the Virgin Mary.

Burberry: trade name of clothing made by Burberrys Ltd., particularly well known for good quality raincoats.

peg-top: a coat that is narrow at the shoulders, flaring to a wide hem.

ma mignonne: my sweet.

electric lotus buds: around 1900 Hector Guimard created Art Nouveau entranceways for the Metro system, some with lotus motifs.

61 *two mourning rings*: possibly indicating that she has been widowed twice.

big wooden sheds: field hospitals.

petit soldat: little soldier.

62 *ma France adorée*: my beloved France.

sabots: clogs.

képi: French military cap.

Merci . . . aimable. Thank you, Monsieur, you are very kind.

We, Sir Edward Grey . . .: this formal authorization is inscribed in the narrator's British passport. Viscount Grey of Falloden was Foreign Secretary; the Foreign Office issued passports at this period.

63 *Toute de suite*: right away.

63 *ah, mon Dieu*: oh, my God.

juste . . . gare: directly opposite the station.

Je . . . tendrement: lots of love.

visiting card: a card with a person's name and address, left when paying a visit, particularly if the host was not at home.

64 *Venez vite, vite*: Come quickly, quickly.

Oui: yes.

Excusez . . . chapeau: Excuse me Madam, but perhaps you have not remarked that there is a kind of seagull settled on your hat.

65 *It means . . . word*: soldiers on active service are executed by their own side if they consort with women who have entered a restricted area illegally.

Non . . . ça: No, I can't eat that.

viséd: stamped with an authorization.

66 *Matin*: morning paper.

Montez vite: Get in quickly.

je m'en f . . .: I don't give a damn.

Bon jour, mon amie: Hello, my friend.

Prends . . . vieux: Take this, old chap.

67 *Dodo . . . dodo*: 'Sleep, my man, go to sleep.' This is the beginning of the refrain from a song called 'Idylle Rouge', words by Saint Gilles and Paul Gay, music by Georges Picquet. Mansfield wrote it out in full for Murry in a letter of 8–9 May 1915 (*Collected Letters*, i.181).

68 *Premier Rencontre*: first meeting.

Triomphe d'Amour Triumph of Love.

C'est ça: that's right.

69 *Sept, huit, neuf*: Seven, eight, nine.

Il pleure de colère: He's crying with rage.

70 *Un Picon*: a bitter aperitif.

Mais . . . ça: But you know it is rather disgusting, that.

V'là Monsieur: There's Monsieur.

un . . . charcuterie: a little prepared meat, such as salami, or prepared salad.

N'est-ce pas: Isn't that so.

bifteks: steaks.

si, si: yes, yes.

ma fille: my girl.

Souvenir tendre: touching memory.

71 *É-pa-tant*: marvellous.

    Mirabelle: plum brandy.

    Café des Amis: Friends' café.

The Wind Blows

First published as 'Autumns: II' under the pseudonym Matilda Berry and with a first-person narrator in *Signature*, no. 1 (4 October 1915), 18–23; *Signature*, a fortnightly magazine, was launched by D. H. Lawrence and Murry but only survived for three issues. Revised in the third person as 'The Wind Blows', it appeared in the *Athenaeum*, no. 4713 (27 August 1920), 262–3 and in *Bliss and Other Stories* (1920). Mansfield wrote of it to Murry: 'I put it in because so many people had admired it. (Yes its Autumn II but a little different.) Virginia, Lytton—and queer people like Mary Hamilton & Bertie all spoke so strongly about it I felt I must put it in' (*Collected Letters*, iii. 273–4). Wellington is a famously windy city.

74 *hat-elastic*: women's hats had a band of elastic attached to prevent them from blowing off; it was usually worn at the back of the head.

    tam: tam-o'-shanter, a woollen beret named after the hero of Burns's poem of the same name, and introduced as a fashion for girls and women in about 1887.

75 *MacDowell*: Edward Alexander MacDowell (1861–1908), an American composer whose own instrument was the piano; he composed piano suites and pieces, characteristically based on folk-songs.

    Rubinstein: Anton Grigorovitch Rubinstein (1829–94), a celebrated Russian pianist and composer who gave concerts and recitals throughout Europe and America.

76 *stave*: set of lines for musical notation.

    allegretto: a musical term meaning somewhat brisk.

    'I bring . . . showers': misquoted from P. B. Shelley's 'The Clouds' (1820): 'I bring fresh showers for the thirsting flowers'.

    Bogey: a nickname that Mansfield used both for her brother and her husband.

77 *ulster*: a long, loose rough overcoat, often with a belt.

    pahutukawas: usually spelt pohutukawa, this tree (*metrosideros excelsa*) is popularly known as the 'Christmas tree' as its crimson flowers appear in December. It grows close to the sea, particularly in the North Island of New Zealand.

Prelude

First published by the Hogarth Press, owned and run by Leonard and Virginia Woolf, as a 68-page booklet in July 1918; hand-set partly by Virginia Woolf and bound by her husband, some copies had line-blocks on the upper and lower wrappers of a woman's head by the art editor of *Rhythm*,

J. D. Fergusson. Then published in *Bliss and Other Stories*. 'Prelude' was a pared-down version of 'The Aloe', an earlier story which was not published in Mansfield's lifetime. The best edition, *The Aloe with Prelude* (Port Nicholson Press, 1982), is edited by Vincent O'Sullivan, giving the text of 'The Aloe' on the recto of each page and that of 'Prelude' on the verso, and including Fergusson's picture for the upper wrapper. The text of 'The Aloe' attempts to reproduce the detail, and excisions, of the manuscript.

79 *buggy*: a light one- or two-horse vehicle.

80 *reticule*: a small bag.

81 *dripping*: fat left over after meat has been roasted; often used instead of butter.

   scullery: a room attached to the kitchen in which dishes were washed and dirty household tasks done.

82 *stay-button*: button from a corset.

   loose iron: the roofs of houses in New Zealand were usually made of corrugated iron.

   dray: a low cart for carrying heavy loads.

83 *Quarantine Island*: Somes Island in Wellington Harbour; named after a deputy-governor of the New Zealand Company, it had been used as a quarantine station for immigrant ships, and was subsequently an internment camp for aliens during wartime.

   hulks: the body of a dismantled ship used as a storage vessel.

   Picton boat: Picton is the northernmost port of the South Island, with a ferry service to and from Wellington.

84 *new roads*: Karori, three miles from Wellington, was the first of the outlying valleys to be opened up for settlement; Harold Beauchamp, Mansfield's father, bought a property there in 1893.

85 *reefer*: slang name given to a midshipman.

   hassock: a thick cushion for resting the feet on.

87 *Pure . . . free*: 'Fair as a lily, joyous and free' is quoted in Henry Lawson's story 'The Songs They Used to Sing'.

88 *Gentle . . . thee*: Lottie has an inaccurate version of the hymn she has heard, which should be: 'Gentle Jesus, meek and mild, | Look upon a little child, | Pity my simplicity, | Suffer me to come to thee' (Charles Wesley, 1742).

89 *eau-de-nil*: literally water of the Nile, pale green.

   adenoids: overgrowth of glandular tissue on the back of the upper part of the throat.

90 *fantails*: small birds (*rhipidura fuliginosa placabilis*; Maori: *piwakawaka*).

   tui: sometimes: called the 'parson bird' because of its white throat feathers, the tui (*prosthemadera novaeseelandiae*) can mimic other birds.

91 *corporation*: slang term for fat body.

93 *wash-house*: outbuilding for washing clothes.

94 *foulard*: thin material of silk or silk and cotton.

   watch-guard: a chain used to secure a watch when it is worn on the body.

97 *box*: a genus (*buxus*) of small evergreen shrub.

98 *picotee*: a variety of carnation (*dianthus caryophyllus*).

99 *Bodega*: wine-shop that also sells groceries.

100 *hire a pew*: to assert his presence and respectability as a newcomer.

   . . . Believers: a misquotation from the Book of Common Prayer, stressed to indicate how it would be chanted in church. It should read: 'When thou hadst overcome . . .'

102 *box ottoman*: a cushioned seat like a sofa but without a back or arms.

104 *rissoles*: chopped meat mixed with breadcrumbs and egg, divided into small cakes, and fried.

105 *kerosene*: paraffin.

   boncer: usually spelt bonzer; Australian/New Zealand term for 'very good'.

110 *stuff*: woollen fabric.

   jetty: jet-black.

   barracouta: a long thin loaf with a rough crust on top, named after a barracouta fish, a snake-mackerel which is about a metre long.

111 *doyleys*: lace mats.

112 *crib*: abbreviation of cribbage, a game using a pack of cards and a board with holes and pegs for scoring.

114 *Chesterfield*: a large overstuffed sofa.

116 *'lock, stock and barrel'*: the entirety of it.

117 *chapeau*: hat.

118 *serge*: durable worsted material.

Mr Reginald Peacock's Day

First published in the *New Age*, vol. 21, no. 7 (14 June 1917), 158–61; reprinted in *Bliss and Other Stories*.

122 *When her . . . wedded*: from a poem by George Meredith (1828–1909), 'Love in the Valley', with 'looping' and 'tying' transposed.

   Covent Garden: the Royal Opera House, opened 1732.

   Lohengrin . . . Elsa: title of an opera (1845–8) by Richard Wagner, and name of the protagonist, a knight who proves to be the son of Parsifal, king of the Holy Grail. He marries Elsa but they separate almost immediately; a mysterious swan appears at crucial points in the plot.

   Voilà tout!: That's all!

123 *John Bull*: the Englishman, first used to name a character in John Arbuthnot's *The History of John Bull* (1712).

127 *Weep . . . fast?*: a slight misquotation of a song by John Dowland from *The Third and Last Booke of Songs or Aires* (1603); it begins: 'Weep you no more sad fountains | What need you flow so fast?'

Feuille d'Album

First published as 'An Album Leaf' in the *New Age*, vol. 21, no. 21 (20 September 1917), 450–2; slightly revised as '*Feuille d'Album*' and reprinted in *Bliss and Other Stories*.

129 *tortoise stove*: wood-burning stove.

131 *as neat as a pin*: from the saying 'neat as a new pin'.

    lamplighter: gas street-lights were lit each night by a lamplighter.

A Dill Pickle

First published in the *New Age*, vol. 21, no. 23 (4 October 1917), 489–91; revised and reprinted in *Bliss and Other Stories*. A dill pickle is a cucumber pickled with dill leaves and seeds.

135 *raised her veil*: fashionable women's hats of the period had veils covering the face which were lifted indoors.

136 *Kew Gardens*: the Royal Botanic Gardens, founded in 1759.

137 *river . . . song*: the Volga is the longest river in Europe; the 'Volga Boat Song' (traditional) was popular in the early years of the twentieth century.

138 *crochet hook*: a hooked implement used for crochet, a kind of knitting.

Je ne parle pas français

First published by the Heron Press, which belonged to Mansfield and Murry; it was set by Murry's brother. One hundred copies appeared in 1920, dated 1919. The story was too sexually explicit for Michael Sadleir, Mansfield's editor at Constable, who insisted on cuts before he would publish it. At first Mansfield resisted: 'No, I certainly won't agree to those excisions if there were 500000000 copies in existence. They can keep their old £40 & be hanged to them. Shall I pick the eyes out of a story for £40. Im *furious* with Sadler. No, Ill never agree. Ill supply another story but that is all. The *outline* would be all blurred. It must have those sharp lines' (*Collected Letters*, iii. 273). Murry persuaded her to give in, but when the story was published in *Bliss and Other Stories* she regretted it and loathed the blurb: 'if Id known they were going to say that no power on earth would have made me cut a word. I wish I hadn't. I was wrong—very wrong' (*Collected Letters*, iv. 137). A fuller account of the circumstances and events surrounding the story is given in Alpers's edition, *The Stories of Katherine Mansfield*, pp. 559–61. The title means 'I don't speak French'.

142 *portmanteaux*: suitcases.

143 *sous*: coins of little value.

144 '*dying fall*': quotation from the opening speech by Orsino in Shakespeare's play *Twelfth Night*: 'That strain again!—it had a dying fall'.

145 *geste*: gesture, in the sense of a highly significant moment.

spill: a slip of wood for lighting candles etc.

bubble of gas: a gas lamp.

147 *passons outre*: let's pay no heed. (Alpers's text reads *oultre*, which seems to be a misprint; I have followed the Constable text and substituted *outre*.)

concierge: caretaker.

148 *bon enfant*: good child.

le Kipling: the writer Rudyard Kipling (1865–1936), author of *Kim*.

149 *photographs*: erotic or pornographic pictures offered to prospective customers by a prostitute.

tweed knickerbockers: the stereotypical outfit for an English gentleman; knickerbockers would be referred to as plus-fours in Britain, and worn when shooting or golfing.

150 *comme il faut*: as it should be, proper.

cubist: coined about 1911; a contemporary art movement based on the form of a cube.

152 *enfin*: lastly, here: for heaven's sake.

153 *ce cher Pinkerton*: this dear Pinkerton. In Puccini's opera *Madame Butterfly* the Japanese heroine yearns for the return to Japan of her husband, the American Pinkerton, and dresses beautifully in her wedding kimono to greet him when he does come.

154 *mignonette green*: greyish green.

155 *Gare Saint Lazare*: a major station in Paris.

158 *flap seat*: folding seat opposite the passengers' seats in a taxi.

159 *garçon*: porter.

pair of boots: guests in hotels could leave their shoes or boots outside their bedroom doors to indicate that they wished staff to take them away to be polished.

164 *morning coat*: formal dress.

167 *gallant*: a man of fashion and pleasure.

Sun and Moon

First published in the *Athenaeum*, no. 4718 (1 October 1920), 430–2; reprinted in *Bliss and Other Stories*, though Mansfield tried to withdraw it from the

Athenaeum: 'Even tho I am as poor as a mouse don't publish Sun & Moon' (*Collected Letters*, iv. 53).

169 *white thing*: a cape to protect her clothes from make-up.

Bliss

First published in the *English Review*, vol. 27 (August 1918), 108–19; reprinted in *Bliss and Other Stories*.

177 *Entendu*: OK.

179 *monocle*: a single eye-glass.

perambulator: pram, baby-carriage.

180 *'Why doth the bridegroom tarry?'*: an ironic reference to the biblical theme expressed most clearly in the parable of the wise and foolish virgins, Matthew 25: 5: 'While the bridegroom tarried, they all slumbered and slept.'

181 *liée*: close to.

Tchekof: now spelt Chekhov. Anton Chekhov (1860–1904) was the Russian author of short stories that were admired and translated by members of the Bloomsbury Group and Mansfield. His plays include *The Three Sisters*, *Uncle Vanya*, and *The Cherry Orchard*.

183 *drunk and seen the spider*: a quotation from Shakespeare's *The Winter's Tale* II. i; Leontes says: 'I have drunk, and seen the spider.' There was a belief that if there was a spider in the cup, the drinker was unharmed as long as he was unaware of it, but poisoned if he saw the spider as he drank.

185 *Table d'Hôte*: literally the host's table, used to refer to the set menu in a restaurant or hotel.

Psychology

First published in *Bliss and Other Stories*.

186 *sommier*: day-bed.

187 *en escargot*: like a snail.

188 *hatter's bag*: possibly a reference to the Mad Hatter, who was preoccupied with bread and butter, in Lewis Carroll's *Alice's Adventures in Wonderland* (1865).

Book . . . good: an adaptation of the line that is repeated in the first chapter of the book of Genesis: 'And God said, let there be lights in the firmament of heaven . . . and God saw that it was good' (vv. 14, 18).

189 *psycho-analyst's claim*: psychoanalysis was a popular fictional theme at this period; when she was reviewing, Mansfield wrote to Murry: 'I am

amazed at the sudden "mushroom growth" of cheap psycho analysis everywhere. *Five* novels one after the other are based on it: its in everything' (*Collected Letters*, iv. 69).

Pictures

First written as a dialogue called 'The Common Round' in the *New Age*, vol. 21, no. 5 (31 May 1917), 113–15; later recast and published as 'The Pictures' in *Art and Letters*, vol. 2, no. 4 (Autumn 1919), 153–6, 159–62. Reprinted as 'Pictures' in *Bliss and Other Stories*.

193 *Brighton*: coastal town in Sussex famous for its raffish entertainments.

my poor dear lad in France: the first version of the story was written and published during the First World War.

194 *washing . . . pointing*: an indication that Miss Moss cannot afford to employ someone to do her washing.

195 *vanity bag*: a small handbag fitted with a mirror and powder-puff.

A B C: around 1890 the Aerated Bread Company (ABC) and the Express Dairy opened hundreds of popular cafés serving drinks and buns.

parmas: Parma violets, named after the city in northern Italy which is also famous for its cheese and its ham.

196 *brahn*: imitating a Cockney accent, meaning brown or sun-tanned.

all found: with everything, such as meals, provided.

lino: floor covering.

197 *'Waiting . . . Lee'*: song with words by L. Wolfe Gilbert and music by Lewis F. Muir, made famous by Al Jolson.

cure: eccentric.

scream: uproariously funny.

provinces . . . West End: shows and plays that begin their run outside London and then move to London's theatreland in the West End of the city.

198 *hop it*: dance.

Hearts of oak: both 'Be brave' (from sea shanties describing sailors as hearts of oak) and rhyming slang for broke, no money.

199 *never pay their crowds*: a film company that does not pay extras who appear in crowd scenes.

aviate: fly an aeroplane.

buck-jump: jump like a horse that bucks.

The Man Without a Temperament

Originally called 'The Exile' (see *The Katherine Mansfield Notebooks*, ii. 188). First published as 'The Man Without a Temperament' in *Art and Letters*, vol. 3, no. 2 (Spring 1920), 10–14, 17–22, 25; reprinted with small improvements in *Bliss and Other Stories*.

202 *brown wooden bear*: an umbrella stand.

    pinnies: pinafores.

    nets: mosquito nets.

    Vous desirez, monsieur?: What do you want, sir?

205 *Vous avez voo ça!*: Did you see that!

206 *drawers*: knickers, with a drawstring.

210 *Saturday Evening Post*: an American magazine.

    a feast . . . soul: quotation from Alexander Pope (1688–1744), *Satires, Epistles and Odes of Horace*, Satire I, Book 2.

212 *bread and wine*: the sacrament.

The Stranger

First published in the *London Mercury*, vol. 3, no. 15 (January 1921), 259–68; the place-names were altered from Auckland and Napier to Crawford and Salisbury when it was reprinted in *The Garden Party and Other Stories*. Alpers restores the original names in his text. Mansfield wrote of the story to Murry: 'Ive *been* this man *been* this woman. Ive stood for hours on the Auckland Wharf. Ive been out in the stream waiting to be berthed. Ive been a seagull hovering at the stern and a hotel porter whistling through his teeth. It isn't as though one sits and watches the spectacle. That would be thrilling enough, God knows. But one IS the spectacle for the time' (*Collected Letters*, iv. 97). The story was first called 'The Interloper', but this was changed on the original manuscript.

213 *Don't . . . harmless*: a signal that might have been sent in the days of colonial exploration.

    A welcome . . . forgiven: the language of melodrama.

    every man-jack of them: every one of them.

218 *costume*: suit.

    state-room: superior accommodation on a ship.

221 *new collars*: shirt collars were buttoned on to the shirt, so that a clean collar could spruce up a shirt that had already been worn.

Miss Brill

First published in the *Athenaeum*, no. 4726 (26 November 1920), 722–3; reprinted in *The Garden Party and Other Stories*. Mansfield told her brother-in-law, Richard Murry, in a letter that: 'In Miss Brill I chose not only the length of every sentence, but even the sound of every sentence—I chose the rise and fall of every paragraph to fit her—and to fit her on that day at that very moment. After Id written it I read it aloud—numbers of times—just as one would *play over* a musical composition, trying to get it nearer and nearer to the expression of Miss Brill—until it fitted her' (*Collected Letters*, iv. 165).

225 *Jardins Publiques*: public gardens.

   tingling: an indication of degenerating health.

   rotunda: circular bandstand with a domed roof.

226 *Panama hat*: hat made from leaves of the stemless screwpine.

227 *ermine toque*: small white fur hat.

228 *English . . . a week*: Miss Brill earns a living by teaching English and reading to an invalid for payment.

The Daughters of the Late Colonel

First published in the *London Mercury*, vol. 4, no. 19 (May 1921), 15–30; reprinted in *The Garden Party and Other Stories*. The title on the manuscript of the story is 'Non-Compounders', a term used at Mansfield's school in London, Queen's College, to refer to older students who did not take the full-time programme. Mansfield wrote of the story to Dorothy Brett: 'I put my all into that story & hardly anyone saw what I was getting at. Even dear old Hardy told me to write more about those sisters. As if there was any more to say!' (*Collected Letters*, iv. 316).

230 *top-hat*: man's silk hat with a high cylindrical crown.

   bowler: a hard, low-crowned, stiff felt hat, named after a London hat-manufacturer.

   '*Remember*': possibly an echo of the ghost of Hamlet's father's saying, 'Remember me' (*Hamlet*, I. v).

   wear black: formal mourning clothes.

231 *Ceylon*: a British colony at that time; now Sri Lanka.

233 *blancmange*: a milky and opaque white jelly.

234 *holding his wrist*: taking his pulse.

   Miss Pinner: a formal mode of address, distinguishing the elder from the younger sister by using the surname of the elder one.

236 *tight-buttoned*: refers to the leather upholstery inside the cab.

239 *Round Pond*: Alpers capitalizes Round Pond to indicate that it refers to the pond in Kensington Gardens.

   drawers: loose shorts with a drawstring.

240 *cork helmet*: a pith helmet or solar topee, worn by colonial officers in hot climates; the veranda and cane rocker are stereotypical images of colonial life.

   Tatler: a magazine published in London about fashionable life.

   Busks: strips of wood, whalebone or steel used to stiffen corsets.

   waistcoats: men wore watches in the fob pockets of waistcoats.

246 *Bertha*: a deep-falling collar, to be attached to the top of a low-necked evening dress.

246 *barrel-organ*: a musical instrument with a pin-studded revolving barrel acting mechanically on the keys; organ-grinders were traditionally accompanied by monkeys, which often wore hats and jackets.

247 *pagodas*: a temple or sacred building built over the relics of Buddha or a saint; this and other artefacts suggest mementoes of colonial life from a colony such as Ceylon.

boa: a scarf of feathers worn by women.

248 *Anglo-Indian*: person of British birth resident in India.

Eastbourne: a respectable holiday resort on the coast of Sussex.

carved screen: another reference to an object brought back from a posting in a colony, possibly Ceylon.

on approval: purchasing things which could be returned to the shop and the money refunded within a fixed time limit.

Life of Ma Parker

First published in the *Nation & the Athenaeum*, vol. 28, no. 22 (26 February 1921), 742–3; reprinted in *The Garden Party and Other Stories*.

250 *jetty spears*: black hat-pins.

toque: small hat without a brim or with a very small brim.

252 *Shakespeare*: Stratford-upon-Avon was Shakespeare's birthplace.

consumption: tuberculosis, the disease that Mansfield suffered from.

255 *lock-up*: police cells.

Mr and Mrs Dove

First published in the *Sphere*, vol. 86, no. 1125 (13 August 1921), 172–3; reprinted in *The Garden Party and Other Stories*.

257 *Rhodesia*: the British colony in south central Africa, named after Cecil Rhodes, which is now independent Zimbabwe.

the mater: public school parlance for mother.

258 *Umtali*: a town in eastern Zimbabwe on the main railway line to Mozambique from Harare, known since Independence in 1982 as Mutare.

Pekes: Pekinese, an ancient breed of toy dog originating in China.

the governor: public school term for father.

trouser pockets: moved out of little boys' shorts to long trousers.

263 *ilex-tree*: holm-oak or evergreen oak (*quercus ilex*).

Her First Ball

First published in the *Sphere*, vol. 87, no. 1140A (28 November 1921), 15, 25; reprinted in *The Garden Party and Other Stories*.

265 *Sheridan girls*: Leila is a cousin of the girls who appear in 'The Garden Party'.

> *tuberoses*: a fragrant, creamy-white, funnel-shaped flower (*polyanthes tuberosa*).

> *Twig?*: understand?

266 *programmes*: men wrote their names in women's programmes to engage them for particular dances.

267 *More pork*: the endemic owl (*ninox novaeseelandiae*), ruru in Maori, found throughout New Zealand; its cry sounds a bit like 'more pork'.

> *chaperones*: married women who accompany young women for the sake of propriety.

> *parquet*: polished wooden floor.

Marriage à la Mode

First published in the *Sphere*, vol. 87, no. 1145 (31 December 1921), 364–5; reprinted in *The Garden Party and Other Stories*. The title means 'fashionable marriage'.

271 *Royal Academy*: in Piccadilly, founded in 1768 with Sir Joshua Reynolds as its first president; a gallery that is seen by Isabel as an establishment institution.

273 *fire-shovel, tongs*: fire irons.

274 *Titania*: the Queen of the Fairies in Shakespeare's *A Midsummer Night's Dream*.

276 *Avanti*: Forward!

277 *sloe gin*: a version of gin made from the fruit of the blackthorn.

> *my Nijinsky dress*: Nijinsky was the male star in Diaghilev's Ballets Russes, an avant-garde Russian company that appeared in cities such as London and Paris at this period.

> *mes amis*: my friends.

279 *marriage lines*: marriage certificate.

> *A Lady reading a Letter*: a popular theme in painting.

At the Bay

First published, carelessly edited, in the *London Mercury*, vol. 5, no. 27 (January 1922), 239–65; revised and reprinted in *The Garden Party and Other Stories* (22 February 1922). Mansfield's family, the Beauchamps (whose name is translated for the grandmother in the story, Mrs Fairfield), spent summer holidays at Muritai or at Day's Bay, on the eastern side of Wellington harbour, which is where 'At the Bay' is set. Contemporary photographs of it appear in *Katherine Mansfield's New Zealand* by Vincent O'Sullivan. Mansfield comments on the writing of the story fully in letters, making one of her most significant comments on the nature of her fiction: 'I have tried to make it as familiar to "you" as it is to me. You know the marigolds? You know those pools in the rocks? You know the mousetrap on the wash house window sill? And, too, one tries to go deep—to speak to the secret self we all have—to acknowledge that' (*Collected Letters*, iv. 278).

281   *bush-covered hills*: New Zealand bush is characterized by lush vegetation and a wide range of trees and bushes, including eucalypts, pines and tree-ferns.

    paddocks: fields; a word in more common use in Australia and New Zealand than in Britain.

    bungalows: one-storeyed houses, here mostly holiday cottages.

    toi-toi: Maori name for native grass, like pampas grass, which has rough thin leaves and tall stems topped with huge silvery plumes that glisten as they blow in the bush.

    frieze: coarse woollen cloth with a nap.

    wideawake: see note to p. 10 above.

283   *whare*: see note to p. 11 above.

289   *Limmonadear*: Lemonade dear.

290   *straight dinkum*: equivalent of 'and hope to die', that is, totally honestly.

293   *stays*: corsets.

294   *turned turtle*: turned over.

    steamer chair: chair for lounging, like those used on the deck of a ship.

    manuka tree: see note to p. 10 above.

    picotees: see note to p. 98 above.

295   *Tasmanian*: Tasmania, formerly Van Diemen's Land, is an island state south of Victoria in Australia, separated by the Bass Strait from the mainland.

    uncovered: doffed his hat, as a gesture of greeting.

296   *something pink*: his toes.

297   *sand-hoppers*: small terrestrial jumping crustaceans with no carapace; buried in sand by day but at night emerging to feed on debris under stones or amongst seaweed.

    pawa shells: see note to p. 12 above.

298   *casting on*: creating stitches on a knitting needle.

    mines: probably on the Australian gold diggings.

300 *leghorn*: straw hat.

perishall: parasol, represented as Alice says it.

larrikin: rascal.

her mosquitoes: i.e. mosquito repellent.

canningbals: Mrs Stubbs's version of 'cannibals'.

301 *johnny cake*: cake made of wheatmeal, baked on the ashes or fried in a pan.

Primus stove: trade name of a stove burning paraffin.

302 *dozzing*: Alice's version of dozen, i.e. twelve.

water-fall . . . snow: the background to a studio photograph, suggesting national identity.

dropsy: accumulation of watery fluid in the body.

mutting: Alice's version of 'mutton'.

Be not afraid, it is I: Christ's words to his disciples when he walked on the water; Matt. 14: 27.

303 *copper*: a copper vessel for washing clothes.

ninseck: child's version of 'insect'.

304 *pinny*: pinafore, apron.

308 *ledger*: a book containing records; Jonathan is a clerk.

do I fondly dream?: Jonathan uses archaic and literary language as a kind of self-mockery; 'Ay me, I fondly dream!' is from John Milton's elegy 'Lycidas' (1637), l. 56.

309 *Jehovah*: the name of God in the Old Testament.

Whose eye . . . simply: the way that Linda imagines the Last Judgement.

310 *greengage*: a green plum.

telegraph . . . wire: see note to telegram, p. 45 above.

wash-leather: shammy or chamois leather.

314 *A cloud . . . still*: in the American edition of *The Garden Party and Other Stories* Mansfield separated the final paragraph from the preceding text, as Section 13 of the story; Alpers includes this revision in his edition of the stories.

The Voyage

First published in the *Sphere*, vol. 87, no. 1144 (24 December 1921), 340–1; reprinted in *The Garden Party and Other Stories*.

315 *The Picton boat*: the boat that ferried passengers across the Cook Strait from Wellington Harbour to Picton, the port at the head of Queen Charlotte Sound in the South Island.

ulster: see note to p. 77 above.

318 *grandma's blackness . . . crêpe*: they are in mourning for Fenella's mother.

   a little something: spirits of some kind.

319 *fascinator*: headscarf for wearing at home.

   plush: cloth with a nap longer than velvet, used for upholstery.

   lace: laced up, and thus hard for a small child to remove.

320 *the Straits*: the Cook Strait.

321 *ferns . . . trees*: tree-ferns and eucalypts.

   lid of a box: boxes decorated with sea-shells were popular souvenirs

322 *bluchers*: strong leather half-boots.

A Married Man's Story

First published in the *Dial*, New York, vol. 74 (January–June 1923), 451–62; reprinted in the *London Mercury*, vol. 7, no. 42 (April 1923), 577–86 and in *The Dove's Nest and Other Stories*. The story was published posthumously and is incomplete.

323 *Mother and Child*: like a painting of the Madonna and the Christ-child.

   cover: a horse-drawn cab; the horse has been covered while the driver waits for custom.

324 *arum lily leaf*: white funnel-shaped lilies (*zantedeschia*), often associated with the Madonna as images of purity and death.

326 *tant mieux pour nous*: all the better for us.

   tant pis: too bad.

327 *stories of little children*: such as the twins Romulus and Remus in the myth about the founding of Rome.

328 *sotto voce*: quietly.

   bravuras: a piece of music written to task the artist's powers.

   confirmation dress: for her confirmation in the faith and first communion.

   Botanical Gardens: this suggests that the story is set in Wellington.

331 *Gregory Powder*: a nineteenth-century laxative named after its creator.

332 *pestle*: a pharmacist's instrument for bruising or pounding.

334 *beads of black*: mascara.

   bust . . . Hahnemann: Samuel Hahnemann (1755–1843), a German physician and the founder of homeopathy.

The Garden Party

First published in the *Saturday Westminster Gazette*, vol. 59, nos. 8917, 8923, (4 February 1922, pp. 9–10; 11 February, p. 10) for Parts 1–11; *Weekly*

Westminster Gazette, vol. 1, no. 1 (18 February 1922, pp. 16–17) for Part III. Revised and reprinted in *The Garden Party and Other Stories*. In the first editions the title of the story was hyphenated but that of the book was not.

336 *Meg, Jose*: the names, and Laurie, later, seem to echo those of two of the March sisters and their male friend in *Little Women* (1868) by Louisa May Alcott.

337 *karakas*: *corynocarpus laevigata*, glossy, bushy trees with big shiny ovoid leaves, reaching 15 metres high, and growing naturally in groves. The fact that the trees are bearing their golden-orange berries (prized as food by the Maori) indicates that the story is set in February.

338 *squiz*: look, glance.

339 *green baize*: baize is coarse woollen stuff with a long nap, often used to cover doors that were demarcation lines; see Graham Greene's account of the door between his headmaster father's house and the school, Berkhamsted, at the opening of *The Lawless Roads* (1939).

canna lilies: ornamental plants (*cannaceae*) thriving in a warm climate with showy flowers ranging from pale yellow to scarlet.

340 *chesterfield*: see note to p. 113.

341 *flags*: small labels attached to cocktail sticks.

342 *traction-engine*: a steam-engine used for drawing heavy loads along a road.

The Doll's House

First published in the *Nation & the Athenaeum*, vol. 30, no. 19 (4 February 1922), 692–3: reprinted in *The Dove's Nest and Other Stories*. Other possible titles for it, appearing in lists of titles for prospective collections devised by Mansfield, were 'The Washerwoman's Children' and 'At Karori'. This is another story about the family of 'Prelude' and 'At the Bay'.

350 *Pat*: Pat also appears in 'Prelude'.

turn: walk.

351 *oil*: the lamp is a miniature version of a paraffin lamp.

352 *art-serge*: probably high-quality serge.

wishbone: the small forked bone in a chicken's breast; traditionally people pull it between them when the meat has been cooked and eaten, and the person with the larger piece makes a wish.

353 *johnny cake*: see note to p. 301 above.

356 *creek*: small river or stream, a word used more familiarly in Australia and New Zealand than in Britain.

wattles: acacias, which flourish in Australia and New Zealand; their flowers range in colour and appear at different times whereas yellow mimosa is the only variety familiar in Britain.

The Fly

First published in the *Nation & the Athenaeum*, vol. 30, no. 25 (18 March 1922), 896–7; reprinted in *The Dove's Nest and Other Stories*.

358 *Q.T.*: quiet, confidential information.

Windsor Cassel: Windsor Castle, on the River Thames, one of the royal residences.

finger: measure of alcohol.

Belgium: at a First World War cemetery.

360 *telegram*: see note to p. 45 above.

A Cup of Tea

First published in the *Story-Teller*, May 1922, pp. 121–5; reprinted in *The Dove's Nest and Other Stories*.

362 *a baby in long clothes* . . . : small babies wore gowns.

Curzon Street: in Mayfair, one of the most elegant and expensive parts of London.

364 *Dostoevsky*: Russian novelist (1821–81) whose passionate sympathy for the downtrodden, often in an urban setting, is reflected ironically in the story.

365 *velvet strap*: the car has luxurious fittings.

women were sisters: Rosemary has heard feminist and suffragette arguments.

lacquer furniture: probably expensive oriental furniture.

368 *The Milliner's Gazette*: an ironic comment implying that he cannot prepare for a dinner engagement as he usually would by checking on the guest in the fashionable or financial press.

The Canary

First published in the *Nation & the Athenaeum*, vol. 33, no. 3 (21 April 1923), 84; reprinted in *The Dove's Nest and Other Stories*.

370 *mock-orange*: syringa (*philadelphus*), a fragrant shrub resembling orange-blossom.

The Oxford World's Classics Website

www.worldsclassics.co.uk

- Browse the full range of Oxford World's Classics online

- Sign up for our monthly e-alert to receive information on new titles

- Read extracts from the Introductions

- Listen to our editors and translators talk about the world's greatest literature with our Oxford World's Classics audio guides

- Join the conversation, follow us on Twitter at OWC_Oxford

- Teachers and lecturers can order inspection copies quickly and simply via our website

www.worldsclassics.co.uk

American Literature

British and Irish Literature

Children's Literature

Classics and Ancient Literature

Colonial Literature

Eastern Literature

European Literature

Gothic Literature

History

Medieval Literature

Oxford English Drama

Poetry

Philosophy

Politics

Religion

The Oxford Shakespeare

A complete list of Oxford World's Classics, including Authors in Context, Oxford English Drama, and the Oxford Shakespeare, is available in the UK from the Marketing Services Department, Oxford University Press, Great Clarendon Street, Oxford OX2 6DP, or visit the website at www.oup.com/uk/worldsclassics.

In the USA, visit www.oup.com/us/owc for a complete title list.

Oxford World's Classics are available from all good bookshops. In case of difficulty, customers in the UK should contact Oxford University Press Bookshop, 116 High Street, Oxford OX1 4BR.